There's an old French saying: "A day without wine is a day without sunshine." There will be plenty of days without sunshine unless retired investigative reporter Aubrey Warder and his unlikely colleague, the beautiful Baroness, can foil the machinations of an international wine cartel!

Books by Les Whitten

Les Whitten

A DAY WITHOUT SUNSHINE

McGraw-Hill Book Company

New York   St. Louis   San Francisco
Bogotá   Guatemala   Hamburg   Lisbon
Madrid   Mexico   Montreal   Panama
Paris   San Juan   São Paulo
Tokyo   Toronto

For the seed of this book's theme and for her advice I am grateful to Sidney Moore. I am also grateful for editorial and research help to Lisa Cannon, Martie Chidsey, B. K. Chun, Perry Knowlton, Bernard Leason, Leslie Milk, Ellen and Richard Miller, William Moore, Natalie Neviaser, Phyllis Chasanow-Richman, Archie Smith III, Manya B. Stoetzel, Thomas Stewart, David Vaughan, Phyllis Whitten, and among others, the Austrian, British, French, and Portuguese embassies, the Library of Congress, the Montgomery County, Maryland, library system.

Reprinted by arrangement with Atheneum

First McGraw-Hill Paperback edition, 1986

1 2 3 4 5 6 7 8 9 A G A G 8 7 6

ISBN 0-07-069961-5

LIBRARY OF CONGRESS CATALOGING-IN-PUBLICATION DATA

Whitten, Les, 1928–
   A day without sunshine.
   (McGraw-Hill paperbacks)
   I. Title.
[PS3573.H566D38 1986]   813'.54   86-7370
ISBN 0-07-069961-5 (pbk.)

For my brothers:
Harvey and Stanley

THE SOUL OF WINE

Within the bottle's depths, the wine's soul sang one
    night:
"Dear disinheriteds, I give you willingly
"From my imprisoning glass which scarlet wax seals tight
"An anthem full of light and warm fraternity!

"I know how much it takes on hillsides turned to flame
"Of labor and of sweat, of cooking suns to fuel
"And fructify my life and give my soul a name.
"I'm not ungrateful, no; my nature is not cruel.

"I'll take enormous joy in pouring like a wave
"Into the mouth of one whose work has made him old.
"His overheated chest is like a gentle grave;
"And I'll be happier there than in the cellar's cold.

"Do you hear Sunday choirs that echo in my throat,
"And hope that babbles in my palpitating breast?
"With elbows by your plate and sleeves rolled on your
    coat
"You'll glorify me as you put your cares to rest . . ."

Charles Baudelaire
TRANSLATED BY LESLIE H. WHITTEN

Contents

One

BETHANY VON MOHRWALD

With a boyish whoop, Franz von Mohrwald called to his wife Bethany as she worked in the sunny shed, transferring young grape cuttings to boxes so they could be taken to the nursery of their vineyard.

"Big business, *meine kleine Bäuerin*"—peasantling—he called her, a nickname she liked for its endearment and, in recent days, silently bridled at for its reminder of the limited life they lived. He waved a letter on cream-colored stationery at her. Bethany looked at her husband's mobile face, smiled back at him, and snatched the letter from his hand. At the top was the engraved name, "William Carnavan Bridsey," and she knew it was going to be big business indeed.

Bridsey was the chief and only operating Bridsey of the House of Bridsey and Sons, Ltd., of London. They were major importers of Bordeaux, owned some acreage there and in Portugal, and distributed French and other wines to Britain, the Commonwealth, and the United States.

Bethany recalled meeting Bridsey at wine convocations, a brash, mustached sergeant major of a man who thundered his opinions on world trade to all who would listen. Given his power, all did. The letter asked whether he could visit them Tuesday next on "an interesting business matter."

No more than that. But clearly it suggested the purchase of wines, and because Bridsey himself was coming, lots of wines. The von Mohrwald's vineyard, beside Neusiedlersee, a lake in Austria's Burgenland, sold its wines through a Vienna shipper. By selling directly to Bridsey at English wholesale prices, they could do without the shipper and make a good 6 to 10 percent more than at present.

Bethany threw her arms around Franz and kissed him soundly on the lips. For the last two years the weather had been disastrous all along the lake: too wet in spring, too cold too early. Their bad crops had occurred simultaneously with low prices for Austrian wines.

She knew the books as well as Franz, for he shared all the business problems with her. Two more bad years would force them to sell off the greatest part of their land if they hoped to keep anything at all.

Their château, Schloss von Mohrwald, had been built during the middle years of the great Austrian wine era from 1526 to 1780. It was modeled on Durnstein, a larger, more famous castle, but had never been finished. Nevertheless, it had a restored keep, a small chapel listed in Baedeker and Fodor, and a dining room whose windows looked out over the vineyards to the placid, aquamarine lake two hundred yards away.

Over the centuries, the von Mohrwalds had neither aspired to nor achieved more than the modest distinction of minor nobility. They produced a singularly fine table wine, Mohrwalder Maximiliansehre, many salable ones, and a strain of industrious, loyal, optimistic wine men and women.

Franz was the present Baron von Mohrwald. Bethany had been a countess, but had taken the lesser rank of baroness when they married. She too, however, traced a family line back to the von Mohrwalds. So, in fact, they were fifth cousins.

He was a handsome, dark-haired man of forty-five who knew his Rieslings, muskatellers, and green veltliners as well as any man in Austria. He and Bethany had moved with the times and their 504 acres were clean and spruce, the equipment modern and well-maintained. Their holdings, among the largest in Austria, were devoted mainly to the more ordinary and thus more profitable pressings. But in the family tradition, they continued to produce exportable quantities of the Maximiliansehre.

Franz's vices were unextraordinary: some overindulgence of a married daughter and of their two sons, the younger away at a *gymnasium*, a classical high school, in Salzburg, the older at the University of Cologne (he would be heir to the vineyard); a five-year-old Mercedes convertible with all the trimmings; and two intermittent dalliances with married women of his own class.

Bethany von Mohrwald had once thought she would do more than grow grapes. She had been reared in part by an English nanny, had the right schooling at the Wiener Musikhochschule, and had earned a degree in art history at Munich. But nothing artistic quite took. With a substantial dowry, she had married the busy, ambitious Franz.

Once she was settled at Schloss von Mohrwald which, though hereditarily Franz's, was bound as close in terms of blood to her, she found her calling. She thrived on the feel of the dirt, the rough twiggage of the cuttings, the sensuous pulp of grapes, the intractable crush of the press, frothing up the wine-to-be. She loved her husband, and though (almost without qualification) she was faithful to him, she was of lustier stock.

Blond, trim, youthful herself at forty-two in a fresh Nordic way, she deftly avoided the advances of Austrians and of foreigners at wine gatherings. Her one lapse into adultery had been brief, discreet, and dangerously romantic.

Recently, however, she had felt an unaccountable restlessness. At its worst, it was a pondering over whether "this is all there is," accompanied by sharp but unspecific yearnings. But with it all, she, like Franz, had remained charming and even naive in a world where so few escape the long stretches of suffering which are the death of both charm and naiveté.

When William Bridsey arrived at Schloss von Mohrwald, worsted-clad, with a tweed hat and a burled cane, he leaned to kiss Bethany's hand. His heavy pomade distracted her. Four generations of middlemanning, she thought, had not made him a gentleman.

Bridsey and Franz, after observing further amenities, took off for a drive in the von Mohrwald

Land Rover to inspect the vineyards while Bethany inspected the luncheon fixings.

In sterling buckets embossed with Hapsburgian eagles, she iced three different commercial wines and one pale green bottle of Maximiliansehre, around whose graceful neck hung a tiny replica of the Paris gold medals of 1889 and 1900.

Recalling her guest's portliness, Bethany and the cook produced a lunch of fresh asparagus, Neu-siedlersee trout, veal quenelles with a light cream sauce, and a slam-bang ending: American Mc-Intosh apples with strong, Austrian goat cheese.

During the meal, Bridsey wolfed the asparagus, botched the deboning of the trout, and gnashed the quenelles as if they were French fried eel chunks.

With the wines, however, he was punctiliously discriminating. As each was offered for his tasting, he rolled it in his mouth and looked ceiling-ward as he weighed it against the countless others he had sampled over the years. Bethany could almost imagine his brain through the slick, thick hair, measuring how well each would sell in the English-speaking markets against Moselles and Rhines, Alsatian Rieslings and Gewurztraminers, the new Yugoslavian and other eastern wines.

It was between the cheese and coffee that Franz said carefully, "Bethany, I asked Mr. Bridsey to put off our talk of his," he paused, ". . . mission until all three of us could discuss it."

"And may I add, baroness," Bridsey purred, savoring the title, "I am delighted to see a husband so very, very much in tune with women's rights."

Bethany nodded pleasantly, thinking "horse manure," and wishing the butler-handyman would appear with the homemade *obstler* fruit schnapps. As if by extrasensory summons, he entered, and poured drops of the clear liquid in fluted crystal glasses. Bridsey, with the same almost feminine precision, picked up the glass, sniffed, and took a sip.

"Superb!" he resonated. "Incredibly Austrian. Royal! Would you were putting *this* up for export."

"We only make three cases a year," said Bethany sweetly. "There would not be much profit for you in that."

Franz cast a blink of disapproval at Bethany, then looked back at Bridsey, less grateful for his praise than expectant. A bit patronizing—the descendant of tradesmen talking from a position of strength to old nobility—Bridsey began.

"Baron, baroness. I will mince no words. More and more, particularly when I visit such historic acres as these, I feel myself drawn again to the soil, the earth, looking for new challenges. Challenges," he reemphasized, finding in that word the tone he wanted to convey.

Bethany wanted to squirm. Challenges? Poppycock. Everyone knew about the variety and extent of his holdings. Drawn to the soil? The only interest he had in soil was in extracting gold from it. She glanced at Franz to see whether she dared risk a bit more tartness, a look that Bridsey, self-important but no dolt, did not miss.

Bridsey went on. "I and some of my colleagues—they wish to remain behind the whiffle trees for the nonce, so to speak—are planning a company to, um, buy up a few vineyards making good table wines."

He looked as if he might again slip into circumlocution but with a sigh that ruffled his grenadier's mustache, he bit into the meat of his proposal. "We are prepared to make a substantial offer for the von Mohrwald vineyards, with you, of course, managing them, and continuing to produce their splendid nectars."

Franz and Bethany were stunned. They had expected a proposal to buy their wines, not their land, vine stock, cellars, and all. Bridsey hurried on, hoping to win them over before they could object.

"In the alternative, we would take a long-term lease on your acres, unless, of course, you wanted to keep apart your unmatchable Maximiliansehre."

"Such a surprise," Franz interjected. "We had thought . . ."

"No, no," broke in Bridsey forcefully. "Do *not* think, not yet. Let me first give you my details, please, please!"

From the inside pocket of his tailored coat, he drew out a paper. Drawing closer to the table, he handed a copy to Franz, then his own talking copy to Bethany. As she read, she realized how formidably his verbal inadequacies camouflaged his pecuniary shrewdness.

The figures on the paper were disturbingly correct as to the financial condition of Schloss von Mohrwald, right down to their burden of loans. The summary of their acreage, their plantings, their past and present production could hardly have been more accurate if they had done it themselves.

Yet the price Bridsey was offering was far above the vineyard's appraised worth, enough above it so they could easily keep up the Schloss and a few acres surrounding it during their and their children's lives. Bethany did some quick calculations in her head. No matter how Bridsey hyped the von Mohrwald's production, he would still lose large sums in today's market.

She started to burst out with a question on it, but deferred to Franz.

"It is generous past all . . . ," her husband began (for a moment she thought he was going to say "past all wisdom"), ". . . what we could have imagined. We would want to give it some long and deep consideration."

Once again Bridsey broke in. "Of course, baron. But I must warn you and you, baroness, that there is a caveat emptor, or rather a caveat seller, whatever that would be in Latin. You would know; I would not.

"I, and my colleagues, would need to know in a week or two, to have it on the bottom line as the Americans say. The financing, you understand: it is here today, solid as a rock, I assure you. But one cannot be sure it will be here tomorrow . . ."

Franz stepped in. "In two weeks? You are asking us to make up our minds in two weeks . . ."

Now Bethany, shaken, could not hold back. "After over four hundred years?"

The unintentional reminder to Bridsey of his plebeian lineage, combined with his present superior positioning, almost made him bark at them. But, face flushed, he said calmly, "In a fortnight, yes. We are making a number of inquiries. Other enterprises such as ours may also be. I do not know. But you, as well as anyone, understand the tumult these days."

"You're making other inquiries in Austria?" asked Franz, rapidly thinking of the economic effect on his acres if his competitors sold out to a cartel. Or if he did and they did not.

"Yes, and elsewhere."

"Can you say whom you are approaching?" asked Franz.

"No," said Bridsey, pulling a long face as if with real regret.

"I cannot. My colleagues would object, as you can imagine."

"I understand," said Franz, courteously taking him off the hook. "We understand."

As they walked Bridsey to his car, Bethany's mind was in turmoil over this strange and strangely ominous visit. Franz did not understand at all, she knew. No more than she did.

Bridsey drove his rented BMW to Vienna and checked in at the Hilton. The lunch, the wine, and his drive had made him drowsy. But he forced himself into alertness. The man he was calling in London, a solicitor named Robert St. Gage, was not the sort of person with whom one dared be less than entirely wide-awake.

When the lawyer's aristocratic voice came on the line, Bridsey reported with uncharacteristic succinctness on his conversations with the Austrian vintners. From St. Gage there came neither credit nor criticism.

At the end, St. Gage dismissed him with a correct but warmthless, "Thank you, that will be all, I think," leaving Bridsey, as in all of his communications with St. Gage, vaguely and unaccountably uneasy.

*   *   *

Bethany and Franz had stood before the Schloss door, hand in hand, seeing off Bridsey. As his car turned from their drive onto the rural road, the couple's grip had tightened, no longer merely a conventional clasp, but one of resolve.

"It's frightening," said Bethany. "You were wise not to tell him no right away. It will give us some time . . ."

"To find out what's going on. It's crooked. We know that. At those prices . . ."

"A lot of people are going to sell."

"A lot of people are not us," he said, shifting his hand to embrace her shoulder. "Better to lose it all in bankruptcy than give him an acre . . ."

"Of nettles!"

"There was a menace in it. You caught it? We may have to fight him—them—with everything we've got left."

"He said they were 'making a number of inquiries.' "

"I'll soon know something about that," said Franz, turning her to the open door.

It took Franz only a few phone calls to discover that in the last two days, Bridsey had approached two of the von Mohrwalds' competitors, one near Gumpoldskirchen, the other at Krems on the Danube.

Traditionally secretive about business affairs, they would confide only fragmentarily with Franz on the offers. But he gathered that, in their cases, too, the inducements had been inexplicably high. And because these two were even more straitened than the von Mohrwalds, both were negotiating with Bridsey.

"Even if I come to an agreement with him," said the grandfatherly owner of the huge Krems vineyard, "it would never be at your expense, Franz."

But Franz knew that once holdings were sold or put out to long-term leases, the former proprietors were powerless to prevent ungentlemanly, and therefore cutthroat price manipulations. Prices could be slashed so much that it would ruin him and Bethany along with other independent winegrowers. Then the newcomers could buy their vineyards for groschen and raise prices all over Austria.

Bethany made her own inquiries of a source certain to be open with her. It was an Italian prince a few years her senior, Claudio Martino e Stelio. They had been at school together in Munich, he as a history major. It was the prince with whom, years later, she had her single affair, conducted with impeccable discretion, ended with wise brevity.

Martino e Stelio had also been approached about his family vineyards, but not by Bridsey.

"By that little cherub of a Frenchman. You remember him, *cara*, his name is Maier. He couldn't keep his eyes off you in Milano last year. But why should he? Who could?"

"Please, Claudio," she admonished him.

"He came to us, with what lip pursing, what smiles. But look, *cara*, what choice do I have? My God, you know the market. So we worked it out.

I keep the *palazzo*, some of our vintage land. He gets the nonvintage, the equipment. I hate to see my coronet on the label, but . . ." He laughed self-effacingly. ". . . you know we've only had it since Napoleon anyway."

The offer had been similar to the one made to Bethany and Franz. It sounded like it came from the same cartel. Yet one could never be sure.

Later that afternoon, Martino e Stelio called her up excitedly.

"More mystery," he said. "I phoned Belz-Arensbogen in the Rheingau; we're related through my mother. He wouldn't lie. He got a visit from the *Witwe* Pfeffermühle"—the widow of a Rhenish magnifico whose vineyards and counting house controlled unending hillsides of German grapes. She had taken over the business with her Prussian hand and was best known and least esteemed for turning the great Marienwagner acres into a mass-produced, sweetly fruity wine for the American market called "The Jolly Priest." "Belz says the *Witwe* is trying to buy up the whole river, from Düsseldorf to Switzerland."

"From Düsseldorf to . . . ?"

"Well, practically," said the prince embarrassed at being caught out in a characteristic excess. "What are you and Franz going to do?"

"Hold out. As long as we can. First, we're going to find out what's going on. Even if it costs money."

"Which you don't have."

"Which we don't have," Bethany echoed solemnly. "Where is this thing, or things, centered, do you think?"

"In London," said the prince sourly. "Where else?"

Of course it would be London. London was the throbbing heart of the wine trade, a freewheeling Casbah of importers and exporters of all the great wines of Europe, of the cognacs, the ports, the exotic brandies of Slavic lands.

In the Connaught Grill and other sedate dining rooms and offices, wine merchants and buyers struck the principal deals of vinicommerce, sealing them with earnest nods or handshakes. Here the forty or so mainly British males who controlled the multi-billion-dollar world wine trade chatted over noble cheese and nobler ports, ruling the oceans of wine as surely as Britain once ruled the waves. And with the same arrogance. Only the rambunctious and renegade American market, whose wines were grown in a quantity and, now, in a quality that rivaled Europe, was outside their purview.

Bethany had family in the Austrian embassy in London, most notably a cousin who was first secretary. She called him and reported what she and Franz had discovered. She said she wanted to find out what was going on and asked him to make some calls.

He telephoned Bethany next morning. The embassy commercial attaché had heard rumors of recent vineyard purchases, options, leases, and lease-buys in France, Germany, Austria. Only vineyards planted more for quantity than quality figured in the reports; none mentioned the *grands châteaux* and *Schlösser*. The commercial attaché did not know whether the activity was merely one of the all too frequent disruptions in the once orderly wine markets or something drastically new.

It was clear to Bethany that the machinations of Bridsey and his allies—or rivals, if that was the case—were too complex for her and Franz to decipher alone. It was also clear that the upheavals could wreck Schloss von Mohrwald, could cave in their lives.

They needed outside help from an expert.

The cousin's recommendation was that if they were determined to make a serious investigation, they should speak with a retired Scotland Yard inspector, Jerome Wheatley-Smith, who had been suggested by a trusted friend in the British Foreign Office.

Wheatley-Smith, who had been Scotland Yard's international trade specialist, was a lifelong oenophile and had written articles on viniculture for trade journals under various pen names.

Franz and Bethany saw no alternative but to hire the inspector and make a full investigation of it. That, of course, would force them to drastically rearrange their lives. One of them would have to take over the entire burden of the vineyard's daily business: orders for equipment repair, for bottles and crates, for fertilizer; schedules for removal of vine suckers, and other vine maintenance; blending wines; tuning cellar temperatures to the young wines; carrying on, in sum, the vineyard's thousand routine tasks. He—or she—would also have to work more diligently than ever to sell the wines, negotiate and sign new contracts, seek out new markets in such places as Sweden, Belgium, Czech-oslovakia.

The other person would have to pursue the investigation, assist the British inspector with research and in any other duties that might save money and time, and allocate funds for the whole distasteful business. In a word, this person would be both supervisor of the investigation and apprentice detective.

The fact was that for all Bethany's verve and independence, Franz was the better choice for both jobs.

"I would gladly try either," she said after supper that night. "And you, I know, would be better at both."

Franz smiled lovingly at her candor. However, there was no real question but that he must maintain the vineyard operation. That was the principal thing and he could not be spared from it.

"If we were Hohenzollerns," he said, reaching across to put his hand over hers, "I could plead madness and let you handle the vineyard while I played international sleuth."

She knew that his taking the arduous daily chores was the only rational course. At the same time, she could not deny a secret feeling of relief, tinged with the slightest bit of shame, that she would end up with the more adventurous role.

Although it was after nine, she called Wheatley-Smith at his home in Sydenham, outside London.

No, he said with a touch of irritability, he would not take the case. For one thing, he had made up his mind not to handle matters centered in England. There were too many potential conflicts of interest—with businessmen whom he had once covertly cultivated as sources of information, with former bosses and colleagues still in the police business.

She pressed him, using every argument, every bit of charm she could filter into the telephone. At last, he agreed to see her.

They met at a pub in Sydenham. Wheatley-Smith, a trim, small-boned man, sipped lemonade and listened attentively as she laid out every fact, every supposition at her disposal. When she had finished, he responded in what Bethany decided was the raspiest voice she had ever heard.

"It is impossible to be definite based on your limited information," he said. "But it seems significant to me that their efforts are directed toward large vineyards which produce mediocre but drinkable table wines plus, in some cases, a few *tonneaux* of superior wines. We must wonder why."

He paused and ventured a chill smile. "In other days I sampled the Maximiliansehre. It is a lovely thing."

"Thank you," she said, pleased at any sign of benignancy in this self-insulated man.

Wheatley-Smith drew a simple block pad from his pocket and rapidly did some computations.

"If I judge correctly, and my figures can only be estimates, the buyers of the prince's lands, and Mr. Bridsey, in his offer to you, are willing to pay twenty-five or so percent above current market value."

"We had estimated twenty-seven percent for

ours," said Bethany, "even valuing it at its most favorable worth."

Wheatley-Smith nodded, took a swallow of the lemonade and went on.

"I am not fond of Bridsey. He has more than a streak of avarice. But I assure you, baronness, he is no fool. I know little of Maier, but understand he is of like kidney. The same, if I do not err, is true of the *Witwe* Pfeffermühle."

He spread his hands and Bethany interjected, ". . . I have heard, by the way, that she is not well."

Wheatley-Smith raised his brows, inserting the possibility of her illness into his equation, and picked up his theme. "So, diverse as these three might seem at first, they have this in common: they do not willingly lose money. Therefore, there is something they know that the rest of us cannot divine, something that will enrich them." He stopped and looked at her piercingly.

"Well, the obvious thing is that they would raise prices once they get the land they want," said Bethany, "but . . ."

"Yes, 'but.' We both know they cannot do that without ruining themselves. They would be undersold by everyone, the Spaniards, the Portuguese, the Romanians and Bulgarians, the Chileans. And, above all, the Americans. Can you imagine how much drinkable wine—if their so-called Chablis and Burgundy can be accounted drinkable—the Americans, indeed the Californians alone, can produce? Why they and these others would rush into the market and wipe out the Bridseys and Maiers and the Pfeffermühles."

"Then what . . . ?" began Bethany.

"The 'what' is what has brought you here," said the inspector. "We do not know the 'what.' We are talking, after all, about an industry of great complexity, one grossing in the vicinity of sixty-five billion pounds a year. Even vineyard owners, if I may be presumptuous, do not often realize the extent to which the world economy is related to wine production. It is the largest single industry in Italy, not much less so in France, Spain, Portugal. Dear lady, in the Soviet Union, hard as some would find it to believe, we are talking about a crop worth seven billion pounds.

"In the United States, gigantic conglomerate firms own very large vineyards. When such companies shudder, the American stock markets shudder with them. There are, in addition, fertilizers, petroleum for transport, glass, banking—there's no end to the other industries which have critical ties to the wine industry.

"In strictly financial terms, there are, conservatively, forty billion pounds throughout the world in outstanding loans to wine enterprises of one kind or another. Indeed, short of the world wheat market there is no single comestible with so much economic stature. And some might argue about wheat.

"The intricacies of this Gargantua are not fathomable." He paused again and said as gently as his gravel voice permitted, "Baroness, I would not dare suggest an answer as to why these people are offering these seemingly outlandish prices. We do not even know if those we have named are acting

in concert. So I come full circle. They know something that we do not know, something that only a
methodical and thorough study might unveil."

"Then, inspector, that is even further reason
for you to help us," she urged, hoping that she
had interested him enough for him to reverse the
decision he had made on the telephone.

With an almost gentle smile, he leaned toward
her. There was a further reason, he said, why he
would not take the case. While he did indeed know
the wine business well, as well anyway as any outsider could, there would be a quality of self-
flagellation in his investigating it.

"Baroness, it was both my beloved and my bane
for many years," he said.

She looked at the cadaverous cheeks, the introspective eyes, thought of the lemonade, and recognized the dedicated alcoholic who drinks no more.
She liked the austere honesty of the man. He reminded her of an old vine that has been tested by
storm, by freezing, and by sun heat.

She wanted him to help her all the more. He
saw this and raising his hand, allowed himself another personal note. "It would be a madman who
having survived a neurotic love affair, goes back,
merely for money, to the same beguiling woman.
I am not yet, I think, crazy. I cannot take your
case."

His no was definite. Involuntarily, tears came
to Bethany's eyes.

Wheatley-Smith did his best to retrench and
become steely.

"Now let's not do that." He directed a stare at

her which held no more warmth than a good police report. Still she sat before him in the little pub with the tears welling in her blue eyes.

"Look here," he said, knowing he was doing something foolish, or worse. "I have a nominee for you, an alternative. I am sure enough of him that if he should not take it, I will, in that event, do a bit for you—ask a few questions."

It was as much as she would get.

"I would prefer you, of course. But I am grateful you are willing to go that far with us."

Wheatley-Smith acted as if he had not heard her.

"He is an American journalist."

Bethany, optimistic a moment before, started to protest. If there was one thing she did not want, it was publicity. If there was one group she disdained, it was journalists. Wheatley-Smith cut off her intent with another look of North Sea chilliness.

"We worked on a major story together, a decade or so ago. We have been friends since then. I trust him. Both of us liked wines; I, a bit too much. His name is Aubrey Warder and he has recently retired with considerable honor, I gather, from his newspaper career. Here is how you can reach him . . ."

Two

AUBREY

Aubrey Warder, fifty-four years old and counting, knelt in the sandy Maryland loam before the grapevines which were a fifth of his age and tried to slip the end of a fresh cut scion into the white vee he had cut in the twisted wood. On the first try, the young graft overlapped slightly. He took it out, inspected the cut and tried again. It slid snugly into place.

The late June sun was overhead. He had sweat through his flannel work shirt and the upper rear of his trousers. He did not mind the smell of his sweat. In his days as a reporter he had always thought that someone was going to discover that deodorants, whether they were the kind that dried up sweat or suppressed it, would be found to be carcinogenic.

In fact, he liked many strong, natural smells. He liked the smell of Gorgonzola and Limburger. He liked the smell of women. He liked the odor of

21

what the French call *pourriture noble*, the "noble rot" that comes in late harvested grapes.

He liked the smell of manure and of decaying grape skins. On these two acres that he had bought a year and a half ago, he had switched to these and other natural fertilizers from chemicals.

By midafternoon he could feel the stiffness in his back. He rolled sideways from his knees and lay face up on the ground. His eyes were half-shaded by the vines. He bent his knees and squeezed in his buttocks, flattened the small of his back against the earth to soothe its discomfort, to strengthen its muscles. He was no fitness fanatic, but two minor heart episodes had contributed to his quitting the newspaper. So, for his heart, for the vineyard, for his bicycling, and because he wanted to ski a few more years, he kept himself in prime shape.

The vineyard, outside Washington, D. C., had belonged, along with many other properties, to Aubrey's late publisher, Mr. March. In Aubrey's more than twenty-five years with the paper, he had brought it honor, including a Pulitzer Prize, and Mr. March's estate had let him have the vineyard and its minimal equipment for a song. He had retired on it early and happily to indulge his lifelong interest in wines. A widower, he was marginally secure on the income from his profit sharing at the paper, his pension, and conservative investments he had made over the years.

His first harvest at Phoebe Hills Vineyards—named after his wife who had died ten years before—had been last fall. Aided by the seventy-year-old self-taught vinedresser who had haphazardly run the toy vineyard for Mr. March, Warder had bottled forty cases of a red, a Chelois, and a white, a Seyval.

His first sampling convinced him he had a toilsome way ahead, but now that the bottles of his initial extract were proudly labeled and stocked in the *cave* of his compact farmhouse, Aubrey was getting down to the business of making serious wine. By the time the century reached its nineties and Aubrey his sixties, his wines, he was certain, would be suitable for entry in state and regional wine contests.

His back exercises ended, Aubrey, still supine, turned his head and smelled the good earth, like an aging Ferdinand the Bull. In fact, zoomorphically, his handsome gray head did have something of the bull in it, mixed anomalously with the curious bright eyes of a chipmunk or squirrel.

Rocking his back, he came adroitly to his knees in front of the hybrid root stock he had been addressing, plucked from his wicker basket another of the Chardonnay grafts with which he was experimenting, and scientifically whittled it to a perfect wedge.

As he did, perhaps from some old reportorial sense of threat, he cocked his head toward the east, the city. Far off, he saw a little burst of dust. A car or truck had turned from the asphalt county highway onto the dirt road that ran past his own land and then deeper into corn and dairy lands to the west.

The dust plume wafted up over the hedgerows, disappeared behind a copse, and appeared again, glowing in the afternoon sun before it was lost nearer behind dark woods. Aubrey returned to his vines.

Yet the dust had left irritating particles in his mind: there had been excitement in reporting. He had liked the feeling of exhilaration in the chase, the exultation when the story was finally in type with his name on it. But that was inextricably entwisted with anxiety, frustration, inefficiency, cowardly editors, corporate red tape.

He took still another of the sturdy Chardonnay twigs between his thumb and forefinger and reached out to his vines.

At that moment, a shadow fell across his back. He pivoted his head, startled and momentarily fearful. The westering sun was directly behind the figure who had so quietly approached him. He could see it only vaguely: a finely woven jonquil yellow linen skirt, and practical shoes below strong, shapely sheer-clad legs. The upper body and face were in silhouette.

"They told me at your paper that I would find you here among the things you loved," the woman said. Her voice was aristocratic. It held a demand in it. Her accent was decidedly Germanic. But for all its earnestness, it had more in it of Strauss waltzes than Wagnerian angst.

Aubrey levered himself to his feet, brushed the dirt from his old corduroys, and, the sun out of his eyes, looked into a lightly tanned and unarguably attractive face.

"Aubrey Warder," he said, putting out his dirty hand. Without hesitation she wrung it in the firm Austrian style.

"Bethany von Mohrwald. You're wondering why

I'm here," she added without a breath, rerouted by his uninhibited look from the set speech she had rehearsed. Her words came out in a gush. "The embassy didn't even know where Poolesville was. And once I was here, I would never have found you except for the help of the librarian." She paused and began again. "Jerome Wheatley-Smith suggested I come to see you. He turned me, my family, down on something very important to us. I would have called, but I was afraid you would say no, too."

"Slowly, slowly," Aubrey stopped her. His inspection of her face done, he invited her in. As they walked toward the farmhouse, he asked her where she had come from, had her repeat her name, trying to remember where he had heard it before. He led her across his faded carpeting, his hardwood floors, and into the large country kitchen.

"My favorite room," Aubrey said as he drew back a heavy captain's chair from the cherry table for her. "Next to the bedroom," he added, to be accurate, then embarrassed by her startled look, he explained quickly. "I get tired at night. I like to read in bed."

She flushed and then smiled. Although she wore a wedding ring and he supposed she was in her late thirties, or even early forties, there was a youthful modesty about her. There was also something outdoorsy, earthy, a rustic quality despite her tailored European suit.

From a rack in the cabinet beside his old-fashioned sink he picked out a bottle of the better of his two products, the Chelois. In producing it, Aubrey had left in a few too many grape stems, exposed the grape juice too long to the skins and kept the fermentation temperature too high. He had hoped these drastic measures would yield a wine of character and intensity, if not of respectability. He was satisfied enough when it proved merely drinkable.

"A glass?" he asked.

"I'd love one." She inspected the label and Aubrey felt in her scrutiny more than a mere laywoman's curiosity.

"Mohrwalder," he burst out. "Of course. Son of a bitch. Whoops," he quickly added, "forgive me. The tongue gets a little salty out here." He smiled, pleased with himself for remembering. "I've heard of your Maximilians . . ." He tried to recall the rest.

". . . ehre," she helped him. "Thank you."

He poured the Chelois and then fetched a chunk of American blue cheese, half a small salami, chilled apples, a loaf of rye from which he cut two generous slices. The food, he hoped, would reduce the wine's brute impact.

She forthrightly tasted the wine and tried to repress a shiver, seeking at the same time some way to soften her judgment.

"It's strong," Aubrey acknowledged. He was hurt. Then he chided her. "Come on, goddamn it, it's my first vintage. I've got some gentler stuff in there if . . ." He had some good California Chardonnays, Cabernets, and zinfandels which he himself drank when his own monsters became too scratchy for his palate.

She nodded off his offer of a substitute, adding

lightly but candidly, "It may take a little time for you to produce any *grands crus* out here in Montgomery County, Mr. Warder."

"I'll be satisfied if I can get them to where they're no worse than Austrian wine," he countered good-humoredly.

She started to defend Austrian wines, but demurred.

"Touché," she bowed. "To the wines of Austria and Montgomery County. May all of them and all of their makers improve with age." She took a solid conciliatory gulp of the Chelois. In spite of her best efforts, her face puckered.

"You have an honest palate, Mrs. von Mohrwald," he said. Her face was still trying to find its original lines. "And an honest face." He laughed, and she, as best she could, joined him. "When you find your tongue, tell me why you're here."

She took another sip of the Chelois, this one circumspect and only for resolution. In chronological order, she told him what she knew, ending with Wheatley-Smith's single conclusion that the vineyard buyers had some mysterious secret that would make them money where no money would seem to be.

Aubrey made no comment for a long minute.

"And you're absolutely sure," he said at last. "You'd rather risk having the old homestead go up for a sheriff's sale than take the big money and run?"

"We don't like the . . ." she looked for words.

"Big guys from outside taking over."

"Yes. After the last two bad years, we've known

something drastic might happen. But the land has been ours . . ." She was afraid to mention the four centuries for fear it would sound like bragging.

"For a couple of hundred years," Aubrey guessed.

"Better than four hundred. And our son, perhaps both of them will want to continue to . . ."

"So you came to me . . ."

"Hoping you would find out for us what's going on. It may be that what appears to be a cartel is actually several competing groups, all buying up different areas. If that is the case, perhaps we can steer an independent road and survive. It might even mean we can sell our wine for better prices."

He wrinkled his brow, thinking, too, what all this could mean to American wines. The American vintage was a half-billion gallons a year, mostly Californian. That was a three billion dollar crop, five if you figured retail.

American wines made up 5 percent of world production. If money was to be made undercutting the competition, that could easily go to 10 percent, maybe more: the Americans had always wanted to crack the European market.

"Wheatley-Smith was right about the Americans," he said. "Imagine the amount of horsepi . . . of cheap wine we'd flood into Europe at say three bucks a bottle if the Europeans really jumped up their prices. Hell, they'd be peddling at five and we'd do to them what Japanese TV sets did to us . . ."

Bethany was watching him shrewdly. Her mind was working on a number of levels. How enthusiastic he is, she was thinking. Yet he's got to be fifty, maybe more. How hard he would work; how fast his mind functions now that it's in gear. Why should a person with his skills vegetate over here with these dreadful reds? And his whites even worse, I'm sure, or he would have served me one. And less definably, there was another consideration: it would be stimulating to help on the case with this shaggy, craggy, open man.

"The kind of investigation you're talking about will cost you a helluva lot of money. I thought you were on the rocks."

She shrugged.

"What choice do we have? We are not going to sit by while these people send the tumbrels for us."

Her pluck made her seem all the more attractive. He wondered whether she was faithful to her husband. Two months ago, Aubrey's lover for years, a woman divorced from a former Speaker of the House, had left the country. She had been a Congresswoman, then a Commerce undersecretary, and was the new ambassador to Sri Lanka. When he dropped out, those flarings of late passion that had so surprised and enraptured them became less frequent, less hot. Now, he had no one.

Aubrey hoped his visitor had not sensed the trend of his thoughts. He poured her another glass of the Chelois. She smiled into his eyes, knowing this third glass was both a gesture of friendship and a dare. She drank it down boldly, in the Russian style, this time not bothering to hide her grimace and her shudder.

"This *verdammt* thing is all of muscles," she said, her English breaking down slightly from the shock.

Then she composed her face, seeing in his that he was making up his mind.

He turned his glass in his roughened hand. The late afternoon sun streamed through the windows, highlighting the coarse bread crust, the pale cheese, the dark wine bottle, setting aglow the yellow linen of her jacket.

Certainly in his newspaper days, he would have jumped at such an offer: unlimited expenses to travel anywhere in Europe, the subject—wine—one he was crazy about anyway, a chance to discommode rich avaricious people, to sort out entangled financial dealings, to unpeel layer by layer an unusually well-concealed mystery.

And here, he thought with a thump of his heart, there was a hint—no, less—a fantasy of romance with a beautiful woman. It tempted him. But not quite enough.

He looked out the window where the sun was throwing a golden light on his land.

"I can't," he said. "If I were going to do this, why hell, I might as well be back in the news business." He didn't want to be the kind of person anymore that he had been as a reporter, shooting the head off a new rattlesnake every day, functioning as a hitman in a world of hitmen.

He preferred to be the spouse of loneliness, sentimentally reviving the memory of his dead wife, of his lover who had left him, tending to the farm routine, the clusters of tiny grapes, and thickening foliage of his vines. He had contentedly toned down to nothing more adventurous than an occasional opera or concert in Washington, a long evening meal at his favorite restaurant, Old Anglers in Potomac, the desultory translation he was doing of Vergil's *Bucolics*.

"No, I won't do it," he repeated. "I can't, won't."

Her face lost its animation. Without that spark, it was young no longer. Aubrey looked at it, a sad, brave forty-year-old face now, one that had its share of disappointment. He sighed, feeling suddenly a coward, and yet protective of her even as he forfeited the right to be.

"No, I won't do it," he repeated. "I can't, won't."

He started to pour her a last glass, but she waved it off. So he poured himself the final glass and drank deeply from it, to make himself feel better about his vineyard, his wine, his present life.

"Inspector Wheatley-Smith was sure you would," she said, her voice small now, no longer confident. "I thought for a few moments you might," she added desolately.

He looked at her, truly liking her, stirred by her intelligence and good looks, her class, her courage, the upbeat quality in her that he had felt from her first words.

"I damned near did," he said almost to himself. "I don't know who to advise you to try."

He had rejected her and her mission after she had come all the way to America. With a dignified chill in her voice, she said, "Inspector Wheatley-Smith was so certain you would take it that he said he would help us out a bit if you didn't. But I'm afraid the emphasis was on 'a bit.' "

"Oh, he'll do more than that. Once he's into it." It sounded so lame. "You're actually better off with him," Aubrey tried again.

"Perhaps," Bethany said.

At her rented car, they shook hands. Aubrey watched the car disappear around a curve, then saw its plume of dust to the east above the darkening woods.

Three

THE WINE PRESS I

Jerome Wheatley-Smith, in spite of his sixty-three years, bald head, and the thin wispy hair that ringed it, was sinewy as a greyhound beneath his light Donegal sports coat and Daks—unseasonable and unfashionable clothes for California in July. He was a stubborn, traditional man. Stubbornness had kept him drinking too long and stubbornness of a different kind had helped him give it up two years ago.

At the end of the Sunday tour of Domaine McIntyre vineyards, on the outskirts of Los Platanos, he nodded pleasantly but negatively to the fellow tourist who offered to fetch him a glass of the vineyard's wine samples. As the group slowly dispersed, he strolled to a bench a hundred yards up a sparsely graveled path that looked out on the wine acreage and the wooded hills.

A bit of breeze caught him, fanning his hair as he wrote down in his notebook his observations

33

on the visit. That done, he scanned the leaflet on
the vineyard which he had picked up inside,
underlining a phrase here, putting down an excla-
mation mark where he found something particularly important to his investigation. Such notes
would help him on his next visit when he came
back not as an unobtrusive tourist, but as an investigator, a private eye as the Americans called
them.

Along the path which he had just trod, he saw
a younger man coming slowly, wiping his face with
a black-and-red bandanna. The man was dressed
in a light blue tennis shirt and spiffy dark blue
slacks. He wore a camera over his shoulder. The
approaching figure's once athletic build was gone
and he was panting. They get that way out here,
Wheatley-Smith thought. He looked back at his
notes.

To his surprise, the muscular young man sat
down beside him with a word of apology. An-
noyed, then instinctively alerted, Wheatley-Smith
started to rise with a murmured, "Just going." But
the man's right hand gripped him on the forearm.

"If you look down you'll see there's a pistol
underneath my bandanna, inspector."

Wheatley-Smith did so. A silencer's snout protruded from under the handkerchief. He looked up
at the open American face of his confronter but
said nothing. His heart tightened. This man, he
knew, in all probability meant to kill him. If he did
not he would have come on him with his face hidden.

"We will get up," said the man distinctly, "you
and I. We will walk toward the wine press shed

up there on the hill. Stay to my left and a half pace ahead."

The gunman gave Wheatley-Smith an instant for that to sink in, then with a firm bump said, "Okay, up!" thrusting the smaller man off the bench with his arm. He shifted the pistol and bandanna to his right hand which he kept casually at his waist.

They walked silently up the path. At the top, near the large shed, deserted now until the harvest, the man nudged him leftward across a bare area of packed dirt toward the fields, equally deserted, today, Sunday.

Wheatley-Smith's mind worked agitatedly, a bat seeking a way out of a windowless room. Sweat, which up to now had not come, dampened his armpits, his hands, his wrists and calves.

Within the vine rows, the gnarly plants grew too close together for two to walk abreast. The gunman commanded him to go first. Wheatley-Smith could almost feel the place in his back where the bullet would enter. The vines brushed at his coat, scraping the notebook and the Domaine McIntyre literature he had hurriedly thrust into his pocket.

Thirty yards into field, and without a change in his careful steps, Wheatley-Smith tensed. It was now. Or good-bye. He would spin and strike the gun with his fist. But before he could pivot, the gunman spoke.

"Stop and hand me backwards the notebook and other things sticking out of your coat pocket. Pick them out with your thumb and forefinger and don't try to dig deeper." The voice was precise, strong, and confident.

For all his forty-one years of police work, Wheatley-Smith had never dealt with an armed man. He had never carried a pistol. In his hard cop's mind this irony flickered: that he should be threatened by a gun only after he retired, and in a foreign country.

Calmly as he could, he pulled out the notebook and the slickly printed pamphlet. He handed them rearward, waving them slightly as if nervous. At the instant before he imagined the younger man was reaching for them, he dropped them in the dry dirt.

"Forgive me," he said, simulating, nor was it difficult, a panicky voice. He turned as if meekly to pick them up.

The gunman was already stooped, left hand downward to retrieve the papers, the small automatic still at the ready in his right hand. The posture gave Wheatley-Smith the momentary opportunity he sought. With bony fist tightened hard as stone, he struck with all his power at the tanned forearm of the gunman.

The impact was like striking a meaty leg of lamb. The pistol went off with a "thwatt." The man clutched at Wheatley-Smith's coattail, but the wiry Englishman wriggled free, broke wildly through the row of vines, and crouching low, rushed up the dirt avenue parallel to the one he had been walking.

There was no time for jubilance, only flight, frantic flight deeper into the vineyard, for the way back led past the gunman. Wheatley-Smith heard his adversary crash through the vines behind him.

Knowing this would give the man a clean shot, Wheatley-Smith hurled himself into the next row. His foot tangled in a vine and he fell, but scrambled up and ran on.

He could hear his pursuer thrashing through the vines behind him. His throat ached. His breath grated. His heart thudded dangerously. Wheatley-Smith did not want to die. He had found a new life in his retirement and in the conquest of his demon. He wanted a few good years to enjoy these unpretentious treasures.

Ahead, the vineyard was crossed by a dirt path. When he reached it at a trot, he saw at its end a paved road. A car flashed by on the road. Wheatley-Smith plunged down the path. It would be a long run. But just maybe! For a man his age, he was in good shape. "I can do it!" he thought feverishly. "I can!" His second wind came with an invigorating lift.

Risking a look over his shoulder, he saw the gunman in the path aiming, both hands outstretched, American police style.

Wheatley-Smith swerved into the weeds beside the dirt path to throw off the aim. On his second stride, he tramped an unseen rock. His ankle canted, pitching him into the shallow overgrown drainage ditch that edged the path's narrow shoulder. Pain stabbed his ankle as he sprawled. He lurched to his feet, but the ankle would not support him and he fell.

Reflexively, he tried to crawl. But that, of course, was futile. Tears of fear, anguish, and anger burned his eyes. He pulled out his penknife, opened the

pathetically small cutting blade. He lay panting in
the short grass of the ditch, waiting like a crippled
bird for the man to do what he would.

The American ran up, his sky blue shirt sopped
to navy with sweat. The gun was in his right hand,
his eyes on the knife as he stopped a half-dozen
paces from Wheatley-Smith. Between his gasps for
breath he smiled maliciously at the older man and
his penknife.

"Don't be stupid," he said. "Fold it up and toss
it on the path. I'm not going to hurt you." He
paused and caught some more breath. Wheatley-
Smith, assessing his face, kept the blade open. He
took no hope from the man's promise. It was always easier to handle a docile man than a hostile
one. He felt contemptuous of the man for trying
this old ruse.

"Okay, fold it up," the man repeated, irritated,
and pointed the tubular snout of the automatic at
Wheatley-Smith. "Quick!"

There was no percentage in defying the gun.
The Englishman snapped shut the blade and threw
the knife up onto the dirt. The gunman walked to
it, picked it up, and pocketed it.

"Leg?" he asked almost amiably, gazing down.

"Ankle."

"Can you walk?"

Could he? Better to try than to die in this ditch.
He came to his knee, raised himself on one foot
and placed the other down gingerly.

"Perhaps," said Wheatley-Smith. He put some
weight on the injured ankle. Pain shot up his leg.
Still, it did not feel broken or badly sprained. He

put some more weight on it. It ached but no longer pierced him with agony. He would be able to hobble.

"Get up on the path. Try to walk," said the American. "Come toward me. But not too close," he added, again almost with good humor.

Wheatley-Smith limped painfully to the path. The gunman moved to the lame man's left and stopped slightly behind him. Wheatley-Smith waited for him to say which way they were going.

He sensed the tension in the man to his rear, then saw the man's right arm come up. He tried to duck as a fist flashed toward the corner of his eye. Too late. The fist hit him stoutly on the temple, and he fell, unconscious even before he crumpled.

The former inspector came to as the gunman flopped him from a rough fireman's carry onto the ground between the grapevine rows. His head ached terribly. He felt a muddled but horrible guilt, an anger, a sense of outrage. He lay on his back and blinked. The gunman was picking up the notebook and the pamphlet from where they had fallen.

Wheatley-Smith was bewildered by the pain in his head, his ankle. But mostly he was confused by this unfocused but intense feeling of guilt. At last his mind cleared enough for him to understand. He was drunk, as drunk as he ever had been in his life. But he had not had a drop to drink.

He saw the man bend over him. He was jerked to his feet and felt even through his wooziness the crushing pain in his ankle. Drunk! He was hideously, incomprehensibly drunk!

"I didn't have a dram," he murmured.

"You got hit in the head. "

No, this feeling was too familiar, familiar in a bizarrely disorienting way, a sickening way.

"No," he slurred, "I'm drunk."

"That's ridiculous," said the American with a cruel laugh.

The man shoved him along and he stumbled, trying to keep his footing. The ankle pain cut through the thick clouds in his mind. His head throbbed. From behind him, the man roughly brushed the traces of dirt from the back of his coat and then from his pants legs.

"Thank you," said Wheatley-Smith inanely.

He walked leadenly on, gradually feeling a mild itch in his groin.

"I must pee," he said and fumbled for his fly.

"Hold it. You can pee in the shed," said the man.

Ahead Wheatley-Smith saw the bulk of the shed weaving vaguely in his intoxicated eyes. Because his eclipsed mind was fixed on urinating, he was almost unaware of crossing the bare yard to the shed's doorway.

The man fumbled with the door and the ex-inspector saw that his hands were now clad in leather gloves. Absurd, he thought. It's summer. It's all absurd. The man pushed him lightly into the dim coolness of the building.

Made obedient by his indecision, his almost infantile confusion, the Englishman let himself be guided to a fuse box. He saw his captor's arm come down, the hand clad in the leather glove. It was odd, Wheatley-Smith thought again, most curious.

He gave a little "hunh" of laughter, but his

mouth was closed and the snort came out his nose along with a little mucus. He attempted to wipe it off with his sleeve but couldn't seem to find his nose. He snorted again.

The man led him to a large horizontal basket press, a Vaslin. A catwalk ran up eight feet to a door atop the huge cylinder through which workers could enter for cleaning. The door was open. Was this where he was supposed to urinate?

"I must pee," Wheatley-Smith repeated urgently, like a child.

The man behind him shoved him roughly up the catwalk. The agony in his ankle made him momentarily forget his most demanding need. He stared fascinated into the empty cylinder.

"Wine press," he said sillily. "I'm going to pee in the wine press." It seemed babyish but appropriate. A sort of payback to the adult world for the things that hadn't gone right. He reached for his fly.

Rude hands took him by the back, lifted him skyward over the guardrail toward the open door of the press. He struggled and screamed and screamed, or thought he did, as he was pushed into the cylinder and fell to its concave floor. He hurt all over but was conscious. There was a moment of quiet. Thank God, he thought foggily. He's gone. He just wanted to hide me away in here. Somehow I will manage to get out.

The wine press roared into operation. A shining steel plate heaved from its position on the side of the cylinder toward the center where Wheatley-Smith lay.

Four

ROBERT ST. GAGE

Barristers' Chambers West, for all its picturesque name, was a gleaming maroon steel-and-glass tower just out of the old legal district of London. On its eleventh floor, one of the city's largest amd most powerful law firms had its offices.

It vigorously represented clients disdained by older firms more careful of their reputations: a pharmaceutical firm accused of deforming babies with a drug known to be dangerous; renegade coal-mine owners against widows and children whose husbands and fathers had been killed in the mine's patently unsafe underground galleries; in years past, the Ugandan tyrant Idi Amin. The law partners were wealthy as a result. For good reason, there was not too much questioning among them.

By a window in the conference room—whose walls were richly paneled with what on close inspection was mahogany veneer—one of the partners, Robert St. Gage, mused on the Thames a diagonal mile away.

St. Gage was in his late thirties, his face lean, handsome yet etiolated as if the feelings had drained away with some of the color. In his hand-tailored double-breasted suit, he had the elegant tension of a race horse, an animal too specialized to do any gainful work, bred only to run a few seasons before he would be sold for meat, or put out to stud and pasture depending on how well his running career had gone.

Through the sealed window, the sound of the bells by the river reached the air-conditioned room ever so faintly, chiming the time. St. Gage thought fleetingly of the poet of bells, Betjeman, whose poems he had first read at Cambridge, memorizing them when others were committing to memory Eliot and Spender and Auden. He looked beyond the Thames at the warrens of small crowded homes, and silently recalled:

"Oh brick-built breeding boxes of new souls.
  Hear how the pealing through the louvres rolls!"

Betjeman's verses spoke with such intricacy and precision, minor but well-bred poems about minor but well-bred people, not unlike St. Gage's own lineage. His direct antecedents were second and third and fourth sons of other second and third and fourth sons. There had not been a titled St. Gage for generations.

But far, far back, in a time toward which both St. Gage and his father had yearned, there were

Hotspurs and Hastings and Tewkesburys. St. Gage felt in himself infusions of these distant heroes' bravery, their quick, sure vision.

In darker genealogical corners, there were St. Gage links with Tyrrels and long-ago Extons, and if St. Gage had been more honestly introspective, he would have acknowledged in himself something of their penchant for cruel impulsions, their pleasure in causing anguish in others, their self-indulgent aberrations.

St. Gage's father, a subcabinet minister, had been exposed in an espionage and prostitution scandal while his son was at Cambridge. In proving he was innocent of the former (and guilty of the latter), the father had exhausted the family's money, then shot himself. Loyal and at least superficially unresentful toward his father, St. Gage had left Cambridge for night law school in London, forsaking Betjeman for Blackstone.

Now, here in the quiet conference room, the telephone buzzed and St. Gage pushed a button. His secretary announced the American visitor that St. Gage had been expecting and for whom he had reserved the conference room which was electronically swept each week out of respect for the British intelligence establishment, *inter alia*.

The man who entered had blond, sun-lightened hair and the tanned reckless look of a surfer. But Pierce Tobb was older than most surfers, in his mid-thirties, and heavier.

St. Gage overshadowed his visitor from California in height, presence, and breeding. Yet Tobb's eyes held no fear of the lawyer, rather a kind of cocky liking, a recognition of equality in some things, superiority in others, inferiority, perhaps, in some few others.

"A long trip," said Tobb. From an inside coat pocket he drew a small newspaper clipping on the death of Jerome Wheatley-Smith from *The New York Times*. St. Gage took it as fastidiously as he might a scorpion one joint above the sting. He scrutinized it rapidly.

"Is there anything else I need to know?" he asked Tobb, his heart beating very fast as he returned the clipping.

"Yes," said Tobb. "I checked out the phone numbers in his notes. Mostly agricultural officials, wine people in London, a few in California, some FBI types. . . . But in the front of the notebook and again on the page with his expenses was Franz von Mohrwald, an Austrian . . ."

"The holdout," broke in the usually sanguine St. Gage. "The von Mohrwalds are the ones Bridsey . . ."

"Would they have enough money to fund him?"

"Yes. And the will to."

"Then you've found your Employer of the Year."

Although St. Gage had known someone had hired the British inspector, he was nevertheless shaken to learn his enemy's name. Like many who do unto others, he was surprised to discover anyone would do unto him.

"What else?" he said finally.

"Nothing," replied the casually dressed American. Using a book of matches on the table, Tobb ignited the short article. He waited for it to burn his fingers, blinked pleasurably at the pain, and dropped the dying morsel of paper into the ashtray on the conference table. Then he tamped it to pieces with his fingernail.

"What about your side?" Tobb asked when the tingle in his fingers diminished.

St. Gage motioned him to a chair at the table and when they were both seated began so softly that the American had to lean forward to understand him.

"It's going very well. Bridsey, Maier, the *Witwe*, all doing fine. Not just the land, but stocks, *caves*, options. Everything."

"Anybody else holding out?"

"A few. No one except these von Mohrwalds doing anything about it." St. Gage's face puckered as if he had bitten an unripe grape. "Sometimes I wish we had ignored Austria. But the potential for increased production . . . like Germany in the sixties, and the shilling so low." His thoughts returned to the von Mohrwalds. "Let us hope these von Mohrwalds will take the hint."

"Hint?" Tobb said sardonically. He raised his hand a few inches from the table to signal that no more be said about the von Mohrwalds. "And the other countries?"

"Bridsey is working on Spain and Portugal. He has holdings outside Oporto in the Douro. He will handle South Africa, Australia, and—discreetly if that is possible for him—the Communist people. The *Witwe* does not wish to extend her efforts beyond Germany."

"Maier . . . ?"

". . . is still working on Italy but will move on to Algeria. I have made a few initial appointments with the Chileans and the Argentines." He smiled coldly. "They are seeing me here. I am paying their airfare. They requested first class."

"The Americans?"

"Almost certainly not."

The two men, so different, looked at each other with solemn mutual understanding. Tobb spoke first.

"Well, we expected it. Still, it's too bad."

Again they paused and again Tobb took the initiative.

"So we," he looked an instant for words, "call in the things that go squoosh in the night."

"Interesting way of putting it," said St. Gage. "Do you think this fellow you, um, encountered in California had any inkling of what we are thinking about?"

"Very little to judge by his notebook. And now it doesn't matter. Why, do you think anybody has any definite ideas?"

"I think not," said St. Gage. "There've been reports of some of our acquisitions, but no dangerous speculation." He thought a moment. "The *Witwe* may be guessing. And I suppose Bridsey and Maier. They aren't idiots. I don't think they *want* to know too much. Just that the money . . ."

"By the time anyone does put it all together," said Tobb, "the Fat Lady will be done singing."

St. Gage smiled lamely at the Americanism and half-humorously knocked on wood, using the lozenge-shaped walnut table.

"When things are firmed up a bit," he said, turning to other matters, "we will want to hold some sort of board meeting. It would give our colleagues a sense of legitimacy. I want to make sure they are unanimous in leaving the executive decisions to us. And I want it done in a forum where all of them bear witness to it."

"Can you do it without getting down to too many details?"

"I think so. And it will serve to strengthen a few backbones."

"Maier and Bridsey?"

St. Gage nodded.

Tobb rose to go. The two men had too little in common to spend time in pleasant small talk. At the door of the conference room, Tobb said, "You can reach me at the number in Cannes." He grinned, knowing that his sojourn on the Riviera would irritate St. Gage. For while the solicitor and the others were on the road or the telephone day and often night, cajoling, bribing, threatening, doing all the necessary things to get the vineyard owners and the wholesalers with the stocks of wine to come around, Tobb was living the sweet life, exempt from wearing work.

"Yes, it's as well you stay over on this side for a bit," said St. Gage in a pinched voice. He did not want to resent Tobb's cavalier existence. Resentment, like hate, worked only against the person who felt the emotion, not its target.

St. Gage had found Tobb through an American gentleman-racketeer he had represented in an English gaming case. Since then, Tobb had been irreplaceable. It was not just Tobb's enormous wealth, left him by his timber lawyer father. There was something more.

In this surfer-skier, this pilot-skydiver, this unexpectedly well-read and sometimes superficially charming sociopath, St. Gage knew his hopes would eventually lie. Beneath the sun-bronzed skin, the solicitor recognized, lay a willingness, perhaps a desire, to do things that even St. Gage would not do.

Five

THE WINE PRESS II

When Bethany von Mohrwald called Aubrey at seven one morning two weeks after her visit, he was at first pleased. Now he would find out how her case was going.

But her voice was tense, and unless he was mistaken by the distant connection, angry. After a perfunctory inquiry about how he was, she asked abruptly whether he had read *The New York Times* yesterday.

No, he said, he never read the *Times* anymore. He read the *Washington Post* and his old paper, the *Washington Eagle*.

"I think," she said, "maybe the best thing is to ask you to find a copy and to call me when you have read it."

"You're calling me all the way from Austria to try to get me to subscribe to the *Times*?" He didn't like playing games, not about anything. "Damn it, Mrs. von Mohrwald, I have to go into Poolesville to get a copy. You've spent your dime to call; read me the thing. Or if it's long, summarize it."

She paused. He thought she would accede.

"My cousin in London saw the paper and called me only a few minutes ago. Something terrible has happened. If we talk about it now, you will have no time to consider what I am going to ask you. And you will say no. I am sorry about the trip to Poolesville. But I implore you to do it."

"No to what?" he asked.

"Please, please," she begged him. "Just go. Just read." She gave him her number, had him repeat it to her, forced from him a promise to do as she insisted.

Forgoing the bicycle which he usually rode when he had no major supplies to bring back, he drove to the high school where the library was located, the only sure spot for a fresh *Times*.

He flipped the pages over, as miffed as he was curious, absorbing the headlines. There was nothing on the front page, on the business pages. Then he spotted it: a small headline on the obituary page. Aubrey could not have been more shocked if it had been an eight-column streamer.

"RETIRED BRITISH INSPECTOR DIES IN CALIFORNIA MISHAP," the headline said.

The story read:

Los Platanos, Ca. (UPI)—Jerome S. Wheatley-Smith, 63, an internationally known Scotland Yard official before he retired two years ago, was killed Sunday when he apparently fell into a wine press here.

Mr. Wheatley-Smith had headed Scotland Yard's

international trade section and specialized in white-collar fraud. Earlier he had won fame on celebrated espionage, murder, and bank robbery cases.

The former inspector's body was found in a giant wine press by an employee at Domaine Mc-Intyre Vineyards here. A spokesman for the vineyards speculated that Mr. Wheatley-Smith had strayed from the tour of which he was a member, switched on the unattended wine press, peered in to see its operation, and fallen into the machinery.

An autopsy was performed at the San Leon County coroner's office. Police sources said a high percentage of alcohol in the dead man's blood may have been a contributive factor. The full autopsy report has not yet been made public.

The body was released to Hillcrest Haven Funeral Home here from which it was to be transported to London for burial.

Aubrey cursed to himself. Through the workings of fate, workings beyond his control, he was an accomplice in this death. He was not guilty, but he was involved. He saw now why Bethany von Mohrwald had not filled him in over the telephone. She wanted his conscience to work on him.

He read the story again. There were far more questions than answers in it. What was Wheatley-Smith doing in America anyway? Europe was the proper place to begin his investigation. Unless he had run up against some imperative American angle.

What about the tumble into the wine press? Sure, Wheatley-Smith had tapped out on booze from time to time, but he had never been a fall-down drunk. Of course he could have slipped on grape pulp, but Aubrey knew how unlikely that was. Ironies like a man accidentally dying in a wine press while he worked on a criminal investigation of wine potentates just didn't happen in real life. Someone had gotten him drunk and pushed him, or, his guile diluted by booze, had knocked him out and then thrown him in.

Aubrey copied the brief story in longhand, drove back home and called Bethany.

"You should have asked me, or maybe I should have told you; he was heavy into the schnapps." He felt cheapened by even seeming to buy the accident theory.

"No," she brought him up positively. "The newspaper is wrong, or somebody is. My cousin at the embassy had a dear friend make sure before we retained him. He had stopped drinking, was very missionary about it as a matter of fact. Besides, I talked with him the afternoon it happened. He was sober, absolutely."

She explained that Wheatley-Smith, from the beginning, had been scrupulous to the penny about projected costs. In the telephone call before his death, he had said he would need a few extra days and had discussed expenses. The talk had been too detailed, too finicky, for him to have conducted it under alcoholic sail.

Aubrey let that new fact percolate in his head. He had assumed that Wheatley-Smith was drunk when he was murdered. But Bethany von Mohrwald seemed so certain that he was securely on the wagon.

"So you're convinced," he said. "Sober."

"Sober."

But goddamn it, that was impossible. People didn't make mistakes in stories about blood analysis. Even if Wheatley-Smith had been sober when he spoke with Bethany, he could have, for some reason, fallen compulsively off the wagon before he was killed three or four hours later.

"What the hell was he doing out there anyway?" Aubrey asked.

"He never quite said. Not even why he wanted to commence there instead of the continent or England. In the last talk, he did say he had come across 'something interesting.'"

Aubrey mulled that over, too. But then his mind snapped closed. These weren't his mysteries to clear up.

"I still can't take it. I won't. Get somebody younger. Get somebody in the business. A private detective. I'll come up with some names for you."

"We don't want anybody else," she said. "We want you. Besides, you . . ."

"Now, wait a minute. I know what you're going to say. That if I had taken the case, he might be alive."

Yes, Aubrey thought, and I might be a crushed body newly shoveled in. Or maybe not. Maybe I wouldn't have taken the steps he did. Or maybe they wouldn't want to have risked killing an American, an ex-gumshoe. Maybe the Pulitzer would have saved my ass, the ruckus my freak death would have stirred up.

"No," Bethany was saying heatedly, "if you think Franz and I are the kind of people who would suggest that, then you aren't very perceptive. If you think we would use extortion on people's emotions, Mr. Warder . . ."

Well, he was sorry he had said it, but he did notice she slipped into "Franz and I" when the going got rough.

"I'm sorry," he said, "you were going to say?"

"I was *going* to say that you are the sort of person we feel we could work with, could trust."

"That's kind. But I can't." He was less firm now. He thought of his good, passive life, this life he had earned by his past derring-do. He thought of mentioning his heart to her. That would get him off. But his last examination had shown his heart in better shape, his body tougher than it had been since his twenties. He could not lie, had never been a good liar.

Could he really *not* take this case? Could he honorably turn his back on it? A residual vanity in him agreed with Bethany von Mohrwald that he —and he smiled at his hubris — *was* the ideal man for it. Who else knew wines as he did, was retired yet still vigorous, and had done the kind of intricate research, the interviewing, the undercover work, taken the chances, written the white collar crime stories that he had?

But might not he, Pulitzer or no Pulitzer, be killed? The murder of Wheatley-Smith had been intended as a signal to the von Mohrwalds. Yet, honestly, Aubrey could not beg off on fear: one did not investigate the Mafia, report on wars, go into ghetto jungles to do drug stories if one worried about personal safety.

Looking at everything, he was trapped. There

was no way out, not if he wanted to retain his self-respect.

"Okay," he sighed at last. "But you don't know what a reluctant dragon you are sending out to battle."

That same afternoon he drove into Washington to the Library of Congress and read up on the organization of the European wine markets, on the financing, economies, technology, botany of continental winegrowing. When he at least knew what was available, he turned to biographical material on the owners of Schloss von Mohrwald.

From a popular wine history, he found that the first von Mohrwald was a grape grower, a commoner born Eberwald. This Eberwald became von Mohrwald in the sixteenth century after the Turks had conquered a substantial part of Austria. As occupiers, said the history, the Turks were bad enough. But their Moorish mercenaries, though small in number, were a particular plague to Eberwald and his Neusiedlersee neighbors.

Far from home in a country then as now of delectable but uncelebrated wines, the homesick Moors had abandoned their abstemious ways. One Sunday, in violation of both the Koran and the Sublime Porte's 1547 treaty with the Holy Roman Empire, the Moors raided Eberwald's cellars, drank or poured out the entire 1566 vintage, carried off oaken kegs containing part of the 1565, raped four peasant wives and daughters and absconded with three more.

The infuriated Eberwald rallied his own frightened grape pluckers and, .. `h some outlay of gold, some promises and some persuasion, got up a militia that afternoon of neighbors and their peasants. Just before dawn next morning, armed with rude spears, scythes, and vine knives, they crept into the Eber forest where the Moors had their slovenly encampment.

Like many a present-day visitor to the Heurigen, the Moors had been beguiled by the sweetness of the new wine and ignored its punch. They were all drunk or drowsily hung over and were no match for the vengeful vintners who slew them almost to the man. A few managed to flee deeper into the woods, later to tell their story to a regional pasha who rewarded the escapees with evisceration as an example to others who might be bewitched by Western ways.

Maximilian II, learning of Eberwald's bravery, seeking a hero from among the gentry whom he was then enlisting against the occupying Turks, satisfied that the sultanate did not countenance the boorish, Moorish behavior, summoned Eberwald from the Burgenland to Vienna. With much pomp, he coroneted him, Baron von Mohrwald—Baron of the Moorish Forest. Franz was a direct descendant of this doughty farmer.

Aubrey clicked his tongue, pleasantly suprised at the history and went on to consult the *Almanach de Gotha* to find out, now that he had discovered Franz's lineage, what kind of baroness Bethany was. The *Almanach* showed her a member of a slightly older line with a distaff branch, or rather vine, reaching directly to the von Mohrwalds.

The numerous crowns and coronets in her background made the whole business a little more romantic for a middle-class American boy who had never quite gotten over Sir Walter Scott. His recollection that she had not even hinted to him about her title made him like his new employer all the more.

As for the case itself, by dint of the macabre death of Wheatley-Smith, it presented him with an unarguable course to follow. Without the death, Aubrey would have begun by concentrating on the corporate relationships of Bridsey, the German woman, the Frenchman; by interviewing their rivals; by reading wine journals; by talking with specialized newsmen who covered wine events, with European wine officials, wine brokers, real estate men who handled vineyards.

The death allowed him, at least initially, an entirely different tack. If he could prove there was foul play, he could enlist the help of California and perhaps other government authorities and thus increase the manpower working on the case. If those buying the vineyards were shown even peripherally involved in a murder, the scandal would blow up their acquisitions, doom whatever was going on to instant financial disaster.

That evening, he made his plane reservations to California, looked out his window toward his night-cloaked acres, poured himself a tumbler of his Chelois and wondered what in the hell he was doing leaving the sweet life of Candide.

Six
_____

CALIFORNIA LOOK

Aubrey was back in a business suit with Oxford shirt and slightly aggressive tie, the uniform he had worn for thirty years. More than that, he was back in the mold of obdurate reporter, sublimating the easy, even kindly side of his character that had begun to bloom since his retirement.

For a while, as the stretch Chrysler rolled along, he stared at the glamorous mountains, the stands of great trees. Then he read a few pages in a dreadfully written book, *The European Wine Industry, 1123–1981*. After a half-hour, head back, lips parted, he dozed.

Michael Duddman, the hip young coroner for San Leon County, efficiently asked Aubrey for his identification. Aubrey had flirted with a breach of ethics: using his press credentials from the *Eagle* on the thin theory that he might convert his investigation eventually into a free-lance story. That would be the perfect cover. But it would also be abuse of a profession or at least a trade in which he had taken pride.

So he had settled, perhaps with even less legal or moral justification, for a credential provided him by a former source, a veteran Virginia private detective. It was adorned with a colored and embossed seal, the motto "Sic Semper Tyrannis," and Aubrey's mug shot glaring out with hostility toward all, tyrants and bureaucrats alike.

Duddman nodded over the impressive credential and told Aubrey he had an aunt who lived in Roanoke. After a minimum of other small talk, they got down to business.

No, said Duddman in answer to Aubrey's questions, there was no suicide note. The police had found the motel where Wheatley-Smith had been staying when the owner called them after the story appeared in the local paper. The police had turned over the room. No, said Duddman, there were no lists of telephone numbers, no notebooks, no investigative notes. Only clothes, personal articles. A second set of false teeth.

No, no sign of forced entry. Duddman shrugged.

"What does that mean?" he said. "Every moron burglar's got the most advanced lockpicking gadgetry now."

The police, he said, had found the Englishman's passport in the wine press. From his entry date they had ascertained he came directly to San Francisco after clearing customs at Kennedy.

Aubrey bored in, but Duddman interrupted. It was his turn. What, he asked, was Aubrey looking for? Well, Aubrey said, distorting Bethany's position a good deal, a business associate of Wheatley-Smith had retained him to make some routine checks.

"Embezzlement?" guessed Duddman.

"No, more a personal thing." Aubrey tried to look up at Duddman guilelessly.

Duddman gave an understanding grin without, behind the grin, a scintilla of eye evidence that he believed Aubrey.

"So what can I help you with?" Duddman asked.

"Just the usual," Aubrey said. "The blood count, according to the paper . . ."

"Well, I shouldn't . . ."

"The body's already gone. What can it matter? He's out of the country. So's the family."

"Point two eight," Duddman obliged.

"Jesus," said Aubrey involuntarily. That was one hell of a lot of booze between Bethany's call and when Wheatley-Smith must have dropped into the wine press. He'd have had to be slugging the bottle nonstop.

"Talk with anybody in the tour group?"

"The police did."

"And did they say he seemed drunk?"

"Well, we didn't have the blood tests at the time."

In other words, no one said he seemed drunk, or Duddman would have told him that the police found witnesses who had remarked on it. Aubrey felt crawly. But he did not want, at least yet, to put Duddman any more on his guard than he was already.

"Can I get a look at the autopsy report?"

Duddman hesitated.

"There ought to be a release from the family, you know."

"Come on. Get me out of your hair. Why make me waste time finding a cop to get it for me? Or some local reporter. Besides, you may need a favor on the East Coast. I'll owe you a big one."

Duddman considered that. It didn't hurt to have a contact back East. In exchange for helping Aubrey at no real risk to himself, he'd have Aubrey's IOU in his pocket for free information or even a bit of free snooping.

"Forget you saw it here," Duddman said.

"Of course."

The autopsy report was a lengthy catalogue of hematomas, cranial to metatarsal fractures, traumatized ependyma, epicardium, and epiglottis, among other things, abrasions on several surfaces and a few minor lacerations. The report also touched unkindly on Wheatley-Smith's liver, and its "precirrhotic state."

Aubrey had seen the jargon enough to interpret it like a doctor.

"Ravages of sin, hunh? No big cuts, no external bleeding?" he asked.

"Nope. Crushing, but no tearing." Duddman scrunched up his face. "The body shorted out the wine press."

"So except for the scratches, the skin . . ."

"Well, it looked like an eggplant."

"No chance of a knife wound or bullet wound getting lost in the bruises?"

Duddman looked at Aubrey disgustedly.

"Oh come off it," he scoffed. "You've been a

private detective too long. You guys see a murder every time there's an unattended death."

"I was a reporter before I was a private eye."

"Then you were a reporter too long."

"I'll buy that," said Aubrey. "Who's the best guy to talk to at the cops?"

"The deputy chief's a shrewd old Mexican mudslogger named Hernandez. Try him," said Duddman.

"The chief?"

"Criminology Ph.D. Berkeley." Duddman could not resist adding, "I don't think he'd find you're his type."

Aubrey walked across the hot square with its ratty palms, their trunks dusty and ringed as old elephants' legs. Elderly men were playing checkers there and blacks and Mexicans were, separately, sitting on the scabby zoysia, smoking. Two blocks off the main street was the Hillcrest Haven Funeral Home, new and expensive, built in the hacienda style.

The portly white-haired mortician looked alarmed when he saw Aubrey's credentials. He started talking rapidly about rights of the deceased's family to privacy, but Aubrey locked eyes with him and warned ominously of lawsuits on behalf of Wheatley-Smith's business partners if information wasn't forthcoming subito.

The mortician wore his watch on the inside of his wrist and when he turned it nervously to look at it as if he had to take a pill, or had a funeral coming up, Aubrey saw the sweat in his palms glistening like oil.

"The best way to get rid of me, Mr. Pernweiser," said Aubrey fixing him with his eyes again, "is just to give me everything I want." The man was intimidated but pouted as if to spar.

Aubrey glowered and continued, "Don't force me to go through all the mangy work of sub-poenaing you to come to a hearing in New York, of grabbing up your records with a duces tecum . . ."

"Can you do that?" asked the older man, rattled.

"Try me," said Aubrey. Resentful, but resigned, the undertaker collapsed with a soft sigh, and answered Aubrey's questions.

Yes, he had personally prepared the body and no, there had been no signs of any unexpected wounds. It had been a terrible job, though, even the face had bruises. He'd spoken with the brother in England before he embalmed, and had even suggested cremation.

"I know how rough that must have been," chaffed Aubrey. Both of them knew how cremations before embalming cut into the funeral homes' profits. The mortician smiled wanly but genuinely.

"We're not as bad as you think. Anyway, they wanted whole interment so that was that."

"Did the brother say anything else? About what he was doing over here? About drinking? Anything like that?"

"Unh uh. The brother was a very cool customer. English, you know."

"Yes," said Aubrey. "Well, he would be, English, that is."

Aubrey recrossed the square to the one-story police headquarters and went directly to the deputy chief. He was past sixty, a cautious second-generation Mexican-American with as much Indian as Spanish in him, Aubrey guessed. He's got to be good, Aubrey thought as he introduced himself, or he'd never have gotten even this far, not with a name and a face both ending in "ez."

Half cop himself, it wasn't long before he'd hit common ground: the deputy chief knew a retired homicide detective in Washington who was an acquaintance of Aubrey. And Aubrey knew the city hall reporter in neighboring Bidlersville who had once been an intern on the *Washington Eagle*.

They chatted with seeming ease, feeling each other out.

Aubrey told Hernandez that he had given up police reporting because of an iffy heart, a mild and only partial untruth, and had taken up private eyeing on a few easy cases to supplement the retirement pay.

"Newspapers are worse than police commissions on pensions," Aubrey said, scratching his chest.

"Oh no man, you don't know." The police official told Aubrey what he would get if he quit. "I couldn't live on it."

"But anyway, you're not thinking of quitting? This place looks like heaven. Sunshine. Good wine. An easy berth."

Hernandez spread his hands, thumbs out.

"Not yet. Not yet."

"Well, if you want to know how retirement is, if you want a list of companies that place old bozos like us, call me. Okay? I got a file an inch thick."

The cop knew what Aubrey was doing, but he

was pleased. Foreplay such as this was a thing of the past. The young reporters, the young private eyes came in and wanted a quick rape of police files.

"I may just want to call you," said the deputy chief.

"Speaking of files," said Aubrey.

The chief smiled.

"I was wondering how you'd get around to that."

"We've both been doing con jobs for a long, long time," Aubrey said, touching the deputy chief's arm.

"So what do you want, man?" he said, his face wrinkling with humor. "You think I got all day to bullshit with has-been door busters?"

"Everything you got," said Aubrey.

In the tiny interrogation room where Hernandez let him sit down with the file, Aubrey took off his coat and tie and began jotting notes.

A vineyard worker, according to the file, had found Wheatley-Smith's body after the master panel in the main building showed a fuse blown at the wine press shed. The discovery had been at six P.M. and the worker had climbed down into the wine press—after switching off the already shorted machinery—to see whether Wheatley-Smith might still be alive. He wasn't.

The police arrived. The detective on the scene noted there was some dirt on the victim's shoes, even a little inside of one. But Aubrey thought, the walk up to the wine press or perhaps an impromptu stroll in the vineyard by Wheatley-Smith could have accounted for that.

At the hospital emergency room just outside

Los Platanos, the doctor on duty had estimated death occurred approximately forty-five minutes earlier. That would have been only fifteen minutes before the body was discovered.

Aubrey took time out to jot down a brief chronology: Bethany had spoken with Wheatley-Smith at about one P.M. California time. The tour had begun at three, ended at four. Wheatley-Smith had been killed at about five forty-five. The body was discovered at six and pronounced dead in the hospital at six-thirty.

That gave the Englishman a maximum of four hours and forty-five minutes to get drunk, assuming Bethany was right about his being sober at the time of the telephone call. Well, if he went at it right, that'd be enough time, even for point twenty-eight.

Aubrey felt drowsy from the heat and because the cross-country trip had elongated his day. He shook it off and tried to force himself back into the bulky file. It showed the deputy chief had called Wheatley-Smith's brother in London and laconically noted that "brother indicated prior drinking history."

Less concise were a homicide detective's interviews with other members of the tour whose names he had taken from the vineyard's guest registry. The cop, efficiently, had put a phone number and address in his report for everyone he had contacted, and for some he had not been able to reach.

Of the five with whom he spoke, four said they remembered the Englishman, because he had worn a tweed jacket and a tie despite the hot day. None thought he was drunk.

One of the four had talked with Wheatley-Smith at the end of the tour. "Mr. Tremsal," said the detective's report, "approached the subject at approximately 1605 hours and inquired whether subject had enjoyed tour to which subject replied in the affirmative. Mr. Tremsal stated that the management of Domaine McIntyre served samplings of red, white, and rosé wines in a large cellar room in the above-identified premises.

"Mr. Tremsal stated he had partaken of one glass of rosé wine and inquired of subject whether he liked the wine. Subject stated he had not imbibed a sample. Mr. Tremsal thereupon offered to bring subject a glass which subject politely refused."

"Son of a bitch," Aubrey said softly. It was not totally impossible that the tour members interviewed were mistaken, that Wheatley-Smith had been drinking earlier. He was taciturn enough not to show it. But Aubrey had seldom seen a drunk who, in his cups, wouldn't take a sip of some other kind of booze if offered it.

If Wheatley-Smith was sober at the end of the tour, that just gave him an hour and forty-five minutes to get bombed out of his mind. But Wheatley-Smith had not been one of your boilermaker drunks, getting smashed all at once. He had been a steady tippler, indefatigably and determinedly drinking, just as he had relentlessly worked on his cases.

So what the hell was going on? Duddman? The man seemed to know his job. That didn't ensure that his lab hadn't fouled up on the blood count. A mistake at the lab would take care of at least that part of the mystery.

Aubrey returned the file to Hernandez, shook

his hand, and gave him his address and telephone number. If it had been Chicago, Aubrey would also have left a fifty dollar bill in a plain envelope and said with a leer that it was for the cop's "favorite charity." But this wasn't Chicago, and Hernandez wasn't that kind of cop.

"*Adios*," said Aubrey.

"So long," answered the Mexican-American.

Aubrey was dog-tired, far more weary than he would have been from physical labor in his vineyard. But he had to keep moving with the momentum. He went back to Duddman's office. This time he didn't get by the secretary so easily.

"Tell him I have got to see him. For both our sakes," said Aubrey. The collective phrase worked. Duddman came out of his office and with a disagreeable but curious look ushered him in.

"I'm not putting any heat on you, honest. I just need the straight. I've got to know that there was no mistake, no possibility of a mistake made on the blood count."

The question should have made Duddman haughtier than he was. Maybe, Aubrey thought, he's checked me out with the local paper and doesn't want to try to outpiss a skunk.

"The lab report said what it said," replied Duddman. "What do you mean you needed to see me for 'both our sakes'?"

"I wondered if you knew that the people the cops talked to said the Englishman was stone sober at the end of the tour and was turning down wine samples."

Duddman looked uncomfortable.

"I saw the whole file," he replied.

"You didn't tell me."

"I don't have to tell you everything I do. I guess you also saw the brother said he'd been a lush. Besides, I don't give a rat's ass what those people said. When I opened him up, the blood smelled like Vat 69."

That brought Aubrey up short. He knew that when an autopsy was done on a person who'd died drunk there was the smell of alcohol. Still, what other avenues did he have?

"Look, I know you know your business. But smelling isn't lab testing. Maybe the lab's count was off. Maybe they goofed and switched specimens by mistake."

"No chance. The other two autopsies that day were a six-year-old kid and a Mormon deacon. Neither had a drinking record." He was pleased with his wit.

"Still, labs make mistakes. Blood from another day. Getting a wrong label on it. I swear I'm not trying to . . ."

"Just what are you trying to do?" Duddman's voice cracked with irritation.

"Look, man. This guy's business associates don't think he was drinking. And the witnesses on the tour . . . I just want to go back with the proof positive."

Duddman was weakening, considering the possibility that some mistake had been made and what that could mean to his career.

"Make a call for me," Aubrey urged. "Jesus, if something turned out to be wrong, better you should make the discovery than somebody else."

Duddman, having reconsidered, decided against helping.

"They don't make mistakes," he said with finality. "I'd be embarrassed to question them. It makes me look like an asshole."

Aubrey saw there was nothing more to be gained by playing Mr. Nice Guy. He had one longshot. Suppose Wheatley-Smith had been drugged, injected with some enzyme that wouldn't show up in tests, and then alcohol forced down his throat as he mindlessly swallowed. Or suppose he'd been injected with alcohol.

"Did you go over him with a magnifier?"

"You're driving at what?" demanded Duddman angrily.

"Just wondering why you didn't really scan the skin on a weird one like this. Nobody asked you not to, did they?"

"Look, I don't even have to talk to you."

"Yes, but you'd rather do that than have my client or somebody sue you or file an official complaint." Duddman still looked ferocious, but Aubrey felt him going on the defensive, smelling lawsuits as the undertaker had, trouble in the newspapers, grief from his boss.

"Okay, for one thing this was the third one that day so the place looked like a battlefield and I was working alone. Two, you noticed, I guess that I ran the blood and tissue and urine through the lab before I closed him up. I'm not crazy, you know. I knew this guy was an ex-cop. And for your prick-ass question, no, nobody asked me to do or not to do anything!"

"Well, never mind that," Aubrey said, tilting

toward the conciliatory. "I had to ask. So you ran the tests . . ."

"All of them. Because the death was unattended. And when the hootch showed up on top of the smell and what the brother said, it looked like that explained it. My god, point two eight!"

"It's high."

"Damn right it's high. So why Sherlock him with a magnifier? When was the last time you saw a guy mainlining J&B?"

Put that way, it sounded pretty lame to Aubrey, too. The logic was on the county coroner's side. But Aubrey moved in doggedly, an old body-puncher who didn't know any other way and had won an awful lot of fights by sheer persistence.

"There was a case years ago where a guy did in his wife with a succinic acid injection. Didn't leave a trace in the tissues. Suppose . . ."

"Sure, the Coppolino case. Once in a million cases, ten million."

"Well, suppose that it happened and the alcohol was just a cover, or even suppose the alcohol was shot in him?"

"Suppose I'm Louis Pasteur?"

Aubrey laughed.

"Recheck the alcohol count. Call the lab. Do it to cover your ass," he said amiably now. "Why not?"

The county coroner smiled. He had won the argument. On balance, too, it was smarter, when challenged, to double-check.

When Duddman called him at the motel, Aubrey knew from the tone of his voice that the lab was accurate. The technician remembered the body. How could you forget it, especially with the added oddity of its being that of an Englishman squeezed to death in a wine press.

The technician had personally labeled the sample and just now had done a second quick run on the blood. It had been off a hundredth, and that in the direction of even greater drunkenness.

"Close enough?" Duddman asked, able now to be as nasty as he wanted.

"I don't blame you for being pissed," said Aubrey soothingly. "I would be too." Leave 'em smiling, if you can, he thought. It's always smarter, particularly if you might want to come back for more.

That night, Aubrey called the vineyard visitors reached by the police, redoing their interviews. When he'd talked to those five, he called another eight from the full list in the police file.

One of the eight, a woman who had been next to Wheatley-Smith, said she had asked him friendly questions about how he liked California and he had answered politely and soberly.

"Poor man," she said, "he talked about how he loved the sunshine here." She had read the report in the paper of his having alcohol in his blood. "I never believe the papers anyway," she said. "The man was as sober as I was."

By eleven o'clock, Aubrey was too punchy to call any more.

In the morning, he tried to chase down the tour people he had missed the night before. By noon, he was left with only a few "don't answers," and some "impossibles," people with names like Brown or Johnson who recorded only towns, not street addresses.

Besides the statements on Wheatley-Smith's sobriety, he got only one worthwhile bit of information. No one remembered any "unusual types." Indeed, Wheatley-Smith with his unseasonable English clothing was clearly the most exotic of the thirty or so tour members.

That afternoon Aubrey planned to take the tour himself. The reenactment made him nervous, but it was necessary. As a reporter, even on war coverage or when he had been looking into the Mafia, he had eschewed weapons. Now he thought of Wheatley-Smith's crushed body and wanted a small pistol.

But California law required a fifteen day waiting period for pistol buyers while a police check was made. He settled, embarrassed and apprehensive, for a knife with a short, ugly spring blade which a novelty store manager sold him furtively from a tray under the cash register.

Like Wheatley-Smith, Aubrey took the tour first as an ordinary visitor. There was the usual trip past the wooden tuns, the stainless steel barrels, the musty cellars where Domaine McIntyre aged its best vintages.

The attractive tour guide, a young viticulture graduate from the University of California, Davis, gave the visitors enough technical information to impress without challenging.

So many gallons exported to so many countries, so many separate steps to produce a wine, so many grapes in a single 1.5 liter bottle, so many varieties of grapes grown in California now as compared to 1900. Aubrey took notes, more by rote than from need.

As he listened, remarking the organization, the modernity of the place, he thought this was surely the kind of vineyard the European combine would like to incorporate into its plans. Was that what brought Wheatley-Smith here? He shuddered, looked over his shoulder.

After the tour he tasted the offerings, his back to a safe corner, and thought wistfully of his own vineyard. He was depressed, and a little jealous of the workaday samples: how long it would take him even to achieve parity with these modest giveaway wines; how long his investigation was putting off the day when he would.

Aubrey drifted to the table where the guest book lay and leafed back to July fifteenth when Wheatley-Smith had died. Rapidly he checked the names against those on the police list. All were the same. Nor was there anything worth noting in the handwriting or comments.

In the waning afternoon, he stood on the veranda of the mission-style administration building behind a giant protective planter and skimmed the slick literature he had picked up inside.

The Domaine, it said, put in some of California's first Chardonnays and Pinot Noirs in the 1860s; was among the belated first to recognize the threat of phylloxera in 1875, and imported from the eastern United States *vitis riparia*, a vine which resisted the oviparous insects; sent five viniculturists to France in 1890 to study vinifera (another first); welcomed President Grover Cleveland in 1896; and lost

ten thousand gallons of wine to an enemy sub-
marine off the Outer Banks in 1942. There was no
hint, though, of why Domaine McIntyre might play
American bellwether for a European cartel.

Aubrey sought out the vineyard manager, an
epicene middle-aged man in stylish jeans named
Cadwalder. With the aid of a flashlight, he was
squinting at the sediment in racked bottles of cham-
pagne. He groaned when Aubrey told him he was
there on behalf of the business associates of the
late Jerome Wheatley-Smith.

At first, he too huffed and puffed, but once
again Aubrey threatened to bring a ravening law-
suit. The vineyard manager sighed his acquiescence. Aubrey had him lead the way to the wine
press shed. As they walked, Aubrey tried to strike
up some talk, but the manager was barely com-
municative.

"Path about the way it was . . . on that day?"
asked Aubrey.

"What do you mean?"

"I mean he had a little dirt in his shoes when
they found him and I don't think there's enough
loose for him to have scuffed it up."

"About the same. It needs graveling," said the
man.

Inside the shed, Aubrey did a sketch of it, wrote
down the specs of the motor from its label plate
and the name of its manufacturer. He was almost
sure the rig had enough power to maim and kill
Wheatley-Smith, but he wanted to be positive.

Outside again, he looked at the miles of grapes.

"Anything special about the fields around this
area?"

"No," said the manager.

"Okay, come on. Why make me ask? What are you growing within a radius of two hundred yards of where we are standing?"

The vineyard man looked hostilely at Aubrey.

In that direction, he pointed to the western quadrant, young zinfandels and vine stocks, and here, Chenin Blancs. Here, he pointed south, were the oldest vine stocks of all.

"The ones you wrote about in the poop sheet, from the east."

"Yes, the old *vitis riparia.*"

"They still bear?" Aubrey asked, more curious now as a viniculturist than as a private eye.

"Yes."

"But don't produce much?"

"No, but . . ."

"Then, why?"

The man sensed Aubrey's shift to mere curiosity and was willing to open up as long as the subject was wine for wine's sake.

"I was going to tell you, if you'll just let me. We use them for experimental purposes. Phylloxera is still a threat, you know."

Yes, thought Aubrey, but much less so since the *vitis riparia* and *vitis rupestris* had saved California and France and just about every vineyard in the world.

"What else do you use them for? You've got lots."

"We export some. And their scions, a dozen or so to Europe this year and last, a dozen to Australia."

Aubrey looked at his watch. Now that he was

talking wine he felt some of his anxieties lift. But he could not indulge himself in conversation for his own pleasure. There was so much else to do.

"Before I go, I'd like to get a list of your top management," he said. The manager went tense again. "Save me the trouble and give it to me," Aubrey said sternly. "And I'd very much like to have a copy of that booklet that companies have with all the phone numbers of employees. And later on I would have to do interviews with your top people . . ."

As intimidated as the winery manager was, this was too much.

"I'd have to talk to our lawyers," he interrupted.

"The list of your top management . . ."

"Oh God," he sighed. This was not his bag, these extraneous things that kept him away from the grapes and the many stages of their juices. "I can let you have that if you'll just go away."

It would give Aubrey enough to start, enough to check out possible cross-ties between Domaine McIntyre and European firms. It wasn't very much, but Aubrey took it, thanked the manager and they parted.

Seven

THE LABORATORY

In summer, Neuilly always seemed cooler to Robert St. Gage than downtown Paris. That was one reason why he had the taxi drop him off a few blocks from his destination: so he could walk beneath the venerable sycamores that shadowed the cracking sidewalks, so he could feel the peace of the suburb seep through him. The other reason was that he didn't want even a taxicab driver to recall someday an Englishman's trip to the huge old house on Rue de l'Horloge.

As St. Gage strolled, he felt buoyantly good about himself. He liked the *idea* of it, a proper Englishman in this refined old faubourg. Tobb, shallow intellectually but a mental jack-of-all-trades, had once described St. Gage as "Richard Cory without the suicidal instincts." St. Gage had nodded as if he understood and appreciated the point. That evening he had found the poem and been pleased by Tobb's perspicacity.

At 14 Rue de l'Horloge, St. Gage pushed the polished brass button beside the high iron gate with its twisted bars and crown of spikes. There was no nameplate to identify it as the home of Dr. Pieter Berkady. On either side of the tall gate, the boxwoods grew eight feet high. Their shiny leaves were so thick that mere speckles of sunlight trickled through, and these only at dawn and sunset.

Withal, the residence was less ominous than it had seemed three weeks ago when he had first visited Berkady. St. Gage had gotten his name from the *Witwe* Pfeffermühle in the course of what he had hoped was a vague talk about authorities on grapevine blights. St. Gage had done what he could to check out Berkady's reputation and, casually using the *Witwe*'s name, had set up that first meeting.

As before, he gave the bell button a sedate push, heard the buzzer sound and swung open the heavy gate. Inside was a flawless furze of lawn, a long flagstone walk, a walnut front door with archaic wrought hinges. Behind its peephole, Mme. Berkady's concierge eyes would be watching him.

Nele Berkady's protectiveness of her husband was neurotic, irritating to St. Gage. He had seen it instantly on his first visit. He was acute about women, although he did not really like them. It was not that he was an invert. Women had their uses. And St. Gage occasionally used them.

The heavy woman let him in with a grimace that did for a smile. The house smelled of the chemicals, formaldehyde, sulfur, and the tubs of molds—the harmless ones—that St. Gage knew were stored in the cellar. At the top of the baroque staircase Berkady, in a long white surgical robe, was waiting for him.

The frosted glass in the squat, old researcher's left spectacle disconcerted St. Gage. Berkady, a Belgian, had been a scientific employee of the Germans in World War II. A war-skewed villager, suspecting unfairly that Berkady was responsible for shipping his wife off to Germany for experiments, had gouged out the eye in 1945 after the allies liberated Belgium.

Berkady had not blamed his crazed fellow townsman so much as he had the Americans whose bumptious entry into the town had occasioned the blinding. In the fifties, unable to find work in Belgium, he had moved to Neuilly to pursue his specialities. It was this background, turned up by St. Gage from biographical data and from his initial interview with Berkady, that had made the solicitor certain that the expatriate Belgian was the right man.

As resourceful interpersonally as he was scientifically, Berkady sometimes removed his glasses as if to wipe his good eye, but in fact to intimidate a visitor with the scarred hollow. It served to interrupt uncomfortable conversations, bring interviews to a close, and stir manic talk during unpleasant lulls. It did for Berkady what nose blowing and sharp coughs did for less advantageously equipped social manipulators.

"You will have more time on this visit, I hope?" Berkady said with an ingratiating whine. St. Gage disliked the scientist even more than he did the wife.

"Yes, of course," he said. "As much as we need."

Berkady opened an ordinary door in the wide hallway. Inside was an airtight metal door, much like a refrigerator's. It led into the laboratory itself, a large room hermetically sealed with thick cream-colored vinyl. A complicated air venting device protruded from the ceiling, its borders thickly layered with sealant.

A huge skylight washed the tile floor with sunlight. In the room's center, like a decorative Japanese garden, four grape vines grew healthily. Others sprouted in rectangular boxes in two of the room's corners.

The rest of the laboratory was neat, but thronged with equipment: a compound microscope and stereomicroscope side by side on a table, an American-made home computer, bell jars, mold trays, burners, test-tube cases, flasks, a wall shelf of bottles whose taped labels were marked in black, backward-leaning script.

Incongruously near a desk in a corner of the room lit by a gooseneck lamp, two old-fashioned leather armchairs were drawn up. Berkady pointed to them and, as St. Gage sat, took off his glasses and began to wipe them. St. Gage, taken by surprise, was confronted by the gaping eye gulch. Satisfied, Berkady put on the glasses and turned to his guest.

"I have done what you asked. I have drawn up the options." He pulled from a coat pocket inside the gown a folded piece of paper and opened it. St. Gage tried to read it upside down. It was in black ink, in the same careful script as the labels. Berkady studied it a while as if he had never seen it before and made a correction or two with one of several old-fashioned fountain pens on his desk.

"Can you let me have a copy of that," said St. Gage, a lawyer who liked his documents first. "It would help me with my colleagues."

"Better not," said Berkady, holding on to the paper as if he was afraid St. Gage might snatch it from him. St. Gage shifted in his chair with annoyance. The scientist's tone was that of a doctor saying, "you have a mild lung condition. If you want to smoke, of course, your physician cannot stop you, but . . ."

Why, thought St. Gage, couldn't the man simply say, I'm afraid to let anything out of here on paper, even for your kind of money?

"Proceed," said St. Gage. No reason to ruffle Berkady needlessly. Tobb, when St. Gage had spoken of Berkady, had sniffed, "mad scientist." St. Gage had not liked the remark, but there was some truth in it. He only hoped the noun was more on point than the adjective.

"I want to say something for the record," Berkady began in rapid Flemish-accented English. "We are doing nothing illegal. We are speaking hypothetically. We did not last time, nor will we this time, speak of any specific country, much less region."

What was going on? St. Gage wondered, hearing this set speech.

"There are, in any case, only laws banning the import of our research products, none banning their manufacture," Berkady went on.

St. Gage was no slouch as a lawyer. He knew

that French laws, like the equally esteemed laws of England and the United States, were what the powers-that-be said they were. Then it struck St. Gage why Berkady had begun this way.

"You're not recording this little statement of purpose, I hope," said St. Gage quietly. "Things like that wind up in the wrong hands."

Berkady looked sick. He started to take off his eyeglasses.

"Of course not," he said.

St. Gage, however, was certain his hunch was correct.

"Get it and bring it to me," said St. Gage, still calmly. "That sort of thing is not only foolish, but the worst kind of breach of contract." He did not want to be more explicit with the unseen reels spinning. He stared at Berkady, his eyes quietly murderous.

The squat man, his face as pulpy looking now as a porcini mushroom, started to argue. St. Gage, lithe as a long cat, came to his feet and stepped to Berkady's chair. His breath coming fast, his actions unemotionally executed, he took Berkady by his ancient, crinkly throat with his left hand. With his right, he removed the glasses and put them on the desk.

Though appalled by the eye cavity, now a shocking pink with fright, St. Gage snatched up the fountain pen Berkady had been using and held the point close to Berkady's terrified good eye.

"Don't ever, ever try to lie to me," he said. "Now, get the thing."

For an instant they were frozen in this perverted ophthalmological posture. Then St. Gage carefully placed the pen by the glasses, released the sitting man's throat, and wiped his moist hand on his pants leg.

Berkady lurched awkwardly from his chair and knelt before his desk. He tinkered underneath its bottom drawer, pulled out a wire and a mini-microphone. The wire ran into the drawer from underneath. Berkady opened it and withdrew a small Sony cassette recorder. He handed the equipment to St. Gage like a bad boy caught with a stolen toy.

"I thought we should have some record," he stuttered.

St. Gage looked at the cassette and pushed the stop key.

"Do you have a second one?"

"No, no," began Berkady, panicky, thinking of the fountain pen.

"All right," said St. Gage. "Now let me give you some advice. One, as a lawyer, whether we mention what might be done with these things or not, you are as guilty of criminal complicity as anyone else. Two, I can assure you that if you ever attempt anything like this again, you will not have to worry about going to trial on that charge. Or on any other charge. Ever." He paused. "You understand?"

"Yes," said the chastened Berkady.

St. Gage plucked out the cassette for future destruction, and dropped the recorder on the tile floor. With a single stomp, he smashed it beneath the heel of his ankle-high boot. Berkady looked at the demolished device and shuddered.

"Now, proceed," said St. Gage.

Berkady sat very still, bringing himself under control. When he began, his voice had a flat duck-like quality. "You asked me for options. I have four to offer. The first is oidium, which you would know about." St. Gage knew the layman's facts: oidium was a whitish mildew that had blighted half, or was it a quarter, of the Bordeaux wines in the middle of the last century. The scourge had been turned back with powdered sulfur.

"How . . . ?"

Berkady held up his hand, some of his confidence coming back now that he was presiding over his particular esoterica.

"You may not know that oidium is an asexual spore," he murmured, "formed by the abstriction at the top of a hyphal branch."

"Pray be less scientific if possible," said St. Gage, able to be gentle now that they had reached the appropriate relationship: stern master to cowed servant. Berkady bobbed his head.

"With oidium the wine has an unpleasant taste, the flavor of the sporophores. In our terms, the wine is conidiatic, oidioid."

"Please spare me the fancy words," said St. Gage, aware that Berkady was using his scientific pedantry as a sort of weapon of revenge. How, he wondered, did the *Witwe* Pfeffermühle, who had a certain sere style, ever even hear of this hateful man.

"As you know," Berkady was going on, "we routinely sulfur the vineyards—two, three, sometimes four kilos the hectare, each time."

"Yes, yes," said St. Gage. "That's the point.

How could oidium serve our purpose when there is a serviceable antidote?"

Berkady signaled the solicitor to follow him to a cork board where he had pinned a number of color photographs.

His long forefinger flicking out from the hinge of his knuckle, the scientist pointed to the top two pictures. The first showed a luxuriance of enlarged spores, a little like a field of purple-and-white tennis balls. The second resembled a dried-up lava crater.

"Ordinary oidium before and after sulfur," said Berkady.

The long finger dropped to the two photos below.

The first was similar to the tennis balls, though the rounded objects, obviously the spores, were mixed with orange tones. In this pair, the after photo showed ugly craterings, but in the main, the field of spores were still plump and revolting.

"*Oidium berkadrax*, as I call it," said Berkady.

"Whoof," said St. Gage with a genuinely admiring exhalation of breath. But instantly he thought of a major problem. What if the oidium got out of their hands, spread beyond their control?

"What if it . . . ?" he began.

Berkady dared a condescending look.

"My dear Mr. St. Gage," he said. "When I reviewed the available options, I turned down many: red spider, black rot, anthracnose, cochylis, altise, millerandage. . . . All for one reason or another were not acceptable, perhaps too simple an antidote, perhaps too difficult to, um, disseminate, perhaps, as you suggest, too complicated to control once outside the laboratory. In this case, I made the monster and I can kill it."

"Like Frankenstein," said St. Gage.

"*Not* like Frankenstein. *He* could not control his monster. In this case, I have developed a carbon by-product." He took another fountain pen from inside his gown and on a pad began a diagram based on a pentagon. St. Gage broke in, "Something to kill your oidium."

"Precisely. Something that would take another specialist a year or two to develop. Assuming he had good luck. Let me move on to the second option. It is as you might have guessed, blue mildew, *peronespora viticola*, a distant relative of oidium."

It had hit the Bordeaux region in the late nineteenth century, St. Gage knew. It was controlled with copper salts, known as Bordeaux mixture. St. Gage had never seen vines afflicted with blue mildew. Berkady was pleased to brief him.

"In this case, the leaves fall, and the grapes, lacking sugar, cannot mature so they are sour, acidulous, doughy. The wine from them is the color of sick urine and musty tasting. Bordeaux mixture controls the mildew." He pointed to another quartet of color pictures.

"In the same manner, Bordeaux mixture would, in sufficient proportions, kill my Peronospera Type B. But," and he allowed himself another smile, "eating the grapes would be like chewing on a big British penny," he said, and cackled, a high barking sound like the gobble of a frightened turkey.

"I'm afraid there aren't any big British pennies anymore," observed St. Gage dryly. "And if there were, they would not taste of copper, I can assure you."

Berkady looked put down. St. Gage went on with his questions.

"Do you have a provision for the peronespora if it should infect vineyards where it was, um, not required?"

"Yes, again, specifics. It would take a year or two before anyone could catch up."

. There was no denying the genius of the man, thought St. Gage, assuming he could deliver on his prognostications.

"Ah," St. Gage went on. "And the third option."

Berkady withdrew a butterfly case from the drawer. On its cotton bed lay four moths with broad wings, the forewings naturally truncated at the tips.

"*Tortricidae*," he said, giving St. Gage a sly, hasty look, "their root name is tortrix, a female torturer."

"Um," ummed St. Gage again. The moths, he recalled, had been a hazard to crops a couple of times in this century but were controlled by spraying. Berkady anticipated his questions.

"For anyone to spray for a plague of the proportions my moth might cause would drive up the cost of wine to enormous heights," said the doctor.

"But it could be done: the moths could be prevented from destroying . . ."

"Yes," Berkady interrupted, conceding the point as he put the cover on the moth case and closed the drawer. With a shrug, he said, "Nothing is perfect."

"Your last option, of course, is phylloxera," said St. Gage.

"Yes," said Berkady. Unwilling to let St. Gage

have any victory unqualified, he added, "to be explicit, *phylloxera vastatrix* or to be à la mode, *vitifoliae.*"

St. Gage needed no recitation on this blight. In his thoughts, it had already seemed an answer. If only all its elements could be juggled into place. The aphidlike phylloxerans had been spotted by entomologists in America in the 1850s on some wild grapes in the Mississippi valley. They looked like nothing so much as small, fat, yellow lice. When a shipment of vine cuttings were sent from America to France in the 1860s, or, according to some, after riding piggyback on American table grapes, the insect appeared one day in Languedoc.

It spread into Portugal and Bordeaux, infiltrated the Rhone valley and ate its way into Germany and Italy. With twelve generations a year, it settled in root nodules, ate them out, then began on leaves. Vines became dwarfed, leaves yellowed and withered, grapes grew hard, juiceless, roots rotted until a veteran vine that had withstood forty winters could be pulled from the ground by a baby.

To combat the plague, a parasitic mite called *tiroglyphus phylloxera* was imported. But in Europe, unaccountably, the mite made an armistice with its enemy. Carbon and sulfur sprays were developed to no avail. Holes were dug beside roots and poisons poured in; fields were flooded. Nothing worked.

At last, the Europeans began laboriously to tear up their own vines and replace them with vines from the eastern United States, *vitis riparia* and *rupestris*, which were largely resistant to the pest. Precious vinifera cuttings were grafted on to these rude American natives. Gradually, the perilously sick European wine industry began to recover, literally, by the grace of the American vine stocks. As a result, today Europe's grapes grew on American vines or on the hybrids and clones which have been produced from sturdy American ancestors.

All this was understood between the two men when Berkady said with unabated pride, "I have developed a new strain of phylloxera. I call it *phylloxera berkadicula*. My phylloxeran is gluttonous toward *all* vines, not just vinifera."

"Bugger a saint," said St. Gage, shocked into crudity.

Like a king introducing two mighty nobles, Berkady led St. Gage to a sunlit corner where a vine grew in an oversized bell jar. St. Gage had never seen a vine so blighted by disease.

The leaves were galled and yellow and, because the roots were also behind glass and thus observable, St. Gage could see their grotesque and necrotic mutilation. They were as bizarre as ginseng or mandrake. On the few remaining leaves—chewing their centers, crawling on their tops, clinging to their undersides—were stout, yellowish insects, a millimeter long. Dozens of the hideous pests, some with wings, all fat on the vine sap, had glued themselves to the sides of the bell jar. Berkady thumped the glass and a squad of two dropped off into the dirt.

St. Gage thought of what these creatures might do.

"You're sure they can't get out?" he asked.

Berkady gave the younger man an impudent glance of contempt.

"We . . ." He meant his wife. Or, thought St. Gage, was he using a royal "We," this monarch of vinicides. ". . . do not make that kind of mistake."

St. Gage was still unnerved. He did not grant anyone that degree of certainty.

"But suppose vandals or housebreakers or an accident in transit, something beyond your control: even that risk . . ."

"Is not acceptable," Berkady ended the sentence for him. "I understand and to that goal, I am working on a formula of disulfides and phosphates which will destroy my *petites*."

St. Gage nodded and walked with the old researcher to the desk. There, one by one, they examined the possibilities. The mildews, promising as they were, would require months to produce in quantity. The moth was the most easily combated.

Phylloxera looked like the best method by far. It could be ready soon. Because of the virulence of Berkady's strain it would destroy rapidly, particularly in the massive doses St. Gage envisioned. But it posed a threat of uncontrollable havoc until (and unless) Berkady perfected his chemical antidote.

"When will you know if your formula will work?" St. Gage asked. "We are under new time pressures to fix a date certain for the completion of the project."

"Two weeks, three at most. I am studying some insecticides used in the nineteenth century which showed promise of success back then but failed for one reason or another. There are some loose ends."

"And won't other researchers come up with the same antidote eventually?"

Berkady removed his spectacles, this time, for a change, not to intimidate, but to wipe the sweat from his face with a huge linen handkerchief he had drawn from beneath his gown. The interview with St. Gage had wearied and upset him and now it was coming to a close. He looked into the handsome Englishman's face with his marred one.

"Eventually they might," he said. "But eventually, Mr. St. Gage, would be much, much too late."

Eight

CONTACTS

Bethany and Franz von Mohrwald, like most people seeking bail-outs from private detectives, lawyers, tax accountants, psychiatrists, expected miracles for their money. The von Mohrwalds were rational, intelligent, fair people. But they were impatient. Their vineyard was at stake; their first employee on the case was dead; unsubtle pressures were now beginning. And they knew that time was running out on them.

The Mohrwalder wines had a modest market in the United States and the Commonwealth countries. The von Mohrwalds, for the last few years, had sent them to an efficient, if expensive, shipper in Vienna who wholesaled them to a London distributor. In fact, it had been their first thought when Bridsey wrote them that they could cut the Vienna shipper and pick up an extra 6 to 10 percent.

Those hopes had not only been wiped out, but were now reversed. The Vienna shipper called them mournfully and told them that the London distributor would no longer handle their wines.

"Why?" asked the startled Franz.

"Lack of sales."

"Nonsense. Sales have been steady!"

"I can only tell you what they told me."

"Can we try someone else?"

"We can try," said the shipper without any great spirit.

"What about the rest of the Austrian market?"

"I shouldn't talk about my customers."

"You mean Dirnbaum and Higgins"—the London distributors—"are still buying some Austrians?"

"Yes. No set pattern, but still buying."

Franz knew how to find the pattern. He called the octogenarian who was his friendly competitor in Krems and the brothers who ran the Gumpoldskirchen vineyard. The old man had decided to hold out against Bridsey; the brothers had capitulated. The former had, like the von Mohrwalds, been cancelled; the latter were still shipping.

"We have hired someone to find out what's going on," said Franz to his erstwhile competitor and now new ally in Krems.

"You are asking me to contribute?"

"Yes."

"Well, we may go broke just as well if we find out," said the Krems owner. "But at least we do not go out like sheep."

"No," said Franz gloomily, "like goats, stubborn goats."

"Better like goats, any day," responded the spunky old man.

Bethany was about to call Il Principe Claudio to

learn whether that worthy had heard anything when he telephoned her. Without the usual charming preliminaries, he began chattering at her in demotic French.

"*Cara*, it is sickening. This French *chameau* Maier has come into the Veneto like the Visigoths, dictating what hectares we are to plant with what. He wants to tear up the old, solid vines, plant new ones to build up production of . . . " She could sense him starting to say *pisse*. ". . . Marseilles sewer water. He suggests, never says—even he must know it's illegal—that our foreman sugar the must like we were making Sacher tortes, that we bring up Calabrian junk, already fortified, anything to stretch out the alcohol over more bad wine."

He stopped to catch his breath and she started to break in, but he was off again.

"Don't sign with them, Bethany. I would have done better to have bankrupted. Believe me. I am so ashamed."

"We have hired a private detective, Claudio," she said.

"You will need a brute, some sort of gangster . . ."

Bethany thought of Aubrey: hardly a gangster, although his talk, even on things of the mind, was sometimes crude. And she did feel in him a capacity for violence. Yet there was also, oppositely and not really contradictorily, an unexpected gentleness.

"We have an American," she said.

"Good, a gangster."

". . . well no. We had a British person." She started to tell him that Wheatley-Smith had died, but then, as loyal as Claudio was, he was so voluble. If any of the conspirators, if that was what they were, knew that the von Mohrwalds were doing anything about their suspicions, then it could not only be disastrous to Aubrey and the investigation, but to them personally. ". . . It didn't work out."

"Better an American," said Martino e Stelio, "much. Tell him this, Bethany. Tell him I will swallow my disgust and try to weasel more information out of this hideous little French spider."

Bethany thought with a remnant smile that for Napoleonic nobility, Claudio certainly hated the French. Or maybe it was *because* he was Napoleonic nobility.

"When I consider the prices they are paying," he was going on, "then I know they know something that you and I do not know. If they do not, then the world has gone *pazzo*."

"Claudio, there is one thing I want to ask you."

"I want to contribute to this, Bethany," he generously anticipated her. "It will be my conscience commission: ten percent of their first payment. I will have it in a week or two, *cara*."

Anxiety pervaded Schloss von Mohrwald. A noose seemed to tighten slowly around its tranquil acres. The two house servants and the vineyard workers spoke among themselves of possible jobs in Vienna or Salzburg. The ragged saws of tension tattered the edges of Bethany and Franz's marriage.

She was irritable, nervous. Usually so open with him, she seemed withdrawn. Wheatley-Smith's death weighed on her. She worried about not hearing from Aubrey whom she knew she had manipulated, shamed into taking the case. If he were hurt, it would be her fault.

Her malaise infected Franz who was working from dawn until late at night to save the vineyard, to find another exporter, to carve a bit more for the von Mohrwalds in the diminishing Austrian market. A good and, for all his intelligence, an uncomplicated man, Franz did not want stress at home. Not finding his accustomed warmth there, he took the classic course. On his hectic business trips to Vienna, he crammed in an hour or two of frantic lovemaking with a young matron in a gentrified flat off the Ring. When he got back to the Schloss he had to work even harder to make up for lost time, with the expectable augmentation of tensions.

During one of Franz's absences, Aubrey called from his vineyard. At the sound of his strong accents, Bethany's hopes, held in so long, ballooned. Surely this resourceful man had news of salvation. But Aubrey quickly disabused her.

"On the central question I don't know any more than I did," he said. "I don't know what they're up to. It's still a mystery. As best I could, I sniffed around the big vineyards out there—Gallo, Almadén, and so on—the ones that'd be the equivalent of what they're tying up in Europe. The table wine guys. Nothing. No contact, or if there is, nobody's talking."

She sighed, unable to hide her instant depression.

"How about over there?" he asked.

"The same. The three of them are buying more vineyards. There's talk of them getting options, of Bridsey particularly investing in wholesale stocks, in distributorships. All of it table wines, none of the *grands crus*. My cousin says some of this is being handled by a big London law firm, but he thinks it's merely the intermediary for the real interests . . ."

"Anything over there about them buying over here?"

"Nothing."

Thoughts of their quandary deepened their dejection. Aubrey turned to the few things he had discovered.

"On the inspector, I have a bit."

He summarized his findings:

Wheatley-Smith, as she had thought, was not drunk at the time the tour ended. Yet the alcohol count was accurate. From Aubrey's own knowledge, Wheatley-Smith was not a down-the-hatch drinker who would build up a .29 in 105 minutes. So unless he was out of character and had guzzled the booze fast, it had been forced down him. If forced down his throat all at once or even drink by drink, Wheatley-Smith, particularly after being on the wagon for so long, might well have gagged. However, there had been no sign of vomit. That left the unlikely probability that the alcohol was somehow injected.

"Injected?" Bethany interrupted.

"Injected. I've checked with friends, forensic doctors. It's not impossible. You'd have to shoot about fifty ccs. of very high proof ethyl alcohol in him. Do it slowly, ten, twelve minutes. He'd be snockered as a result. I know it's nutty, but . . ."

"But that's just a theory. There's no proof." Her voice was small with disappointment.

"Yeah, well it may be our only chance," said Aubrey. "If we could show somebody tried to make a murder look like an accidental death, then the authorities in California would damn well reopen the case. That would expand our manpower about one thousand percent," he added sardonically. "Ten men working on it instead of one. Besides, it would scare hell out of the bunch over there if they found out they were the subject of an official criminal investigation. One of them might just break and start talking to save his tail. Things like that happen."

"Yes, but how?"

"Well," said Aubrey, "let's just take a look at what we have." Concisely as he could, he laid it out.

Obviously Wheatley-Smith was in California because he had scented some tie between the European vineyard purchases and the California wine industry. Aubrey's suspicion, even though he couldn't prove it, was that one or more Europeans were soliciting the Domaine McIntyre bunch to sell out, perhaps even to help get others in California to do the same.

If the stakes were high enough, and if some illegality was involved and Wheatley-Smith had uncovered it, then it could be that an "accident" had been arranged.

But Aubrey had tried every computerized and printed list of business executives he could find: the Securities and Exchange Commission, the Commerce Department, Standard and Poor's, Moody's, Who's Who, The New York Times and Wall Street Journal indexes, Barron's and Forbes's files, several State

Department license rosters. And not one tie be-tween Domaine McIntyre and any European firms in the same field had popped up.

Oh, the American company had sent executives to conferences in Europe and who could say what private meetings might have taken place. And there had been some commerce with Europe—the export of a few cases of wine to a piddling number of restaurants and distributors, a scientific shipment or two of vine stocks, but nothing that amounted to anything.

"So I've run down every lead over here. That leaves just that one long shot of proving death wasn't accidental. It means my coming over there."

"Well, we've budgeted for that. You would have to do the financial investigation over here anyway. But you were saying . . ."

". . . that the San Leon County coroner in California did a mediocre job. He didn't check for needle holes. He did pull out—that is he removed—the esophagus and there wasn't any trauma from a tube being forced down."

"What in Europe would . . . ?"

"Europe, well London, is the place to let the victim prove it wasn't an accident."

For a moment she thought she had misheard him.

"The victim?"

"We've got to get his family to, uh, raise him up so he can be reexamined."

Disinter the body of Wheatley-Smith? She re-coiled.

"Oh no."

"Oh yes. To check for an injection."

"But how?"

"We go see the family. You or your husband should be there. It's going to take some convincing from somebody more respectable than I am, and maybe some signing of court papers as plaintiff if worse comes to worst; something I can't do."

She said nothing. And he, thinking she disapproved of his plan, continued a little nastily.

"Listen, do you want me out of this?"

Her nerves, her time, and her money were all fraying. Neither Claudio nor the Krems vineyard owner had yet sent their bank drafts. And the von Mohrwalds' investment in Wheatley-Smith and Aubrey had produced so far only death and speculation. As if that weren't enough, her marriage was eroding.

"I wish you would stop whining so," she snapped at him suddenly. "It's beneath you, beneath both of us."

She heard his gasp. Then there was silence on the line except for the cracklings of the 5,000 miles between them. She could imagine Aubrey formulating a reply. Perhaps he would quit. Right now. She was not sure she cared. At last he cleared his throat, and his voice was matter-of-fact.

"Try to make it you who comes to London," he said.

In the midst of so many woes, the ambiguously provocative invitation gave her an unanticipated but not entirely explicable lift.

Nine

MAIER'S FOLLY

Auguste Maier, a short man with carefully styled hair and a pouty angel's face, was injudiciously impressed by titles. He yearned over the fact that he had nothing in common with Prince Claudio Martino e Stelio except a mutual admiration for Stravinsky. The prince had let drop his taste for the Russian composer during their long vineyard negotiations.

It therefore seemed to Maier a coincidence made in heaven that on the very day when he and the prince were meeting in Venice to sign the final batch of legal and financial papers, *The Rake's Progress* was being performed at La Fenice.

To Martino e Stelio, it was more opportunity than coincidence. True to his promise to Bethany, he wanted to search out what the Frenchman and his accomplices were up to.

He recognized Maier's genius when it came to the paperwork of financing. There, Maier was as unshakably competent as the prince was, by constitution, baffled. The urbane Italian's brow wrinkled during talk of beneficial second liens, unrecorded debenture options, flexible and periodic balloon payments. The prince, however, aware of his weakness, hired lawyers and accountants to make up for his lacks.

Maier's failings could not be rectified so handily. For in his dealings with his social superiors, he was pathetically susceptible to kindness, to open generosity, to acceptance, even to tolerance.

The prince had catalogued these vulnerabilities in the lazy but keen mind that lay beneath his graying hair and tonsurelike bald spot. But his slightly feral Venetian face gave no hint of guile as he and Maier left the marble-columned main conference room of the Gran Banco Ducale di Venezia.

"Agosto," said the prince familiarly, "I can tell you I am glad this business is done. And in time for a decent lunch."

Maier had prayed for such an invitation. He had expected to dine thriftily and alone, to buy a cheap ticket to *The Rake's Progress*, to retire to his category two hotel and to catch an early plane to Algiers the next morning to tie up some new vineyards.

"Ah, *principe*," he said. "How good of you. But, please, on me."

The prince cordially dismissed Maier's counteroffer with a patrician nod. "Harry's," he said. "Or maybe the *motoscafo* to Cipriani's? We could stop off at San Michele."

Maier melted. A private motorboat to Cipriani's! And by way of San Michele! For San Michele was the cemetery island in the lagoon where the beloved maestro was buried. Maier visited the Stra- vinsky grave each time he was in Venice, but al- ways by public *vaporetto*.

"Perfect. Perfect," said Maier. "But may I stop an instant by La Fenice? I must pick up a ticket."

Again, the prince nodded imperially, but amiably.

"The maitre d' can call from Cipriani's. Take my two regular seats there, I beg you." The prince smiled, a warm man-to-man look. "Or if you have not already arranged to go with some *petite amie*, I will accompany you. I never grow tired of the *Rake*."

A thousand rough-handed vinedressers could not torture Maier into a disadvantageous deal on *vins rouges ordinaires*. But the prince's smile of com- radeship, the two orchestra or box tickets to La Fenice and the offer of a fine meal made him feel as deferential as a provincial courtesan in the Sun King's antechamber.

"Ah, *principe, la bella Italia*," he exhaled again as they crossed under the portico and into sunlight on the Piazza San Marco.

The motorboat sat back on its stern and skimmed the lagoon's wavelets. It darted in at the Fonda- mente Nuove while its young captain rushed ashore at Martino e Stelio's request and returned with a dozen lilies.

On San Michele, the tall Italian, English-dapper in his blue linen blazer, his light gray Egyptian cotton slacks, and the Frenchman, sweating in his solidly bourgeois brown synthetics, walked past tombs and cypresses to the Orthodox section.

"Even *his* genius came to this," said Martino e Stelio staring at the simple monument with its timeless name. Maier thought this a little dramatic, a little *Italian*. It is the kind of sentimentality, he thought with self-satisfaction, that has let me sew up your vineyards and leave you with little more than your title.

"But think what he has left behind for us, *principe*."

"I wish you would call me Claudio," said the Italian, looking with mournful kindness at the shorter man.

"Yes, Claudio," said Maier, trying it out, and loving it.

On Torcello, as they sat beneath the arbor at Cipriani's waiting for their first course, Auguste Maier drank two Scotches with water. He was a wine commerçant who disliked wines. Yet his tasting abilities were consummate. With the agnolotti and the delicate fenneled fish, he drank Italian beer. He felt wonderful.

They talked easily and intelligently of why they preferred Russian, Italian, and French music to German. Maier dismissed Bach, Beethoven, and Mozart with an airy hand wave that swept past his after-lunch brandy and out eastward toward Mother Russia.

In the cooling late afternoon, they returned by motorboat to Venice and let the day languidly die as they sipped more spirits in the Piazza. They listened to rival but equally schmaltzy orchestras stringing and reeding show tunes from six countries and two centuries.

By the end of a light supper, the prince felt safe

in putting an initial painless tap on Maier's dulling circuits.

"You cannot know, Agosto, how free I feel to be rid of that acreage. You don't know how grateful I am to get that extraordinary price from you. But I cannot help but think, dear fellow, that you have a Gallic trick or two up your sleeve for those two cutpurses, Bridsey and the old crone, Pfeffermühle."

Maier looked slightly melancholy, not so much at mention of these two, but because it reminded him of St. Gage in whom he suspected and feared unknown darknesses.

"It is something of a gamble," he said guardedly.

Martino e Stelio noted Maier did not deny that he, the *Witwe*, and Bridsey were acting in concert. The prince smiled sympathetically.

That evening's operatic tale, of an Englishman falling from grace, told by a Russian through the good services of a Venetian theater, moved the Frenchman Maier deeply.

Martino e Stelio, for his part, was woozy from the liquor he had consumed in order to keep Maier from becoming suspicious. Still, he rallied after the opera enough to invite his blissful moonfaced companion to the Danieli bar for a nightcap.

Full of music and the reflected gleams from the welcome given the prince by the hotel's senior staff, Maier made the best of his freeloading and ordered Old Rarity.

"We have been corrupted by Britannia's whiskey," observed the prince with an expansive but distasteful slug of his own glass of Scotch. "We should call it the English disease."

"It is the only thing they make worthy of export," sneered Maier. The prince shook his head, seeming to ponder his drinking comrade's attitude.

"I do not understand, Agosto, how you could have joined with this English buffoon, this German hag. True, it has worked to my benefit. But why, tell me my friend, why this pair when there are so many of us, so many Italians, French who are more knowledgeable, more honorable."

"Ah," said Maier, looking around him and lowering his voice. "I can tell you that they are not the worst." He wished he could tell the prince about the English lawyer, wished he had some strong Latin ally against him.

The prince looked casually around the sumptuous little bar, disguising the leap his heart made despite its burden of inadequately converted sugar. Too smart to ask for names, he merely said sympathetically, "Why you among these disgusting Teutons? Neither of them would know Bizet from . . . the Beatles."

Maier shrugged. The alcohol had inflated his self-importance. He tried to look shrewd, the international man of affairs instructing a dear but naive friend.

"They are hatching an interesting proposition. It has advantages for me."

The prince sensed the big fish was at last near his hook. He let out line.

"Perhaps we Italians, you French should never go into business anyway. Not that you are not a master in that world. But we are artists. I wanted to be a painter. You should have been a musician."

"I was, I was," said Maier with the excitement of remembrance. "I won two gold, two silvers, for oboe at Lyon in the Prix de la Jeunesse. I could have . . ." Once more, but less steadily, he waved his hand toward the vastnesses of the east. "I had talent, my friend. But my family. I was born to commerce."

"You could quit, even now."

"After this, yes, why not."

The prince looked at him with admiration.

"How lucky if you could. It must be stupendous. Do not lie. I know it is you who have put this deal together. What could English, Germans do in wine. No one trusts them. I wish I had a head for business. I would love to be in on this thing with you. But be careful, Agosto. You must also watch out for the Americans. They are pirates, believe me."

"The Americans are pirates," Maier agreed emphatically.

The prince pressed, but gently. "I say the Americans, my friend, because in California they produce such huge quantities. True, it is like dog piss beside your Burgundies and Bordeaux and our Barolos . . ." The prince scowled, not in fact at the thought of California wine, but at his dissembling: not two days ago he had drunk a California Merlot that made all but his best Merlot *riserva* taste like rosewater by comparison.

Maier, despite his personal distaste for wines, took professional umbrage at the prince comparing Barolos with the great wines of France. But the prince, his friend, was making a point.

". . . even the California Cabernets, they are uneven. And these *maledetto* Chardonnays that keep winning medals in France—France!—are freaks, even if admirable. What is one to drink them with . . ."

The prince's present tendency to ramble made Maier feel secure, superior. The prince was saying, "But these California growers . . ." The prince looked fraternally at the Frenchman and leaned as if to confide in him. ". . . Believe me, Agosto, if you have any large international enterprise going, you must bring them in. Whatever we may think of their wines, you cannot establish a stable market in Europe without them. They would destroy you with low prices."

The prince was guessing, but it was a guess based on what he knew of the wine industry and his intuitions about what Maier was hinting at. He made a quick sign across his own throat to indicate what the Californians might do.

Maier paused a moment, on the brink. Why not trust this well-meaning friend, at least a little? He would say nothing that was not already rumored in the wine industry, or would be soon.

For the rest, Maier saw that the prince had already surmised something from the buying patterns. Had the Italian known of the secret talks with the Latin Americans and Communists—and at least so far the absence of the Californians—his speculation about the Americans might have quickened even more, Maier mused.

Indeed, while Maier himself did not know (or really want to know) the details, St. Gage's total financial and other commitments had convinced Maier—and he was certain, the *Witwe* and Bridsey—that the solicitor had found means to make absolutely sure America did not or could not undersell the cartel.

Maier looked meaningfully at the prince and said self-importantly, if not entirely informedly, "No, my dear Claudio, I assure you we do not need the Americans."

"Come, come *compagno*"—countryman, a stretch of national boundaries, but an intimacy that pleased Maier—"you must have them. You must. Unless you can curse California with seven wet, wet seasons in a row." Engagingly, but feeling foolish, he made the Italian curse symbol with fingers at forehead in the direction of the United States.

Maier smiled fondly at the prince and, dropping his voice to a whisper, said, again more in surmise than certainty, "I think it would be safe to say, and you must swear on your title, my good friend, that California will not have a sufficiently competitive wine crop to threaten my enterprise for quite a few years."

Beneath the patina of his mock tipsiness, Martino e Stelio was alarmed. Did these madmen plan to monopolize California out of business? Or to control the California weather somehow? Seed clouds? Set off a nuclear bomb in the stratosphere? What did this scurvy French troll know?

"You have a meteorological mastermind who can forecast the future! Is it safe to risk all on such insubstantials?" The prince's eyes popped now with genuine apprehension.

"Allow me to let it go at that," said Maier smugly. He took a deep pull at his Scotch and felt the beam-ceilinged bar reel. "It has been an incredibly satisfying day, my friend." His speech slurred but his soul soared.

"I will walk you to your hotel," said the prince, conceding to himself that he dare not push Maier further.

Through the switchboard of the Danieli where the prince was staying, he reached Schloss von Mohrwald. It was past one. The phone rang and rang until finally a sleepy servant answered. Martino e Stelio asked for Bethany.

"The baroness is not able to come to the telephone," said the man with haughty if somnolent irritation.

"It is a matter of life and death. This is Claudio Martino e Stelio."

"*Il principe*," said the servant almost to himself. There was a pause. "She is on a business trip, Herr Prinz. Must I wake the baron?"

"Yes. Apologize to him for me. But get him up."

Franz von Mohrwald had fallen asleep only a half hour before after another of his eighteen-hour days, four of them making an unsuccessful pitch to Scandinavian wine importers. He had it fixed in his slumberous mind that Claudio Martino e Stelio was at the local station wanting a ride to the Schloss. He mumbled as much.

"I'm in Venice, Franz. *Venedig!*" the prince interrupted him.

Von Mohrwald went silent, struggled his wits together.

"Bethany is in London," he said. "What can you tell us?"

"Much," said the prince, "I think. To begin with, things are moving far more rapidly than we had imagined . . ."

Ten

THE *WITWE*

In the dying light, the *Witwe* Pfeffermühle's dark eye pouches bespoke an internal illness that kept her awake at night or in uneasy narcotized sleep. Only the most careful and sympathetic scrutinizer could discern in her wasted face the beauty that had been there in her youth.

Yet even aged, cruel, sick, and ugly faces soften, take on warmth and liveliness in the presence of former lovers who remain friends. So with the *Witwe* on the terrace of Schloss Löwenfels. So with the wrecked visage of Dr. Pieter Berkady.

The Schloss had been renovated by the Pfeffermühles during the thirties, the crumbled twelfth-century stones used in the walls of the restored castle, this terrace built from rock quarried nearby.

The ruined tower that pointed like a black finger to heaven had not been rebuilt. Instead, the Pfeffermühles' master bedroom had been constructed inside its shell. It was there, surprisingly to her, but irresistibly, that she had wholeheartedly given herself to Berkady more than forty years ago.

The wiry young scientist had been doing apolitical work in botanical entomology for the German government. Frau Pfeffermühle's husband's millions came from agricultural and fertilizer interests, and they had put Berkady up at the Schloss during the Belgian's visits to the Rhineland.

Frau Pfeffermühle had found this serious, dedicated specialist vastly different from her pompous husband. Herr Pfeffermühle, while capable, was also a blow-hard. He constantly inflated himself by dropping the names of German leaders who visited the Schloss. In bed, he fancied himself a Schwarzwalder boar.

Berkady, on the other hand, although aware of his merit, neither overstated it nor buttressed it with the names of important scientific colleagues. And in him Frau Pfeffermühle divined a sensual subtlety that would have been unthinkable in Hans Pfeffermühle.

When the industrialist was away, his wife and Berkady had found ways to meet and chat, first about wines which they both loved, then about their spouses which neither of them loved. One night, when the husband was off at a meeting with other businessmen, she and Berkady had shared a 1935 Schloss Johannisberger Spätlese and the Franck symphony.

Berkady had risen midway through the music to flip the records. On the way back he had swooped impulsively to kiss Frau Pfeffermühle on the mouth. By the third movement's paean to joy in the brasses and strings, they were embracing. She had led Ber-

kady to her room where she had served him a
kümmel and he had served her slight, angular body
as it had never been served before.

The last days of the war, the rude, brief occu-
pation of the Schloss by the Americans, her husband's denazification trial, which while it acquitted
him ruined his health, had embittered her forever
against the United States. These things and the
blinding of Berkady's eye, his inability to find work
as a result of his German employment, and the
general postwar woes had forced a decision, a painful one. Frau Pfeffermühle and Berkady had broken
off their affair and practiced fidelity to their spouses,
to whom they were manacled in misery.

Herr Pfeffermühle had died ten years ago when
Frau Pfeffermühle was sixty-five. Berkady, five years
her junior, had begun seeing her again, but they
were by then set in their ways. Now they were
friends, bound by memories but not by lust.

As the sun dropped down behind the Rhineland and France on the far horizon, Berkady told
the *Witwe* of his unpleasant dealings with St. Gage.

"I am ready to intercede if you wish, Pieter,"
she said.

Moved by this sympathetic offer, he nibbled on
his marzipan and took tiny sips from his long-
stemmed glass. He could look at it more calmly,
even the incident of the fountain pen at his eye.

"This St. Gage, who seems so controlled at first
encounter, he is not an entirely rational man," he
observed.

"None of them are," she said, meaning all Eng-
lishmen. "There is an American, Pierce Tobb, who
I sense is even more dangerous. I met him only

once when he came in brashly and I think to St. Gage's dismay while I was speaking with St. Gage."

"He is the one, perhaps, who delivered the vines. A blondish, thick-chested fellow . . . ?"

She nodded and he went on, "I wish it had been possible not to become involved." He was not blaming her. Quite the contrary, he was speaking for them both.

"We had the choices," said the *Witwe*. "We could have ignored this opportunity to hurt those who hurt us."

The complex matter of revenge against the Americans stirred old thoughts.

"We would have done better," he said, "if we could have forgiven them all those years ago, gotten on with life."

"It was not possible," she reassured him.

Involuntarily he touched the frosted lens which hid his mutilation. The day it had happened, he had sought the Americans' protection from the madman. They had sent him away.

"I only meant that if we had been *able* to forgive them, then . . . ," he said.

She laughed, a girl's laugh.

"Then we would have become lovers again," she finished for them.

They watched the long dark forms of the barges on the Rhine far below them. The river's chill, borne up to her, made her shiver.

"I am not well, my dear friend. It is a question only of time. I would like to see this business finished before I . . ."

He held the gnarled old hand more firmly.

"In a few weeks, maybe less," he interrupted.

"I am working night and day." It was time for dinner, but still he lingered, the thought of her death making it urgent that there be a summation.

"If we had become lovers again," he mused, "who can say if it would have been better than this life we have had? Even as sick as he was, if Hans" —her husband—"had discovered . . ." He smiled with brave rue, ". . . he would not have stopped with just one eye."

"Jealousy was his only real strength," she agreed. "And Nele . . ."

"Is so loyal," he finished for her. "If she had found out, she simply would have faded away. It would have been like shooting a pet rabbit."

The *Witwe* Pfeffermühle rose, feeling dizzy as she did nowadays when she got up. Bypasses three years ago had given her a brief armistice with death. Now she had cancer. She had demanded and had gotten from her doctor the full measure of its march into her abdomen. She sighed.

He touched her upper arm where the skin hung like an ancient, failed pennant on a windless day. She felt a stirring toward him. No matter what I say, she thought, the flesh does not die until it is dead.

Catching this spectral whiff of longing in her, in his abominable German he gallantly quoted Goethe. *"Das Ewig-Weibliche zieht uns hinan."* The Eternally Feminine draws us on.

Eleven

ENGLISH SOIL

Aubrey and Bethany met the survivors of Jerome Wheatley-Smith at tea in his elder brother's newly painted house off Russell Square, evidence of recent successes in the plastering business. The Sunday clothes that the brother and his two sisters wore said for them that this was a solemn and unpleasant duty.

Aubrey, his hair freshly nonmodishly cut, looked all sincerity in his subdued blue pin stripe, last worn at his retirement party. Bethany, in her black nubby silk suit, was dressed primly and beyond her years.

The conference had been set up by Aubrey in his posture as the von Mohrwalds' business representative. Bethany had flown in as Aubrey had suggested to give the vital meeting both weightiness and tone, for Aubrey was sure that the Wheatley-Smiths would be impressed with a member of the nobility, even the Austrian nobility.

It was Bethany who presented their case. She gave their evidence on why they were sure Wheatley-Smith had not been drinking, on how they knew the autopsy had been mishandled. She pussyfooted around for precisely the decorous amount of time before saying the only way to prove an "untoward event" had occurred was a "reexamination."

Even with such euphemisms, a triple shudder went through the Wheatley-Smiths. But Bethany gallantly pushed on, offering to have a British solicitor get up all the necessary papers, gracefully accepting responsibility for costs because their brother had been working for the von Mohrwalds.

At mention of the paperwork and costs being taken care of, there were noddings of appreciation. But not acceptance. Wheatley-Smith's years of alcoholism, to which the family had been exposed so painfully, appeared to weigh more heavily on the family than their brother's distinguished accomplishments and the need to bring out any undiscovered truths.

When Bethany had finished her appeal, the lean elder brother spoke for them all. "We knew, of course, baroness, that Jerome had, um, desisted for some time." He looked at his sisters, who were nodding now with even greater vigor, and this time in agreement with their brother, not just in understanding. "So many times," the brother went on, "he made these efforts." He parted his hands, palms up as if to emphasize the numbers. "So, I am sorry to say, it is difficult for us to believe that this time, too . . ." He left the rest of the sentence unsaid, but redolent of negatives.

To Aubrey it seemed these stuffy people were almost relieved that the family shame was now quietly buried. Remembering his shrewd and observant friend, Aubrey privately hated these smug siblings.

As if hearing the brother's verdict, his diffident wife wafted in like an unprepossessing gray ghost with scones, bits of ham, home-made jam. It was a signal. Bethany had done her best. Aubrey made one last try, hoping the bludgeon would work where kid gloves had failed.

"But, Mr. Wheatley-Smith," he said, "my inquiries have convinced me that your brother was murdered." There was an almost audible twittering among the family members.

"But confess," said the older brother, at last, "you and the baroness do not have any proof, do you? If you did, of course, duty would dictate a different view on our parts. But . . ." Again he spread his hands, letting the unconsummated conjunction do the rest.

Muggy London, the pollution, the squawking horns, the growling gear boxes of rush-hour traffic, closed in on Aubrey and Bethany where they sat glumly on a bench in Russell Square.

For a few minutes they inveighed against the surviving Wheatley-Smiths. Both felt their best hope of reopening the dead inspector's case was as defunct as he was.

Now their only avenue was the routine investigation of the white collar aspects of the case, digging through corporate and real estate records, talks with government and industry officials, the sort of laborious piecing together they had hoped to avoid by going directly at the criminal possibilities.

"It could all turn out to be legal," Bethany said dispiritedly. "And if we do find something, it could all be too late."

"We could still try for a court order to raise him," Aubrey said, thinking aloud. But what chance? The Wheatley-Smith survivors were right. There wasn't enough evidence. Aubrey thought of a case twenty years ago where a coroner had discovered an ice pick puncture in a disinterred woman's hair so small that the undertaker had missed it when combing the supposed cardiac victim's tresses.

"A really good pathologist is a guy with a magic touch," he said dismally. "He could have settled things once and for all."

"Well, we can't get him disinterred," said Bethany with irritation. "So why even think about it." She rubbed at a spot of sugar icing on her black suit, ready to get up and write off this no-outlet avenue.

Aubrey felt her annoyance, but sat brooding silently. Was all his investigatory work really wasted? Years before, a reporter had dug up the grave of Senator Avery Lenneman to get some documents buried with him. They proved the senator had sold out to the investor-owned utilities. Aubrey told his restless companion about the case.

"Graverobbers," she said, thinking of how little she liked the press.

"Well," Aubrey countered, "I wish we had a graverobber like that." He scuffed at the ground with his shoe.

She was silent for a few moments, then looked at him seriously.

"You don't know anyone over here who . . . ?" She stopped.

"Jesus, no," he said. What a thought. How deep her anger must go over what they were doing to her vineyard, he thought. Then he grinned without joy at his own hypocrisy. Hadn't he wanted to provoke her into something with his story of Lenneman? "I am not saying I wouldn't see it through if there *were* someone," he said to her, more to get right with himself than with her.

Even if they did find a cooperative shoveler, though, what about a pathologist? Well, thought Aubrey, his mind beginning to run with dangerous efficiency, that wouldn't be so hard. He had enough friends in the seedy English press to find some down-and-outer. Finding a criminal in the professional classes was always easier than finding one in the working classes. Finding a gravedigger who'd risk a crime was the problem.

"You know I am not asking you to locate . . . ," she began to back away.

"Be quiet just a minute, Bethany," he said, his thoughts marching along double time. The reporter who had raided the late senator's coffin had been in his sixties. But he had only had to feel around for the documents, not lift out a body. Two men would be needed for that. "He's lying there just a couple of feet underground with all the answers," Aubrey said at last.

She waited now for him to go on.

"I wish there were a little more Lady Macbeth in you," Aubrey said, trying to lighten things.

"There may be enough," she came back.

"I can't figure how to get anyone to dig him up," Aubrey blurted it out. "I'd be willing to risk it. But it's a two-man job."

He didn't really have that much to lose. He'd never minded the publicity that had surrounded stories he'd done. Once he had helped a disgruntled employee drill a safe so he could get evidence on a crooked oil company. He'd been arrested and jailed, a hero to his colleagues for weeks. The second man had to be someone with a lot of emotion invested in the case. Franz von Mohrwald? But Aubrey would be damned if he was going to make the nomination.

Bethany gave him a shrewd, quick look, picking up his thought. But why Franz? she thought.

"It's horrible," she said, thinking suddenly of being a graverobber: someone who stole the jewelry from buried people and sold the bodies to medical schools.

She saw Aubrey's dark brown eyes go angry and hastily added, "I'm not saying I'm against the idea. I'm simply saying that . . . that it's horrible."

Now Aubrey waited for her.

"I'm going to do it," she said.

Aubrey took her gently by the lower arm, impressed.

"Blond Baroness Nabbed in Grave Crime," he said, a last warning, a chance for her to reconsider.

"Not funny," she replied.

They skipped supper, separating on their individual tasks. Bethany's was to find a neighborhood library where she could consult the *Times* for the small death notice that would tell them where Wheatley-Smith was buried.

Aubrey's was to meet with Varner Leason, an old acquaintance on the *Globe-Informer*. Years before, they had covered the London trial of a cuckolded British general who had inflicted the crime passionel on a U.S. Secretary of Commerce.

Leason, when Aubrey met him at El Vino's, was all talk of his latest scandal. It was only after the British reporter's second after-dinner cognac that Aubrey felt the relationship was resolidified enough for him to bring up his need for a pathologist.

Leason, his fox face suddenly alert in spite of the spirits, waited for Aubrey to explain. Cautiously, Aubrey told him that an American businessman had died in London supposedly from coronary insufficiency. His insurance company wanted to check out the possibilities of an overdose—which would trim the payout under a "by-the-insured's-own-hand" clause—before the businessman, at the family's request, was cremated and sent back to Battle Creek.

"Not much of a story," sniffed the Fleet Streeter.

"You're right. I'm doing it as a private investigator."

Aubrey paused, remembering the yarn about the English publisher, Lord Somebody, who when asked whether his reporters took bribes, replied, "Why would they when you consider what they'll do for nothing." Better, in this case, to pay the bribe and be certain, Aubrey thought. A little baksheesh would assure Leason's silence. He would not dare double-cross Aubrey lest Aubrey reveal the unethical payment.

"There'd be a consulting fee in it for you," he said.

Leason waited expectantly.

"A couple of hundred dollars," Aubrey smiled. "In unreportables."

The reporter smiled at the double pun.

"I'll telephone him for you myself," he offered.

"Set me up for breakfast," said Aubrey, fumbling with four fifty dollar bills under the table for the British newsman's hand.

"How tall is your uncle? What is his weight?" asked the fusty sixty-plus saleslady, standing beside Aubrey and Bethany late the next morning. Behind her, the wheelchairs were lined up like antique race cars revving for a contest.

Aubrey and Bethany looked at each other.

"Shorter than I am by a couple of inches," said the five-foot-eleven Aubrey. He had not seen Wheatley-Smith for several years, could not guess what weight he would be. Then he remembered the autopsy report. "Maybe a hundred and forty-five pounds," he said.

"And his ailment?"

Bethany pulled a long face. They were prepared for that.

"We would need a gentle restraint at the chest, I'm afraid," she said. "His motor control is, well, enfeebled."

"Muscular dystrophy," said the saleslady commiseratively.

"A related ailment."

"Poor dear," said the saleslady. "We have the perfect thing."

*   *   *

Minutes later in an orthopedic shop two blocks away, Aubrey asked the clerk whether he had something a little cheaper than the fancy doughnut of latex and stainless steel that lay on the counter.

"Just an ordinary neck brace," said Aubrey.

"National health will cover it, sir, if you've a prescription."

"I'm a tourist and it's just a temporary crick."

"Well," said the man, reaching in a drawer and pulling out a simple collar of styrofoam with a plastic strap and flimsy metal snaps, "this might do if the condition's not too serious."

"Nothing a little rest won't cure," said Aubrey.

At the hardware store down the street, Aubrey asked the jolly-looking proprietor for two shovels, one regular weight, one light.

"For snow?" asked the man.

"No," said Aubrey, "not for snow. For digging in the garden."

"*Spades* then," said the proprietor. "Spades are for digging; shovels here are just for moving things about."

"Right, then spades, a pair of pliers, a large screwdriver, and a crowbar, or do you call them pries?"

"No, no," said the proprietor jovially. "Pries are nosy people. You want something for stuck doors, windows, etcetera, yes?"

"Right," said Aubrey.

"Then a crowbar is right," said the proprietor, "and a mask and a flashlight?"

They all chuckled at the ironmonger's wit.

They loaded the tools into their rented car, and by the time they got to Hyde Park, their anxieties had largely turned to excitement. Aubrey unfolded the wheelchair. With Bethany playing rag doll patient, Aubrey strapped her in, adjusted the neck brace, and practiced getting up and down curbs and negotiating the park's low marble steps. Other visitors to the park clucked sympathetically at the couple: loyal husband, crippled mate.

They were too nervous for a real lunch so settled for buns and tea. Then they moved from the Dorchester to an American-style motel two miles beyond East Hounslow, near the churchyard where Wheatley-Smith was buried.

That afternoon they drove to the churchyard. Its stone wall was low enough for them to climb even if the gates were locked at night. They found the grave, the dry earth not yet turfed, scraps of asters and rotting lilies still on its gently convex surface. Before the verger had removed them, there would have been layer on layer of flowers. Cops always gave their own a big sendoff, particularly when the death was violent.

Bethany stared at the raw grave and Aubrey sensed her apprehension returning. God knew his was beginning. He gave her arm an understanding pat. How deep do they bury in England? he wondered. Labor costs being what they were, he'd bet it was no more than three feet from surface to coffin. He wished they could dig now and be done with it.

"I'm mad to be taking any part in this," Bethany said. "I wonder if I shouldn't talk with Franz first after all." Aubrey said nothing. If Bethany wanted an excuse to get out of the gravedigging, he wasn't going to interfere.

"Franz would say no," she tried Aubrey again, wanting a word of urging to stay in. This time Aubrey told her matter-of-factly, "You're a big girl now, Bethany."

She looked at him with mild irritation. But she did not call her husband.

Aubrey had specified a double room for himself on the first floor of the motel. Bethany was a floor above. They both took late afternoon naps, he so exhausted that when she jarred him awake with a call to his room, he trembled for a half minute.

As he got dressed, he looked sourly out the window. London was foggy enough when you didn't want it to be. This evening was pristinely clear, boding a full moon.

After eating lightly, they drove to East Hounslow at ten and parked near a small playground, a spot where the car could be left unobtrusively. The neighborhood was made up mainly of snug two-story semidetached houses. The only sign of life was at a pub a block and a half in the opposite direction from the church. There a few loud week-night regulars were closing things down.

Aubrey quickly removed the wheelchair from the back seat and opened it. Bethany, while they looked to left and right, plopped into it. She wore the least stylish of her summer frocks and low-heeled shoes, but still looked too dressed up for this part of London. Once she was settled, Aubrey handed her the wrapped tools and neck brace.

They left the doors of the car unlocked. They

might need the minute that would save. Despite
the darkness, Aubrey donned the long-suffering
expression of a tweedy resident taking his disabled
wife for a late evening walk. He trundled Bethany
briskly toward the cemetery. Once there, they
pivoted their necks in all directions. Then Aubrey
whisked his passenger into the weeds and shadows of a small vacant lot adjoining the churchyard's rear wall.

He urged on the chair as if he were a child
pushing a heavy lawnmower in deep grass, not
thinking how much easier it would have been to
tell Bethany to step out, and she too nervous to
think of it. At the wall, she got out and Aubrey
boosted her over. He passed her the tools and the
brace, then folded the wheelchair and they lifted
it across.

He climbed over and they stood together for a
moment beside the wall, catching their breath, eyes
and ears straining.

Faintly on the evening breeze, they could hear
the voices of people leaving the pub and the cars
in streets a block or so away. Nearer, they heard
the cheep of swifts and the interrupted chitter of
bats.

With a jerk of his head, Aubrey indicated Bethany should follow him. The moonlight was cold
and hard as plate. Their shadows extending across
the tombstones ahead of them, they walked toward
Wheatley-Smith's grave. It was partially shielded
from the street by a small copse.

Bethany put down the tools and Aubrey the
chair. He had not rolled it in order to prevent unnecessary tracks. He could feel the sweat prickling

out of his underarms and back. He looked at the grave. Up to this point they were only plotters. When he put the first shovel blade into the ground, he was a graverobber, a felon. Why had he gotten into this mess? He glared at Bethany in the half-light, saw the brave set of her shoulders, and felt ashamed.

They dug deeply into the soft, dry earth, depositing their spadefuls carefully at the foot of the grave just shy of where the grass started. That way it could be returned without leaving telltale crumblings on the lawn for the verger to discover tomorrow.

Bethany, muscles as tuned by her work as his, matched him shovelful for shovelful. Their breath soon came in pantings, loud as alarms in the stillness of the graveyard. The recessed windows of the church, anthropomorphized into eyes, seemed to watch them with ominous disapproval.

From time to time, a car's headlights turned the corner and moved across the trees, turning passive shadows into accusatory fingers. At such instants, they went rigid to prevent any observant driver from noticing motion.

Before they were down a foot and a half, the perspiration was running from under Aubrey's arms and down to his waist. Bethany, hair wisping now onto her cheeks and clinging sweatily there, dug, methodical and unwavering.

Her spade was the first to hit the casket. It thudded woodenly but solidly, as if there were the same thick dirt within as without. They used their shovels gingerly, scraping the last bits of earth from the lid. The coffin seemed long enough for a giant. As they worked on the final few inches, another set of headlights traversed the trees.

Aubrey and Bethany froze. This time the lights did not move onward. The luminance stopped outside the cemetery wall, shone a moment, then blinked out. Breathless as they were, Aubrey and Bethany made no sound, taking in the air silently through open mouths.

One car door, then the other, slammed. Two cops, thought Aubrey, nearly panicking. Some neighbors had seen the suspicious workers in the graveyard and had called the police!

Aubrey slowly crouched and Bethany imitated him. Both strained their ears for a voice or other sound that would identify the interlopers. There was nothing. Aubrey sensed that the police, if that was what they were, were scanning the graveyard. Noiselessly and by degrees, he flattened himself on the ground. Bethany, too, eased down. At last, they heard a man's low voice, youngish and insistent. "Come on, Emma," it said. Aubrey could have cried with relief.

"No," a timid female voice replied. "Maybe the car. In the car."

The worst danger, that of police, was past. But discovery by anyone could still lead to disaster. Their fate could depend on whether or not this young woman agreed to a romp on a tombstone.

"No. Not the car. It's not the same. I can put my jacket down," he argued.

Aubrey heard nothing again. He prayed the girl would show some seemly determination. The seconds passed. It was clear the man was kissing the woman. "Umm," he murmured. In a moment, there was an answering "umm." Aubrey internally groaned. The jig was up. Emma was succumbing.

"Yes, darling?" the man asked, hardly a question anymore.

"For a tiny bit," she acceded. "That's all."

"My jacket. I'll get it." The door opened. Aubrey raised his head, saw in the moonlight the whites of Bethany's terrified eyes. He rolled across the earth and into the grave. With a motion of his hand, like a vampire's summons, he gestured her after him. She snaked across the dirt, and silent as a python plopped in atop his back.

His face against the cold wood, Aubrey felt Bethany's 125 pounds or so as a ton. Oh God, he prayed again, you let them come into the graveyard, but now please let their lovemaking be quick.

Bethany's stiff body seemed almost to apologize for its weight. Where was the other graveyard couple now? Face to face, he was sure, not back to face. While they rutted, he and Bethany lay still and sexless as two mummies in a single sarcophagus.

On the other side of the copse, he could hear the quiet rustle of clothes and whispers of indecipherable speech. A minute or two more and the man tentatively emitted a series of sharp aspirants. The girl's small animal grunts made a duet of it.

Seconds later, the man gave a single muted cry of passion and a few instants later a soft curse. The woman was silent. Precipitant man, disappointed mate, Aubrey thought, with grim relief. In his salad days, he had known all about that.

In less than a minute, the two doors slammed again. The starter turned over, the gears grunted in low and the lights disappeared.

"*Sakrament!*" Breathed Bethany, easing herself from Aubrey as gently as she could. He tried to bend his creaky joints. She leaned over and firmly took his hand to help him.

Once he had clambered out, he started to make a lewd newspapery crack about preferring it—on balance—missionary style, but decided that was in bad taste even under the extraordinary circumstances.

"Thank God you go light on the strudels," he said instead.

They brushed themselves off, whisked the last of the earth from the coffin top, then dug a small canal around it so Aubrey could reach down with the screwdriver and loosen the lid enough to insert the crowbar.

Even then, the lid stuck. Aubrey pushed the crowbar under the edge and circumspectly pried it up along both sides. He glanced quickly at Bethany.

She nodded, giving her dress a last nervous brush. Aubrey lay on the ground, reached to the top of the coffin, and, delicate as a surgeon, pushed the lid up.

Half-shadowed by the sides of the grave, Wheatley-Smith lay waxen as an unburnt candle, smelling slightly of perfume on a base of something else, formaldehyde if Aubrey's guess was right. Within the large enceinte of the coffin, the policeman looked small and pathetically respectable in his best black suit, two rows of police and war ribbons over his breast pocket. Aubrey reached in and unpinned the ribbons, thinking of how vulnerable the corpse of this once dynamic man was, who now had been twice assaulted, once by an unknown enemy, now by a friend.

"We'll put the ribbons back on as soon as all this is over," he whispered to his old comrade, slipping the multicolored bars into Wheatley-Smith's breast pocket.

Twelve

THE PATHOLOGIST

Plucky as Bethany had been in helping to pull Wheatley-Smith shoulders first from the coffin and in lifting him over the wall, she had been unable to bring herself to assist Aubrey in bending him at the elbows and knees to accommodate him to the wheelchair.

With rigor mortis gone and the body more or less limp, the late inspector sagged slightly even with the wide restraining strap around his chest and the neck brace. But by pausing to prop him erect, Aubrey was able to give him a guise, if not of life, at least of moribundity.

While they wheeled the body under the street lights, an auto slowed and the working-class youths inside stared at them. At the rented car, two more cars passed as they carefully slid Wheatley-Smith onto the back seat. But they went efficiently about their loading and were soon underway.

Aubrey wished they could pull their car right

up to their room as could be done at some American motels, or that they dared get out of the car in the motel lot. But there was still too much coming and going by guests. He parked the car four blocks away on an unlighted street off Hounslow Road.

Bethany had been pinch-faced ever since Aubrey had muscled the late inspector's limbs into a natural wheelchair position. Now Aubrey glanced at her.

"You all right?"

"Yes," she said in a small unconvincing voice.

They sallied out of the side street, an ordinary looking couple pushing an invalided relative or friend at an unusual hour on a moonlit night. Aubrey's mind was working agitatedly. He had cased the motel and was sure the service entrance would be locked. He feared the emergency exits would sound an alarm at the desk. They would have to go in the main entrance.

"I'm worried about the clerk," Aubrey said as the motel lights hove into sight two blocks away. "You're going to have to distract him."

"Saying what?" She was rapidly losing her nerve. Aubrey took his own anxiety out on her.

"Bethany," he admonished her, "in theory you're the boss of this operation." She stared back at him with an angry pout. "Tell the clerk," Aubrey went on, "that my brother's got advanced polio or M. S. or some damned thing. Keep the guy's eyes on you. Try to look vivacious."

"Vivacious?" she said with exasperation. "Vivacious?"

They passed semidark shops, the motel only a

block away now. From the final cross street, a policeman appeared at a leisurely stroll. The bobby
looked first toward the motel, then back in their
direction.

Oh shit, Aubrey said to himself, stay cool.

"Talk like we've been married twenty years,"
he said in a low voice to Bethany. "Everything
natural, okay?"

"Shall we go to the British Museum tomorrow?"
she said with only a touch of hysteria. "Is Uncle
Jerome up to it? The mummies . . . maybe he'd
like to see the mummies."

"Fine," said Aubrey.

". . . unless," she said, most of the squeak gone
from her voice now, "we'd visit the Tower of London or Reading Gaol or drop in at Madame Tus-
saud's to see how the competition is doing."

"Very funny," Aubrey replied conversationally
as the bobby approached. The officer, he hoped,
would pass them by with a simple "good evening."
But as the trio and the uniformed man converged,
the bobby said, "Fine moon tonight," looking hard
at Aubrey and indicating he wanted a word or two.

"Yes," said Aubrey, gulping. "Gives us a little
light."

"Less pollution," said Bethany. "At night,
that is."

"Very much so," picked up Aubrey, then
dropped his voice to a whisper. "Only time of the
day for asthmatics."

The bobby nodded, copping a glance at Wheatley-Smith's motionless form. "That it, unh."

"That's the least of it," said Aubrey sotto voce.

"No matter," said Bethany, "the poor darling's asleep."

"All tuckered out," said Aubrey.

"Poor devil," echoed the bobby, not looking quite content with all this, but willing to assume that the three of them were respectable. "American, right? Going to the motel?"

"Yes," said Aubrey with a weary smile.

"Enjoy yourselves," said the bobby with a last look at Wheatley-Smith, and bid them a good evening.

"Well-patrolled streets," observed Aubrey to Bethany to keep the tenor of their talk alive until the bobby was out of earshot.

"Keeps down the criminal element," said Bethany, looking at him with a mix of humor and desperate relief.

At the motel Bethany held the door while Aubrey wheeled in the dead man. Bethany walked briskly to the desk, seeing from the corner of her eye Aubrey moving into the long hallway that led to his first floor room.

"Any messages for me?" she said, drawing the clerk's eye from the receding figure. Then, seeming to confide in the callow clerk: "His uncle, a terrible stroke two years ago."

"Ah," said the young man sympathetically, then with an assessing but veiled look at Bethany that had nothing to do with dead bodies, said, "No messages, madame. And a very good evening."

Bethany went to her room, called in a wake-up to allay any suspicions she might be in Aubrey's room, felt silly about caring what hotel personnel might think of her personal life, and hustled down the rear staircase to join him.

"Thank God," she said, looking almost fondly at the hapless exhumant. "We made it."

Aubrey had never seen her looking so worn.

"So far," he corrected her, not unkindly. He fumbled in his pocket, found a number and dialed the pathologist. Aubrey spoke with him in a quiet voice and then looked up at Bethany, his eyes perplexed and upset.

"The son of a bitch is drunk," he said.

Raymond Foscott, quondam fellow of the Royal College of Pathologists, was not drunk, Aubrey recognized as soon as he saw the contracted pupils in their visitor's bloodshot eyes. He was doped. Aubrey only hoped it was something benign and predictable like morphine. Bethany looked appalled at the man's slack face and disassociative smile.

Unlike most addicts, Dr. Foscott was dressed nattily, a clean, tan light cord coat with a navy vest. In spite of the air conditioning, he was sweating. He took off his coat with an apologetic look at Bethany. His hips were pear-shaped, his chest tiny, giving him the appearance of a lardy bowling pin. His voice was as unsinewy as his body.

"Isn't this man dead?" he said to Aubrey, pointing to Wheatley-Smith who was still in the wheelchair with his back toward them. He giggled at his joke. "My understanding was that you wanted a pathological examination, not a resuscitation. Why isn't he laid out? Hunh?"

He waddled around the wheelchair, bent at his

high waist and peered with dark-rimmed eyes at Wheatley-Smith's face.

"Fine," he said. "Very good."

Aubrey felt betrayed by his Fleet Street acquaintance, and angry at this sickening little man. He looked at Bethany and saw confusion where he sought support.

"Can you do this?" he harshly asked the doctor.

"Certainly," the man said defensively, trying to rally. As Aubrey continued to glower at him, he added, "Oh, you mean *this*," spreading his hands as if to indicate "this" was himself.

"At this point," he said, closing his eyes perhaps to further his self-assessment, "it will be fine. Forty-five minutes from now," he paused, smiled again at something interior, "or forty-five minutes ago"—obviously before he had taken the injection—"I might not have been, um, your man."

Aubrey considered for a moment aborting the whole scheme, returning his old comrade to the grave without further outrage. But he shook off the idea.

"Okay," he growled to the physician, "let's go."

"Fee in advance," said the man.

Grudgingly, Aubrey gave him the thousand dollars they had agreed to that morning. "Where do you want him?" he asked.

Foscott looked quickly but probingly around the room.

"A door would be best. But these'd be hard to take off. Empty that chest of drawers and put them bottoms up across the bathtub." He looked at Bethany with petty cruelty. "And open the drain. We'll have to wash things down afterwards."

Bethany, who had been almost all that Aubrey could have asked from a fellow graverobber, made a stifled sound over this implication of noisome fluids and rushed to the bathroom. Behind the closed door Aubrey could hear her vomiting.

"Morning sick?" asked the pathologist unkindly.

"I should break your arm for you, you filthy little dopehead," Aubrey said, moving toward him threateningly. The doctor backed up behind Wheatley-Smith.

When Bethany came from the bathroom, she looked ashamed. Aubrey took her arm, still furious at their visitor.

"Go get some rest. I'll come for you when I need you."

She started to protest. But he shook his head assertively.

"C'mon, boss. No time to argue."

Wheatley-Smith's mouth popped open when the two men put him on the makeshift examining table, or as Aubrey preferred to think of it, catafalque. It was as if the dead policeman was surprised to find himself there, his naked, hairy body exposed, the hideous autopsy cuts, sewn but unhealed, his limp sexual organs blatantly tendered for inspection.

Foscott had brought a leather case not much bigger than a child's watercolor set. In it were a scalpel, a small stainless steel saw, a straight probe, scissors, and long tweezers.

From his coat pocket, he drew a cheap, high-powered magnifying glass with a plastic rim. While Aubrey sat on the closed toilet, the pathologist lowered his unshapely body beside the tub as if in prayer. Aubrey sensed that this was not Dr. Foscott's first operation under juryrigged conditions.

Sensitive pink fingers moving with swift efficiency, the pathologist started on Wheatley-Smith's feet, spreading the toes with one hand while he inspected the skin with the glass, checking under the nails.

Seemingly unaffected now by whatever tutti-frutti of drugs he had taken, the pathologist moved rapidly past ankle, shin, and knee. His exertions made his inhalings and exhalings heavy and uneven.

He worked up the hirsute thighs.

"Get me a pillow, will you?" he said to Aubrey. When Aubrey returned with it, the doctor said abstractedly, "Slip it under my knees, will you. That's a good fellow."

At the genitalia, Foscott took Wheatley-Smith's flaccid member between thumb and forefinger, turned it back and forth like a sausage grader and dropped it, then held the testicles in his hand as if they were leather-sacked marbles, lifted them, bent to look narrowly underneath, grunted with discomfort and moved on to the groin.

For the pubic hair, he had Aubrey hold a small flashlight fetched from the second coat pocket. Foscott peered closely into the miniature forest, poking the hairs apart expertly, occasionally shaving a few with the scalpel to bare a spot of skin.

On the left side he stopped, went tense and alert as a butterfly on a sippet of honeysuckle, febrile, swaying, determined.

"Un hunh," he murmured to himself in subdued triumph. "Un hunh." He stared through the glass, his artistic fingers pressing the hair away from a spot of skin just to the leg side of the groin. "Yes sir," he said, his satisfaction growing. "Yes sir."

"A needle entry?" demanded Aubrey, almost beside himself.

"A teensy-weensy hemorrhage in the cutis," said the pathologist, fixing his eyes on Aubrey now as if he were an interloper.

"But . . . ?"

"It *could* be a needle intrusion, Mr. Tough Guy. And now, let's you just get out of here. I'm feeling nervous emanations from you. They are making me fidgety. I am tiring and I want to move on. Go. Scat. I'll call when I need your help to turn the body."

Aubrey obeyed. He had seen this kind of remission in drug heads. He knew it was temporary. He wanted this rotten man who had given him hope on this impossible case to hold together as long as he could.

A half hour later, Foscott came out, done with his centimeter by centimeter scrutiny of the corpse. He had sweated all the way through his cotton cord trousers. His shirt was drenched. His blotched, unhealthy face looked as if he had just come in from a downpour. He was panting.

"Nothing else," he said. "Nothing in the body cavity. Nothing."

"What do you mean nothing?" said Aubrey. "What about the injection hole?"

"What about it? It's probably an injection hole."

"Probably?" said Aubrey angrily. "Probably is not goddamn good enough!"

"Well," said Foscott, "probably is all you get."

"You mean that's all you can say: probably?"

"Without cutting."

"I want to *know!*"said Aubrey, still upset.

"Even if I cut, I won't know until I get down to the vein. And maybe not then."

Aubrey could see Foscott's face going dopey, dull.

"Nobody said I'd have to cut," he went on. "It'll cost you."

He looked at Aubrey with crafty, tired eyes. "Make up your mind fast. My body's running out of time."

Aubrey felt anxious. In a few minutes the physician would be too shaky, too numb, too something to cut.

"How much?" Aubrey asked.

"Make it two thousand more," said the doctor, "and I'll give you the evidence."

"The evidence?"

"The specimen."

"A thousand more," said Aubrey, "or screw it. I'll take it out myself with a razor blade."

"And muck it up." Foscott put on his coat as if to go.

Aubrey stood over the pathologist and took him lightly by the shirt collar.

"You dirty shitpoke," he said. "You came here *expecting* to take us for another two thousand. Take the extra thousand and be damned lucky."

"Fifteen . . ."

Aubrey dropped his big hand and took the fore-finger of the doctor's right hand, holding firm even when the man started to recoil.

"Sonny boy, I'm going to give you the two thousand. And then I am going to break each fucking one of your fingers, at two hundred dollars a snap." He stared in the frightened man's face and began to twist the finger at the joint. The man tried to pull away. Aubrey twisted until the pathologist went down to his knees. Aubrey let go and the doctor rubbed his finger, not looking at his assailant.

"Now get in there and be happy we're giving you anything at all." Aubrey moved toward him again. "Or do you want that two thousand?" The man shook his head no, cowed.

"And take it out neat as a goddamned bouillon cube," said Aubrey. "I've got to show it to medical people at home and if it isn't perfect I'll come back personally and take care of those little pussy hands of yours and then I'll throw you to the cops."

"You're as guilty as I am; you couldn't," the pathologist began, a little spunk still left in him. Aubrey moved toward him again. Foscott backed away, too far gone into his obsession, too much the coward, too needy. He held up his hands weakly.

"Come in and point the flashlight for me," he said.

At the end of a flurry of meticulous incisions, Foscott lifted out a two-inch cube of flesh and held it daintily with thumb and forefinger. Aubrey looked at the livid cavity in Wheatley-Smith's groin and then at the specimen.

With the magnifying glass, Foscott studied a

cut he had made in the cube while Aubrey waited, holding his breath.

"It was an injection," said Foscott with quiet pride. "Take this and look at the vein." Aubrey did as he was told. "You'll see where it's punctured, right there beneath the discolored adventitia, the darker flesh. It was a sloppy shot."

"Holy shit," said Aubrey admiringly. "I see it."

"Your friends over there will want to put the vein and some of the adventitia under a scope. They can try a lab test on some of the tissue. It may or may not be worth a zinc farthing. With luck you'll get an educated guess on what went in there."

"Alcohol would show?"

"Well, that or something chemically like it just might, if it's there."

The pathologist wrapped the specimen in the plastic from a drinking glass and dropped it in the glass.

"Freeze this as fast as you can and keep it at least damned cold until your people look at it. And *don't* put it in any fixative—alcohol or anything like that. The adventitia and fatty tissue are mucked up enough from the embalming fluid."

"Freeze?" Aubrey asked. Where would he freeze it? How would he get it all the way to California frozen?

"Your problem," said Foscott, waiting nervously for Aubrey to pay him. Aubrey could see Foscott tightening, trying to fight off the second wave of dope symptoms that were beginning to clutch him.

Holding the roll of money in his hands, Aubrey said, "I'm going to need you to testify."

The flabby face twisted and squirmed. The voice squeaked. "Testify? Are you bloody insane? Testify that I came here and committed a felony? That's what it is, you know. For us all. I'd be so fast back in Pentonville . . ."

"Back in Pentonville?"

"Prison, for Jesus sake. Didn't Leason"—the reporter—"tell you? Why in god's name do you think I'm doing this instead of working for the National Health or some Harley Street nob?"

Aubrey started to interrupt. The doctor was falling apart.

". . . because of this, you imbecile." He pulled up his wet sleeve. Aubrey had seen railroad tracks on addicts' arms, but never the match for these. The loose flesh at the inside of the elbow looked as if it had been lined laterally with thick white fluid which had dried into miniature mountain ranges. "Do you think I'm here to solve some fancy case for you so I can put my head into three years and six? Why, man . . ." He stopped, out of breath.

"Then what good . . . ?" Aubrey started to argue.

"Well, the good is that you can go back to America and prove to your people, whoever they are, that this man had an injection before he died. That's what you paid for. And the satisfaction of knowing your hunch was right."

"Jesus, it could be a vitamin shot."

"In the femoral vein?" Foscott sneered.

Aubrey looked at the perturbed man. He thought fast. But there was no way he would ever get Foscott to testify or even give an affidavit. He peeled off twenty fifty-dollar bills from the roll.

"Thanks," said the physician. This and the other thousand would hold his terrible habit for a while. He giggled, much as he had when he came in. "I'd get this fellow back where he came from before I did anything else," he said.

The combination of formaldehyde and perfume Aubrey had smelled in the car filled the motel room. But there was still something nagging his mind.

"What the hell are you using?" he asked the doctor.

"Smack," the American slang for heroin.

"That's not all," said Aubrey. "You needed some kind of upper to get done what you did."

"Well," said Dr. Foscott, "you start with two parts dextroamphetamine . . ." He smiled, foolishly but proudly. "After that, I make it a point to forget the formula."

When the pathologist was gone, Aubrey, rather than ringing Bethany through the switchboard, hurried upstairs.

"He found it," Aubrey whispered exultantly when she opened the door. "The hole. The injection. In the groin."

"My God," she said. "They *did* kill him. They'd kill us."

Aubrey nodded, sobered by her reaction. She was right. But he quickly put that aside and considered it from his own perspective: this was the evidence he needed to get the California authorities to reopen the case.

Thirteen

DUDDMAN REVISITED

Freezing the specimen proved no problem. Bethany simply had the clerk switch her to a room with a mini-refrigerator while Aubrey dressed Wheatley-Smith for retransit to his resting place.

Keeping the cube frozen, or near frozen, all the way to California was not as easy as the druggie pathologist had made it sound. The airline galleys had no freezer and would not permit passengers to use the small refrigerator. Aubrey opted for dry ice, but in England as in the United States, frozen CO_2 had gone the way of the player piano.

Finally, from the phone book, he located an ice-cream store that used it at the bottom of its cans. He bought three pounds, packed most of it around the well-wrapped frozen cube in a six-pack-sized Styrofoam cooler and stashed it in his luggage. He went straight to the airport. The luggage was stowed in the plane's bay, a cool forty degrees Fahrenheit as Aubrey had determined from the airline.

An hour away from landing at Kennedy, a stewardess passed out the U.S. Customs forms. They warned of "fines or other penalties" for smuggling meat or "meat products" into the country. The stricture gave Aubrey a minor stomach spasm.

In the Customs room, Aubrey slipped the cube from the cooler, from which the dry ice had evaporated and put the specimen in his coat pocket. He shoved his toilet kit into the cooler as if that were his usual mode for protecting small bottles.

Customs passed him without inspection of either baggage or person. He rushed by cab to a dry-ice supplier in the Bronx, then, his refrigeration intact again, he flew on to San Francisco.

At Los Platanos, he put the evidence in the room refrigerator for solid freezing. That done, he called Bethany. She told him animatedly of Martino e Stelio's talk with Maier and the latter's strange reference to the California wine crop, his hint that something dramatic was going to happen—and soon. Aubrey telephoned long-range meteorological scientists, vineyard owners, and California agricultural officials. As far as they could speculate, California was in for good, or at least not bad, weather for the next few years.

Groggy with jet lag, he nevertheless returned to Domaine McIntyre and reinterrogated the manager. He got the names of the vineyards to which McIntyre had exported vine stocks, two in France, and one each in Italy, Germany, Australia, and Chile. It was thin stuff, but still the names of the four European vineyards were the only tie he had been able to establish so far between the Domaine and the continent.

Now he called Duddman. The county coroner could hardly have been unhappier to hear from Aubrey Warder again. But the alternative to seeing him—evading him—could, Duddman suspected, result in Warder endangering him professionally.

This time at Duddman's office, Aubrey did not have to be nice. He had the goods.

"You've got a classic fuck-up on your hands," Aubrey told him. "It's a shame for me, but lucky for you that I'm not still in the newspaper business."

They sat in Duddman's small air-conditioned lab off the examining room. Between them on an enameled tray was the cube of human flesh slowly thawing.

"I could claim it was a put-up job, a needle puncture made after the body left me," sparred Duddman.

"You know damned well there wouldn't be any of that bruise tissue, any inflammation if he'd been injected after he was dead. I'd make a laughing stock of you."

Duddman looked as liverish as the fragmentary remains. He held the magnifying glass again above the needle puncture. His rubber-gloved hands carefully turned the piece over to where Foscott had slit the grayed vein to show the tiny puckering made when the needle punctured it.

"How could I have missed it?" Duddman asked himself.

Aubrey felt a cautious sympathy. The stubble on the skin side of the specimen made it look like a small, untidy square of golf course rough.

"Anybody could have. The poor bastard was

hairier than an ape." Familiarity with the grisly item had bred insensibility.

"Who killed him?" said Duddman. "Any ideas?"

"No, not really."

Duddman closed his eyes and put the thumb and forefinger of his right hand lightly to his lids, examining whether there was any way out. Aubrey could almost read the way his thoughts went: a murder had occurred; something, probably alcohol was injected to make it appear accidental; he, Duddman, had been successfully misled; now, this private detective was ready to identify the telltale cube of flesh as coming from the corpse. If his word did not stand up, there was the exhumable body to testify mutely, precisely, indisputably to the authenticity of this same missing cube.

Sure, Duddman would be thinking, Aubrey and his accomplice or accomplices had committed a crime, probably a felony, in England. But Duddman would bet that bodysnatching, particularly on such a sampler basis, would not be grounds for extradition. Besides, while such a revelation might disgrace Warder, assuming he was capable of disgrace, it would not save Duddman's good name.

Duddman rocked back and forth slowly. When at last he opened his eyes, they were hostile but resigned.

"I would need a way out," he said.

Aubrey relaxed.

"I'll find it," he said.

"I would have to admit I missed the hole," said Duddman, assessing his damage potential aloud. "That would hurt. But I could say that after you came to me the first time, I tended to believe you and urged you to come up with proof so I could ask that the case be reopened. I had no idea you would come up with this," he gestured at the cube of flesh.

"You could say you were shocked when I came in with it," said Aubrey, wanting to make it easier for Duddman because that would make it easier for Aubrey. "I would take the heat on it. You could speak of the body's extreme hirsuteness."

"I could point out it was a rushed day. Three autopsies."

"You could talk of understaffing."

"I would still look like an asshole," said Duddman realistically.

"I would talk about the scientific way you worked on the specimen, how you were able to determine that it was alcohol or a like substance that was invasive, assuming that's what you find. How you immediately took the responsibility and insisted it be brought to the police and prosecutor's attention. I would express awe at your integrity in a world often lacking it."

Duddman smiled in spite of himself.

"Enough bullshit," he said. "It will fly. Barely."

For the time being, Duddman would confide only in the county prosecutor, the police chief, Deputy Chief Hernandez, and the single homicide detective on the case. Interviews would have to be reconducted and broadened to include all the top Domaine McIntyre officials, plus some of the workers, all the visitors listed in the guest registry.

Eventually, the local paper was going to get on to the fact that the investigation had been reopened. But Duddman thought that the reopening could be explained with statements that Wheatley-Smith's relatives in England had sworn to his tee-totaling, that the other tour people had seen him cold sober shortly before he died, that new computations on the possible alcohol ingestion and the amount in his blood had raised suspicions. Perhaps there might even be some imaginative suggestions by police that the dirt in his shoes came from an area of the vineyard removed from the wine press, suggested Aubrey helpfully.

The real evidence of murder—the morsel of Wheatley-Smith—would not need to be surfaced until the case got to the grand jury stage, giving Aubrey time to try to identify the killers and the details of the conspiracy that led to the murder.

Nevertheless, any report of the renewed investigation, no matter how toned down, would get back to the murderers of Wheatley-Smith. They would increase their endeavors to cover their tracks. Still, even that had its positive side. For in covering up they could well do something to flag themselves as the culprits.

Perpetrators often hanged themselves that way. Nixon, he thought, might never have had to quit if he had not tried to conceal Watergate but had simply thrown his top aides to the dogs, apologized, and gotten on with the business of being president.

"You'll let me keep the corpus delecti?" Duddman asked.

"Just enough of that advent . . ."

"Adventitia . . ."

"To run a test for the booze on. You got a blowup lens in there?" Aubrey jerked his head at the lab room. "Take a photo of the vein and the puncture. But I'm keeping the meat. I got it at some hazard."

"I'll bet," said Duddman acidly. "You're asking me to do a lot on faith."

"I have my own ass to think of," said Aubrey. "And my client's." For an instant he thought of his client's trim hindquarters. He grimaced at this unseemly turn of mind and quickly righted his thoughts. "I've got to keep the proof where I can get to it. Sooner or later your cops will pressure the English to disinter the body. That's when I'll have to prove it was worthwhile for me to . . . have dug him up. I've got to show I *had* to do it, to prove the murder took place."

"But if anything happened to you?" asked Duddman plaintively.

Aubrey shuddered. It wasn't all that unlikely.

"I'll have a note in my safety deposit box about where the cube is. It'll say to turn it over to you."

"You know I could get a court order here and try to get it enforced over there to disinter the body right now, then subpoena that thing the hell away from you."

"Sure you could," said Aubrey scornfully. "You'd have one complete murder victim and zero suspects. Wait. I'm not going to spin you. When I get it pinned down, you'll get it. Hell, Michael," he said, risking the first name for the first time, "you may be the hero of this thing yet."

Duddman smiled sourly again. But now that he could see he would survive, he relaxed a bit.

"Have you the faintest idea what the hell is going on?" he asked Aubrey. "Gotta be a lot of money in this to kill so elaborately. Where's it coming from?"

Aubrey outlined what he knew, then went on, "I got nothing but theories. I've thought of a hundred angles. What I do know is that they can't make their investments back on the present wine market. That means a gouge, a scam, something with felony written all over it. Are they over-insuring all this land and wine stock so they can destroy it and collect? Or some kind of multinational tax write-off? Or selling short the wine market and the banks doing the financing; then bankrupting on purpose? Mafia extortion to make wholesalers buy at super prices? A miracle fertilizer in the closet, or some kind of dream pesticide to multiply the amount of wine they can produce? That could figure because they're already jacking up production to the maximum on some of the land they got, jacking up their profits at the same time provided they can peddle all the cheap stuff it'll make. Man, I've thought of everything. You name it."

"Maybe they're buying up all the vineyards in the world. A monopoly to end all monopolies."

"No goddamn chance. There's too many. You can lay down a billion bucks and get maybe eight billion in leverage, but even that's not enough for everything. What they might do is buy up enough of the table wine market to monopolize, but that gets complicated, too."

"How about torch jobs on all the vineyards they *don't* have a piece of?" said Duddman. "Arson is very much in with businessmen this year."

"Very funny," said Aubrey. "Let's take the picture, and I'll give you your tat of . . ."

". . . adventitia . . ."

". . . and I'll be on my way. "

They rose, the morsel of Wheatley-Smith back in Aubrey's custody. When they were done in the lab, Duddman walked Aubrey to the door, not uncompanionably.

"Just make sure you put that piece of the late inspector in a safe place, okay?"

"Of course."

"Make that a safe, *cold* place," said the coroner.

In the square outside, the noon heat was thick and gummy. There was no breeze to cut it even for a second. Aubrey felt the same apprehensions in Los Platanos he had last time. Out there, someplace, were people willing to kill. Maybe the old guy on the park bench; maybe the kid in the car with the marshmallow racing tires; maybe, and most likely, someone he didn't see at all.

He went back to the motel and restored the morsel of Wheatley-Smith to the ice section of the room's refrigerator. In the morning he would call ahead to San Francisco and locate dry ice for the trip east. Once there, he would secrete the specimen in a rented meat drawer in Rockville.

Next he called Bethany to report on the four European vineyards which had gotten Domaine McIntyre vines. That done, a little embarrassedly, he pulled the knife from his luggage and put it on the night table before flopping heavily onto the bed.

Bethany reached him during the week after he got back to his vineyard. From the names of the four wineries, she had come up with the principals.

One of them was Bridsey, a fact not difficult to uncover considering the jingoistic dedication with which the French recorded foreign investments in *La Patrie*. The Englishman was a partner in Château Ambourg-Repose, classified as a fourth growth in 1855 and now producing about eight thousand cases a year.

Aubrey was excited by her discovery. It could not be mere coincidence that the vineyard Wheatley-Smith had been investigating when he died had shipped vine stocks to a French vineyard owned in part by one of the cartelists. Aubrey was sure that the location of the vines and the use to which they were being put would shed light not just on what Wheatley-Smith was doing in Los Platanos, but on the whole conspiracy.

Hoping that the lead on Bridsey might signal his case was on a roll, he quickly called an old crony at the State Department to see whether any of the four vineyards' management, especially Ambourg-Repose's, had visited the United States before or during the time Wheatley-Smith was in California. But there was none.

At last, though, he had something solid to work on. He called Schloss von Mohrwald to make arrangements for meeting Bethany or Franz in Paris from whence they would journey to Rutheville, where Château Ambourg-Repose was located.

Fourteen

THE SUSPECT

Once again, St. Gage and Tobb leaned over the walnut table in St. Gage's law offices, the two of them as confidential and nervous as an imprisoned client and his attorney. Which was client, which attorney, would have been hard to say. Their desire for utmost secrecy was, however, unambiguous.

"Bridsey called last night," whispered St. Gage. "An American, his name is Aubrey Warder, a private detective, has visited Domaine McIntyre twice."

Tobb drew his breath and grunted as if he had been hit. St. Gage tightened his face. He did not like interruptions.

"The McIntyre manager called Bridsey's partner in Bordeaux. The detective is aware their vine stocks have been sent to France . . ."

Impulsively, Tobb broke in, gripping the edge of the table. "The silly bastard at McIntyre must have volunteered it! Must have bragged about it . . ."

160

St. Gage shrugged with real annoyance.

"On the first visit the McIntyre person did not notify Bridsey's partner. The rootstocks had only come up incidental . . ."

". . . I'll bet."

". . . to the detective's inquiries about the late inspector. On the second visit the questions about the vine stocks were pointed."

"Does the detective know they went to Bridsey's partner?"

"Yes, along with three other European vineyards." St. Gage looked disgusted. "It seems this Warder threatened the manager and the manager told him."

"Threatened him? With what?"

"With a nasty suit of some kind."

"I'll fly to California. We'll have a second pressing."

St. Gage smiled in spite of himself. Yet he could never be sure with Tobb when he was deadly, as it were, serious and when he was not.

"Not yet," said St. Gage. "And not out there. Two, uh, coincidences would really encourage suspicion."

"Then the von Mohrwalds. They're the root of it. If not them personally, then they have children if I'm not mistaken. A nonfatal accident to one of them at night, maybe a minor assault, a broken arm, or a few ribs. It would make the point."

St. Gage appeared to be impassively studying Tobb's proposal. In fact, he was thinking about his dead father, how he would have suffered if St. Gage had been beaten in an alley as a pressure tactic against him during his days of trial. He felt a flash of anger against Tobb, this American brute. But he hid it.

"I think not," he said smoothly. "But there is still the worst of it: at the end of the talk, this Warder asked almost casually what kind of crop Domaine McIntyre expected and the manager said fine and Warder said, 'and I guess that would go for the rest of California, too,' and the manager said, 'yes, everybody.' "

"Doesn't sound like just small talk," said Tobb.

"No. The manager didn't think so either, and of course he has no idea."

St. Gage, generally so calm, burst out peevishly, "My God, the schedule is tight enough already. And I *can't* push our Belgian friend any faster on the antidote. But if this fool stumbles on something, then . . ."

"Then we're diddled. So set a day."

"How? When somebody inside may be . . . ?"

Tobb's tanned face flushed into swarthiness. "We've got a leak," he agreed.

The two men, usually so glib, brooded. The American spoke first.

"Who besides you and me and your Dr. Strangelove knows where those vine stocks wound up?"

"Well, the *Witwe*, if she was told by Berkady. And Bridsey knows you picked them up at the vineyard. But he doesn't know where they are now. He's saying, even to his partner down there, that they went to Portugal as part of a secret government project to grow decent Cabernets. Bridsey doesn't *want* to know."

"It wouldn't be him anyway," said Tobb. "But, shit, who can be sure?"

"The *Witwe*'s too old. Too smart. Too close," said St. Gage, "but she could be playing her own game somehow."

"The mad scientist?"

"Mad, not suicidal."

"Maier," Tobb spat out.

"He's too frightened," St. Gage said. Yet it could be Maier as much as any of them. St. Gage thought of Maier, nodding, bowing at the wine conventions. He knew everyone. A very industrious operator.

He would have met the von Mohrwalds at one place or another, and St. Gage was sure that it was they who had hired the American, just as they had the Englishman. But Maier was too timorous to have betrayed them to the von Mohrwalds. Indiscretion maybe; malice never. And if not them or another holdout, then whom?

Into St. Gage's recollections of the European wine meetings, the tall Italian, Martino e Stelio, drifted. He had been a big coup for Maier.

"That Italian," St. Gage said to Tobb. "Maier's catch: the prince. I have seen him, a balding movie star of a man, playing the gigolo to von Mohrwald's wife at wine do's."

Tobb mused on that a moment.

"There's a big jump from that to Maier's blabbing," said Tobb, for a change assuming the cautionary role. "Call them all in," he said. "You've been talking about a general meeting anyway."

"Yes," sighed St. Gage. "There's no other way to do it."

Tobb pushed back from the table, graceful and menacing as a large, angry leopard.

"Do you know who this Warder is?" he asked.

"No time to find out. Not yet."

"His name is vaguely familiar," said Tobb. "You have an American *Who's Who* in the law library here, don't you?"

Two days later, in the same conference room, four of the cartelists awaited the arrival of the fifth, William Bridsey. He had nervously called in late. His commuter train had failed to stop at Chislehurst for the second time this week. He was taking a cab.

On one side of the walnut table, Maier talked weather with the aged German gnome, Matilda Pfeffermühle. They had already reviewed the folders of commercial documents before them and wanted to get on with whatever the meeting held.

Across from them, Pierce Tobb studied his folder, a scowl twisting his open California features. He had arrived only moments ago, having crossed the Atlantic and come back since he last saw St. Gage. He had not had time to review the material and he was irritated. He turned the pages like a schoolboy doing last minute cramming for a semester exam he knows he is going to fail. His schoolmates, his resentful expression seemed to say, had already prepared for the test and could afford small talk before the exam began. He could not.

At the window, alone as he often was, St. Gage looked at the Thames and thought about which of the four conferees, not excluding Tobb, might be his betrayer.

Bridsey entered all in a rush, with apologies for everyone and a cautious look at Tobb. The American rose briefly when St. Gage introduced him to Bridsey, then went rudely back to his papers. The others awaited, ill at ease, the *Witwe*'s withered mouth pinching tighter and tighter with annoyance.

When Tobb's dog-in-the-manger performance had gone on for several minutes, St. Gage said to him mildly, "Are we ready?" Still Tobb kept his nose in the papers.

"Mr. Tobb is still doing his homework," the old German woman said malevolently. "He is, I believe, what you in English call a lip reader."

Tobb glared up at the *Witwe*.

"Widow Peppermill, be careful that you do not become my homework," he said, his voice the soft snarl one hears from a dog trained to kill.

St. Gage tightened his lips almost imperceptibly. In such enterprises, he sighed to himself, one does not get the conviviality of family Christmas dinners. As cordially as if Tobb had never made his ominous remark, St. Gage indicated the meeting would begin and signaled Bridsey to give the first report.

Bridsey, usually so bluff, seemed tense from the contretemps between the *Witwe* and Tobb. He reported progress in Spain and Portugal. Prospects were also good in South Africa and, at the other end of the political spectrum, in the Communist lands.

The Communists can always be counted on to put the cuckhold's horns on Karl Marx, St. Gage thought, when there are a few extra pounds to be made by luxuriating in the arms of Adam Smith.

"I have made no inquiries on Australia yet," said Bridsey, "but they are on my immediate agenda." He began to expand on his Australian plans and Tobb yawned. "In Austria," Bridsey went on, trying to hurry, "we can expect about sixty, seventy percent of our quota, giving and taking a bit. We cannot count on the Krems and von Mohr-wald holdings. But I'll . . ."

St. Gage scowled at mention of the von Mohr-walds, but the mustachioed Bridsey thought it was an expression of annoyance with his wordiness and struggled to wind up.

". . . I'm working on the rest."

When Bridsey had finished, the *Witwe* Pfeffer-mühle looked up at St. Gage with bright rat eyes that held no fear nor even respect, eyes that long since had stopped seeing the ordinary run of people as entities with souls, and now saw them merely as pieces in her own game of life. Her English was guttural, economical.

"In Germany, enough at this stage. Forty percent. The other"—she sought in the dry old attic of her mind for the word—"targets will come. We have the ones we wanted most."

"The groupings around Bingen?"

"Next week I find out," she said, then added, the tartness giving an almost attractive chiding quality to her tone, "*Langsam, langsam*, Robert," as a mother might restrain an impulsive son.

"Koblentz?" he asked, a small smile acknowl-edging her reproof, a plating of approbation on his voice.

"Fine," she nodded. "Everything in Koblentz is lovely."

Maier, the next around the table, was clearly

intimidated by St. Gage. His bent for theatrics and his present effort to draw his face into its most nearly statesmanlike lines, made him seem more fraudulent than he really was.

"In France and Algeria, you already know, *ça marche*. Nothing new. In Italy," he smiled at his colleagues, savoring his next announcement as a man might a sniffed but still undrunk Margaux, "we have signed the Martino e Stelio acreage, and at a good price. In the rest of the north and Tuscany, etcetera, it will be fine when the lire drops . . ."

"*If* the lire drops . . . ," St. Gage interrupted.

Maier's nose quivered like a frightened rabbit's.

"It will drop," he said softly but did not press the point. "In Sicily," he recommenced, feeling again the proddings of Calliope, "the 'black hand' remains outstretched but rather in demand than in agreement. I . . ."

St. Gage cut him short.

"I will talk with them."

His mouth open, but his stage air of bravery gone, Maier shut up. St. Gage went on coolly with his own reports.

"On the overall financial arrangements"—St. Gage's primary concern—"Very good news. As to the purchase and lease agreements in Chile and Argentina, seeming willingness to go along with us, not to interfere, though some resistance on the details. On the matter of increasing the yield on our new acreage, the vinicultural advisers are very optimistic indeed. This, of course, is as vital to our profitability as our, um, other plans for raising profits."

He paused, his face clouding.

"Nothing good can be expected from the United States," he said.

For the first time, the American looked up.

"Try another way of phrasing that, Robert. Okay?"

"Point conceded, phrase amended in re 'nothing good from the United States' to exempt Mr. Tobb." The American nodded and St. Gage continued.

"There is not the slightest chance we will get any cooperation from them," he said. "They are still obsessed with their spirit of seventeen seventy-six. They turned me aside as I began my suggestions."

"There are the criminal antitrust and monopoly laws for them to worry about, Robert," said Tobb.

St. Gage was too good a lawyer not to know that these could be circumvented. He recognized the dig Tobb was giving him. But he did not choose to take umbrage.

"Right. Well, for several reasons, then, we can't hope for anything at all there." He breathed deeply, his only sign of pressure, or indeed of any other emotion.

No one at the table missed either the significance or the finality of what St. Gage had said. "Does this," he asked them, "change the resolve of anyone?"

He looked at each in turn.

Tobb might not be very good on account books, but he was fine on people. His relaxed expression gave way to something with undertones of reckless cruelty, the look of a schoolboy with an aptitude for dirty tricks.

"No," said Tobb. "Not in the least."

"No," Bridsey echoed.

"There is no intermediary we could use to try to bring the Americans around, Robert?" asked the *Witwe* Pfeffermühle. "No other course? It would so simplify things."

"No way at all?" parroted the Frenchman. Had the *Witwe* not spoken, Maier would have cringed silently.

"I am open to other avenues," said St. Gage. "I agree it would all be so much easier if the Americans would cooperate. Without them, we will have to act so much more rapidly. But . . . ?"

He left the question hanging, waiting for explicit suggestions from the two reluctant partners. Hearing none, he shrugged. "Then I assume, in spite of your—all our—misgivings . . ."

"So Robert has our proxies to do with the sword what all of us would rather cowardly do with a kiss," interrupted Tobb with a leer.

The *Witwe* Pfeffermühle's eyes flashed like a sudden reflection of light in an old, dim mirror. St. Gage saw it and winced. Tobb got things said, but his irreverence did not appeal to the lawyer, at least not to his most coldly rational aspect.

Still, St. Gage thought, one deals with what is. At least Tobb's remark had given St. Gage the opportunity to get a formal ratification of total executive power.

"We all do understand that Pierce and I will act forthwith then, and I do assume that the rest of you prefer to remain . . ." He looked for the precise word. ". . . sanitized from the details."

The meeting was over. As they rose, Tobb covertly eyed St. Gage who glanced at Maier, bent now over the table. Tobb did no more than smile faintly in agreement.

"Auguste," said St. Gage pleasantly, "could you stay over for a moment or two? There are some few trivial details that need not delay the rest of you"—meaning Bridsey and the German woman.

Maier was sweating through the armpits of his suit coat. The perspiration also oozed from his forehead, filling the shallow wrinkles there until they looked like tiny irrigation ditches.

As he exchanged *à bientôts* with Bridsey and the *Witwe*, he tried to sound calm.

"Here?" he asked St. Gage as Tobb closed the conference room door.

"Yes, some coffee?" St. Gage smiled.

Sourire du cobra, Maier thought.

"We wanted to get caught up on the fine points of France, Algeria, Italy," said the solicitor. "We needed to talk with you confidentially about Latin America."

The mention of confidentiality gave Maier some comfort, but still he wondered why he had been asked to spell out minutiae on his assignments while Bridsey and the *Witwe* had not.

Nevertheless, over the coffee, brought to the room by a young secretary, Maier unrolled his reports on acreages and purchases, on *caves* and warehouses and they listened intently as he spoke.

He finished with France and commenced Algeria where, he said, he had consummated most of their contemplated deals with O.N.C.V., the state wine monopoly. He then began running down the status of the vineyards from the Tyrol to south of Rome. St. Gage nodded reflectively. Tobb sat inscrutably.

"Auguste," said St. Gage, as Maier wound up his summary, "our main reason for inviting you here was to ask you this: is there anyone in Italy? Anyone we could trust enough to use as a coordinator? We would not confide much in him, but he would be our day-to-day factotum.

"I tell you this in great confidence, my friend. I have not been doing as well as I had hoped in neutralizing the South Americans. Argentinian interests have raised the old Falklands issue, unfairly, against me. I thought perhaps if you could find a temporary Italian deputy, we could free you up for a trip to Buenos Aires."

Maier's heart bumped with sudden assuagement. There was nothing then to fear. How logical it was. St. Gage, despite his words to the full meeting, had failed in Latin America. He, Auguste Maier, would succeed.

"The Argentinians have not forgotten that the French missiles were most successful against our ships," said St. Gage churlishly. "You will know how to parlay that fact."

"Of course. Immediately after Algeria, but . . ." Maier went through the names of the big Italian owners who might serve the conspiracy, if unwittingly, as proconsuls. Cautiously he mentioned Claudio Martino e Stelio toward the end of the list.

That done, he waited Gallically for the two Anglo-Saxons to indicate a preference before giving his own.

They talked among themselves of the list and St. Gage asked, "What of this Martino e Stelio, the prince. Would his title help us? I believe I've met him somewhere. Isn't he a bit of a playboy?"

Maier felt a tremor. He knew he had been indiscreet with the prince, no doubt of that. But he saw it as minor, speculative, not substantial, at least as best he remembered that liquid evening. Nevertheless, it would not do for St. Gage and the prince to get too close. The prince, precisely because he was a lightweight, might reveal that, in fact, Maier had spoken of California, of the possible downtrend in its wine production.

"He is somewhat empty-headed," said Maier. "The better choice would be Treado from Verona, or Sergio di Toni if you prefer a nobleman."

St. Gage seemed to consider the choices.

"Do you know these people on a social basis, Auguste? By that I mean, have you ever seen them outside the financial dealings, been able to assess them over a table, a social drink. It is important that I have your most personal views on them."

At that instant, whatever manliness existed in Auguste Maier died. They *knew*, he surmised with deathly fear. They *knew*. Or did they? Conflicting fears and desperate hopes clattered about in his head.

"Never socially," he said, praying his guess was right. "Yet one could always make that kind of approach with an Italian, if you wish for me to. When the price is correct . . ." He wanted urgently to sound sophisticated, appropriately contemptuous, but not overly so, toward the Italians.

"Let me think about it," St. Gage said suavely. "Let me discuss it with Mr. Tobb. Now, I want to tell you from the heart that you are moving beautifully, Auguste. How much longer will you need for Algeria, do you think?"

Maybe, thought Maier, I am only being paranoid. Still, he wished he had never gotten into this affair. He wished he had never heard the name St. Gage, never looked at the deceptively healthy Medusa face of Tobb. It made him cold as a stone inside.

When Maier had made his adieus and St. Gage had graciously shown him to the corridor door, Tobb and St. Gage returned to the conference room.

"I don't know," said Tobb when they were inside, both by the window. "There's nothing, really, not enough anyway for me to . . ."

He left the sentence suspended in the air like the blade of a guillotine.

"Did you notice how he hesitated when I asked him if he had met with Martino e Stelio socially?"

"No," said Tobb. "I thought he didn't. He sounded clean."

"Well, we can't ask the good prince whether Maier compromised us," said St. Gage peevishly.

They coursed back and forth across the question of Maier's guilt. Had Maier and the prince met in some social, intimate way outside the encounters at the vineyard and the bank conference rooms of Venice? If they had, then Maier had lied and was the culprit. They would need to look no further for the leaker.

"How long would it take you to find if they met socially?" asked St. Gage.

"A couple of days," said Tobb, "if it's provable."

"It's worth it," said the solicitor. "But how . . . ?"

"Trust me," said Tobb.

In a French wine-trade publication, Pierce Tobb found a picture of Maier standing with a French agriculture minister. Tobb had the face blown up to three-by-five. Armed with copies and a wallet full of money, he flew to Venice.

It did not take Tobb long to learn that for all Venice's past grandeur, there were not many places where an Italian prince would entertain an important visitor. Besides, the trail was fresh, and from the financial documents he knew to the day when Maier and Martino e Stelio had cinched the deal.

Posing as an American federal agent seeking a Frenchman who defrauded rich American tourists (and was suspected of trying the same thing with well-to-do Italians), Tobb made his rounds of maitre d's, headwaiters, and bartenders.

His approach was crude, direct, designed to allay natural and protective suspicions with hard cash. After he had introduced himself as an American government detective, he asked to be shown to a table for one, slipped a folded fifty thousand-lire note into his surprised host's hand and began his spiel.

As part of it, he showed the maitre d', the waiter, the bartender the photograph of Maier. But despite his diligence, his plea, "to help us with law enforcement, *signore*," he got no leads. Too many years of discretion had shaded the spark that the initial fifty thousand lire produced. He passed through the bar of the Danieli, as with the others, without a hint of Maier's recent presence.

By the time he was down to Cipriani's, the last of the fine restaurants, Tobb was discouraged. He was reluctant to make the long trip to Torcello, the island in the lagoon where it was located. But ill-temperedly, he decided to go. There, perhaps in a zealous desire to protect his guest, the prince, the maitre d' chose to remember the man in Tobb's photo.

"You are certain," Tobb said, hiding his excitement behind a professional tone. The maitre d' nodded, "yes, *signore*," but called over a waiter to be sure. "*Sì*," said the waiter with certainty. "I tell you it was hot, but he sat there, a Frenchman in a two-piece business suit."

"Do you remember his companion? An American? A well-to-do Italian, one, perhaps, of high respect."

The waiter looked at the maitre d'.

"Yes," said the maitre d'. "A patron of long standing."

"May I . . . ," said Tobb.

"I do not think I should," said the man.

"We would wish, through the Italian authorities, of course, to warn him, perhaps even to solicit his help."

Now the maitre d' looked at the waiter.

"It was Prince Claudio Martino e Stelio," said the maitre d'. "I would prefer you did not say I told you this. But we wish to cooperate with your government. We wish to avert harm to the prince." The maitre d' was obviously agitated.

"You acted wisely in telling me," Tobb said soothingly. "This man would prey on just such a nobleman. But God be praised, fraud artists, the best of them, do not hurry things. We will be in time."

"Should I not notify the prince," said the host, clearly now of two minds. "He has eaten with us for many years. His family . . . "

"I tend to think these things should stay in police hands. But of course, Italy is a free country. The Italian police will have this information by late this afternoon. They will call him this evening."

The maitre d' and waiter both nodded uncomfortably. It was not the sort of thing that usually happened at Cipriani's.

On the way back to Venice, when his anger at Maier had subsided, he thought how easy it would have been for the Frenchman to have simply said he had a few social dinners with Martino e Stelio, among others. Fear had made him lie, fear, obviously, that Tobb and St. Gage would discover what had been discussed by him and the prince.

Tobb had the motorboat take him to the Rialto where, at the tourist telephone room in the main post office, he could call St. Gage without any record of the call.

"Maier had a lunch with the prince on an island a good ways from Venice. I don't know if they met anyplace else."

For long seconds, St. Gage said nothing. Then he replied, "Maier is back in Algiers. I am genuinely sorry about all this."

"Where in Algiers?" asked Tobb, irritated at what he saw as softness in St. Gage.

"My guess is the Hotel Moretti. You will, uh, first confront him with his lie, satisfy yourself that it was he?"

"Of course," said Tobb, not liking to be told his business.

When Tobb had paid for his call, he noted that he had used up all but two of his fifty-thousand lire notes. Only the maitre d' at Cipriani's had given him back the gratuity when he realized it was for information, not a good table. Tobb liked that kind of probity.

Fifteen

THE MYSTERY OF EL KEBIR

In the intense Algerian sunlight the vineyards of Mostaganem seemed to run directly into the Mediterranean, the green vines and the blue sea fusing in a band of shimmering color.

For a century, France siphoned off most of the produce of these vineyards for blending with their own *vins ordinaires*. Yet in the dusty Arab-modern town of Mostaganem there were also cellars full of wines of quality, honored by the French appellation, *vins délimités de qualité supérieure*, or V.D.Q.S.

The Algerian wines' heritage went back two millenniums to when the Romans prized them even over the wines of Campania. Under the centuries of Moslem abstemiousness, the Christian minority kept viniculture alive in church closes. Now, under socialism, it was a money crop.

The Algerian vineyards grew hardily on seaside hills and from oases by lifeless wadis. Their vinifera scions blossomed on desert vine stocks called Farhana and Hasseroun. Beside them, where one would expect irrigation ditches, stone spillways kept water from seeping into the thirsty sand.

In the wineries, next to the most modern glass-lined barrels, oddly shaped native tuns aged heavy reds and luscious whites. A number of these huge old wooden tuns had bulged gradually over the years from a climate which was often too dry in summer, too rainy in winter. Making them even more fantastic were the archaic mouths on their top sides through which the juices and skins were poured. They were capped with lids of wood the size of manhole covers.

One of the oldest of Mostaganem's cellars—a ramshackle warehouse in the workers' quarter of Sebra Ishwari—was built over a branch of the stream Oued Cheliff which cooled the wines as it ran.

The largest of the tuns in this cellar had its own name, El Kebir—"The fat one." Over the years this oaken giant had sagged grotesquely as its boards weakened with the weathering and the decades of vintages. But the resultant leaks had been plugged with the ingenuity and skill of Moorish master carpenters.

Some of the finest of Mostaganem's V.D.Q.S.'s were given their initial fermentation in "the fat one." Its seasoned oak gave a special distinction to the Pinot Noirs, the pick of the neighboring vineyards. And its extreme age encouraged the romantic belief in Mostaganem that vintages whose life began in El Kebir had magic medicinal and vigor-restoring qualities.

Thus when a young Bedouin-cum-vineyard watchman heard strange slow bumps coming one night from "the fat one," it was natural that he would fear something unworldly was going on. On this moonless night, his fundamentalist Muslim abhorrence of alcohol at odds with his job anyway, he was frightened that Allah or a more vindictive member of the hagiology might be visiting some curse on him.

He wakened a supervisor who, knowing the youth to be honest and free of any disposition to dip into the liquids he was employed to guard, stumbled to the warehouse. Sure enough, the bumps clearly sounded near the top of the gigantic cask.

In the morning, the supervisor passed on the word to the cellar manager who called the state wine chemist for the western region. They tapped the tun at its old wooden bung. By then, the sun was warming Mostaganem, and the tun and the wines that labored within were as silent as they had been all its numerous and productive years.

As to the wine itself, their sampling showed perhaps a hint of early richness, but such minute variations from year to year were by no means uncommon.

The manager had his assistant spend the night on a cot beside the elderly tun. Its contents were too valuable to risk inattendance. Sure enough, as the cool of night touched the cavernous warehouse, there were low, periodic bumps from the upper quarter of El Kebir.

During the day, the management considered what to do. To unseal the cover atop the cask could throw off the work of the precious juice and skins inside.

A trans-Mediterranean call was made to the cellar's chief importer in France. He suggested that gas may have formed in the cask and was actuating a piece of board that might have broken from the cask, or might even have been left inside during one of its many repairs.

"Ingenious," said the Algerian cellar manager. "But, monsieur, where would such gas have come from?"

"Ah," said the French expert. "Who can say? I am a mere purveyor of wines, not a gazer in crystal balls."

The manager, using a cloth-wrapped hammer, pounded on the cask to see whether the hypothesized pocket of gas could be released in a way that would replicate the bumps. Nothing happened.

The manager decided that if the bumps continued that night, there was nothing to do but unseal the heavy cover on top.

By nightfall, a small troop of wine workers and officials and a number of townspeople were gathered in the low-ceilinged warehouse. For two hours, as the heat left the steamy littoral, the gathering theorized on the causes of the thuds, all the while casting concerned glances at the silent wooden tun.

Just before eleven, the manager heard a tentative thump up by the cover. He shushed the crowd.

In the shed, lit only by dim lanterns, the audience listened, their faces as intent as if they anticipated a miracle. Again, there was a light bump, no mistaking it. A collective "aaahhh" went up from the waiting men.

"A flashlight," said the manager to an assistant. "The big American one."

In a moment, his assistant was beside him,

handing him the electric lantern. The manager shone
it on the top of the barrel high above their heads.

"A ladder," said the manager. Two workers
brought an old-fashioned scaling ladder used to
ascend the sides of casks. The manager climbed up
and slightly loosened the wooden cover. There was
a gentle whiff of gas from inside which he sniffed
as it vented, but the minuscule bit of gas was not
enough to have caused the bumping.

The manager descended, leaving the cover on,
half-sealed. In the silence, the motley group listened keenly. Suddenly, as pronounced as the
opening chords of Beethoven's Fifth, the thuds
sounded defiantly. It was as if some imprisoned
spirit demanded liberation from the cask. The crowd
jabbered.

The manager jerked the light from the hands
of the open-mouth aide with whom he had entrusted it, and flicked on its beam. A town consta-
ble nervously fingered his pistol holster. The crowd
scrambled to find a cart, a keg, a railing where they
could stand to see the top of the cask.

The manager fixed the spotlight beam on the
wooden cover. The bumps increased in power. Then
abruptly, the lid sprung from the top of the tun
and cartwheeled down its side. The crowd gasped
as if with a single throat.

Simultaneously, a head appeared from the aperture. Its hair was a mass of grape skins and must,
like a hideously tonsured Bacchus. It seemed almost that it might rocket from the cask as if it were
a Polaris.

But one shoulder or the other struck the side
of the opening; the body was never positioned so

exactly in the middle of the hole that its torso could spring out. Like a jack-in-the-box, the head bobbed up and down in the flashlight's rays. Its eyes were white, its mouth slightly open, but twisted as if it would entreat the multitude below to release it from its vinic cell, to end somehow its ghastly jig.

The crowd was agog, paralyzed by the apparition. As the manager began to collect his thoughts, the head uttered an unearthly sound, a loud, drawn-out belch, accompanied by a tremolo vibration of the lips. The gas within the strange corpse which had caused it to rise and fall had been released.

Then, slowly, like an ocean liner, it sank, first the chin, then the face, and finally the tangled hair. The congregation was frozen for a few moments, as if they expected the form to rise again. But the body was at rest.

There was nothing to do but grapple the corpse from within the tun. That was quickly done. The horrified warehouse workers hauled the body down ladders. It was laid on the ground and those still able to stomach the gross spectacle, gazed into the face, eerily illuminated by the electric lantern.

The skin was too stained with the burgundy coloring of the grapes for one to be sure of its race. But its battered features, insofar as one could discern them, were European rather than Arabic.

It was days before collaboration between Algerian and French police led to identification of the man as Auguste Maier, a prominent French vintner, vineyard owner, and commerçant. Even so, it was impossible to say how he had died.

A skilled autopsy, performed at the University

of Algiers, determined that the head was fractured in twenty-six places. It could not be said with certainty whether the massive skull damage had occurred before or after submersion.

What was certain was that yeasts and other natural ingredients in the cask had stimulated production of large quantities of gas within the body cavity. The corpse had, over several days, risen to the top of the cask and remained pressed there until the chill of evening set in. Then it had submerged slightly, been instantly rewarmed by the wine, and pistoned to the surface again.

The body was sent to Maier's widow. Its burgundy pigmentation was beyond the skill of any cosmetician to coat. The death certificate read *"décédé pour des causes inconnues,"* although the Algerian authorities, not wanting to have an unsolved murder on their hands, suggested Maier might have been copping a clandestine sniff of El Kebir's contents and fallen in, with some worker resealing the tun when he saw the cover off the hole.

The fine Pinot Noir of El Kebir was drained into the branch of Oued Cheliff which ran through the warehouse. The cask was broken up by the management and distributed in pieces to the poor of Mostraganem for firewood. When they burned it, the villagers noted a peculiar bluish hue, due to the natural chemicals it had absorbed during its many decades of beneficial use.

Sixteen

THE VINES OF AMBOURG-REPOSE

Aubrey's French was awful and, avid amateur viniculturist though he was, he was not confident he could discriminate ages, health, and varieties of American wines at Château Ambourg-Repose.

Both the von Mohrwalds, like many educated citizens of small countries, spoke a half dozen languages well. And both had the requisite knowledge of vines. Aubrey was unqualifiedly glad that under their division of labor, Bethany got the Ambourg-Repose assignment.

Aubrey and Bethany arrived in Paris on the day after Maier was identified as the victim of El Kebir. Rather than the breezy outdoor café where Aubrey had hoped to meet Bethany, he went to her room in her moderately priced hotel on the Right Bank. Maier's death had scared them both, and they did not want to flinch at every passer-by.

The gamy French papers were strewn on her bed when he arrived. The opinion of the journalists, unsupported by any specific facts, was that Maier had been murdered either by anti-French terrorists or by the lackeys of some business associate to whom he had done the dirty. The means of his demise, not surprisingly, overshadowed the motives.

For Aubrey and Bethany, the new death engendered a sense of greater momentum, a feeling that the conspiracy was moving ever more rapidly toward radical—if unknown—action.

"If we just knew," she said.

"Well, we're gaining on it," he said. "We know a few things we didn't know before."

But it wasn't enough to curb her anxiety.

"I get this awful feeling that they're moving so fast and that the Schloss, all of us, are being swept along in the night. I'm afraid we'll go over the waterfall before it even gets light enough to see the river."

"Are you sure you don't want out?" Aubrey asked her, seeing the concern in her face, pale even beneath its usual healthy tan. "I have to level with you: any of us could be killed by these guys, Bethany, even your kids. People who crush bodies in machinery and drown them in wine barrels aren't the same kind of murderers who just panic and kill somebody in a stick-up."

Before she had begun to read his moods, she might have thought he was merely seeking a way out for himself. Now she took his warning at face value.

"No," she said. "We want to follow it wherever it goes."

*   *   *

Bridsey, although but one of four partners in Château Ambourg-Repose, controlled it through liens on the personal holdings of his three French associates. He had bought into it three years before, and it produced superior reds and whites. Both facts distinguished it from the cartel's recent buy-ups of vineyards that concentrated on table wines. Yet Aubrey was certain that Bridsey's interest in the château now tied in somehow with the conspiracy. There was just too much coincidence.

To save money on their trip to the château, Aubrey and Bethany rented a Citroën Dyane. They rolled back the top and, even given the danger of their mission, the summer morning air from the fields rushing in on them lifted their mood.

They talked easily, comrades tried now in adversity. Aubrey told her of his reporting days, how the big stories had thrilled him, but how, as time passed, things seemed to repeat themselves until finally he left the business. Now, he laughed dryly, he had come back to it in a different form, and with a vengeance.

Bethany recounted the absurdities she and Franz had encountered in the wine trade; she spoke of her three children. The talk grew personal. He ventured that he and his wife had never had any kids, mentioned that they had dreamed years before of dropping their work—she was a teacher—and buying a small vineyard.

Suddenly, catalyzed by a combination of the sun, the dark green foreign fields, the clean, gusting air and this good, interested woman, his feelings precipitated.

"I got the vineyard too late," he said. He wanted to go on, but could not. His wife's death from cancer ten years ago was the first real wrench life had given him. With her dying, he had understood the grief he had so often casually written about.

"I'm sorry," she said, knowing it was inadequate, then risked an intimacy she would otherwise never have ventured. "Women are fortunate when they have good men in their lives. Your wife was fortunate, Aubrey, in all the years she had with you. As I am with Franz."

He looked quickly and gratefully at her. She had carried them back to safer ground. Yet, there was a twinge of regret. His talking of his wife was rare. How few people would want to listen? And now it was too late for him to go on.

They were only a few kilometers away from Rutheville, a medieval town of ten thousand which was bounded on two sides by the Ambourg-Repose vineyards. Aubrey drove slowly, eying the bar-restaurant, the tobacco store, a fancy wine emporium, the greengrocer, the bus-train plaza, the two-star hotel with its dressy restaurant sign outside, the winding streets twisting out from the main drag.

He left Rutheville and drove along the road bordering the Ambourg-Repose vineyards. Its weathered wooden fences were intertwined with wisteria and with grape vines that had returned to wildness. Behind them in the fields, the cultivated grapes grew in thick, healthy clusters, stretching in rows toward forest lands. At a gravel road entrance, a weathered metal sign slightly atilt on its wooden pole said, *"Au Château."* Beside it, a newer, larger sign stuck in the ground like American real-estate placards said, "DEFENSE D'ENTRER"—"Do not enter."

The road, arched by scraggly poplars, ended about a quarter-mile away at a faded, stuccoed three-story building, the "château." As they drove on, they could see a cluster of outbuildings, including to their surprise a greenhouse—for greenhouses were not common in European vineyards—and beyond, a small lake. Still further they saw the low cone of a hill, tufted here and there by unkempt trees and bushes.

Bethany and Aubrey scrutinized the fields as greedily as appraisers. At the crest of a hill, they stopped and looked back. To be sure, there were vines of different maturities in the vineyard, but no patch of dissimilar plants which might be there solely for innovative purposes.

"The greenhouse?" asked Aubrey.

"Not likely. That would be for flowers, vegetables."

"Let's try anyway," said Aubrey.

To get to it, Aubrey and Bethany would have to wait until the vinedressers had left the fields, and sneak in from behind the greenhouse to avoid being in the line of sight of people inside the manse.

"There goes our supper date," said Aubrey.

Bethany was sure Bridsey did not spend much time at Ambourg-Repose. But on the odd chance he was there, she did not want to be seen on the streets of Rutheville. They went by car to the wine shop, pausing outside it on foot only long enough to note the display of Château Ambourg-Repose vintages in its small show window.

Aubrey knew how he wanted to proceed with the lanky wine merchant, but he did not trust his French enough to try. Bethany obliged as translator.

First, Aubrey bought a half-dozen wines of recent vintages. It was a nice sale for the storekeeper. As the man put the bottles into separate plastic bags, Aubrey had Bethany ask him whether it was possible to tour the vineyard.

"No. Not possible," said the merchant, waving a finger. The château, cellars, and fields, he explained, had been open by appointment under the old owners. The new ones—including an Englishman, he said neutrally, testing Aubrey—believed visitors would disrupt the operation.

"My husband is American. I am Danish," said Bethany quickly. The tall storekeeper smiled, showing gapped teeth. "We had looked forward to seeing it. We have visited châteaux all over the Bordeaux."

"I wish I could be of help," said the man. "In the old days, I would merely have called them on the telephone for you. Believe me, the château is nothing spectacular. I have visited it in the past many times."

"We think we saw it from the road. A square building with a large greenhouse?"

"Ah yes, the greenhouse," said the storekeeper as if he were talking of the first automobile in town, "it is novel, is it not?"

"Perhaps they are using it to develop a secret

wine to win the market away from all the other fine wines of Bordeaux," said Aubrey jokingly. As Bethany translated, the merchant, who had begun with a pruny look, smiled even more widely. He was unlimbering fast.

"Monsieur, like all Americans, has a fine sense of humor. But no, it is, I am told by the men of the château, merely a place where—along with the flowers and other plants—they nurture vine stocks."

Aubrey hid his excitement.

"A sort of hospital for sick vines," he said. He was hitting it off fine with the merchant. He looked at him man-to-man. "I must consult with my wife about something," he said, and turned to her. "I think I ought to buy a seventy," he said. "If things work out, it goes on my expense account. If not, I pay."

The storekeeper heard the date in English and understood it; his eyes took on a gleam of bourgeois greed.

"My husband insists on buying a seventy," she said eying Aubrey coldly.

The store owner found one on a lower shelf and carefully put it into still another sack, without disturbing the dust on its shoulders. "It is a lovely wine," he said. "Produced under the old management."

"But," said Aubrey, "I do not understand. If this Englishman is so injurious to Ambourg-Repose, why would he go to the trouble of putting in a new greenhouse to nurse back vines? Such buildings are expensive, no?"

"Ah, well, I will explain. The greenhouse, as I

understand it, is not just for flowers and vegetable seedlings. Nor is it just a hospital for vines, as you put it."

"Oh?" asked Aubrey.

"The greenhouse, I am told, is for vines which come from other countries. They are cared for, revived from their long trips, then shipped out."

"The vines are resold then," said Aubrey.

"Probably. I am not privy to their finances."

"Then the Englishman sells not only wines but vines."

Aubrey's rhyme did not translate out, although it came out nicely alliterative in French and the merchant looked appreciatively at Aubrey.

"Monsieur is a poet."

"A mere lover of wines," said Aubrey, "unlike your friend the Englishman who is a lover of the revenue which wines bring, perhaps even an excessive lover."

"You have put it precisely," said the merchant, beginning to tote up the sizable bill.

At lunch in the hotel restaurant, Aubrey ordered a bottle of the Ambourg-Repose white. After the meal, he and Bethany praised the food and the wine to the skies. It was not hard to do.

"I cannot understand why this fine white is not widely known," said Aubrey. "It is not expensive."

"You must ask the boss of Ambourg-Repose," said the waiter as Bethany rapidly translated. "He is an Englishman."

"I am an American," said Aubrey.

"Ah, but the messieurs speak the same language."

"Not always," said Aubrey with a meaningful look.

"Ah, very good," said the waiter. "Monsieur is a wit."

"Besides, I cannot ask him. They do not permit visitors. We would love to tour the vineyard."

"There is a resident partner there," said the waiter. "My cousin is his butler. This resident partner is French. He is less intractable than the other. If you ask this partner, he might make an exception."

"Is the resident partner always there? But no, he would be out in the fields. Perhaps we could catch him just before supper?"

Instead of translating, Bethany said rapidly, "Are you out of your mind? We don't dare meet anyone out there."

Aubrey masked his irritation behind a smile.

"Bethany, shut up and translate."

The waiter sensed discord. Bethany grudgingly translated.

"I would go at six-thirty," said the waiter. "He will be into his first apéritif. Praise his wines. He might oblige you."

"And his name?" said Aubrey.

"D'Edouard. Olivier d'Edouard."

He must be new, Aubrey thought. His was not one of the names Bethany had come up with. One more dud to run through the State Department.

In the town's principal bar, Aubrey remarked to the man beside him that he had seldom seen a town so picturesque. As Bethany once again patiently translated, Aubrey inquired whether one could hike to the top of that hill to which he pointed.

"What a place for a photograph," said Aubrey.

"Ah no, monsieur," said the man. "It is not permitted."

The bartender, his ear cocked, joined them.

"It is owned by one of your countrymen," explained the bartender.

"An American?"

The bartender looked embarrassed.

"Oh, monsieur, pardon. An Englishman."

"But why," Aubrey smiled winningly. "I would not pluck his grapes. Is he hiding something? The atomic bomb, perhaps?"

The two Frenchmen chuckled.

"More important than that," said the bartender. "The hill is the *cave* of our local château, Ambourg-Repose. It is hollow. They have all their wines aging inside the hill."

That afternoon Aubrey and Bethany drove out toward the vineyard, looking for a place off the road where the car could be hidden. There was none: this part of France had been under continuous cultivation for more than two thousand years and at every turning there was a cottage. Aubrey drove back to town and they parked in the railroad depot lot with other vehicles.

They walked back out to the vineyard, and with looks both ways, cut off the road and into the Ambourg-Repose estate. Aubrey, in his casual clothes and she in her slacks and English walkers could make a pretense of being simply presumptuous tourists if they were caught by a late-lingering worker.

The summer sun, though slanting now, was still hot on the rich green vines and fattening globes of grapes. The flinty soil, roughed by hoeing, made walking difficult. When they crossed the hillocks on which the rows ran, Aubrey took her hand and she held it firmly, uncoquettishly, letting it go when she no longer needed support.

For about an hour, using the hill as a marker so they would know the direction of the manse, they trekked the fields, looking for recently emplaced vine stocks.

As the sun began to sink, they drew to within sight of the greenhouse. It was larger than it looked from the road. Aubrey glanced at her to check her mettle. She smiled back.

"It beats body grabbing," she said.

"Snatching," he corrected her with a grin. "Body *snatching*."

From their hiding place, Aubrey and Bethany saw a pair of workers in dusty blue coveralls wheel the antique bikes from a shed and ride down the gravel road. The last to go, they hoped.

They waited uncomfortably for a few more minutes, then Aubrey nodded at her. They circled the greenhouse so as to come at it from the lake side, hidden from the house. Bethany's face was tense. Aubrey looked at her with admiration.

"You're a brave lady," he said to her in a whisper and she smiled back dubiously.

Although the main house was eclipsed now by the greenhouse, Aubrey cautiously dropped to his hands and knees and signaled her down. They left the protective cover of the vineyard and crawled through low weeds to the side of the glass-walled building.

Cleaving to its rear, they crawled to the first corner. Halfway down the side, still largely shielded from the house, was a large door with hinges at the top. Aubrey was sure it was a work door through which plants, fertilizer, and tools could be brought in and out. He touched her, indicating she should wait, and crept to the door.

It was secured only by a hasp whose staple was pegged, not locked. He signaled her to him and swung the door upward just enough for her to enter.

"Stick to the wall inside," he told her. "Otherwise you'll leave tracks in the dust."

She nodded, squirmed in and wriggled sharply right. He smelled the sharp, strong scent of natural fertilizer at the same time he heard a muttered oath.

"Kruzifix!"

In explanation, a white hand came out from the crack of the door for his inspection. It was covered with fresh cow manure. The hand withdrew. Aubrey rolled under the door, well wide of where Bethany had crawled in. She was sitting against the wall, rubbing her hands on the packed dirt floor. The knees and shins of her slacks were splotched.

The manure box was against the wall to the right of the door, conveniently located for a farmer, not so much so for a house-breaker. Bethany left off her hand-wiping and put her lips to Aubrey's ear.

"Some detective," she whispered.

He drew back to see if she were smiling. She almost was.

"You smell awful," he ventured. "Franz ought to buy you a new scent for Christmas."

Aubrey thought about the marks on the dirt Bethany was leaving, but said nothing. When she was done with her primitive cleanup, she came to a crouch like an efficient rabbit sniffing the air. In an awkward kind of stoop she proceeded down the rows, ignoring the flowers, the bean, tomato and lettuce shoots in their thin wooden boxes. She reached the grape vines, some mere shoots, some mature, a few gnarled centenarians.

This was Bethany's world, not his. Phoebe Hills Vineyards had no greenhouse, no imported vines. Aubrey duckwalked behind, careful to keep his bobbling head from rising above the vines where it, or a shadow of it, might be spotted by someone outside.

The sun was falling fast. Its last rays gave the air a strange artificial greenish glint. Aubrey peered into corners, felt at the foot of the wall, looking for scraps of paper as avidly as he had once looked in government files for documents.

But the greenhouse was scrupulously neat. The tools were ordered, the extra clay pots, cartons, balls of twine, were all in their places, the burlap root wrappers as meticulously piled as a French housewife's quilts, the sacks of chemical fertilizer stacked evenly, the natural manure in bays such as had greeted Bethany.

She was finishing up the first row and beginning the second. Aubrey waddled up behind her. She turned, anticipating his query and nodded no.

On the third U-turn, a vacant area of soil greeted them. It stretched for six, seven yards down the center of the greenhouse: prime ground. It was pocked with holes as if small bombs had cratered it at regular intervals.

Bethany bent down like a supplicant to sniff the soil. She rubbed it lightly with the palm of her hand, plumbed the holes, crumbled it, then moved along its border, repeating her almost medical examination of the earth. At the end of the section, she waited for Aubrey. Her hand cupped at his ear, she said, "Whatever they had in here has been gone some weeks. I don't know what kind of vine stocks they were, but the roots went down far enough for mature ones. They turned the earth to receive the plants—well, it's hard to be sure—maybe a month ago, maybe two; if it was two then the Domaine McIntyre vines could have been what was here."

"Why haven't they filled in the holes?" Aubrey whispered.

"Maybe some more are coming in."

"Any way to tell if the crumbs of dirt in the hole are different from what's around it?"

She shook her head no. She turned back to her survey of rows.

Aubrey's back was stiff when they finished the circuit of the greenhouse. He wished he were home doing his back exercises in his own fields or on the floor of his bedroom on his big shag rug. He was sweaty and his companion reeked of cow shit. He felt old and uncomfortable. He caught up with

Bethany. She had come to know him well enough to feel his irritability.

"Did you find anything yourself?" she asked, hoping to disarm him by putting him on the defensive. They were developing the debits of a close marriage without getting any of the assets.

"Nothing," he said grumpily.

"No twigs? No tags? Nothing?"

"Nope, Bethany, damn it, nothing."

"Bills of lading, piece of binding wire, straps, cloth wrappings . . . ?"

"Goddamn it, nothing but burlap . . ." Even as he realized what he was telling her, she cuffed him on the forearm.

"*Dummerl. What* burlap? Where?"

Seventeen

ST. GAGE'S CHOICE

Once more, Robert St. Gage made the trip to Neuilly. He would have preferred to see Dr. Berkady in England. But Berkady's Grand Guignol of wine scourges was not set up for a road tour.

As St. Gage walked briskly toward 14 Rue de l'Horloge, he thought of how well, on balance, things had gone since the board meeting.

The dependable *Witwe* Pfeffermühle, in spite of signs in her of a progressive ailment as avaricious as its carrier, had now negotiated with the Argentinians and Chileans at St. Gage's insistence. Both countries had always shown an affinity for Germans. Their deputy ministers for agriculture had agreed that if European wines went up in price, theirs would too.

The *Witwe* had implied that she had a secret concordat with the Californians under which they would do likewise. The old woman's name was well enough known for the Latin Americans to believe a pan-European monopoly was possible. And why should they not go along? When their own wine companies began to make money, there would be that much more cash available for bribes.

The death of Maier, although St. Gage felt uncomfortable about it, had been necessary. His unfinished business in Sicily with the Mafia had been resolved by him and Tobb. There had been a heartwarming instant understanding on both sides in spite of language differences. In Austria, Bridsey had put all their prospects under contract or option agreement save for an unpleasant old kulak from Krems and the importunate von Mohrwalds.

When St. Gage thought of the von Mohrwalds, particularly Bethany, his blood seethed. "Goddamn her," he allowed himself. The whole scheme threatened by this disruptive, snooping woman!

He remembered her from the International Dessert Wines Conference in London many years ago. There had been an *Auslese* quality about her even then or he would not now be able to recall her. She and her husband had exhibited a late harvested wine, fruity and sweet, as St. Gage was sure she herself would be under the best circumstances.

"Under the best circumstances" meant a good deal more (and less) to St. Gage than it might to more ordinary men. For St. Gage, while he enjoyed conventional sex with women, had found a practice, which, as their fetishes do for all fetishists, carried intercourse to apotheosis.

St. Gage's father had collected several pieces of armor worn by his ancestors in historic and bloody combat and had placed them around the house as if to remind himself and visitors of his noble blood.

On the walls behind the armor were weapons once borne by St. Gages. There was a fifteenth-century sword, its blade worked crudely with Old English Ss and Gs, a knight's mace tooled as an eagle's head and beak, a lance, its leather grip aged and torn.

St. Gage, however, loved most a scabbarded dagger, its sharp blade decorated with gold, its hilt shaped like a helm. It had been a gift to a St. Gage diplomat from a Doge in 1679. Young Robert had been forbidden by his father to touch it: the point tapered to needle sharpness.

When St. Gage was fourteen, a female cousin two years his senior had stayed with his family and the two had stolen serious kisses when left alone. On a day when his family and servants were gone, and with her adventurous acquiescence St. Gage had dressed her in armor.

He had taken down the old sword and the proscribed dagger and they had lightly smacked each other's cuirasses, childishly reenacting their forefathers' combat. St. Gage had been excessively thrilled by the play, even dizzied by it.

As the girl, heavier and as tall as he, seemed to be getting the better of him, he had fallen and struck upward with the dagger, piercing through the ancient jointure of cuisse and fauld.

The girl had howled. Robert had helped her from her belly and thigh armor and discovered he had drawn a drop of blood from her leg. The sight of it had given him a rush of sexual feeling.

His cousin had taken his possessed expression for guilt and had assured him she was all right. He had touched the tiny wound as if sympathetically, been thrilled even more, and had kissed her mouth with adolescent passion.

She had responded fervidly; they had hastily taken off the lower parts of his own armor. For St. Gage it was his first experiment with coition.

Although they had never repeated this *combat d'amour* in chain mail, they had made love several times over the next few years. In each case, he had inflicted and she had accepted and then enjoyed a tiny prick of the antique stiletto which had drawn a droplet or two of blood.

At twenty, however, she had married a stuffy viscount and had abandoned St. Gage to his intercourse, generally unembellished, with other women. Occasionally, though, he had sought out partners to temporarily slake the fires of his mild, but specialized sadism.

After St. Gage's father's scandal and death, the armor and weapons had passed on to St. Gage. The shame of his father, particularly the sexual aspects, had inflicted a cruel impotency on St. Gage for almost a year.

It was with a woman again slightly older than himself, Lady Montfalcon, that he had regained it. A dabbler more than a fetishist, she had willingly and frequently pandered to his unusual need because of the augmentation of intensity it gave his lovemaking.

After she and her husband had left for Brazil, St. Gage had, from time to time, hired prostitutes to play her role. In one episode, when the woman began to renege, he had gotten rougher than he intended and had been obliged to buy her off after her pimp threatened to expose him.

He accurately regarded his aberration as the only dangerous crack in his integrated, if amoral personality. And it was, after all, far less reprehensible than rape, child molesting, or truly violent sadism. And, importantly for St. Gage's self-image, it was in better taste than such disgusting deviations as cantalophilia, cucumber abuse, and—a practice he had read about in an American novel—liver defilement.

On this day, in this warm suburb of Paris, he let his fancy run to Bethany. Her defiance had made her attractive, her title doubly so. And she, like his two principal amours, was, he suspected, a few years older than he.

He imagined her unclothed, then partially clothed, her breasts perhaps in a cuirass, her legs in greaves—shin armor—and the rest of her naked. He saw himself bring the point of the dagger to the soft flesh just outside her armpit or to her groin where thigh joined torso. The thought gave him a vertiginous few seconds.

"This is ridiculous," he murmured and with a determined shudder, shook off his momentary seizure.

From Bethany, his thoughts moved, very much without eroticism, to the journalistic has-been she had hired. The man had lucked into some uncomfortable facts in California.

Still, even if the American inquired about the vine stocks here in France, he would find they were all shipped in accordance with law, and the trail would run out at Ambourg-Repose.

Tobb himself had removed the vine stocks by truck; Tobb had inspected the premises to make sure not one shipping label, not one scrap of paper, not one seal was left behind. As a back-up, the cover story that the wines had gone to an unspecified vineyard in Portugal for research would stand up.

With a chilly feeling even in the warmth of the Parisian day, St. Gage speculated on what would happen if Aubrey followed the trail to Portugal. He would, if he were nosy enough, find out about Bridsey's holdings there. If they could learn the detective was on Bridsey's acreage, then Tobb. . . . St. Gage turned away from thinking of the details.

Finally, St. Gage considered the publicity. There had been unwelcome stories about the purchase of large European table wine holdings in the *Financial Times*, *Le Monde*, the *Frankfurter Allgemeine Zeitung*, the *Neue Züricher Zeitung*, and the *Wall Street Journal*. None, happily, had been very detailed. They had spoken of high prices paid by various parties for several vineyards and some speculation that this might mean another round of price rises for wine.

But the joint venturers' financing had been sufficiently diverse, their financiers sufficiently discreet to keep reporters from putting all the purchases together. St. Gage and Tobb had not been mentioned. The *Witwe* Pfeffermühle, Bridsey, and Maier had been, but they had not been tied up in the same combine. Maier's death had been cited in several of these good papers. Unlike the French popular press, they might follow up on it, and this had made St. Gage briefly uneasy. But now nepenthe had closed over Maier as completely as the Pinot Noir of Mostaganem.

*   *   *

When Dr. Berkady had settled St. Gage in the leather armchair again, he cast a fake look of benevolence from his good eye at the younger man and puffed his chest in the manner of a proud first-time father of a son.

"I am sorry to have been so evasive on the telephone," he said, not sorry at all. "As you must have suspected, the insecticide I spoke of is perfected."

He waited for the Englishman to react. St. Gage obliged.

"I am delighted, doctor. I expected no less, but that is more a tribute to your abilities than a presumption on my part, I assure you."

Berkady beamed. Baroque compliments pleased him most. "Well," he said expansively, "I thank you." He went on professorially, "I assume you have considered all the other options: the oidium, the tortricidae, the peronespora."

"Yes," said St. Gage. "Thoughtfully, thoroughly. I believe if your phylloxera antidote works in the field . . ."

Berkady cut him off with an amiable but efficient nod.

"I guarantee it," he said.

"Then," said St. Gage, "please proceed."

"I have set up a little *cirque des puces* for you," commenced the elderly scientist. "Only the actors are of a slightly different order of insect."

He rose and St. Gage accompanied him to a table under the skylight which held two grape vines under large bell jars. In the first, a healthy mature vine grew, its grapes as round and firm as if they were in the vineyards of Bordeaux or Chile or California.

In the second was a specimen which, at first sight, seemed as infected by the phylloxerans and their galls as the vine on St. Gage's previous visit. As before, the ravenous insects were fixed on the underside of the leaves, on the stems, and on the sections of root that could be seen through the glass. But in this case, the vine was whole. It had been afflicted by, but had not given up to, its nemesis.

"Here," said Berkady, gesturing to the first vine, "is one of the plants delivered to me by your American." Berkady made a face as if he had bitten a gingko fruit. St. Gage accepted this silent disapproval of Tobb, but did not acknowledge it.

"As you can see," continued the Belgian, "it is a normal, healthy vine. In here," he picked up an atomizerlike device with a bottle of yellowish matter attached, "are our sturdy little friends." The yellow, St. Gage now saw, was thousands of insects, alive and asquirm. "We use a very, very low pressure. Just enough to waft them out," said Berkady.

Berkady attached a small air tank to the atomizer and carefully adjusted the pressure gauge. He put the nose of the atomizer to a nipple in the side of the bell jar. He looked at St. Gage who was both revolted and fascinated.

"You are thinking of the temperature in the bell jar. Whether it is the same as that of an average day," said Berkady pedagogically.

Actually, St. Gage was thinking that Berkady might just be *too* crazy. Might not his pride lead him to boast to the wrong people? But Berkady was lecturing on.

"No, the temperature is considerably cooler than the average of winegrowing districts five weeks before the *vendange*. I have calibrated it low to show you the hardiness of these specimens."

"I can see why we are paying you so well," said St. Gage.

Berkady fiddled one last time with the gauge, then opened the valve. A low hiss sounded. Like a living spray of dull golden rain, the insects streamed from the nipple and dropped down on the healthy plant. Berkady cut off the air.

"Observe," he said.

For some moments they appeared dead. Then, those that had fallen to the soil beneath the plant clumsily came to life. With minute movements, they crawled in all directions. As St. Gage watched, he saw the general course of their slow creep was shifting toward the vines as if they were drawn by some slow-acting magnet.

The few already at the base of the vine wobbled onto its surface, while others began to disappear along the root into the soil. On the leaves and upper stems and branches some fell off, but others determinedly affixed themselves as if already scenting the plant's sap, its—and their—lifeblood.

"It's almost as if they were carrying out separate assignments," said St. Gage, entranced.

"And so they are," said Berkady smugly. "Our friends are at various developmental stages. Note some have begun to grow their wings."

"The better to move on with," said St. Gage.

"Exactly," said the doctor. "Now, let us assume

that a month or so has passed. The *phylloxera ber-kadicula* have begun their work." He moved to the bell jar covering the contaminated plant. Using another atomizer, but the same compressed air container, Berkady inserted it in the nipple.

"My disulfide and phosphate formula," he said, patting the jar under the atomizer. He adjusted the gauge. "It can be dusted by plane or by a worker in the field."

He efficiently released a puff almost the same color as the bugs. The powder sifted down on the busy insects, some of it sticking to the side of the glass. Berkady thumped it off so St. Gage could peer in.

At first the chemical had no effect. The sap-satiated pests remained glued to their feed. Then, the faint diastole of the horrible little creatures seemed to cease. A few dropped from the glass. Most simply grew still with the tiny stillness of death in small animals.

"Not dormant?" suggested St. Gage.

"No, dead," said Berkady sepulchrally. "The disulfide."

"These?" asked St. Gage, pointing to those on the roots. They were very much alive.

Berkady did not deign to answer. Instead, he hooked up a third canister and nozzle to the compressed air. This time, a spray of water fell inside the jar.

"Rain," said Berkady. "Or if there is no rain, then heavy watering of the vines." Gradually the water soaked down the side of the glass into the soil, carrying with it the soluble yellow chemical. "It enters the roots, goes into the stems. When they suck the sap, even if they are inside the galls, they are feeding on the phosphate side of my formula. It is called a systemic insecticide."

The underground parasites clung stubbornly to the roots, then gradually gave up their hold and their life.

"Like Lilliputians," said Berkady, seeming to take a depraved pleasure in the insects' demise. "Just like gassing . . ." He started to say something else, but quickly amended it to "little people."

St. Gage shuddered internally. Suddenly, he hated this disgusting old man. It was not Lilliputians that the entomologist was imagining in the skins of these arthropods. It was Jews. Some of the anti-Semitism of his former employers had obviously rubbed off on Berkady, and permanently. St. Gage knew he himself had done improper, even evil things. He accepted the responsibility for them. Such crimes as the deaths of Wheatley-Smith and Maier troubled him although they had been unavoidable. Certainly he had felt no joy in them.

Berkady's satisfaction, on the other hand, in comparing these revulsant insects to humans made St. Gage suddenly loathe the scientist. He almost risked alienating the repugnant little monster for good by saying, "A sort of *Endlösung* for your bugs, you mean, Doctor Berkady." But he forebore.

"And it would have the same effect on the freshly emplaced specimens?" the Englishman asked instead, no trace of his thoughts in words or tone.

"You anticipate me," said Berkady. He moved back to the first bell jar and repeated the procedure with the newly sown phylloxerans. They died by the hundreds, on cue.

St. Gage's lawyerly mind ran through the possibilities.

"They would not build up an immunity to the formula?"

"Absolutely not. No time to. Do people build up immunity to, uh, cyanide?"

St. Gage churned again inside. The man had almost said Zyklon B; St. Gage was sure of it.

"And you said last time that no one could develop their own antidote, an insecticide of their own . . . ?"

"I am all but certain."

"All but certain?" St. Gage interrupted. Goddamn it, there was always a hitch. "What do you mean?"

"Please, please, Mr. St. Gage," said Berkady holding up his wrinkled hand. "I had planned to come to it in my own time. But since you ask now, I will tell you now. In the 1884 and 1885 vintages, Château Rossant, a small, fine second growth, you must know it, produced wines free of phylloxera.

"Most of their crop, like their neighbors', was infected. But experimentally, the Baron James de Rossant, a chemical engineer, you understand, used some kind of disulfide-phosphate solution that saved this small, really insignificant quantity of wine, a matter of a few hundred cases in each of the two vintages.

"He cautiously publicized the compound. It was tried elsewhere, but failed abysmally. And in his own crops subsequent to 1885, it did not work. Whether he was not able to replicate his own formula, I do not know. In those days there was not the precision we, some of us, have been able to master today."

St. Gage wished the doctor would get on with it, but knew he had a major point to make and did not, in this instance, hurry him.

"Well, to make a long story short . . ."

"Shorter . . ." St. Gage could not resist reminding him.

". . . most of these wines were sold and drunk. But some few have become collector's items. I have looked for such bottles and found none. But now, an auction in, of all places, Washington, the American capital, is offering a bottle of the eighty-five in two weeks."

"And you want me . . ."

"Yes. To buy it. If I can find a way to extract Rossant's formula from trace elements in the wine, then perhaps I can better my own, although that is hard to imagine. More importantly, I do not want such bottles at large where someone seeking an antidote to our little workers can use modern spectroscopic and chemical methods to try to uncork its secrets, to find a shortcut to an antidote."

One more damned detail to deal with, thought St. Gage. But at least it would not slow things down. And at worst the freak would cost him a thousand or two.

"We will have someone at the sale," said St. Gage. He jotted himself a note. "Now, another thing," he recommenced, "the taste of wine when treated with your disulfide. There is a limit, as we know, to how much sulfur can be put on European acreages. Will your compound do the job within those limits?"

"No question; and with no more taste than ordinary sulfur."

He led the Englishman back to the old-fashioned desk and from a cabinet took eight cheap wine glasses, two bottles of dark liquid and two of light. He put the bottles and glasses in a neat row on the desk and from a drawer drew out two laboratory chemical jars, each labeled with his distinctive cursive.

"Here we have two bottles of juice, one from white grapes, one with skins in the pressing from black grapes. And two bottles of unsulfured wine. It is execrable wine, grown by a natural foods lunatic. I had almost as much trouble finding it as I did in developing my formula."

He waited for St. Gage to utter an appreciative chuckle. Then, with separate laboratory measuring spoons, he carefully put minute quantities of the two powders in each of the two rows of four glasses. Pouring alternately, he put the white and dark juices and the white and red wines in the glasses. Using a fresh pair of spoons, and even then rinsing each in water after each stir, he thoroughly mixed in the powder.

"*Prosit*," he said. "Follow my directions exactly."

First, Berkady had St. Gage taste the two white grape juices. There was in each the faintest taste of sulfur, the same in both glasses.

Berkady produced a roll from the drawer, gave it to St. Gage to clear his palate, and then pointed to the pair of dark grape-juice glasses, then the red and white wines. Except for the white grape juice, there was no taste of sulfur.

"One of each pair," said Berkady, "had the maximum sulfur allowable by the French government. The other had the equivalent of my disulfide."

St. Gage pondered all he had seen, heard, and tasted. Were there any other drawbacks? In his mind he ran through the questions he had thought of in the last few weeks, then consulted a memo pad on which he had noted them.

"The prognosis of the phylloxerans on a, um, host area?"

"I am speaking now only of the alates, the winged female form. They would lay eggs producing males and females who would mate, and, in turn, lay what we call an 'over-wintering' egg. The galls would begin in late spring, summer."

"Not before?"

Berkady shrugged.

"You would get some consumption of the plant before late spring, but not a great deal."

St. Gage jotted more notes.

"Suppose you were called on to produce the alates in very large numbers?"

"Easily. Do not forget phylloxerans naturally achieve twelve generations a year. I could breed them to procreate up to sixteen, although of course the equipment would be costly. I could produce some here, some at a location nearby."

"Would not the alates die in transit?"

"The jar, purposely, is a worst case. *In vivo*, containers would be half-filled and would have layering shelves to keep the insects from crushing. Standard apiary containers could be modified for this in a few days."

"Could they be transported in ordinary cargo planes?"

"To be safe, the temperature should be slightly above five degrees centigrade. But it is not a problem. There are some theories that even the ordinary strains have been carried from one country to another in the wheel wells of airplanes."

St. Gage nodded comprehendingly. He closed his eyes and leaned back in the comfortable old chair to think through the prospective operation.

"The thing will work," he said aloud, almost with wonder.

Berkady's thoughts developed in a different direction.

"I read of the unfortunate death of a Monsieur Maier," he said, taking off his spectacles, startling St. Gage with the gaping socket.

"I, too, know only what I read," St. Gage said evenly, trying to meet the Cyclops gaze.

But Berkady was not listening.

"I have no plans to go to Algeria," said the old scientist doggedly. "But things happen even in France."

St. Gage tensed. Berkady sensed it, but went on, nervously now.

"What I am saying, Mr. St. Gage, is that I have assembled certain notes." He stammered on rapidly. "I have taken the liberty of photographing you as you came up my pathway." He drew back as if he expected a repetition of St. Gage's earlier violence and St. Gage rose from his seat as if to oblige.

Like an aged crab, Berkady scuttled behind his chair.

"Don't do anything, I beg you," he said, thoroughly frightened, but not voiceless. "I tell you this for both of our protections. If I should die by any unnatural means, the details of our project will be made public. It is my only form of life insurance and I wanted you to know so you would not miscalculate."

"Who?" demanded St. Gage impulsively, the figures first of the *Witwe* Pfeffermühle, then of Berkady's disgusting wife, flashing in sequence on his mind. But St. Gage could not be sure it was either. Perhaps it was some old scientific chum, obscure and undetectable by St. Gage.

"A trusted friend. That's all I can say."

"But, dear Jesus, man, suppose you are hit by a car? I mean innocently hit by a car?"

"The friend will make the determination." He felt the course of St. Gage's thoughts. "And if something happens to the friend, then a provision has been made for it to be made public in another way." He had talked so rapidly he was out of breath.

St. Gage was braced on the arms of the chair behind which Berkady cowered. For an instant, hollow socket or no, St. Gage glowered at him. At last, St. Gage moved backwards.

"You are right," he said, his voice pinched. "You would have been a fool not to. I wish that you had not. I promise you that you are as safe with me as if you were my own father. But I understand. Still, it makes the whole thing so much more dangerous; suppose someone stumbles on your, uh, insurance. It could ruin you unnecessarily."

"No one will stumble on it," said Berkady. "I assure you."

"Well, I cannot blame you," St. Gage said pacifically. But in his mind, he was wondering whether he and Tobb could come up with a safe final solution for Dr. Pieter Berkady.

Eighteen

THE CELLARS OF AMBOURG-REPOSE

Bethany felt as knowledgeably through the pile of burlap as a housewife at a clothing counter sale. Even in the fading light, Aubrey could see that they were of different sizes and weaves. Those with the looser weave, he was sure, were American. It meant that American vine stocks had been here.

The sweat popped out on his forehead. These missing vines had to be a clue to the cartel's mysteries, to everything, just as he had theorized. Otherwise why were they being shuttled around? There was not one chance in a million of its being mere happenstance that Wheatley-Smith was murdered in a vineyard shipping experimental vines to one of the conspirators. Did this mean Bridsey was party to Wheatley-Smith's murder, to Maier's?

Bethany, too absorbed in her counting for such speculation, was carefully toting up the pieces of burlap with looser weaves.

"Eight," she said. "I'd have thought more. The

rest . . ." she shrugged. There were any number of uses good burlap could be put to around a vineyard. Aubrey was getting nervous.

"Is there anything else we can get out of here?" he asked. "If not, let's go."

They waddled back to the work door and slipped out. Bethany crouched close to Aubrey. In the otherwise night-sweet air, she smelled Augean.

It was now dark. Overcast skies hid the moon and there was a restive breeze. They crawled swiftly back along the wall.

As they approached the corner, they heard a door slam in the direction of the manse, then the amiable snort of a smallish dog. Aubrey was alarmed. What if the dog picked up a scent on the wind? He came slowly to his feet to peer toward the porch and bumped his head on something above him. He ducked down, but it was too late. A greenhouse window had walloped shut. He had knocked out the prop.

At the noise, the dog's first conversational bark rose an octave and became a series of frantic yips. Aubrey cursed himself under his breath. The door slammed again, obviously someone coming out to see what was going on. The dog continued his loud barks, but no nearer perhaps because the animal was too timid to investigate.

"*Qui est là?*" demanded a man's deep voice from the porch. At that, from the other side of the house a great barking went up. A kennel of hounds must have been aroused by their master's interrogatory cry. Adding to the tumult, the maddening gobble of turkeys erupted from behind the manse.

Aubrey grabbed Bethany's hand and jerked

her into a run, not toward the road, but away from it.

"Aubrey," she hissed in fright. "We can't outrun dogs."

"I know. The lake! Just do as I say."

There was no time for her to argue. Stumbling, they rounded the far side of the greenhouse. The baying and barking increased in volume, but grew no closer. The resident had not yet cut the dogs loose.

Please, Aubrey prayed, let them be beagles and bassets and not Dobermans or German Shepherds that might tear us to bits. In a moment, he speculated as they ran, the resident and whoever else was inside would have hunting pieces and would be opening the kennel door to free the dogs. Already Aubrey could hear through his panting the jumbled sound of excited male French voices.

A ribbon of road ran to the lake side, then circled it toward the hill. With Bethany's hand in his, he loped toward the water, trying to adjust to her shorter steps.

"What?" she demanded breathlessly.

"Oh, goddamn it, Bethany, shut up and do what I say," he whispered. "Please," he begged her.

At the shore, he swerved and dragged her parallel to it, then looped back toward the greenhouse with her still in tow.

"Have you gone crazy, Aubrey?" she whispered.

"Please, Bethany," he pleaded.

When they had crossed their own path, he jerked her sharply toward the lake again. There, he waded in, dragging her with him. The bottom was muddy and reeds and rushes sprouted unevenly.

Steadily and quietly he pulled her out through the rushes. The dogs were barking wildly now, anticipating the approach to the kennel of the men, sharpening for the hunt.

"You've gone mad," she said, slapping at his hand. He clutched her arm so hard it hurt.

"Now be quiet," he commanded, pushing, half-carrying her out further. There was no madness in his voice, only anger and resolve. "And don't fucking splash."

Behind them, the dogs' voices had taken on a new tone. Liberated at last, the beagles, for clearly that was what they were, bugled and the bassets sounded their full, mighty bays. Gallic voices urged them after the unknown quarry.

Half-crying in frustration, Bethany stumbled behind her determined companion. The shallows, with their floor of stagnant mud, still held some of the heat of day. Out further, the spring water feeding the lake made it cold.

In seconds, they were deep enough to lie down behind the rushes, out of sight from the shore. The younger dogs were yipping frenzily.

The water was terribly cold. She heard Aubrey groan, trying to adjust his posture to some kink in his older body and she felt a flash of sympathy for his bad back, his repaired heart. How did I get him into this, she thought, then, oh dear God, how did I get myself into it.

Their heads just above the cold water, they could see the flashlights through the rushes. Only now, her body seeming to shake loose from her head, did Bethany understand what Aubrey had been up to: he was depending on the dogs to save them from their masters. For she could hear the peeved, confused note in the hounds' voices. The men's shouts also seemed less certain, like questions and responses. And now the lights were playing on the greenhouse and fields as well as the water.

The cold made her shake all over. She balled up, putting her hands between her thighs to warm them. But there was only the cold, wet cloth. Aubrey's face beside her was like a craggy piece of marble statuary at rest on the water; his plastered hair gave him the look of an antique Roman general, one brave but not wise.

She could distinguish among some of the dog voices. One deeper than the rest was an old basset she was sure. It wolfed ponderously, positively. Follow me, its querulous bass seemed to say. Follow me and you won't go wrong.

Amid the accompanying yips of younger dogs, she heard the senior dog's persuasive voice go from bark to ululation and back to bay. It grew more distant. Back this way, it seemed to argue. The men's lights began to play more in consensus in the direction of the greenhouse. Some of the younger dogs took up the old basset's theme: back to the greenhouse.

Bethany momentarily forgot the cold. It was the crucial moment. If it were only a humiliating thing like sniffing around a vineyard where they were unwelcome, she would have given herself up. But intrinsic to her determination not to be captured was the implacable fact that two men were already dead in this mess.

Soon she saw the weird greenish glow of lights from inside the greenhouse. The muffled barking of dogs came from within the building. But other dogs were already to their right, out in the fields, and some lights were flashing there, too, among the vines.

Whatever else, they had given up on the lake.

We're going to be all right, she said to herself, stirring on the cold muddy lake bottom.

Aubrey's hand touched hers. She started. He had been so silent that she had all but forgotten him. She looked over. With his other hand, he was signaling her to stay put. How long? she formed with her lips. But it was too dark to see and she dared not even risk a whisper that might carry to the dogs and men over the placid water.

By the time the searchers of the greenhouse also went off into the fields and the last dog was called away from the lake, Bethany's teeth were chattering so that she was afraid they could be heard.

She looked at Aubrey again, ready to go. But he lay in the water, surely as cold as she was, until the lights were all as distant in the fields as fireflies. That trail would end, she knew, at the road where the carbonics of cars would have eradicated their smell.

At last he moved his head next to her ear to whisper and she reached up to move her sodden hair from her ear. She touched his lips by mistake.

"I want you to take off your belt and tie your

shoes on top of your head," he said. She pulled her head from his mouth and whispered back, "Swim?"

"We can't cut through the fields until before dawn. And we can't stay here. At least I can't." She nodded agreement in the darkness. "If the *cave* under the hill is open, or if I can open it, we'll be safe there." He paused and listened, heard no one, dog or man, and went on. "Before dawn we'll swing back wide and into town for the car."

She shifted ever so slightly in the water. What else could they do? Give up? Risk the fields with the damned hounds and men with guns all over the place?

"Dog paddle," he whispered to her. "Keep it quiet."

Although the fifty-yard swim to the shallows on the other side of the lake warmed them, their waterlogged clothes made it seem a mile. Once there, they crouched together in the rushes under the shadow of the hill which loomed over them. They listened, but heard no more than the faint sounds of insect and summer night bird.

He stood up in the water, turned his back to her and took off his clothes. To avoid leaving telltale puddles ashore, he wrung them out in the shallows. The drops sounded loud as slaps in Bethany's ears. As he waded ashore to dress, Bethany looked at his naked back. He's just a man, she thought. So what. Once she was almost to shore, she did as he had done, feeling vaguely immodest.

At the door to the *cave*, Aubrey felt the padlock on the thick, main double doors. He inspected the hinges. To the side was a smaller door. It was also padlocked. There were no windows in the wooden wall that closed off the *cave*.

Aubrey silently cursed himself. A more provident private eye would have a Swiss army knife with its screwdriver. All he had was the useless thin-bladed knife he had bought in California.

"Do you have anything that'd do for a screwdriver?" he whispered.

"Blunt end of a nail file?"

He nodded and she found it in her wallet. When she gave it to him, she smiled. They had not put on their shoes. Hers were in her hands; Aubrey's were still on his head, giving him the look of an unusually tall Japanese noble.

"You look ridiculous, Aubrey-san," she said.

"So do you," he hissed back. "Zip up your fly."

Her face dropped and so did her shoes as she hastened to comply.

The rounded end of the file didn't work, but Aubrey slipped its blade under a hinge strap and neatly snapped it off to make a serviceable screwdriver. With disconcerting squeaks, the first screw turned. He was at work on the third when the mosquitoes found them.

The light wind that had kept the insects on the far side of the lake had died and they came now in legions. Aubrey steadily murmured curses as he labored. Bethany gallantly tried to fan them away from him, using her shoes.

When the hinges were off the jamb, he lifted the door and eased the tongue from the lock with another scary creak. Then he let Bethany into the *cave*, threw the latch on the inside of the door and carefully put it back on the jamb.

That done, he hurried inside. Remembering, he opened the door again, felt the ground around the door, and brushed dirt over the slight dampness where her shoes had dropped.

The *cave* was dank. Because of their wet clothes, it seemed almost as cold as the water. Aubrey, doubly uncomfortable, felt like one huge whelp from the mosquito bites.

"God," he moaned, "this is miserable."

It was pitch black. They sat on the ground, shivering, their irritations, both physical and mental, festering in the dark now that they were comparatively safe.

"I wish to shit I'd never let you talk me into this," he mused petulantly.

She did not respond but the more she thought of it, the more she resented it. *She* had kept a stiff upper lip and here he was whining. They wouldn't be here, they'd be driving up the road to a warm hotel, or already there over a good meal if he hadn't knocked out the prop.

"Well, if you feel that way, I wish you hadn't either," she said. "If you hadn't bounced up like a guilty schoolboy when that dog barked . . ." She didn't need to finish. It was on target.

Aubrey stewed for a while. He grew angrier.

"You know, Bethany, your heavy Teutonic manner is not the least bit amusing. Or fair."

"Well, that's a racist thing to say," she struck back.

He didn't like that either. If there was one thing he prided himself about, it was being free of prejudice. Even against Germans, he thought mean-spiritedly.

"Bethany," he rejoined unpleasantly, "I hate to say this, but it's small wonder you aren't getting on with your husband, who sounds like a fine man." It was a surmise he had made, and one all too accurate. "How I wish he were here instead of you." He began to wax fierce. "Look what you put me through and now this goddamn remark about the window. Without me you'd be blubbering back there in the field with a bunch of dogs sniffing you."

"Well, you're being pretty damned presumptuous, Mr. Private Detective." Her accent thickened with her anger. "Who says my husband and I don't get along. That's a pretty insolent thing to say for an . . ."

If she had said "employee," he was going to tell her to take her job and shove it up her ass. He could feel steam about to come out of his ears, cold cellar or no cold cellar.

"Nobody has a right to say cruel things like that," she softened it, feeling the deep precipice she was inviting. "I've tried to be helpful," she began and then went silent.

There, in the blackness, she sat without a word. Aubrey felt, as he had before, a sudden sympathy for her, uprooted from everything she had done before. Damn it, he had hit her a mean one, talking about her husband. He heard her sniffling.

"I'm sorry," he said remorsefully. His wife had almost never cried, even at the end. And when she had, in good health or bad, it always tore him up. "I'm really sorry, Bethany," he went on. "What I said about you and Franz was skunky." He thought about it some more, listening to her wordless sniffling. "Really skunky," he said again. It made him feel good to apologize.

But she only sniffled harder, trying to end her tears. He imagined her thoughts: the conspiracy, the possible loss after all these centuries of their vineyards, the spatting with her hard-working and decent husband (about which he saw he had correctly guessed), the danger to her, to her children, to Franz; these adventures for which her life had given her no preparation whatsoever.

"I feel like a grade A shit," he said, ever more contrite.

"It's all right," she finally managed in a small voice. "I shouldn't have provoked you. It's just that everything. . . . I guess I just want to be home, just want things to be like they were before all this began." She started to cry again.

He reached toward her and touched her hand. It was icy.

"You're freezing," he said. "I'm going to crawl around and try to find something. Maybe there's burlap in here too, or an old rug if there's a room they use as an office."

He crawled gingerly around the floor, feeling its perimeters. At one side it stepped up two inches to a wooden platform and a door. He crept into a small office—from the feel of chair legs. There was not even a scrap of rug. Still, it was better than dirt.

"Bethany," he whispered. "Crawl toward me. Slowly. There's a little office here with a wooden floor."

*　　　*　　　*

They sat on two chairs in the office, both shaking from the cold.

"I'm frozen," she said. "Colder than in the lake. Colder than on the dirt." She got out of the chair and rolled up in a ball on the wooden floor.

He thought for a moment or two. He was sure he was being honest with himself when he got down on his knees and vigorously rubbed her back. His only motive, he was certain, was to warm her. She continued to shiver, almost violently.

"Here," he said, "lean your back against mine."

She hunched around and leaned against him. But there was too much soggy clothing between them for it to make any difference. They sat that way a while. Then, he could feel her sturdy body shaking as uncontrollably as before.

"It's not working," she said. "I'm probably just making you colder without getting any warmer." The cold was pervasive, the interior of the hill a refrigerator for the wine. It might make lovely vintages from young wines, but it did not make healthy humans.

"No," he agreed. "It's not working. It's worse."

Trying to sound as much like a disinterested gynecologist as he could, he said, "Take off your outer clothes. Drape them over the front of you. Put your back flat up against mine. I'm going to take off my shirt and jacket and put them over the front of me."

For a long moment she did nothing. Then she got out of her wet shirt and pressed her back against his.

They were both clammy and he was mosquito-bitten as well. At first they were colder than ever. But gradually, he felt a tingling in his back. There, at least they were both warming. He handed his sports jacket to her.

"This might be drier than . . ."

"But you . . ."

"Well take it, I think you're a little colder."

They bunched their clothing on the front of their bodies and scrunched against each other to get as much of their backs touching as possible.

"Bethany," he said, "could I ask you to noodge up and down a little to take care of some of my mosquito bites?"

She rubbed up and down, glad to oblige.

"Yes?" she asked.

"Better."

"Warmer?"

"I think so. You?"

"Yes," she said. "How much longer must we stay?"

"A few hours at least. I'm sorry."

"It isn't your fault."

"Well," he said, "it is. I bumped the window."

"The little dog might have come on us anyway. Perhaps it was good to get that much time and space to run."

Aubrey thought about that a while.

"It's nice of you to say it," he told her.

They were genuinely warm in back, if cold in front. But at least it was bearable. The musky smell of the maturing wines was more pronounced now they were not so brutalized by the cold.

They reran their plan of escape, then talked about the case. Words began to come easy, as they had in the car. He spoke again of his newspaper days, the big stories and the little funny ones, and how he had failed on some and succeeded on others.

She talked of her college and how she had thought about the arts in Munich, but knew she would never be a good artist. Art history had been too derivative, too remote from anything creative and so Franz and the vineyard had seemed a good thing to do.

"And it was a good thing to do," he said.

He told her of Hamilton College and how he had thought of being a novelist but had drifted into newspapering. He had met his wife at a party and they had had a good life together. And after she died, he had been in love only one other time.

She did not ask him who or how, but told him instead that she had been in love too, and that the man had been almost too romantic and a bit flighty and that Franz had never known. She asked Aubrey if he were still in love with the woman whom he had loved after his wife died.

"No. It was wonderful, really dramatic while it lasted in that particularly crazy, heated way. She and her husband were breaking up and after they did, well, we could have married, but . . ."

"But . . . ?"

"Well, she got into politics herself, but it came late and so it still had that kick for her. But not for me. I wanted out of the news business. I wanted the vineyard. And she was out there, as a friend of mine once said, wrestling the bear."

They talked on, now about their parents, she of her children, of God, of their marriages again, and circling back, to how it had been when they were in love with people who were not their spouses, and whether their spouses had had affairs. Aubrey was sure his had not; Bethany thought hers probably had.

The dampness began to creep up on them again. They pushed together harder.

"How much longer?" she asked.

"Still a couple of hours."

She felt sleepy, but too cold to sleep. The only warm part of her was her back. Franz, she thought, had a smooth back, like Aubrey's. Claudio's was hairy. In his embrace she had loved the feel of the hair on his back and his buttocks.

"Aubrey," she said. "Would I be requesting too great a favor if I asked you to let me snuggle my front to your back?" Surely, she thought, it would be more comfortable for him, too. "We could lie on the clothes, even if they are damp." And that would warm more of him, too.

"I'd be flattered," he said.

She thought he sounded a little tense about it. Well, she thought again, so what?

It was no more than a moment's work to make a wet bed of their shirts and his jacket. The loss of warmth from the clothes on her front was minimal and—after the initial clamminess again had passed—the gain of warmth, on balance, was prodigious. She nestled snugly against his big back.

They talked on, about whether Aubrey would forever tend his grapes, about whether she would always be the madeleine of the Schloss and their fields, if indeed the land could be saved. Increasingly, her talk was drowsy. For instants she drifted off, then for minutes and suddenly she was asleep, snuggled tightly against him.

She could not have slept very long, she thought, waking with a start in the blackness. Where was she? Then, a quick waker, she realized where she was. Her left arm was thrown around his chest the better to press his warm back to her breasts. She had awakened because her back was cold, very cold. She also thought commiseratively of how cold her wet bra, which was chilly enough on her, must feel to him and how patiently he was taking it. Was he asleep? she wondered. She took the arm from his chest and put it along her side. He moved, and fearing she had awakened him she said, "I'm sorry. My back was so cold, Aubrey."

"My back is wonderfully warm," he said, more awake than she had expected. After a pause, he said, "My chest was warm where your arm was. The rest of me in front is cold."

"Maybe we should switch," she suggested, wondering a bit about the delicacy of that position. For answer, he turned his body and took her in his arms. She stiffened, thinking she should move out of his grip, get back to a more conservative position. But his chest was cold, clammy, really, and hers was warm, warm with his warmth. Still, she felt a statement of purpose was needed.

"Aubrey, I want to warm up your chest. But I think we should merely reverse the positions we had before."

She wanted to be, at the same time, sympathetic, firm, and warm. Usually so willing to discuss anything, he now silently began to rub her back with his hands. Ostensibly, she thought, he is doing that to warm my back. And it feels good, unthreatening. His hands are big and rough, but comforting like a large, expensive Turkish towel.

She was sorry again about her brassiere being so damp against his chest. In the best, the most innocent of worlds, she would take it off. Then, also, his wonderfully warm hands wouldn't be forced to jump over the strap but could sweep her back in one long luxuriously warming caress.

Yet, another part of her mind was thinking simultaneously and at odds with her growing warmth: this sly Aubrey knows exactly what he is doing.

The top of her back and her chest felt warm, the buttocks and the back of her legs cold. Still, soothed by his touch, she relaxed, not so much toward slumber now, but toward a luxurious torpor.

There was no doubt that Aubrey's hands had a secondary effect. They encouraged her, with seeming innocence, to press even more closely to him, to his large warm body. Her breasts, even within the cold cloth, began to tingle. His back would be cold, too, she began to think. Why should she lie chastely with her arms at her sides while he rubbed her, made her feel so delicious.

She gave his back a tentative rub with her one free hand. It was chilled, like a piece of meat fresh from the refrigerator. She gave it a quick efficient little rub. He said nothing. She rubbed his back more firmly.

Now her nipples stirred within the wet brassiere. How smooth and clean his skin was, fresh from the lake. She felt a very slight slickness inside herself, and made, or thought she made, an ironic little "hunf." But he gave no evidence he was attracted to her, at least none sexually.

Maybe all of this tonight was too much for him, she thought, not disappointed, really rather proud of his forbearance, unless he wasn't interested in her at all that way. But then why would he still be easily, familiarly rubbing her back? Her breasts felt pinched by the wet brassiere. She might pretend to herself she was taking it off because it was uncomfortable for her and because its wetness wasn't fair to him. But, in fact, she thought, her breath beginning to come faster, that wouldn't be the reason at all.

With a swift, ordinary movement, she shifted and unhooked the brassiere, slipped it from her arms, and her ears ringing slightly from her sudden decision, moved her body heavily against his. She felt him harden rapidly and unequivocally.

Aubrey dropped his head and kissed her lips. His hand dropped to the rear of her slacks. She broke from her lips, keeping her cheek to his, to give a little gasp of pleasure. She was tingling all over, except for her icy feet.

Even as she thought it, he began to rub his feet against hers.

Whether on purpose or not, and Bethany did not worry about which, his rubbing her feet made his loins move excitingly against hers. My slacks, she thought, should I just pull them off, or let him? Or leave them on?

He was breathing very hard and so was she. His hand slipped inside the cloth and he began to tug the clothing over her buttocks. There was, however, no way he could get it from her body without cooperation.

For a moment she felt hesitant. But stronger in her was the peasant strain that came down directly from the Eberwalds, from summer haystacks and barns redolent of livestock and feed.

She wondered, feeling at times the cold rough clothes beneath her as he roamed over her body, whether he was keeping back from his climaxing so long because while they were making love, they were warm. If that were the case, she thought, so much the better.

Aubrey said nothing to her during all that long hour, or could it have been more, of love-making. Although her body down there was hot, fluid, she still knew she would not make it to the very top of the mountain. Yet, still she wanted, waited for him to thrust up into her definitely as opposed to the many thrustings and withdrawals he had risked with her, teased her with.

She reached down at last, unable to delay her want for him any longer, and taking him by the stem, slipped him into her. With absolute determination, she gripped his waist with her legs and grunted as he put his whole weight on and into her.

Only then did he speak. As he exhausted himself in her, he said her name and as the long climax waned, "thank you." She lay there, warm, yet wishing she had been there, too, because it had clearly been so good for him.

They slept for an hour or two, she more than he. Aubrey hearing her breathing so regularly, did not move lest he wake her. He was grateful, but a little confused about how this changed their relationship. It was not the kind of thing one could simply pass off as an expeditious way of staying warm. Were they now lovers?

At fifty-four, it was not the problem for him it would have been at twenty. Life would take its course, one way or the other. He hoped they would make love again; but if they did not, he was content that this person of quality had paid him the enormous compliment of loving him, if only for this one night.

On his watch he saw that it was nearly five and stirred her gently to wake. She stiffened, about to look for her clothing, but he held her for a few moments more.

"I want to say something, Bethany," he whispered. "You can pay the expenses from now on. But I can't take a fee."

"Aubrey," she said, "that's silly." But her objections were pro forma. She knew he was giving her an odd gift of love, making a statement to her about his pride and his respect for her. Abruptly, she was too moved to answer him further. She turned, kissed him a last time on the lips and hugged him to her.

In their walk westward, then northward, and at last back toward town, some, but not many of the creases came out of their garments. Their skins were cold and scratchy. It was still dark. They were apprehensive of every sound as they reached the road. And when dogs barked from a farm they passed, she gripped his hand in panic.

At last they reached the station plaza and the

car. Both were too much on edge for more than the rudiments of talk until they were well beyond the town and Ambourg-Repose. Even then there was no mention of the unexpected turn in their relationship, only conjecture on where the vine stocks might have gone and how lucky they had been in escaping.

With the air-blast heater on, Bethany, dry at last, fell into a fitful sleep. Aubrey looked over at her, her hair combed as best she could, her make-up gone and thought with a pang about what a fine wife Franz von Mohrwald had.

Nineteen

BUCKWHEATS

By the time Bethany and Aubrey reached Versailles, their relief over escaping had become fear. It would not take long for the resident partner, d'Edouard, to hear from the townspeople that an American man and a foreign woman had been asking about the château on the day of the trespassing.

If the Domaine McIntyre manager, a Nervous Nelly anyway, should tell the owners of the four vineyards to which he had shipped vine stocks that a detective had the vineyards' names, then Aubrey and Bethany were in even deeper trouble. The conclusion Bridsey would certainly draw was that the same detective, no doubt in the hire of the von Mohrwalds, was one of the interlopers at Rutheville, and that the foreign woman might well be Bethany.

"I feel like somebody threatening is in every car we pass," Bethany said as they drove through the environs of Paris. "I feel like they're waiting at the hotels, at the airport . . ."

Aubrey did not pretend they were not in danger.

"Best you head back to Austria," he said. "Tell Franz about . . ." He started to say "everything," then smiled bleakly at her and went on ". . . their discovering trespassers."

"If there was something I could do here to help out . . . ," she began, but her heart wasn't in it. She wanted some respite from tension: the security of the Schloss, of her husband. Aubrey sensed it, but even beside the Neusiedlersee she would not really be secure.

"When you get back," he said, not wanting to alarm her but aware he would not be able to forgive himself if he did not urge her to take precautions, "you and Franz may want to get down the hunting guns and use your best old-timers to set up a night watch for a while."

He risked a glance at her. Her face looked bloodless. But she tightened her lips with determination.

"How about you?" she asked.

"Scared, too." She knew him too well now for him to be glibly tough. They drove on in silence.

In the afternoon smog, they saw the apartment houses and office towers that have become, along with that last monumental holdout, Sacré Coeur, the landmarks of Paris.

"Oh God," he said, almost to himself, "I know what's next."

The trail of Wheatley-Smith's murder had gone cold with the disappearance of the vines. It left him two choices. He could take a swat at the death of Maier by going to Algeria in whose foreignness it would be difficult to operate. Or he could attack the case in the way he had planned before the disinterment of Wheatley-Smith had let him bypass it: going from one European capital to another and studying the land purchases, the company records . . .

"Better the cartel's finances, the land . . . ," Bethany suggested, knowing what he was thinking.

She was, of course, right. But what depressing work, trying by interviews, by public and hidden records to put together a criminal linkage between Bridsey, the late Maier, the old lady, Pfeffermühle.

And was there time? He could not escape the feeling that events in the enemy camp were moving faster than he knew.

"*Bubkes*," he said, thinking of all the effort he had put into the case and, for the time being at least, all for nothing.

"*Bubkes?*" she looked at him questioningly.

"A Yiddish word. It means 'beans,' but really it means something that's nothing." He explained. A mobster named Joe Valachi had testified about another Mafioso who had been given an assignment to kill someone. The newly appointed torpedo had been good at extorting money from small Italian grocers for supplying them with artichokes, but not murder. Instead of killing the victim, he had lost both heart and stomach and thrown up. Ever after that, the extortionist had only been given "buckwheats"—fourth-rate assignments.

"It just hit me that Valachi meant *bubkes*," said Aubrey. "And this case so far makes me feel like that's all I'm fit for."

*   *   *

Buckwheats was also what came of his inquiries in Paris, along with a semipermanent crick in his neck from looking over his shoulder. If anything, the case backslid. He discovered that prices for wine land in Europe were drifting higher. The amounts paid by the cartel for the acreages, therefore, seemed less exorbitant, more like the moves of shrewd investors and thus less mysterious.

About the cartel itself, Europe's bankers and insurance men were even more tight-lipped than their confreres in the United States. Indeed, many of the deals were not even being handled by the principals, but by a British lawyer whose identity remained equally mysterious.

From all his theories about the conspiracy, Aubrey was coming to believe tentatively in the first one he had mentioned to Duddman. The cabal, he was coming to think, might be set up to fleece Europe's insurance companies. Millions could be made by increasing their insurance on their holdings, then inducing drastic crop failures through managerial manipulations, faulty fertilizers, overly late or early harvesting, even something as crazy as *creating* bad weather, or of somehow destroying the crop. Not only did this seem logical, but he did find the newly bought lands were being well-insured. And yet he knew, too, that this could merely be good business practice by careful owners. The American vines, Maier's hint about California? Both could be part of some effort, pending or even unsuccessful, to do the same thing in the United States.

Before he left for London, he had a talk with

Mme. Maier, a small, bony woman with the face of a vine-pruning knife. She was glad enough to talk with anyone about her husband, particularly a man who represented himself as a detective for the British and American wine merchants. Aubrey said his clients had contracts with Maier and thus were interested in uncovering the facts about his death. The fickle French papers had long since forgotten him.

Aubrey had her give him what few names of Maier's business associates she knew. None were familiar to him. He went on with his routine questions, and she answered eagerly.

No, she had never heard her husband talk of recent dealings with Bridsey or the Pfeffermühle woman, although, to be honest, he seldom talked of his commercial work. Yes, of course she had heard of Château Ambourg-Repose, but she did not think it was a vineyard whose wines her husband handled.

Ah yes, she nodded vigorously, indeed she had premonitions about his trip to Algeria. But when Aubrey pressed her, she said she always had premonitions about his trips to North Africa.

"I tell you, monsieur," she said. "Nothing good ever came from there. Neither wines nor people."

In London, he could not have worked harder or had less success. He swung like a pendulum between blaming it on the unfamiliar turf and telling himself he had lost his touch. His only progress, if it could be called that, were names he had picked up from British wine industry officials of Bridsey's partners, past and present.

He called Bethany to run past her the eighteen

names he had come up with in London and Paris. None meant anything to her. For her part, she had found out the three closest business associates of the *Witwe* Pfeffermühle. With Olivier d'Edouard, that made twenty-two names, and not a single one of them tied to anything solidly suspicious.

With his pathetic little list of names, he flew back on the cheapest flight he could find to Montgomery County and his vineyard.

Twenty

THE SURVEILLANCE

Aubrey's State Department friend was reluctant to run the twenty-two names. It would mean another set of queries to the American embassies in Paris, London, and Bonn; visas weren't computerized in Washington. Aubrey felt the constraint. As a reporter he had cachet, a derivative power. As a private eye he was just another sneak, an annoyance.

Finally the State Department agreed. But none of the twenty-two popped up as visitors to the United States within the past year. A goddamned provincial bunch, Aubrey fumed unhappily. Two days later the State Department man called back, abashed, but even more irritated by all the trouble this was causing him.

"We have your friend d'Edouard filed under Olivier D. Edoudard. You said Rutheville, right?"

"Right," said Aubrey, tightening his grip on the telephone.

"He applied for a visa last month. He's coming

next week. Or so he says on the application. Staying here at the Swansea House. Purpose: business and pleasure, says he."

Aubrey's heart bumped with fear. Assassin! But he immediately calmed. The man would hardly give his hotel, and when and where he was visiting—all optional on visa forms—if he intended anything criminal.

"You're beautiful, even if you've got some creative file clerks over there in Paris," said Aubrey.

"Yeah, and I plan to stay beautiful," said the State Department man, "so next time find a new pigeon." Then, relenting, he added, "How's life out there?"

"This could make it a little better," said Aubrey.

He called Marge Tyler, the food editor of his old paper, the *Eagle*. She was a cadaverous woman who looked like she didn't know where to cadge her next meal, but who, in fact, consumed Brobdingnagian dinners and draughts of good wine without metabolizing any of it into fat.

She told him the only thing going on the week d'Edouard would be there that had to do with wine was an auction, an uncommon event in Washington. It was being held at the Shoreham.

Aubrey called the Swansea House, a large downtown hotel light on both charm and the pocketbook. They confirmed that d'Edouard was due in next Tuesday.

Early on that day Aubrey telephoned again and the desk clerk said d'Edouard wasn't expected until after eight. Nine hours later, at six P.M., Aubrey called still again, this time with a tube made from typing paper on the mouthpiece to give the call the right hollow long-distance sound.

This was the travel agency for Mr. Olivier d'Edouard, he said, carefully but quickly spelling the name. The hotel was aware, was it not, that Mr. d'Edouard would not be there until after eight P.M.?

"Yes," said the Swansea House operator after a moment. "It is guaranteed by you. Firstway Travel, right?"

"Right. We're getting him a cab out to LaGuardia this minute. Are there any messages for him? Briefly, please. And then hold them for him, okay?"

There were three calls for d'Edouard: from London, France, and Chicago. Aubrey hoped the hotel would not tell d'Edouard of the call from the "travel agency." Probably not. At these big impersonal hotels, the telephone operators scarcely talked with the desk clerks.

From overseas information he got the numbers for d'Edouard's manse in Rutheville and for Bridsey's office and home. They matched the calls to the Swansea House—Bridsey's from his office. The Chicago caller had given his last name, Eisen. Aubrey dialed and the number was answered by a recorded message: Aaron, Gallagher, and Eisen would be open at nine A.M. Chicago information told Aubrey that Aaron, Gallagher, and Eisen was listed under law firms; and at the same address and number there was a Conrad B. Eisen.

Aubrey called back the *Eagle* food editor.

"Marge," he said, "please, can you phone whoever the wine person is on the *Chicago Tribune* or the *Sun-Times* and find out if he or she knows a lawyer named Conrad B. Eisen. And anything about him?"

Unlike the State Department contact, Marge Tyler was never going to run dry on him. In the newspaper business the debts were complex, deep, and lasting. In Marge's case, years ago a famous restaurant had sued for an injurious and slightly inaccurate review. Through a city health inspector, Aubrey had found patrons who several years before had reported that they had gotten mild cases of food poisoning at the restaurant. They were still willing to go public. When Aubrey had called the restaurant and threated an exposé, the owners had howled blackmail. But they had dropped the suit.

"Tonight?" she asked. It was almost seven.

"If you can. I'll call back before midnight."

Aubrey sat in the open lobby bar, a sad imitation of the Plaza or the Algonquin with plastic foliage in the planters. He scrutinized the registrants but could not guess which ones were French, much less which one was d'Edouard.

At 11:10 he called Marge Tyler.

"What the hell are you up to?" she demanded.

"Don't even guess," he jollied her, knowing from her tone that she had found out something intriguing.

"Let me try. You're going to buy some fancy wine and pass it off as that Château Potwater you're making out in the country?"

"No, Marge, close but . . ."

"This Eisen is a lawyer for some bookstores out there," she began, teasing him with an irrelevancy.

"Yes, and . . ."

"And he's what's called an auction bidder. He bids on rare books, paintings, and wines at auctions. Out there, and in New York, San Francisco."

"Wines?"

"Just like in the movies, Aubrey. He sneezes, or picks his nose, and that indicates a bid. And that way nobody knows who's bought the item and even if they find out, it's just some lawyer acting on behalf of a client he won't talk about."

"Holy shit," he said wonderingly.

"Does it help?"

"Jesus yes, but I don't know how yet. What's he look like?"

"Sixty-fivish, heavy, with a big Chicago voice. Dapper. He's quite a figure around town. They did a feature on him once."

"Wonderful lady," he said, meaning it.

"Is it something I can write? It is, right?"

"Right and if I tell you I could get hurt."

"You mean libel?" It was a reporter's first worry.

"No, bullet."

She paused and he could feel her caring about him. Suddenly he was touched over how good she was and how many good people like her he had left behind in the newspaper business.

"Be careful, Aubrey," she said.

On the house phone, Aubrey got d'Edouard and, dropping his voice a half octave, said, "Mr. Brown?"

"No, no. No Brown here," said the heavily accented voice.

"Isn't this room 512?" Aubrey demanded.

"No, no."

"Well, what number is this?" Aubrey asked disbelievingly.

"Why it is . . ."

"Right there, on the telephone dial," Aubrey bullied him.

"It is 417," d'Edouard said self-justifyingly.

"Ah, this insane hotel," said Aubrey. "I am truly sorry."

"Not to worry," said d'Edouard. "It happen everywhere."

Aubrey took the elevator to the fourth floor and located room 417 on the avenue side of the hotel. Downstairs, he told the desk clerk he needed a room and didn't want anything higher than the fourth floor because he got dizzy when he looked out the windows. He would like to face the avenue, he said. The second floor was all meeting rooms so he figured he had a fifty-fifty chance of hitting.

"The third?" asked the clerk. "I have . . ."

Aubrey looked pained.

"I'd have a little better view from the fourth. And a little less noise."

The clerk pecked again at the computer. He had seen them all at one time or another. And a floor freak was a blessed relief from some of the crazies, for example the inch-thick-bed-board nuts and the wool or air-conditioning allergenics.

"Four forty-three," he said, ringing for a bell hop. Aubrey raised his briefcase; the clerk waved off the bell hop; Aubrey ascended to find he was about as far from 417 as he could be and remain on the same hallway. To see anyone leaving or entering he had to pop into the hallway and peer past the elevators.

*   *   *

Jet lag could mean that the Frenchman would rise early. Aubrey was fully dressed and ready to descend by 6:45. He left his door open, darting out every few seconds, then slipping back inside.

At eight, twitching from the regimen, he saw a skinny man, perhaps six-three, come from 417 with an old-time European briefcase in hand. As the man preened, pressing down a thin mustache by the mirror next to the elevator, Aubrey got a good look at him.

When he disappeared inside the elevator, Aubrey rushed down the stairs and spotted him headed for the hotel restaurant. Hungry as Aubrey was, he did not follow. For one thing, the less the man saw of him, the better.

For another, Aubrey smelled a break. If he could stick with this guy, he would learn something important. He gave d'Edouard almost time to finish breakfast and then went out to the cab stand, stared at the first two cabbies, rejected them on instinct, and stooped to the window of a third who was reading a paperback.

As unobtrusively as he could, he showed the hack driver the private detective's shield, and said he needed someone followed. He knew he'd drawn a no-help when the man closed the book and Aubrey saw it was Thucydides.

"Unh-uh," confirmed the cabbie.

Aubrey started down the line again. The next cab was driven by a large, elderly black man, too middle-class looking for what Aubrey wanted, but the man hissed at him, "What you looking for? You a cop, right?"

"I'm a private detective," Aubrey said. "You . . ."

"I saw you throw the shield."

"I want somebody followed."

"How far?"

"I don't know. Probably in town someplace."

"Seventy-five if it doesn't take more'n forty-five minutes."

"Fifty," said Aubrey.

"Thirty down," said the man.

Aubrey peeled off a twenty.

"The other thirty when we get there. How long you been hacking?" He didn't want a newcomer.

"Long enough," said the man without a smile, taking the twenty. "Where you want me?"

Aubrey told him to position himself out on the curb so that when d'Edouard came out they could quickly pick up his cab or car as it pulled from the hotel's porte-cochere.

"That twenty'll keep me waiting for twenty minutes," the cabbie said.

In ten, d'Edouard stepped out of the hotel briskly. The doorman handed him ceremoniously into a cab. Aubrey's driver stayed two cars behind, an easy tail on broad Connecticut Avenue. Ten minutes later the Frenchman's taxi turned left toward the sprawling Shoreham.

"Wait for me, okay?" Aubrey told the hacker, grabbing the door handle to be ready to jump when they stopped.

"Another fifty," said the man.

"A buck a minute'd be better."

"No deal," said the driver.

"Jesus, you charge more than a goddamned psychiatrist," Aubrey told him hastily.

D'Edouard's taxi pulled up before the Shoreham's glass doors.

"I do more good," said the driver, the first real smile breaking up his face.

Aubrey lingered far enough back to see d'Edouard round the corner of the expansive lobby and head toward a bank of elevators. The ex-reporter hustled to the elevator panel and watched his quarry's elevator stop at the third and sixth floor. Aubrey legged it rapidly to the desk.

The auction was taking place next day in the Blue Room at 10 A.M., Aubrey learned. The printed material on the auction was available in 318. That would be what d'Edouard was doing there.

Slumped low in his cab, Aubrey waited for the Frenchman to emerge. God, he thought, all this is costing so much. And what had he produced? He reminded himself that, at least, he was no longer charging the von Mohrwalds for his time.

Suddenly the car jerked forward. Aubrey had let himself daydream but the driver had spotted d'Edouard jump into a cab and had moved out after him.

"You must have been a cop," Aubrey said with some admiration.

"Prison guard," said the hacker. "When I was young the police didn't want my kind."

Back at the hotel, Aubrey got the clerk to transfer him to room 423 when they couldn't get him in 421. The new room might give him some fresh vistas for photographs out the window, explained Aubrey.

One last time he called Marge Tyler and asked her whether she would Xerox for him everything she had gotten about the wine auction, and send it by messenger to his hotel room.

"I want to pay for the messenger," Aubrey said.

"Let the *Eagle* do it," she said. "They owe it to you."

Aubrey cracked the door so he could hear anyone coming or going from d'Edouard's room. Then, his pillow toward the door, he lay in his room's entranceway, and waited, doing a few of his back exercises against the day when he would return to his own vineyard.

D'Edouard might be reviewing the stuff he had picked up at the Shoreham or conferring with Eisen, or Bridsey or someone in Rutheville, or just taking a snooze. But whatever it was, Aubrey did not dare let himself doze. D'Edouard right now was all he had.

The messenger with the Xeroxed material came. As Aubrey eased himself back on the floor to study it, he heard d'Edouard's door slam. He cracked his door and saw d'Edouard going by. Again Aubrey rushed down the stairs.

The lanky European paused outside the hotel, studied a map, then struck out toward Fourteenth Street. To Aubrey's surprise, d'Edouard briskly traversed the numbered street to Ninth, the city's seedy T and A district. There the man stopped before a rundown dirty-movie billboard.

From across the street Aubrey could read its gaudy lettering: "Shamrock Sexpot." A promotion banner on the marquee said in emerald green, "Screw Magazine: '. . . A shillelagh-filled romp through Irish clover . . .' "

D'Edouard glanced around, bought a ticket, and entered. Aubrey sidled across the street and asked the old woman in the cashier's cage how long the movie lasted, marveling that they could get $6 for an hour and a half of porn.

To follow d'Edouard into a sparsely attended cooze show could alert the Frenchman. Instead, Aubrey waited across the street in the Bronco Love Goods shop.

When the clerk asked him whether he wanted to buy anything, Aubrey picked up the nearest dirty book, a Beauty and the Beast classic for $7.50 that was wrapped in clear plastic to foil dirty fingers. Its cover featured an aroused boar entering a Victorian room in which a fat, cretinous woman wearing only an inviting smile lay on a sofa.

Across the street the first of the blue flick idolators straggled out. Most of them were neatly dressed and averted their eyes from the busy street as they left. D'Edouard, whose height made him conspicuous, pretended to be looking at the wall. Aubrey exited the porno shop and followed him at a distance back to the hotel.

Auction material beside him, Aubrey, head on pillow, lay just inside his door, continuing the vigil. The catalogue was the heart of the data and Aubrey quickly leafed through it looking for mention of Château Ambourg-Repose. A big sell-off of the château's older vintages would at least give a logic to d'Edouard's visit. But there was not a single Ambourg-Repose offering.

Aubrey thought of the other possibilities.

D'Edouard could be shilling there for some other Bridsey interest, perhaps his Portuguese holdings. The House of Bridsey made a market both in ports and Madeiras and the latter, particularly, were coming back into fashion. Aubrey noted that the oldest wine in the catalogue was a Terrantez Madeira from 1795. The rest ranged all the way up to 1940, a dazzling spectrum, next only to the Bordeaux in importance at the auction.

Might Bridsey be buying up Madeira acreages through the Portuguese interests that had controlled them for centuries, expecting the current fad to become a serious world demand? A sampling of the hoary vintages offered at the auction would give him incomparable guidance in blending his new Madeiras. It was, Aubrey thought, at least a long-shot guess at what d'Edouard was doing in Washington.

Aubrey turned back to the Bordeaux, studying the tentative price and the march of the years. The oldest was an 1832 Lafite, followed by other golden oldies up to the great drinking clarets of the 1860s and 1870s. The prices reflected the legendary quality of the wines.

From an 1880 Mouton Rothschild to an 1888 Leoville Barton—the terrible time of the phylloxera in Bordeaux—there was a leap, with only a single bottle of 1885 Château Rossant offered for the entire eight years. How had the Rossant survived?

It was priced at an opening bid of $1,500, $100 more than the glorious 1874 Mouton Rothschild. Aubrey turned to the back of the catalogue where a brief paragraph was included on each of the stellar offerings. For the Rossant it said:

A collector's item for the unorthodox oenophile. Survived both the mildew and the phylloxera. Not recorked; bin-soiled label; low shoulder fill; unknown drinkability.

A freak wine for the freak collector. Aubrey passed it by and leafed onward, through the Americans, which all seemed so overpriced, and into the Italians, the Germans, the sherries, the cognacs and Armagnacs. Nothing jumped out at him.

Desultorily, he turned back to the write-up on the Terrantez. It said the entire Terrantez crop had been wiped out by phylloxera when the pests chewed through the Madeira Islands in the 1870s. It added that Terrantez had never again been commercially grown.

Funny about both the Rossant and the Terrantez being tied into phylloxera, the one a survivor, the other an anachronism. Aubrey tried to imagine some link between Domaine McIntyre providing vine stock to Europe in the nineteenth century and now, again, for some experimental purpose to Bridsey and d'Edouard's vineyard, Ambourg-Repose.

That was stretching like hell. What auction of old wines would not have some relation to the scourge of nineteenth-century wines? He could make the same sort of connection with oidium, which had originally afflicted Europe before phylloxera completed the job.

Aubrey pulled the telephone as close as he could to the door and dialed the Library of Congress.

"I am partially disabled," he said to the public inquiry clerk, embarrassed by the lie. "I can come to the library if I must, but I wonder if you could just provide me with a fact or two. I don't need much. It's on a couple of wines . . ."

Aubrey called the man back late in the afternoon. The inquiry clerk had taken a cursory look and found only one reference to Terrantez. The entry added nothing to what Aubrey knew from the catalogue. There was more substantial stuff on Aubrey's other query: the Château Rossant.

The vineyard, said the clerk, was named after the Rossant family and had been producing at least since 1792. A chemical engineer, Baron James de Rossant, had once been hailed as the discoverer of a remedy for phylloxera, one based on carbon disulfide.

Either the *formule Rossant* as it was called, or luck, had kept some of the Baron's vines from phylloxera blight in 1884 and 1885. Thereafter the Rossant vines, too, succumbed and, as with neighboring châteaux, only began to recover with the planting of American stocks. That could make it damned interesting, thought Aubrey, if d'Edouard bid on the Château Rossant bottle. Tied up with the import of the American vine stocks by Bridsey, it could mean the cartel had something fancy going that involved phylloxera.

Aubrey let his mind play over it. What could they want with the Rossant? Well, it was a bottle of wine that had survived the insects either because of this formula or because of dumb luck. And the formula, if that's what had done it, had pooped out after two years and not been duplicable.

In theory the Rossant secret was still locked inside this old bottle of Bordeaux. The microscopic vestiges of carbon disulfide and other chemicals that had—maybe—warded off the blight were in there.

Couldn't they be analyzed? Sure they could. The FBI did magic with spectroscopy. Their experts could turn up and pair infinitesimal bits of hair, dirt, semen, cloth. Why not the same kind of high technology pizzaz on old wine? Couldn't spectroscopy determine what proportions of what trace chemicals distinguished the 1885 Château Rossant from all other wines in the whole world?

Aubrey stopped breathing. Holy shit. If you could do that, then you just might be able to knock out phylloxera permanently. Although the American vines had brought it under control, they were not impervious to it. Millions were still spent to fight the pests in Italy, France, Germany, Spain, elsewhere. There were often stories in the trade magazines about the insects' survivability.

He speculated further. People had always said that the great wines of Europe were never the same after the American root stocks were brought over. Suppose the cartel planned to replant European vine stocks. It would cost a fortune. But without the threat of phylloxera, it just might be worth it. It was possible.

Perhaps the cartel was developing antidotes for oidium, for blue mildew—remedies that would make the present costly spraying with sulfur and copper salts unnecessary. It would revolutionize wine making—and wine finances.

Now I'm getting somewhere, Aubrey thought. But where did the missing Domaine McIntyre vines come in? Well, might not the cartel be using them to learn whether *current* American wines were protected by their phylloxera antidote—although there was damned little phylloxera left in America—and by the antidotes they were getting up for mildew and other blights that American wines *were* susceptible to?

If the cartel came up with such findings, then that would be the time to start buying American lands. And Wheatley-Smith's death? Had the British inspector discovered something of what was going on—the string of yarn that might have unraveled the entire conspiracy?

Yeah, Aubrey cautioned himself, and you might just have a bucket of blivits. This bottle of Bordeaux may be the furthest thing from their minds.

Nevertheless, he had begun to speculate on other possibilities for the Rossant when he saw a sweep of suit go past his room. He heard a firm knock at d'Edouard's door. When it opened, greeter and greetee would be eying each other for an instant and Aubrey took the opportunity to cop a look.

The man walking into d'Edouard's room had a saggy face like Sneezy of Seven Dwarves fame, was older than Aubrey, was stocky and well dressed, and was nearly bald. Aubrey heard his confident "Hello, wonderful to . . ." as d'Edouard closed the door. It had to be Conrad B. Eisen.

Aubrey's heart gave a solid thump. Whatever d'Edouard's role here, it was going to cost somebody some important money. He had summoned in an expert from Chicago either to guide him, or to do the actual bidding. That meant the purchases would be crucial and that the true buyer's identity had to be concealed, or both.

Aubrey went back to the catalogue, studying in

vain for some new insight. How he wished he could
have bugged the hotel room. But it was one thing
to defy an English law against body snatching and
a Department of Agriculture regulation against
smuggling in illegal flesh—and quite another to
risk two high-grade felonies: a federal one for the
tap, a local one for the break-in.

Eisen left after more than an hour with
d'Edouard.

At nine, a trim woman in her thirties, dressed
stylishly but with just the slightest taint of tart,
swung by Aubrey's room and knocked ever so gently
on d'Edouard's door. He must have been expecting
her, for the door swung inward almost instantly.

An hour and a half later, room service arrived
at d'Edouard's door with a rolling cart full of food
and surmounted by a wine bottle. At three A.M.,
the woman left. Aubrey rose creakily from the floor
and went to his cool, empty bed.

Twenty-one

THE AUCTION

The Shoreham's Blue Room had once been a sedate cabaret that featured Mark Russell, the political comedian, nineteen-fifties-style jitterbugging, and what in Aubrey's day had been called the fox trot.

Now it was a meeting room with low ceilings, indirect lighting, gray-blue ornithic walls, square columns and pilasters. Outside it a crowd was gathered in the lounge, sampling American wines at token prices, and waiting for the auction to start.

Aubrey's blue pin stripe blended sartorially with the wine enthusiasts. They were an intense, well-to-do bunch, cliquish as most such specialized groups are, craning their necks to see who was and who was not on hand.

Nervous, wondering even at this late moment whether d'Edouard might unaccountably skip the auction, Aubrey sipped a late-harvested St. Jean Johannesburg Riesling. God, he thought, his mind wandering to happier days in his own vineyard, if I could just have the time to make a wine like this.

More than half of the participants had wandered into the Blue Room before d'Edouard arrived alone. Aubrey followed him in, watched him sit well back from the front of the room, then sighed with relief when Eisen came in and unobtrusively sat even further to the rear.

Just as unobtrusively, Aubrey shifted far to the left where he could see both men's faces. They had planned their positions, Aubrey was sure, so that d'Edouard could signal Eisen with an ear scratch or collar pull or some such code they had worked out the night before. Eisen would then do the bidding, keeping d'Edouard anonymous. That was the pro way to do it, Aubrey was sure.

The auction got off on the nose at ten A.M. The enthusiasm and inventiveness of the promoter, a Japanese-American importer from San Francisco named Dr. Yatatiko, said a lot about why so many people drive Hondas, Datsuns, and Toyotas.

For one thing, Dr. Yatatiko had cranked in some suspense by decreeing that the dessert wines would be auctioned before the celebrated Bordeaux, a reversal of the usual progression. For another, while case lots of wines were all, as was usual, in warehouses in New Jersey or someplace, single and odd lot bottles were on hand for exhibition and immediate delivery. Actually seeing these ancients made them all the more exciting—and pricey.

While Washington is not exactly a Mecca for wines, the novelty and deft advertising had drawn 750 wine buffs to the Blue Room, a near-capacity crowd. Dr. Yatatiko stood before them until they quieted, then introduced himself and the auctioneer, a gaunt Englishman of sour mien whose credentials, according to the promotional literature, went practically back to Saintsbury.

The auctioneer explained Dr. Yatatiko's innovations with a slightly disapproving look. Then he rapidly described the standard ground rules, no more necessary for the real aficionados in the crowd than a referee's instructions to a couple of old pugs.

It was all new to Aubrey. He did note that the importer's shake-up of the rules would mean that he would find out early whether d'Edouard was in Washington for the ports and Madeiras. Under the Yatatiko Dicta, the 1795 Terrantez, as the senior bottle, would be first.

An anxious-looking man with short arms poking from his brown suit coat came from a door to the left of the stage. He seemed out of character with the Japanese-American's class act. The man's hands held a bottle by neck and base as tightly as if it were a barbell. He mounted the stage and put the bottle on a small marble-topped table lighted from above by a restrained baby spot.

The auctioneer looked at this Yatatiko innovation, too, with faint distaste, then began to describe the virtues of the 1795 Madeira. The label, he pointed out, was intact though a bit soiled. A similar bottle had been sold in 1980 in Los Angeles for $1250 and drunk "to considerable acclaim."

Terrantez, the Englishman recounted, was a wine no longer made. Only a few wild vines were still grown in the hills above Funsal, harvested by peasants, and drunk as a table wine. Aubrey wondered nervously what the peasants would charge for *their* Terrantez.

The bidding began at $850. Aubrey's eyes moved back and forth between d'Edouard and Eisen. No signals passed, and although the bidding was brisk, neither of the men entered a bid. The wine went for $1350, and the buyer, who had been indicating his bids with a candidly raised arm, moved out of the crowd to claim it.

The factotum in his brown suit came from his lair beside the stage with a miniature duffle of vinyl and some bubble plastic. The auctioneer, rather grandly, presented the Madeira to the buyer who inspected it. The auction functionary took it carefully from the buyer's hand, wrapped it tenderly in bubble plastic, and inserted it in the duffle bag.

Dr. Yatatiko, sitting near the rear of the stage, had on his face the ecstatic look of the visionary. The wine had sold for well over its opening bid. The ceremonial presentation had been carried off with oriental aplomb. Yatatiko Groundbreaker, Aubrey imagined him thinking.

Aubrey held on to the thread that d'Edouard and Eisen were after some specific bottle of Madeira or port, but an 1842 Terrantez, then an 1864 Gran Cama do Lobos, then each of the ports went off without a sign from the Frenchman or the Chicago lawyer. They didn't even take notes on the purchases.

Aubrey felt as if he had been unfairly doused with water. He had come to believe in his Portuguese theory, and suddenly it was nothing, con-

fetti. Now, if they didn't bid on the Château Rossant
he was totally at a loss.

It was lunchtime before the first offerings of
Bordeaux could begin. Aubrey avoided eating at
the Shoreham or the tony restaurants across Connecticut Avenue. He just might meet someone who
had known him when. Instead he went up the
street to a local bar of long standing and ate a tortellini salad from its newly eclectic menu.

While he munched, he tried anxiously to figure
out something new on the Château Rossant. But
it was no use. He would just have to wait.

Returning from the lunch break, Aubrey passed
the Shoreham's bank of public telephones. Thinking of an old reporter's trick when a reserved telephone could be important, he slipped up to a pay
phone, jammed a dime far under the metal tongue
of the phone cradle and affixed a scrawled "out of
order" note.

Back in the Blue Room the auctioneer moved
suavely through the 1832 Château Lafite, an ancient Château Bel Air, and the Bordeaux boomers
of the 1860s and 1870s. The bids were high. The
1880 Mouton Rothschild went off at $1200.

As automatic now as one of those figures that
come out of an ancient town clock to strike the
hour, the man in the brown suit made his entrances
and his exits.

Soon it was the Château Rossant's turn. Aubrey
stiffened.

The first bid was verbal, $1550, $50 over the
minimum. It came from the right side of the room.
In the second row a woman, one of the handful
there, pushed it to $1600. Her offer, too, was open.

The auctioneer began to close the bidding. Suddenly he stopped himself.

"We have a bid for sixteen-fifty," he said. By prearrangement with the auctioneer, a perfectly legal tactic, someone in the audience had given a bid with a secret signal.

Eisen! Aubrey thought excitedly. He had been watching both the lawyer and d'Edouard, but he was sure he had missed some subtle movement. Now he fixed his attention on Eisen. The woman took the bid to $1700, the man on the right to $1750. Again the auctioneer began to close things out. His gaze played across the audience, then at the last moment Eisen blinked his left eye. The auctioneer's face relaxed.

"A bid for eighteen hundred has been made," he said.

Now Aubrey was all but certain. They wanted the Rossant!

The woman took it to $1850. The auctioneer paused before he began his closing litany. This time he did not have to speak. Eisen, with seeming naturalness, blinked his right eye.

"Nineteen fifty," said the auctioneer. "We have a bid for nineteen fifty." The audience swiveled this way and that, looking for the secret bidder. But Aubrey had no need to rubberneck. He knew a blink from Eisen's left eye meant raise it $50, from the right eye, $100.

Okay, he thought. They want the wine. The wine ties in somehow with an antidote for phylloxera. And maybe so do the Domaine McIntyre vine stocks. Aubrey was certain now he was on the right track with his theory that the cartel planned to develop antidotes for phylloxera, and maybe the other wine diseases. That would net them hundreds of millions—billions!—in profits.

The bidding was at $2100. This wine might be the elixir of success for the cartel, but the money, the power it could generate would be poison for the von Mohrwalds. If they were destroyed it was the end of Aubrey's efforts, his attempt to pacify the ghost of Wheatley-Smith.

But how did his theory tie in with Maier's strange words about California? Well, of course: if the cartel could conquer vine blights, their wine could be sold so cheaply they could annihilate the American wine industry.

The blight-free lands of the cartel would make *any* California crop, indeed any vintage anywhere, insufficient. General antidotes to wine diseases were the oenological philosopher's stone, the means to enormously greater and cheaper production, to incalculable wealth.

The bidding had slowed. The man to Aubrey's right had dropped out. It was at $2300 and creeping up by $50s. Aubrey was getting more and more excited. No wonder d'Edouard had been sent over. No wonder they had hired the veteran hotshot from Chicago. This auction was, well, everything.

Could he let this bottle be bought by d'Edouard without a fight?

The room had suddenly quietened. Eisen, his identity unknown to all but d'Edouard, Aubrey, and the auctioneer, had offered $2450. The woman was not responding. The auctioneer was calling the bid in the cartel's favor.

"Twenty-five hundred," said Aubrey, his voice cracking.

At that, he saw the first reaction in d'Edouard, a flinch, but no more. Behind them, Eisen took it up to $2600. Aubrey, inexperienced and cautious, schooled only by what he had seen in the auction up to now, went up to $2650. He was thinking fast. Probably Eisen had open instructions to go to a certain level. Only then would d'Edouard give him a sign. Aubrey kept his eyes on the Frenchman and hiked it fifty dollars.

Eisen bid $2750. Aubrey queasily deliberated. Suppose his whole theory was cockamamie. He'd be stuck with a $2800 bottle of wine which he couldn't even properly store, much less drink, one whose resale value—except to his enemies—was precarious.

"Twenty-nine hundred," Aubrey said, in his nervousness going up $100 more than he intended. But it didn't matter. Eisen confidently raised the ante. The crowd was still turning and speculating on who was giving the mysterious signs.

"Three thousand," suddenly chimed in the woman's voice. It was all too confusing. Was she an ally of the conspirators? A loner? Her looks told him nothing: a handsome, horsy face, an expensive hairdo, a businesslike chalk stripe but feminine ruffled blouse.

Eisen was silent, so Aubrey took it up. The audience strained for the next bid. The drama came not just from the amount. Indeed, the 1832 Lafite had brought $6100, the 1868 Lafite Rothschild $3900. But these prices were not that much higher than the opening bids. They were not surprising. The Rossant had already more than doubled its minimum.

Aubrey fretted anxiously with his catalogue, bending back one page corner after another. D'Edouard gave nothing away, nor did his artful surrogate, Eisen. The stop-and-go three-way bidding went all the way to $5000 before the woman dropped out. With cool intensity, she began conferring with a youngish man next to her.

"Fifty-five hundred," Aubrey said, partly to try to end it, partly to try to flush a dramatic reaction from d'Edouard or Eisen. There was a murmur in the crowd and the man next to the tailored woman, as if Aubrey's bid were the release on a jack-in-the-box, sprung up, bent low, and scurried from the room.

The Japanese-American organizer's eyes swept back and forth across the audience, he, too, looking for the silent buyer. The bids were going up by hundreds now. At $5900, d'Edouard smoothed his black-gray hair. Eisen took it to $6000 and Aubrey quickly offered $6100. He sensed he was forcing some issue.

D'Edouard arched his neck, somewhat exaggeratedly, Aubrey thought, and looked at the floor. Eisen immediately went to $6500. There was an outrush of breath in the audience.

Aubrey was riding a wave now, feeling headstrong and in control. The unorthodox had always stimulated him and while his responses had sometimes in the past been foolish, he had responded. His mind was clear: he would go to $8000. At this level he had the cartel's representatives in a Catch 22 situation.

If they didn't bid him up, they would lose what Aubrey was convinced was a keystone in their empire building. If they did, it was going to cost them dearly. In any case, with every bid they proved to Aubrey how much the hundred-year-old-plus bottle of wine meant to them. He was sure now that in it lay the vinous answer to the land buy-ups, the missing vines, Wheatley-Smith's and Maier's deaths.

The two men, one aloud, one silent as a hidden snake, took the bidding to $8000. Aubrey's euphoria had been short-lived. He could not go higher. And yet . . .

"Eighty-one fifty," he said compulsively.

What signal would d'Edouard give now? Aubrey watched him with attention. The Frenchman decisively touched both his ears at the same time. Eisen quickly came to his feet. He was surfacing. "Mr. Chastleton," he addressed the auctioneer in his bold Chicago voice. "May I respectfully request a short recess?"

The Englishman looked surprised for the first time in the auction.

"You are ill, sir?"

"No," said Eisen. "I would wish merely a brief recess, perhaps with the," he nodded at Aubrey, "gentleman's forebearance. And with the other gentlemen and ladies'."

"I am afraid that without cause, we cannot. It would be quite outside protocol, sir," said the auctioneer.

But he had not reckoned with Dr. Yatatiko's understanding of suspense. The little man to the auctioneer's rear began to hiss like a teakettle or a small dragon. When Chastleton turned, the Japanese-American gave him a beckoning look.

The two exchanged words at the rear of the stage, the promoter excitedly, the Englishman without a change of expression unless it was a tightening along the jawline. At last the auctioneer returned to the podium. He poured himself a glass of water from the large glass pitcher, his first sip of the session, and cleared his throat.

His voice now seemed pipier, a little nervous itself.

"Dr. Yatatiko has asked that we suspend the usual rules if we may do so without dissent." He looked first at the woman, then at Aubrey, then the audience. No one demurred. After seconds of dead silence, the auctioneer excused the session and there was an outbreak of chattering, of rising and milling about.

Aubrey watched d'Edouard move rapidly to where Eisen had pushed his way into the aisle. They exchanged a few words before d'Edouard worked his tall frame out of the Blue Room. The reporters on hand closed in on Eisen, and on Aubrey.

Marge was the most pressing. Eyes a-dance, she nevertheless did not say his name. It was the one fact which she and no one else at the auction had exclusively.

"Could you identify yourself, sir?" an effeminate little man in a modish suit asked. New York

epicurean magazine, thought Aubrey with the ac-
culturated disdain of the general reporter for the
specialist.

Marge was looking at him pleadingly. She
pointed to her thin chest with a discreet finger. My
exclusive, he read her gesture.

"Absolutely," Aubrey said, nodding forcefully
at Marge, but his words seeming to answer the
diminutive fop. "My name is Frank Buck of Tiger
Imports." The two younger reporters in the clutch
jotted it down, the questioner looked disgusted,
and Marge grinned.

Aubrey shoved one of the reporters aside and
made for the door. As he broke free, he saw another group around Eisen.

"I am sorry," the Chicagoan was saying in his
loud tenor, "I cannot. No, I cannot. I am sorry."

Outside the Blue Room Aubrey rushed up the
lounge stairs to the bank of telephones by the elevator. D'Edouard was already at one on the end
and looked up with unconcealed wrath at Aubrey.

There was at least one person waiting behind
each of the operating phones. Only the disabled
one was free. With some embarrassment, Aubrey
pried out the dime with his nail clipper and, finger
to his ear to blot out the cacophony, called Schloss
von Mohrwald. It would be just before eight P.M.
there.

Both Franz and Bethany, summoned by their
servant, came on the telephone. Feeling defensive
toward Franz, Aubrey tried to sound all the more
efficient, the matter-of-fact cop explaining his theory about why the cartel wanted the Château Ros-

sant: part of an effort to discover antidotes for all wine blights, to find the mother lode of wine-making. He said nothing of his own bids.

In strongly accented English, but with firmness, Franz picked up on Aubrey's idea. "You may be on point, Mr. Warder. In Frankfurt the Germans are already doing related research. They are spectroscopically examining table wines to find out the content of sulfur which exists in the longer-lasting wines and in those which disintegrate earliest. I saw it in *Die Presse* a few weeks ago."

"You understand," said Aubrey, "my theory is just a stab in the dark."

"A . . . ?"

"A guess, just a guess. I could be all wrong."

"Bethany," Franz said without patronizing, "we could use the money from Claudio, from Krems . . ." Politely, Franz was speaking English to his wife so Aubrey would not feel left out.

"You're suggesting we should buy it ourselves?" she asked to bring it to a vote.

"A counterattack," said Franz, "a *Gegenangriff*," he repeated in German, liking the martial sound of the word. "The cartel already knows we are their enemies. Why not test their mettle? If we bid more than they, then we can seek the phylloxera antidote ourselves. Mr. Warder is right. It could be worth a great deal. It *could* be used in a variety of ways."

Bethany frugally intervened. "It could also come to nothing. In any case, we cannot match their bid if they are determined. We must decide how high we can go."

Jesus, Aubrey said to himself, I'm already in for $8150 with my own money.

"To ten thousand?" Franz asked Bethany.

"That high?" she replied doubtfully.

They were all silent for a few moments. Then Franz said, "Bethany, I want to make it twelve thousand. If we don't try, if we don't push them, we will have a long time to be sorry."

Aubrey admired this stubborn man. But twelve thousand was crazy. Even with Aubrey charging only expenses, it would use up the money they had been able to raise among their allies for the investigation. Bethany said as much, but Franz was adamant.

When they had hung up, Aubrey crumpled the out of order note and thought. D'Edouard must know a good deal about the cartel or he would not have been entrusted with buying the wine. In America, he was vulnerable. A subpoena, a warrant, something official could hold him here where, with a little intimidation, he might turn pigeon.

Wheatley-Smith's ounce or two of flesh had given Aubrey leverage. A criminal investigation was, after all, in progress. He dialed Duddman's number from his little black book of listings, a carryover from reporter days. He laid out d'Edouard's presumptive place in the cartel and asked what Duddman thought.

"You don't have shit tying this guy to our case," Duddman said. "Just that the vines from Domaine McIntyre went to his vineyard."

"And then disappeared from there."

"So?"

"So, it isn't much. But it's all there is and this guy is going to be long gone by late tomorrow if not before. Besides, air fare for Hernandez is only a few hundred on the el cheapos. I can feed him and put him up."

Aubrey sensed the county coroner considering it.

"We don't lose much," Duddman conceded. "Suppose the papers find out? It'll look like a wild goose chase."

"Bullshit. It'll look like you're leaving no stone unturned."

"No, goddamn it, it's not enough," Duddman said firmly. "Nowhere near, not unless there's something you're not . . ."

"There is, but, Jesus, don't let it get in the papers out there. Another Frenchman in this cartel, or whatever it is, turned up a few weeks ago in a big barrel of Burgundy with his head bashed in. I'm telling you this d'Edouard could be the key."

"Can I use this, uh, coincidence of the new dead guy to get the D.A. out here to free up the air fare for Hernandez or somebody?"

"Yes, but discreetly. And not 'somebody.' Hernandez. Look, I'm on a short leash for time. Let me call him right now."

"This is nuts," Duddman growled, assenting.

"That's what you said about Wheatley-Smith being murdered."

"That *was* nuts," Duddman said.

"Yeah, but not the way you thought it was nuts."

Hernandez, when he heard what Aubrey was up to and that Duddman would back him, was enthusiastic. There's nothing better than an honest cop—God's noblest work, thought Aubrey, because it's so hard to stay honest and be a cop.

"I'll be in room four twenty-three at the Swansea House," he said. "And for God's sake take cabs. I'll pay for 'em. Call me if there's any hitch. And make sure you've got the subpoenas in your pocket and not in the luggage. And, oh yes, if you can get any fancy seals legally put on them, do it. This guy's a Frenchman. For lack of a nail . . ."

"Oh, for Christ's sake," Hernandez interrupted him.

"And bring along the police and autopsy photos of the inspector's body. And handcuffs. And your pistol."

"No pistol," broke in Hernandez. "It's too damned much trouble getting it on the airline."

"Well, try," said Aubrey.

On the way back to the Blue Room, Aubrey saw d'Edouard also moving fast toward the stairs and drew up to him companionably.

"Frank Buck, Tiger Imports," he said, sticking out his hand.

The Frenchman looked furious, ignoring Aubrey's hand.

"That Rossant eighty-five is gonna be outta sight with deep dish pizza, isn't it?" Aubrey said.

Eyes belying his otherwise cool look, the Frenchman increased his speed at the top of the stairs, sending Aubrey into an awkward collision with a column.

"*Pardon*," said the Frenchman without a glance at the stunned Aubrey.

"Prick," said Aubrey, rubbing his aching left knee.

As he entered the Blue Room, a half-dozen reporters converged on him again. The *Washington Post* food person, a youngish reporter, must have recognized Aubrey from some long-ago picture or some chance encounter at a newspaper party.

"Mr. Warder, what is your interest in this wine? Does it relate to your vineyard?"

Aubrey looked apologetically at Marge Tyler. There went her exclusive. He'd try to make it up for her with some good story further down the road. They're so damned smart, he thought, these little Ivy-League types on the *Post* and *The New York Times*. The squirt probably called her morgue and had them punch up a minihistory on him.

D'Edouard and Eisen had already taken their seats. Aubrey shut up and took his, irritated at the reporters, trying to tell himself that investigative reporters were somehow different from this breed, knowing that it wasn't really so.

The woman bidder must have gotten her finances straight, for she joined back in. Maybe she had the idea, too, of trying to decipher the encrypted contents of the old bottle. Whatever the case, her stakes were less than those of the von Mohrwalds. She dropped out at $10,000, permanently, Aubrey suspected.

"Ten thousand one hundred," Aubrey bid doggedly, rubbing his sweaty hands on his pants. Behind him the Blue Room had filled with guests from the hotel. They must have heard reports of strange excitement at the auction.

As more pushed in, exceeding the fire rule limits, those already there slid along the walls toward the front, silent as mud. Dr. Yatatiko retained his fixed smile of enthusiasm, but his eyes had gone a little glassy. The tension was getting to him too.

Eisen moved calmly through the $12,000 barrier, his Chicago voice matter of fact. There was no need for blinks or other gestures now. Aubrey had the choice of holding to the von Mohrwalds' limit, or risking his own money again. This time there was hardly even a question. He took it up.

At $14,500 even Eisen's tranquility cracked and he became jittery. Perhaps wishing it were so, he bid fifteen hundred dollars, drawing an uncomfortable chuckle from the audience. The mistake set off a flurry of signals from d'Edouard, a little like a third-base coach running his commands to a runner with two outs and the count two and two.

When it reached $14,900, Aubrey, almost robotized, made his terminal bid: $15,000. The crowd was utterly still. Aubrey glanced nervously at Eisen. He sat stoically. D'Edouard stared at the floor. For all the world they looked like they had given up.

"Going now for fifteen thousand," the auctioneer said. "We have a bid. Is there any further bidding? Then, going, going . . ."

Holy shit, thought Aubrey. They are going to stick me with the Queen of Spades. The tortellini salad had turned to steel wool in his stomach. Goodbye investigation, he thought. And good-bye my $3000. Along with all the hours of work he would never be able to bring himself to bill them.

Jesus, what the hell would the von Mohrwalds *do* with this ancient horsepiss? Even if they came up with the money to get it analyzed, it was unlikely anyone would find anything practical to do with the analysis. And he had paid $15,000 . . .

Eisen intervened at the ultimate second with perfect timing.

"Fifteen five-hundred," he said. There was a flash of wild cheering from the audience and the tyros who had congregated from the hotel joined in. Eisen was one of the audience's own, the professional. Aubrey was the disrupter, the outsider.

D'Edouard and Eisen had correctly read Aubrey. This was their massive knock-out bid. Still, one last time, his head spinning, Aubrey thought of overriding them. But he could not. It was too mad, too nerve-wracking, too unjustifiable.

The auctioneer, veteran of a dozen such episodes, also sensed Aubrey's resignation. This time he recited the terminal litany knowing he would not be interrupted. Still, cautiously, as he went into "going, going . . ." he glanced at Aubrey and the woman bidder.

"Gone," he said, pounding the gavel, and the room roared with applause, as much now for the drama as for the winner. Eisen, wiping his hands on a handkerchief, stood and those in his row rose, clapping, to let him pass. One man gave him a congratulatory pat. Smiling tightly but gratefully, Eisen moved to the podium to claim his $15,500 treasure.

By morning, Aubrey knew, it would be on the way to some European laboratory, perhaps there to guarantee the cartel's victory. But he had done what he could; he had done his best.

On the platform Dr. Yatatiko rose to make the presentation of the bottle himself. Three photographers moved from their seats to catch the critical instant.

Eisen, at the foot of the platform, looked uncertainly at the auctioneer who returned the look. The two men understood the rituals and did not take easily to breaches of them. But the little Japanese-American had paid the piper. The man in the brown suit emerged with one of the plastic duffles and the padding.

The photographers chose their positions for the best angle. Dr. Yatatiko looked at them with a gracious smile, an Asian Prometheus bringing fire to the West. His attention still on the camera lenses, Dr. Yatatiko went to the marble table and picked up the wine. Eisen mounted the platform. As the oriental entrepreneur extended the bottle, Eisen reached for it, an unhappy participant in this p.r. production.

The cameras flashed, blinding for a moment everyone but Aubrey. Long ago he had learned the right moment to blink when photographers circled a target. Thus he was perhaps the only one to see Dr. Yatatiko drop the bottle of Château Rossant past Eisen's outstretched hands.

Eisen heard it hit the platform. He bent, his hands abruptly gone wild, clutching nothingness like a prestidigitator trying to summon the bottle back up into the air.

But it was beyond saving by even the most talented magician. Like venous blood, its contents ran on the edge of the platform and off onto the floor.

Dr. Yatatiko's face was a Nō mask of horror. He stared at his damp palms from which $15,500 had newly slipped. The auctioneer gaped at the wet carpet. The audience, sensing some awful event, came to its feet.

Besides Aubrey, only d'Edouard reacted with alacrity. The soigné Frenchman and the tough ex-reporter both bulled out of their rows and down the center aisle toward the spilled wine. The Frenchman had a large handkerchief out of his pocket by the time he reached the podium. Aubrey was tearing at his necktie.

The carpeting on the platform and the floor at its foot had sponged up most of the wine. But a shallow pool on the platform, two or three inches across, had not yet been absorbed by the thin carpet. D'Edouard, with no more regard for dignity than a cleaning woman, went down on his knees and began sopping up the pool with his handkerchief.

Aubrey's instincts were to use his tie to do precisely the same thing. But his rival had preempted the wet spot as protectively as a thirsty lion at a meager watering hole. Aubrey lurched over d'Edouard's shoulder to grab the handkerchief. Eisen, athletic for all his years, thought Aubrey was trying to assault his client.

With a quick move of his thick shoulders, he heaved Aubrey away from d'Edouard. Aubrey banged his head against the podium, but rose and stepped back onto the platform.

D'Edouard was sopping up the last of the red fluid. Obviously d'Edouard would have to squeeze the handkerchief *into* something. There were only two glasses on the podium and the large pitcher of ice water.

With a quick sweep, Aubrey dashed the two glasses to the platform and grabbed up the pitcher to smash it, too, on the floor. But instead, impetuously, he sloshed the whole pitcher onto the reddened handkerchief.

The icewater soaked d'Edouard's head as it poured down. Stunned, he looked up, then down at the handkerchief. Trying to retain one spot of unsaturated wine, he squeezed the water-soaked part of the handkerchief but hydraulic action simply diluted it all. The pale fluid dripped to the carpeting.

"Ah, merde," d'Edouard flashed out in anger and frustration and began dabbing at the rug.

Still on the platform, Dr. Yatatiko stood with his hands to his cheeks. His voice had risen an octave as he jabbered incomprehensibly in Japanese. Eisen brayed like a Chicago stockyard ox at the slaughter gate. The photographers fired away.

Twenty-Two

MIDNIGHT SUMMONS

Bridsey did not like the idea of being summoned by St. Gage to London just before midnight, and the purpose of his journey made him particularly unhappy, in part out of fear. It was not that he was a man easily made afraid. His grenadier's manner was authentic. He had been put in for a Military Cross for his heroism in the Korean War and had proudly settled for the Military Medal.

It said something decent about a not overly decent man that in this area, he never bragged, never used his career to his advantage. It was related to a patriotism which was genuine. His fear tonight, however, was of a wasting kind, and thus not contradictory to his impulsive fearlessness in battle.

Bridsey's cab pulled up to the town house in Eaton Square. He knew, of course, about both Robert St. Gage's father's scandal and the family's aristocratic past.

It galled him that a family could be caught out as the St. Gages had been and yet could recover and live again in this baronial way. When the Bridseys of this world went down, they went down for the full count, and the rest of the family went with them.

St. Gage was in a dark purple paisley dressing gown. He ushered the older man into his study. They were surrounded by books, by the small pedestalled statues of Florentine origin. A Romney painting of some gorgeous St. Gage woman peered mysteriously from the wall, lit only by the dimmest of light fixtures atop it. In opposite corners of the room, full armor seemed ready to issue into the center of the study if a jousting horn would but sound.

The antique roll top spoke of some long ago St. Gage diarist or essayist. Bridsey, to his wife, would have described the study as "too-tooish."

"Horrible news," said St. Gage when Bridsey had filled in the details of the auction which St. Gage had not allowed him to go into on the telephone. "My understanding is that the stronger the concentration the better the chance of spectroscopic analysis. You say the liquid he recovered is . . . ?"

"Very dilute," said Bridsey. "Very."

"Still . . ."

"Anything is possible."

Bridsey realized that St. Gage held him responsible for the loss of the Château Rossant. Good plotters covered every eventuality and the integrity of the bottle was the primary concern. D'Edouard could so easily have prevented the accident by having Eisen rule out the pretentious bottle-passing ceremony.

St. Gage's summoning him to this meeting, both for reasons of security and for planning, as St. Gage had explained, was too much like Maier's visit prior to his death for Bridsey's peace of mind. But surely Bridsey's dereliction was not in a class with Maier's apparent treason. In any case, Bridsey was glad Tobb was absent.

"This man Warder is resourceful," said St. Gage. "He was the second bidder from your man's description. I am sure it was he at Rutheville and at the château."

"The second person at Rutheville . . . ," said Bridsey, glad to move the conversation away from the debacle in Washington.

"Was the baroness. No doubt of it," finished St. Gage. "And if they have enough money for this bidding, for that kind of travel, then they are tenacious opposition."

"Can't you cut off the money? Find the bank . . ."

"I suspect it is from friends. That abominable Italian perhaps . . ."

The question of whether St. Gage could cut off their air supply, however, hung in the dim, faintly leathery atmosphere of the study. St. Gage approached it elliptically.

"They will be looking again for the vines."

"Yes," said Bridsey.

"Your partner—d'Edouard—honestly believes the vines were taken to Portugal? He would assume that they were replanted for some confidential purpose on one of your holdings there?"

"That is what you told me to tell him. I, you may be sure do not know where they went."

In fact, while he did not know the location, he was sure they were being used for research by Tobb and St. Gage. He had made a point, following the unsettling general meeting in London, of taking a cup of tea with the *Witwe* Pfeffermühle. There had seemed good reason for their making common cause.

Without going into details, he had told her that some American vine stocks had been removed from a French vineyard in which he had an interest. The trucker, he now believed, had been Tobb.

She, seeing equally good reasons for cautious exchanges of confidences, had told him they had gone to a researcher. Neither had wanted to go much beyond that, but they had agreed to stay in touch when it might serve them mutually.

To St. Gage now, Bridsey added, "I may say I do not want to know where the vines went."

"Come, come, William," St. Gage assured him, "I am not going to harm you. We all fall short of perfection. Now, I assume d'Edouard was aware we were more interested in the Rossant's research potential than its bouquet?" He allowed himself a smile.

"I had advised him to send back immediately half of the bottle with a bit of sediment via two different air express services and to divide the remaining half between his hand luggage and his checked luggage. He is doing the same with the dilute solution."

St. Gage nodded.

"There is only one conclusion that d'Edouard could draw from that," he said.

"Of course," said Bridsey, wondering if he had erred there, too.

"No, no," said St. Gage picking up Bridsey's apprehension. "You did right there. He would have known anyway we didn't plan to drink the stuff. Not at fifteen thousand five hundred, and with a most potable Mouton going for a mere twelve hundred. And you instructed d'Edouard to do what?"

"To get half the, uh, watered wine on the way, to make tentative reservations to fly out, then to stand by his telephone until he heard from me."

St. Gage thought about that. Warder must be neutralized somehow. To do it crudely in such a way that a body could be found as in the first two deaths would be too risky. He must simply disappear. And *not* in the United States where in view of his Pulitzer Prize so many questions would be asked by so many fellow reporters.

"My mind works slowly at this hour, William," said St. Gage self-deprecatingly. "Bear with me."

Well then, St. Gage decided, America was out because of the fuss. But Portugal? St. Gage imagined Warder tramping the fields along the Douro, that strange isolated area east of Oporto with its mists in the mornings, its dark, clouded night sky, its deep ravines, its depopulation.

Would Bethany von Mohrwald go with him? There had been, after all, the scuff marks outside the *cave* under the mountain at Ambourg-Repose, and the dust and bits of dirt on the floor within.

The two had probably picked the lock. American reporters, no better than English reporters, criminal minds, all of them, would know how to do that sort of thing. They had spent the night there. Goddamn it, he thought. If only this idiot Frenchman had caught them. Were they lovers?

St. Gage had a disconcerting thought, just as he had that day at Neuilly on the way to Berkady's, of Bethany naked except for some ancient, cold piece of armor on her shins, or perhaps her thighs or chest, and him over her with his antique dagger.

The image made him dizzy, breathless, as it had then. He put his hand over his eyes, as if thinking, pushing this vision of Bethany out of his head while he appeared to Bridsey to be considering a course of action.

At last, the apparition banished, he looked up, still angry with himself, feeling foolish for what he regarded as less an obsession than a usually vanquishable indulgence.

"I would prefer that d'Edouard *not* fly out tonight," said St. Gage. "You are *certain* he thinks the vine stocks went to Portugal?"

Bridsey was taken aback. He realized that St. Gage was using d'Edouard as a Judas goat. It was a dangerous game, one that frightened Bridsey for it meant, he feared, more bloodshed. He started to protest. But he thought of Tobb, unstable and unassessable.

"I am certain," he answered St. Gage.

"Call him and tell him tomorrow is soon enough for his departure. We do not want a hasty exit to raise suspicions unnecessarily."

Bridsey called d'Edouard from St. Gage's study

and carefully passed on the instructions as St. Gage stood by nodding. At least tonight, Bridsey thought, wishing he were out of the whole mess, my skin is safe from these bastards.

When Bridsey was gone, St. Gage put in a call to Tobb in California. The American's answering service reported him out for the evening.

"Tell him," said St. Gage, "that his English lawyer telephoned him and would appreciate a call regardless of the hour."

At three A.M., St. Gage was jarred from nervous sleep by Tobb's call. For a moment he had a hard time getting a handle on where he was or who was on the telephone. When he did, he spoke slowly. "Do you have some airline contact who could make fairly extensive queries during the next few days about the possibility of our newspaper friend flying to Lisbon?"

"At a price," said Tobb. "Those things are always iffy. You know, connecting flights and so on."

"It could be most important. If you find he is doing so, we should plan, you and I, and I suppose my English merchant colleague, to meet at the merchant's holdings in Portugal."

"Ummph . . . ," grunted Tobb, wanting to hear a bit more.

"We would want to greet the famous reporter on his arrival to the merchant's holdings."

"It's going to happen? He's going there?"

"So I suspect. I may know more later."

"Alone?"

"That also remains to be seen," said St. Gage.

"I suppose you understand what all this pressure means."

"It means D-Day is sitting on top of us."

"Yes," said St. Gage, feeling a tightness all over his body now that it was all about to begin. "I would think three days from now. Are things ready enough there . . . ?"

". . . for me to go to Portugal? That makes things difficult. I must get back here to set everything in motion."

"Then four days."

"That's better," said Tobb.

"So you can leave . . ."

"Tomorrow, say by noon or a little later." Tobb's voice had also taken on an edge of excitement.

"And I think until then we had best leave word at our answering services as to where we can be reached."

Tobb did not take even the gentlest rebuke easily. But there would soon be more important things to think about than being nettled by St. Gage's occasionally superior tone.

Twenty-three

MUMMY AND DADDY

As soon as Aubrey got back to his room from the auction, he called Schloss von Mohrwald and filled in Franz and Bethany. Then he waited nervously for d'Edouard. There was no way, now that he was known to the Frenchman, that he could have kept him under surveillance. It was more than two hours before d'Edouard returned and Aubrey was anxious about where he had been. Not at the dirty movies.

Aubrey was resolved that if d'Edouard tried to check out before Hernandez arrived, one way or the other, he would detain the Frenchman. Nor had he any reason to be tender about it. The man was connected to a group which had murdered twice. And this same suave vineyard owner, if told to, would surely have turned Bethany and Aubrey over to killers had they been captured at Ambourg-Repose.

When the telephone rang, Aubrey jumped from

his post beside the door. Hernandez was on the house phone. Minutes later he came into the room, wiping sweat from his Toltec face. Aubrey hugged him with delight.

The subpoenas Hernandez handed Aubrey were unadorned except for a county seal squeezed onto the paper by some clerk and a judge's signature which, at least, had a grand flourish to it.

"No ribbons," observed Aubrey critically.

He flipped through the photos. They were as grisly as he could have asked. "Beautiful," he said. In urgent words he briefed Hernandez on what needed to be done.

The two aging gumshoes fretted nervously for thirty minutes, then an hour, hoping d'Edouard would leave his room so they could accost him without knocking on his door. To knock would mean that d'Edouard could thwart them simply by not opening.

A bellhop arrived at d'Edouard's door with supper on a cart surmounted by a pail with a bottle of white wine. Beside it stood a bottle of red. Either d'Edouard expected a guest or he was getting full relaxation from what had to have been a terrible day for him.

When it was 10:30 P.M. and no one had entered or left, they knew they had to take direct action. They also knew they were skating on thin judicial ice: they should be notifying the local police that an out-of-state subpoena was being served and requesting the United States Marshal's office to serve it.

Hernandez rapped smartly three times on d'Edouard's door while Aubrey flattened himself along the wall. D'Edouard asked from inside the door who it was.

"Police," said Hernandez firmly but not loudly. "For Mr. Olivier d'Edouard of Rutheville, Republic of France."

D'Edouard opened the door with the chain in place. Hernandez held his badge, a handsome gold-eagled affair attached to expensive black leather, up to the Frenchman's eyes, his finger over "Los Platanos." He took the badge down as soon as it had its effect.

"Police?" repeated d'Edouard to give himself a moment or two.

"I am Deputy Chief Hernandez," said the Mexican-American. "A valuable bottle of wine was broken at an auction today. We have reason to believe you can help us with information about how it broke."

"Ah, monsieur, that was not my fault," said d'Edouard.

"So I believe, sir. If you had waited at the auction as the other gentlemen did, we could have talked with you and been finished. As it is I have found you with considerable difficulty. Your lawyer, Mr. Conrad B. Eisen of Chicago . . ." Hernandez dropped the name glibly, then went on ". . . he is also, we are satisfied innocent of the damage."

"You spoke with Mr. Eisen?"

"We are obligated to speak, even if briefly, with all the principals."

"I am a French citizen."

Hernandez was used to wrigglers. Aubrey could see his cordovaned toe easing into the crack in the door. He braced himself to give the policeman a shoulder if that was necessary to pop the chain from the jamb.

"Now, sir," said Hernandez still more firmly, "we know you are French. But I have this court document." He held it up long enough for d'Edouard to see the seal. "It gives me authority to demand that you answer questions, and if you refuse, to take you into custody."

"But, sir . . ."

"I am standing in the hall, Mr. d'Edouard. My visit will take only a few minutes. This episode is embarrassing this fine hotel, the other guests. I beg you to cooperate in this simple procedure . . ."

"I only saw what everyone saw . . . ," began d'Edouard.

"Please, Mr. d'Edouard, let us not argue. Open the door or I must summon a group of our uniformed men to take you to headquarters. We know you are involved in the wine's purchase. We know you rushed to the platform and dipped your handkerchief into the wine after it spilled, perhaps as a souvenir. It is no crime in America. But we have our rules, our formalities, just as you do in France."

"I know nothing."

"Mr. d'Edouard, if I must, I will put you under arrest. It will be a scandal, in the newspapers, perhaps even in the French press."

"*Arrêt?*" said d'Edouard, flinching at the key word.

"Arrest, yes sir."

D'Edouard after a moment's hesitation opened the door.

Hernandez marched in and Aubrey rounded the corner and swiftly came in behind him. The château owner looked sick when he saw his adversary of the afternoon's bidding. He said with heat, "Why is this man here?"

"He is a complainant in the case," said Hernandez.

He put the subpoena in d'Edouard's hand.

"He is also here to be a witness to the fact that you are served."

"Served?"

Hernandez pointed to the document.

"It requires you to give me a statement."

"But I have done nothing. You said it was about the broken bottle."

"It is about the broken bottle," said Hernandez. "But it is also about other things. This paper," he said, pointing to the subpoena, "requires you either to speak to me, or to go back with me to California and appear before a grand jury. Do you understand?"

"California? I must go to France tomorrow. I have reserved the space. I am to buy the tickets."

"Mr. d'Edouard," interrupted Aubrey with menacing calm. "You aren't going any goddamn place tomorrow except into court unless you talk to this gentleman."

"Let me read the paper," said d'Edouard. All three men stood while d'Edouard nervously put on his glasses and read the subpoena.

"It says in the death of . . ."

"Of a Scotland Yard inspector, Jerome Wheatley-Smith," said Aubrey. "The murder of Mr. Wheatley-Smith. So I don't think you are going to be seeing *la belle France* for a long time unless the deputy chief here says *oui.*"

"Murder? *Meurtre*?" said d'Edouard.

"*Meurtre*," said Hernandez.

D'Edouard turned pale and moved toward the couch to sit down. Aubrey was sure he knew of the death of Maier. Who in the French wine industry would not? But clearly this second death in the case was news to him. When d'Edouard sat, the other two drew chairs up to the coffee table. Hernandez laid his briefcase on it.

"Now, Mr. d'Edouard," said Hernandez, at home with a witness who had felt the pressure and was yielding. "I want to tell you why I am here. I want you to see some photographs."

"You said no arrest," said d'Edouard. "Only questions."

"Just so," said Hernandez. "Only questions."

From the folder he pulled the pictures taken by the police and county coroner's photographers. One by one he handed them to d'Edouard. They were ghastly.

The first of them showed the crumpled form of Wheatley-Smith in the well of the wine press as the ambulance crew bent over him. The next, taken at the hospital after he was pronounced dead, showed his dead face with its bruises, the eyes open. Then there was the naked body from all sides. Then the close-ups of the bruises, and the body after it had been opened up for autopsy.

Not your usual porn show like yesterday, uh Olivier, Aubrey thought. D'Edouard looked sick.

"Do you know this gentleman?" Hernandez asked.

"No, never," said the shaken Frenchman.

"He died in a wine press."

"I never saw him."

"He was last seen alive at the Domaine McIntyre vineyards in California. You have heard of Domaine McIntyre."

D'Edouard started. He said nothing. He did not need to.

"Now you understand why I have come from California to see you," Hernandez said very quietly. "You have heard of Domaine McIntyre?" he repeated.

"It is a vineyard in California," said d'Edouard. "I would like to call my embassy."

Aubrey broke in. "Take him out to California," he said angrily.

"Please," Hernandez said to Aubrey. "He"— he nodded to Aubrey—"was a friend of the decedent. I am handling the case," he said to Aubrey again. He turned back to d'Edouard.

"You say you are aware Domaine McIntyre is a vineyard? You are the proprietor of Château Ambourg-Repose, located at Rutheville, France?"

"One of them. There are several owners."

"You are aware of the purchase from Domaine McIntyre of certain vine stocks by your château?"

D'Edouard looked somber, frightened.

"You need not deny it. The owners of Domaine McIntyre have confessed to my detectives." Hernandez made it sound worse than it was—like the whole lot had been arrested and were about to stand trial. "Where are the vines now?" he went on.

"I don't know."

"You goddamned well *do* know," Aubrey broke in fiercely. "You . . ."

Hernandez glared at Aubrey.

"If you keep interrupting . . ."

"You're going too easy on him. This guy can tell you who . . ." Aubrey grabbed up a particularly lurid picture of Wheatley-Smith, ". . . did him in. This guy . . ." he gestured with the picture at d'Edouard.

"I may have to ask you to leave," said Hernandez to Aubrey. A classic mummy-daddy situation had shaped up and the two experienced investigators fell into it as naturally as if they had been born to it. "If you keep this up, you must go."

Aubrey seemed to seethe with fury at the Mexican-American. D'Edouard looked at Aubrey with outrage.

"I assure you," he said to Hernandez. "I swear to you, deputy chief, I know nothing of this man's death."

"But you purchased the vines from the place where he died and only shortly before the inspector's death," Hernandez suggested.

"I was asked to."

"By?"

"Our proprietorship," he waffled.

"One of your partners is an Englishman," said Hernandez consulting a little notebook in his pocket as if that made it graven in stone. "He is William Carnavan Bridsey of the London firm of House of Bridsey and Sons, Limited. He is the principal partner at your château."

"Under French law, he . . ."

"Come, come," said Hernandez.

"Take his ass out to California. Jail him."

"Sir!" Hernandez said sharply to Aubrey who seemed to withdraw like a chastised cur.

"I will not press you," said Hernandez as Aubrey glowered. "You would swear that it was not personally your decision to buy the vine stocks from Domaine McIntyre?"

"Yes," d'Edouard said.

Hernandez nodded.

"And the vine stocks did reach the château?"

"They came. Yes, and we replanted them."

"So they could get their health back before being shipped elsewhere?"

D'Edouard thought for several moments. If Aubrey was the intruder at Ambourg-Repose and had informed this policeman the vines were gone, then it was futile, even dangerous, to dissemble. Aubrey could see the thoughts going through the Frenchman's mind, the need to be allowed to leave for France, yet the need not to reveal too much.

"Yes," said d'Edouard.

"In transit to . . . ?" asked Hernandez.

"I cannot say."

"You will not say," Hernandez spoke very quietly, seriously.

D'Edouard said nothing.

Hernandez sighed, and as if reluctantly, reached in his pocket and pulled out a pair of handcuffs. He put them on the table.

"One of your coproprietors ordered them removed?" said Hernandez.

D'Edouard paused. The second death obviously preyed on him. Maier, and now this English inspector. Aubrey could see him wondering just how dangerous Bridsey might be to him.

"I do not wish to say."

"We are at a dead end," said Hernandez, unconscious of the pun. "I truly believe you when you say you did not murder the Scotland Yard inspector. I believe you are an innocent party. But . . ." The handcuffs on the table spoke eloquently of what the Mexican-American planned to do. "I have been patient," he said, as if self-accusingly.

"But you said . . . ," murmured d'Edouard. "You said there would be no arrest."

"If you cooperated, answered my questions."

"The vines are not in France," d'Edouard said. "They were sent to another country, I understand for a research project."

"That country is?"

"I cannot tell you," said d'Edouard.

"You *will* not tell me," Hernandez corrected him again.

They sparred some more, and at last without further words, Hernandez went to the telephone. Aubrey was surprised at the action. There was no more chance of getting a legitimate arrest warrant against d'Edouard than against the president of the United States. Even the subpoena had stretched the law to the limits.

Hernandez was finishing up his dialing on the touch-tone. Aubrey saw his fingers move, one-two, one-two, and smiled. The Mexican-American had dialed the weather service and would soon be hearing a weather recording.

"Hello, chief," said Hernandez to the weather report. "I'm sorry to report that Mr. d'Edouard, while he was helpful at first, is no longer cooperating. I do not believe he killed the inspector, but . . ." He paused to listen. His Indian face went morose.

"I am sorry, chief. I have done my best . . . Yes . . . Yes . . . Yes . . . Well, the procedure is for you to telex a warrant for the arrest of Mr. d'Edouard" —he meticulously spelled out both first and last names—"to the Washington police. Yes, charging him with murder. That will permit them to hold him in a cell until I can get him out there tomorrow."

D'Edouard shivered. Hernandez looked at him apologetically, but went on talking.

"Chief, I am sorry that you feel I have been too lenient. I have done my best."

He hung up the telephone and Aubrey watched as he redialed the weather bureau.

"Yes, the Washington homicide squad, please."

Hernandez explained that a warrant would be on the way from California for the arrest of a French gentleman ("no, absolutely no diplomatic immunity. None of any kind") for the murder of a British police inspector. The inspector, he said, had been crushed to death. Aubrey could feel d'Edouard thinking that in France, as everywhere, the most heinous crime in policemen's eyes was the murder of another policeman. And why not?

"No, captain, I do not think force will be necessary," Hernandez was wrapping it up. "I would prefer a cell for him, apart from the ordinary criminal population if that is possible." He listened and looked again hopelessly at d'Edouard. "Then, if it is not possible, at least not with anyone who is prone to violence. After all, Mr. d'Edouard is a visitor to our country. He seems a gentleman . . . yes, I know, I know, the case involves the murder of a fellow officer."

D'Edouard was looking sick. The reputation of French police, the flics, for brutality was notorious. Hernandez was pulling a long face.

"But, captain, couldn't you send an officer over to the Swansea House with the papers? I have no one to leave the suspect with but a private investigator." He paused again, then nervously scratched at his hairline. "Whatever you say, captain. I will be right over."

When he hung up, he explained to d'Edouard that he must swear out the incarceration papers at police headquarters.

"I would rather go . . . ," began d'Edouard.

"Unfortunately, under American law I cannot take you."

"Then . . . ?"

"This gentleman will, uh, stay with you."

"No."

"Yes, I am sorry."

"My embassy," said d'Edouard. "I want to call them." He looked at Aubrey. The Frenchman was badly frightened now.

"I am sorry. Not until the warrant arrives."

"But I am a French citizen . . ."

"Fuck your French citizenship," Aubrey said.

"My chief told me to wait for the warrant before I let you call," repeated Hernandez helplessly.

D'Edouard appeared nauseous. Overrulings by bosses were the sort of thing all Frenchmen understood. There it was a national pastime.

"I am sorry," Hernandez said, picking up the handcuffs and looking around the room, then the bathroom. While he was out of the living room, Aubrey contemplated d'Edouard the way a cat would a caged canary.

"Please," said Hernandez when he came back in, indicating that d'Edouard should stand. Docile now, locked in his own fears and his submission, d'Edouard stood and Hernandez led him to the bathroom as an executioner might conduct a man to the scaffold.

The sink pipes were concealed in a cabinet. The only exposed pipe was the shower curtain bar. Hernandez efficiently popped one cuff on d'Edouard's right wrist. The wine grower involuntarily tried to pull away.

"It will be awkward," Hernandez said. "I apologize."

In a command voice to Aubrey he said, "I do not want any harm done, you hear? When his arm is tired of being raised from the blood running out, you are to allow him to put his other hand up." He handed the key to the handcuffs to Aubrey. "No monkey business!"

Leaving the photographs on the table and Aubrey sitting on the closed top of the commode, Hernandez left the hotel room. Aubrey quickly jumped up and began ransacking the room, carefully replacing each drawer, each suitcase compartment as he inspected them. That done, he came to the immobilized d'Edouard, patted him down, and found the man's wallet in an inside coat pocket. In it were two air express receipts.

"Shit," he said. "Did you send it all?"

D'Edouard, doing his best to look dignified, ignored him. Aubrey again patted him down, this time more carefully, held his foot briefly like a blacksmith with a sulky horse, and pulled off one shoe, then the other.

In the second, between the tongue and upper where it wouldn't break was a little plastic vial such as perfume samples come in. D'Edouard must have found it in the specialty store downstairs. Its contents were a very pale purple, and Aubrey opened the vial and sniffed it. Too dilute even to give off a fragrance.

He closed the container and popped it in his pocket. There was no way he could catch up with the vial's two congeners. But if there was a possibility that the cartel's scientist could dope out the Rossant formula, maybe Franz von Mohrwald's could, too.

Aubrey would air freight his vial in the morning. Whatever was to be found in the watered-down sample, Franz had better hurry with it. From the way d'Edouard had been rushing to get the vials to Europe, it was evident the cartel was moving fast on something.

Aubrey turned to d'Edouard and studied his face with somewhat disoriented malevolence. The effect was to turn d'Edouard's fragile sangfroid to fear. Still Aubrey stared at him. At last, as if he had decided on a course of action, Aubrey came close to the Frenchman and said softly, "You know now who it was out there in your vineyard . . ."

D'Edouard made no answer.

"You tried to hunt me down with dogs and guns like a field rat."

D'Edouard cleared his throat, but his eyes began to blink rapidly.

"And now I discover you conspired in the death of my friend," Aubrey paused. "You saw the pictures."

"I had nothing to do with this matter, monsieur," said d'Edouard, trying, but failing, to sound starchy.

"You're about to be arrested for murder."

"But your colleague does not believe . . ."

"What does he know? If *I* were doing the job, I'd already have a confession for murder out of you, Froggie. One way or another."

"But no," d'Edouard said, then went silent. Aubrey felt him thinking: this, surely, is not a balanced person; better not to incite him. "My arm is tired in this position," said d'Edouard to break Aubrey's gaze. "Could we change arms as the deputy chief suggested?"

Aubrey looked at him with cold contempt.

"Murderer," he said, breathing into the slightly older man's face. "You want to switch arms, do you? You want a rest?"

"Please," said d'Edouard, trying to sound both placating and haughty at the same time. It came out as a bleat.

"You didn't think about rest for my friend when you and your friends pushed him into that wine press to be crushed to death."

"I swear . . ."

"Or that other poor Frog you drowned in wine in Algeria after you beat him to a pulp."

"I know nothing . . . ," said d'Edouard, looking panicky. "My arm, it is so . . ."

"Yes," said Aubrey fiercely and quietly. "Oh yes, murderer, I will help you to change arms." He plunged his hand into his coat pocket, pulled out his knife, and flicked out the blade.

Hoping his eyes looked crazy enough, Aubrey put the point of the knife up to where d'Edouard's wrist protruded from the sleeve of his shirt. Aubrey felt a brief discomfort, not liking himself because he was taking a sadistic pleasure in his threats even though they were fakery.

D'Edouard's eyes bulged and he slid the handcuffs along the bar to distance himself from Aubrey. But Aubrey stalked slowly across the tiles and repositioned the knife by his wrist.

"We will change arms nicely. I will free this arm completely. I will liberate it from the rest of your body and it will be at rest. Oh, it will be at rest."

D'Edouard squawked in sudden fear.

"Oh, you do not want your arm freed that way?"

"No, no," said d'Edouard.

"Then perhaps I should free your head." Aubrey dropped the knife to the squirming man's throat. D'Edouard froze. "How would that do? The perfect way for you to avoid arrest."

"Murder! *Meurtre!*" said d'Edouard gagging on his own sudden rush of saliva.

"You do not want to lose your head?" said Aubrey. "Then perhaps a less fatal liberation." Feeling in spite of himself a clutch of self-disgust, he dropped the knife to the level of d'Edouard's groin. "Perhaps we will liberate that part of you which took so much pleasure last night with one of our local coquettes."

"*Dieu*, no," gasped d'Edouard.

"And then send them to your wife with a note about your infidelity."

"*Sadist*," said d'Edouard in terror.

"Yes, the very kind of man to take care of a murderer."

He grabbed at d'Edouard's belt and the man looked like he was going to faint. At that instant the door opened and Aubrey quickly snapped shut the knife and put it into his pocket.

"Deputy chief. Help me," d'Edouard managed in a terrified gurgle. Hernandez hurried into the room and looked suspiciously at Aubrey.

"What's happening?"

"He try to kill me," said d'Edouard.

"I was about to change his arms for him. He made an effort to escape."

"Liar," said d'Edouard. "He have a knife."

Hernandez looked confused.

"I forgot my briefcase. I had to come back." Hernandez demanded the key from Aubrey and recuffed d'Edouard by the other arm. "No monkey business," he repeated, eying first Aubrey, then d'Edouard.

"But you are not going again?" asked d'Edouard in a pathetic voice.

"I must."

"He has a knife," gasped d'Edouard.

"In America, that is his right," said Hernandez to d'Edouard mildly reproving.

"No," said d'Edouard fearfully.

"Yes, I must," reiterated Hernandez. Aubrey stood behind the policeman with what he hoped was a manic leer on his face.

"No, oh no," said d'Edouard, looking at Aubrey, then at the policeman. "He have the knife. He threaten to cut my throat, my"—he sought for the word in English—"*organes génitaux*," he said, hoping desperately it was close enough.

"Hunh?" asked Hernandez.

"He's crazy," said Aubrey.

"I must go," said Hernandez. "No tricks, now." He turned. D'Edouard's face was almost white, his eyes bugging.

"Portugal," he said.

"Hunh?" asked Hernandez.

"They go to Portugal."

"The vines," said Aubrey. "He's saying the vines went to Portugal."

"It's too late," said Hernandez. "I have to go."

"Please," said d'Edouard. "I will help you. The vines were taken to Portugal."

"Who took them? They were stolen?"

"No, no," said d'Edouard, the words coming in a rush now. "If you can let me go. If you can let me go back to France, I will tell you. All this is a nightmare. *Cauchemar*," he added for emphasis.

Hernandez took the key from Aubrey and released d'Edouard. The Frenchman slumped down on the toilet seat and held his head. Hernandez waited for him to recover some of his aplomb and then signaled him to the couch. The policeman put down his briefcase and called the weather bureau.

"Captain, there is a delay. I will telephone you shortly . . . No, no. Do not process the papers yet . . . Ah, the arrest warrant is there? It is possible it will be unnecessary . . . I am sorry . . . I will call you as soon as possible. I assure you I am truly sorry . . ."

Hernandez looked hostilely at d'Edouard for the first time.

"You have caused me a great deal of trouble; you have humiliated me with my chief and with this large and important police department. I can advise you, Mr. d'Edouard, that it will not go easy with you if you betray me now. Even my patience . . ."

"Please," said d'Edouard. "I am grateful. Ask. I will try to help."

"You say they were taken away. How?"

"A truck came and they were taken to Portugal."

"You are sure?" asked Hernandez.

"I was told."

"By . . . ?"

"By my, by our partnership."

"There is an Englishman and another Frenchman in your partnership."

"Two other French citizens."

"But the Englishman has holdings in Portugal."

D'Edouard paused. Clearly here was a policeman who had done his homework.

"That is correct," he said formally.

"So the vines went to these holdings?"

"One could assume so."

"You were not told?"

"I was not told."

"You sent the vines in a truck from the château. Surely you . . ."

"No, no. Another truck."

"But one of your drivers?"

"No."

Aubrey gave a low growl.

"You are withholding information, Mr. d'Edouard," said Hernandez. "Please do not disappoint me. I am, as we say here, out on a limb for you."

"An American drove the truck. I have never seen him before and I have never seen him since."

Aubrey started. An American? He had thought this was entirely a European operation.

"An Englishman?" interjected Aubrey.

"An Englishman? Could it have been?" echoed Hernandez.

"He looked American. They look different. He sounded like an American. Ah, ah, ah," he tried to imitate the American "a." Hernandez looked at him curiously and d'Edouard wanting, above all, to oblige, said, "Of course, I could be wrong."

"How old was he? What did he look like?" asked Hernandez.

"Thirty-five, forty years old. Not too large, but . . ." The Frenchman held out his arms bent at the elbows with fists clenched ". . . *forte.*"

"Hair?"

"He wore a beret. But light, I think."

"And you have heard no more of the vines?"

"Until now, no," said d'Edouard.

"And the auction?"

"Oh God," said d'Edouard, as if he were saying he wished he had never heard of it, indeed, never heard of America.

"The wine was interesting to you because it was a survivor of this plague of bugs?" prompted Hernandez.

"Phylloxera," said Aubrey.

"I was told to arrange for the American from Chicago to bid on it. Not to make my presence known."

"And the purpose of your bidding up so high?"

"To buy the wine," said d'Edouard with a trace of disdain. He was recovering a little of his haughtiness.

"Please," said Hernandez. "Please do not be smart with me. The wine was not to drink."

"Hell no," interceded Aubrey. "He sent two samples of the stuff he sopped up to this Bridsey. I have the third. In a vial."

"So the wine, as I suspected, was for research into this affliction of vines?" said Hernandez.

"Phylloxera," Aubrey supplied again.

There was a coldness in the air. How much did they know? d'Edouard wondered. Suppose they found out somehow? My God, they knew so much. Supposed that Bridsey or someone else whom he did not even know had revealed this to some other police here? Or in Europe? Was this sly Mexican trying to trap him?"

"That is possible," said d'Edouard.

"It is more than possible," said Hernandez, waiting for affirmation. D'Edouard paused a split second that gave him away.

"Yes, it is likely."

It was a major concession. At some point, Hernandez knew, particularly now that d'Edouard was in control of himself, he would call their bluff. D'Edouard's fear of death from Bridsey or the mysterious force he must sense behind Bridsey would conquer his fear of Aubrey. But, Hernandez reasoned, why not press on until that point was reached?

The policeman inquired about the organization of the cartel, about Bridsey's partners and associates in the cartel's purchase of the vine fields, about the *reasons* for the phylloxera research. But it was clear that d'Edouard, even had he wanted to be helpful, had no knowledge about these matters.

The policeman glanced at Aubrey and saw accord in his eyes.

"Mr. d'Edouard, at considerable embarrassment to myself, I am going to call my chief and recommend that you be allowed to proceed to France. I am going to write up what you have told us in a brief fashion. This man"—he nodded at Aubrey—"will locate an all-night notary, and when you have signed the statement I write up, you will be free to go."

D'Edouard took the news stolidly. In order to escape from this cunning flic and this American murderer he had imperiled himself with dangerous men.

He was already thinking of his telephone call to Bridsey, how he could best present his case. Perhaps he could say that if he had not gone some short distance down the road with these people, they would have sent an arrest warrant to England for Bridsey in the death of this accursed Scotland Yard inspector.

Even as Hernandez worked on the handwritten affidavit, d'Edouard wondered whether his story would pass muster. He thought of Aubrey's knife at his wrist, his throat, his genitals. Again he shuddered. Why had he ever joined with Bridsey in buying Château Ambourg-Repose and gotten himself involved with all these terrible foreigners?

Twenty-four

THE VINEYARDS OF DOURO

On the dilapidated train from Oporto to Régua, while Aubrey studied a large map of Iberia, Bethany looked out the window at the slate-colored Douro running below. Despite the hot morning air that rushed into the second-class carriage, she was already aware of his male smell, something not unpleasant beneath the shaving lotion that he must have used that morning.

She smiled: curse of the vintners—an overdeveloped olfactory sense. She thought of Aubrey that night in the *cave* at Ambourg-Repose and was somewhat miffed with herself. She had not invited him to visit her room last night in Oporto. His feelings, she sensed, had been hurt though he, too, must have seen the good judgment of her decision. She did not linger on it; it was easier to think of other matters.

She had debated about how important it had

been for her to come to Portugal. Franz had needed her. She could have shepherded the vial of diluted wine through the laboratory in Frankfurt, among other urgent things. On the other hand, Aubrey, like most people from *grandes nations*, was a linguistic ignoramus. Bethany's Spanish was a workable substitute for Portuguese. And again, there was the absolute necessity of her identifying the imported American vines.

She smiled to herself, all too cognizant of a third factor: her desire to see her attractive employee-colleague-instructor again.

The train climbed and the hillsides grew steeper, the earth barren and cracked like the skin of a rhinocerous. In a few miles the first vineyards began, unlike any she had ever seen before. From a distance they looked like small mountains made of corduroy, the contour lines clinging even to the steepest slopes.

As they came nearer, she saw the vines snaking around olive trees that jutted almost straight out from the hillsides. The broken slate of the fields was the color of the river. Here and there low, fallen stone walls, the remains of aqueducts betokened the countryside's antiquity. Traces of mist swirled past the train.

"Weird," said Aubrey beside her.

She nodded, jarred from her thoughts.

"I wish there were some other way," she said.

"There isn't," he said.

Their plan was bold, perhaps desperate. D'Edouard would have immediately called Bridsey to report on his inquisition by Aubrey and Hernandez. Bridsey, therefore, would assume that Aubrey would be on the way to his Portuguese holdings.

To sneak in as they had at Rutheville would invite being bushwhacked, perhaps shot as trespassers. Aubrey had suggested they fly quickly to Portugal, survey the place as best they could in a rented car or taxi in broad daylight, question workers if possible, and then drive up and talk with the resident manager. If Bridsey were there, Bethany would baldly and implausibly lie and say she had come because the von Mohrwalds were at last ready to talk business.

Her language and Aubrey's skills, they hoped, might elicit something about the vines. If they failed at the vineyard, then they could try in the neighboring village, Armanda. The Douro area had been hit by phylloxera a hundred years ago. The vine growers had at first thought the plague was from excessively hot, dry summers. They had delayed import of the American vines. As a result, the pest had been even more disastrous than in France. To this day, anything touching on phylloxera or American vine stocks would be the subject of intense speculation and gossip.

Neither she nor Aubrey was satisfied with this scattershot plan. She was doubly uncomfortable about the pistol he had in a holster inside the waistband of his wash-and-wear seersucker suit. She knew Aubrey would not have risked smuggling the ugly little thing in his luggage if there were not real danger.

"I hate this being lost," Bethany said.

"Not knowing what the hell they're up to, aimlessly following these goddamn vines, hoping for a break," he picked up morosely. "When you look at it, we sure don't know much."

"Well, we know a cartel has bought a great many vineyards, a lot of wine stocks, invested in other wine enterprises. We know it expects to make an enormous amount of money, and without any competition from the Californians, the Americans. We know their success depends somehow on these American vines we're chasing and on some kind of research into phylloxera." These were things they both knew, but recited to each other cabalistically as though it might produce some unambiguous answer.

"That they're only interested in table wines and are going to squeeze every gallon they can out of every acre they've got." He brooded for a few moments and added dismally, "That they are willing to kill people and that we're running out of time to put the puzzle together."

When the train reached Pinhão in the port country, Bethany and Aubrey got out. They cautiously studied the other passengers who had dismounted. No one looked suspicious.

In the station yard stood a tiled fountain. In its bowl was a metal model of the Douro sailboats that carried port to Oporto. The fountain was waterless. The flowers around it were cooked dry.

Aubrey found them a taxi and Bethany negotiated a respectable price for the day's travel. The back of Bethany's blouse was wringing wet by the time the old Opel had covered the thirty-two uneven miles to Armanda. The small village, with its circular town center, the brown grass, and once again, the baked-out flowers, seemed almost deserted in the dry heat.

Even the few men under the faded chartreuse canopy of the café seemed more part of the architecture than of humanity. The taxi driver, a heavy, wheezing man in his mid-thirties, unloaded himself from the driver's seat and inquired inside the café for directions to the vineyard.

Two miles up a dirt road between scabby, eroded banks, the vineyard's fields opened up, well-kept but parched. Bethany had the driver slow in order for her to study the vines, get the feel of them so she would note any departure from the ordinary.

At the driveway into a cluster of buildings, a sign said De Dona Armanda, the name of the vinelands, but Bethany had the hacker drive on until she saw a rough work road leading in. The driver, when she told him to take it, was disbelieving. He looked at the two tire ruts, no better than a fire road. Not until she asked him firmly a second time would he nose the Opel across a shallow ditch and into the vineyard.

The port vines sloped upward on the left, downward on the right. Each sat in its own slate-filled ditch where precious rainwater could collect.

Deep inside the vineyard two workmen stared in wonder at the old taxi. Bethany and Aubrey bailed out and she asked them in her best and slowest Spanish if there were any American vine stocks at De Dona Armanda.

"Why yes, *senhora*," said the oldest of the two, smiling gummily. He wanted to be helpful. Excitedly, she asked them where they were. With a dignified sweep of his arm, he indicated that the

American vine stocks were all around them. "Our great-great-grandfathers put them in here at the time of the lice," said the old man.

Bethany's heart fell. Weren't there any new American vines?

"Why no, *senhora*," he said with patient courtliness, "why would we need to put in more American vines? We have the finest now of any *quinta* along the Douro."

The two tracks came out at last on the original packed earth road that had brought them from the village. They followed it to the barred gates of De Dona Armanda. The taxi driver looked back inquisitively and Bethany said that he should open the gates and take them up the graveled driveway. It led to a two-story building whose front porch was shaded by olive trees. In front was an old Jeep.

As they moved toward the building, they saw further up the hill a mansion in the grand eighteenth-century style. Both of them peered from their windows hoping to see some plot where the vine roots had been replanted. There was nothing.

"Uh-oh," Aubrey said. Ahead, two Portuguese workers, from the looks of them, had come from inside and were on the porch, both of them so stern-faced that Bethany and Aubrey could discern their expressions even at this distance.

Aubrey touched his pants over the holster. Bethany shivered. His involuntary action made her aware of how seriously he assessed the situation. She screwed up her courage. This was not her métier, but she was damned if she would let Aubrey, or anyone, know how frightened she was.

The taxi driver handed Bethany out of the back

door and got back into his seat while Bethany and
Aubrey walked toward the two men. As they approached the veranda, a third figure came from
within. It was William Bridsey, as much the retired
guardsman now in his synthetic linens as he had
been in worsteds at Schloss von Mohrwald.

"Welcome, baroness, to De Dona Armanda,"
he said with a bow when they stepped onto the
porch. Turning to Aubrey, but not extending his
hand he said, "You must be Mr. Warder, making
us a visit this time by the front door." There was
no humor in it, only cool anger and a hint of contempt.

Aubrey and Bethany were too taken aback for
a moment to speak. They had thought it possible
that Bridsey might intercept them here, but the fact
of it still startled them.

"I thought we might have something to talk
about, a continuation of our talk at the Schloss,"
Bethany said, unusually gauche as she tried to put
into effect their contingency plan.

Bridsey seemed almost ready for her words.

"I would have been happier to take up that
matter some weeks ago," he said. "And in Austria
over your lovely wines rather than here where my
port is most unready, baroness."

She started to rephrase her request, but he went
on, "Still, talk can only be helpful." She moved
toward the door, anticipating Bridsey, but he did
not budge. "While we talk, baroness," he said,
"perhaps Mr. Warder would like to wait here on
the porch?"

Bethany looked at her companion.

"We are staying together," said Aubrey.

"Come, come, Mr. Warder," replied Bridsey. "I am not putting myself at your disposal. You are an unwelcome guest and I am trying to be obliging nevertheless."

Although Bridsey stood unwaveringly stolid in the doorway, Aubrey tried again.

"It may be the baroness will need my counsel," he said.

Bridsey gave a dismissing snort through his nose.

"I do not think you are a party to our negotiations for the Schloss." He turned to Bethany, "If he insists on being present, baroness, I am afraid neither I nor my partners would want to speak with you. It would be better in that case if you went back the way you came."

Bethany thought fast. Something threatening was in the air. But what? She and Aubrey could go back to the village and see what they could discover. But wasn't that her cowardice speaking? Shouldn't she spar with Bridsey? What harm could come of it? She felt herself smarter than this pompous smart *Engländer*. Maybe she could squeeze a fact or two out of him which would fit into the growing mosaic of their case. Bridsey would not dare do anything to her and to Aubrey. The taxi driver was expected back in town with two foreigners. Franz knew where they were. There would be no logic to hurting them, no excuse.

Bethany glanced again at Aubrey. He met her eyes and tilted his head slightly in a "why not?" gesture. If, on her own, she wanted to abort this meeting with Bridsey, this was her last moment.

"We will be done shortly, Mr. Warder," said Bethany.

Bridsey seemed relieved. He bent rather than bowed and held the door for her. The two Portuguese men on the porch, one blondish, one dark, both menacing in their impassiveness, followed Bethany and Bridsey into the building.

Twenty-five

THE GARBAGE GULCH

Aubrey sat on the edge of the unpainted porch. The sun was hazy but scalding. The taxi driver, at the invitation of one of the Portuguese vineyard workers, had pulled his cab to the shady side of the house. Now he would be dozing or drinking wine or beer inside with his new acquaintances.

Aubrey's suit coat which he could not take off lest it reveal the bulge of the gun was sweated from armpit to waist. He wiped his face with the sleeve and peered hopelessly across the fields. If the American vine stocks were there, he was certain he and Bethany would never know it.

After fifteen minutes he was half-dazed by the heat. He felt dirty and even more discouraged, ready at this moment to be done not just with this long-shot trip but the whole case.

Aubrey was stirred from his enervation by the sound of the door behind him opening. He touched his pants again over the pistol. But it was only the

thuggish blond worker carrying a case of empty
bottles. The man stooped to put them down outside the door. Aubrey gave him a disgusted look
and turned his gaze back to the cooking fields.

A board creaked and as Aubrey pivoted on his
seat, he felt the worker's foot in the center of his
back and was shoved sprawling into the gritty dirt
of the front yard.

Aubrey righted himself and turned to curse the
man. But in a flash, the assailant's hand dropped
to his overalls pocket, and his excited blue eyes
fixed on Aubrey. His fist snapped out of the pocket
with a long-nosed foreign automatic.

Aubrey blinked with astonishment, trying to
get his thoughts together. But all he could do was
curse himself for his stupidity. He had let himself
be bushwhacked in the very place he should have
been most careful. As a result, both his and Bethany's lives were instantly at hazard.

With a gesture of the automatic, the man ordered Aubrey to the Jeep. Aubrey's thoughts fas-
tened on his own pistol. He knew that if he could
not get to it, he was within a few minutes of being
dead.

Still using the automatic as a pointer, the man
signaled Aubrey to the passenger side of the Jeep.
There, the gunman warily came up behind Aubrey.
With a quick, precise motion, he pulled the back
of Aubrey's suit coat from his shoulders and onto
the top of his arms, pinioning him in the old-time
police style.

With a poke in the back, the man directed Aubrey into the Jeep's passenger seat. Swift as a wol-

verine, he circled the Jeep and started the vehicle. Gun and wheel both in his left hand, he shifted into low, took the wheel with his right hand, and drove out the gate. From the main roadway he turned into a field road, his right hand dropped long enough to shift into second, and they roared off between the vines.

The lesser roads of De Dona Armanda made the earlier ones look like interstates. They alternated between rock-hard dried mud, steep miniatures of the Sierra Madre, and slippery stretches of unevenly broken slate. The kind of land that made good port did not permit good dirt roads.

The driver silently and venomously swung them into the raw ruts, all but sending Aubrey out of the Jeep. They jounced again through the green, dusty rows of vines, stands, and wires.

They turned into a byway so narrow that the fibery leaves brushed Aubrey's face; it wound through the enfolding plants in a maze, sometimes straight for two hundred yards, then with a series of right-hand turns, one of which was so abrupt the gunman had to back up and turn to negotiate, never for a moment taking the gun off his passenger. Then, still without a word, he accelerated, and they sped westward.

All of a sudden they broke from the vineyard and onto a reasonably level dirt road. It ran along the brink of a gulch that plunged down to where some tributary of the Douro must have run centuries ago.

From the precipice's almost vertical sides, sharp slate outcroppings gave it the look of stegosaurs' spines. At the bottom two hundred feet below were dwarfed shrubs, stones, branches of failed trees blown in over the decades.

Aubrey braced a knee against the dash of the Jeep as it ripped along the cliff side. Only when, unaccountably, the Jeep slowed did he relax, looking up the road to see what had impeded the driver's breakneck speed.

As he did, the Jeep braked to a stop, hurling Aubrey forward. He avoided hitting the Jeep windshield face-on only by taking the impact on his right shoulder. The motor died and the driver jammed the gear shift into first to keep the Jeep from rolling backward on the incline where they had stopped.

The driver turned and smiled almost amiably. Before his first words, Aubrey sensed he was American, the American whose shadow had cast itself across the entire case.

"I am sorry to have to restrict the freedom of the press, Mr. Pulitzer Prize Winner," said Pierce Tobb mockingly. "Get out, and slowly."

While Aubrey's body responded sluggishly, still shocked from the drive, his mind pumped. This was the man d'Edouard said had picked up the vines at Ambourg-Repose. He was the gunman, to judge by the California look of his tan face, who had killed Wheatley-Smith. He may also have killed Maier.

And, thought Aubrey, he is going to kill me.

"You have a knife," said Tobb. "The baroness seems to equip all her detectives with knives." He dismounted and came around to Aubrey's side of the Jeep. Jerking Aubrey's coat back up to his shoulders, he said, "Take it slowly from your pocket and toss it seven or eight feet away, please, where I can pick it up."

Aubrey obliged, thinking desperately of the revolver and how he might get at it and fire before Tobb shot first.

"Take off your clothes."

Aubrey felt the dark wings of panic in his chest.

Tobb's face took on a malevolent look, then wrinkled in amusement as if he had just thought of a very good joke.

"You were going to take care of the masculinity of our French friend in Washington, no? Let us see how brave you are now in such matters, *Senhor* Reporter."

Aubrey had felt when he made that threat in Washington that it was shameful, that there would be some discomforting psychological payoff down the road somewhere. Now it had come, and not just psychologically.

"I would not have . . . ," he said, his voice breaking.

"*You* did not have the guts to," said Tobb. He picked up the knife and snapped it open with one hand, keeping the automatic pointed at the still-clothed Aubrey. "*I* do."

Aubrey felt his bladder release. He was mortified by the wetness of his pants, unmanned by both this act and the terror that had caused it.

The Californian's face broke up in merriment. He began to laugh so hard that the gun shook in his hand. Aubrey tried to get control of himself and finally did. The urine reek, accentuated by the heat, angered him even as he quaked at what Tobb seemed to be planning.

"I never would have . . . ," Aubrey stammered again. Tobb was getting control of his laughter.

"No, no, my friend," he said companionably, as if he liked Aubrey for giving him the gift of such unaccustomed laughter, "I am not into that kind of business. I will make it nice and easy for you. Now take off the clothes. Drop them in a heap, right there."

The man is crazy, Aubrey thought. He may not mutilate me, but he is going to kill me. And conversationally, the way you might ask someone for a cigarette or what the weather is going to be like.

"Nothing about dying is nice and easy," he mustered, wanting to keep the talk going, at all costs. He bent over to untie his shoes, then put them together as if they were an orderly child's. "Do you mind if I leave on my socks?"

"I once heard you can spot a Princeton guy because he screws with his socks on," said Tobb. "You went to Princeton?"

"No," said Aubrey. "Hamilton."

"Never heard of it. Take off the socks."

"You?" asked Aubrey as he complied.

"UCLA. Two years."

"What'd you take?"

"Can the shit," said Tobb.

Aubrey took off his coat and held it in his hand, turning as if modestly to undo his belt. He lowered the pants and underpants at the same time, shielding the holster with the coat as he stepped out of them. He dropped shirt and T-shirt on the pile, concealing without encumbering the pistol.

"Touching modesty," said Tobb. "But turn around."

Years ago Aubrey had been jailed in a First Amendment contempt case and three inmates had threatened to rape him. It was not so much their roughness that had angered him, but the outrage of it all. His anger had saved him. He felt that same anger now, remembering this man's outburst of laughter.

"Okay, waggles," said Tobb. "That way."

Naked Aubrey followed the order and moved toward the cliff. He walked as slowly as he dared across the sharp edges of chipped slate.

"Keep going," said Tobb. "I mean you can look down at where you're going. But don't jump yet." He laughed again, though not as enthusiastically.

Aubrey felt a run of prickles up his left arm. The last time he had felt them was in the city room when he was working on the story that had gotten him the Pulitzer. When the hard pains had begun in his left arm, he had known it was time to get the desk to call the ambulance. He waited for that pain now, thinking how ironic it would be if he saved this man the trouble of killing him by dying of a heart attack. But this time no pains came.

The sweat ran down Aubrey's skin. It was utterly quiet in the sunlight. Behind him were the road and then the acres of grapes. Above him was the hazy blue sky. And below now, almost vertically, was the side of the gulch with its eroded, slate-bladed side.

Two hundred feet down he could see why Tobb had brought him here. It was a huge garbage dump: cardboard boxes, old bags of trash spilled over each other, tires, a rusted automobile body, rotten fencing, pieces of broken vine props, the off-white gleam of some ancient appliance. Here at the edge, only a few feet away from him, was a giant pile of accumulated cut brush and household trash left by those too slovenly, too lazy to shovel or throw it in. This, he knew, would be his shroud after he fell.

"A newspaperman is something you wrap your trash in," said Tobb self-appreciatively with a chuckle.

Aubrey no longer listened. I am going to make him shoot me, he was thinking. He wants me simply to jump or let myself be pushed. That would make it too easy for them. They will tell Bethany a hokey story about me taking the Jeep to look at the fields, assuming they do not kill her too. How can she prove they are wrong? My body, naked as it is, will be bones in a day courtesy of rats and vultures, scattered and unnoticeable in the trash. Even if some peasant spots them eventually, there will be no clothes to identify their nationality. Only a bullet, stuck by a fluke into a bone, could stir up anything.

But am I simply going to give up, Aubrey thought, force myself to be shot? Am I just passively going to join the miscellany of trash down there?

"Shit, no," he said quietly.

"What's that? What did you say?" asked Tobb, wanting to hear it all, savoring the possibility of a brief conversation with a man he was about to murder, as he had enjoyed his last few words with Wheatley-Smith.

"I was going to say that since you're so full of

little jokes and gestures, maybe you'd like to grant the prisoner his last request."

"A cigarette and blindfold?" asked Tobb.

"No blindfold. Just a cigarette."

Tobb thought a moment. Why not? There was a piquancy in seeing this guy, a classy guy in spite of his pissing himself, going over the brink after a drag.

"Sure," said Tobb, finding new matter for humor. "But don't smoke it down so far that it endangers your health."

"Funny as hell," said Aubrey, his heart pumping, his arm tingling like crazy. But he paid no attention to the symptoms. Let 'em come, he thought. "You got one?"

"Nope, don't smoke."

"I got them in my pants," said Aubrey. He lowered his arms, just enough to let the blood run back into them, then raised them again. Without asking permission, he walked back toward his clothes, making a big thing of his feet hurting to distract any serious thinking by his captor.

Tobb moved carefully with Aubrey, ten feet away, the pistol pointing at his naked prisoner. Aubrey knelt by the clothes, keeping one hand up and his eyes on Tobb as if he did not trust him not to shoot.

"Don't worry," said Tobb agreeably. "You don't think I want to have to *drag* you back there. Get your goddamned cigarettes."

Aubrey dropped the other hand as if complying with the gunman's concession and fished in the coat pocket.

Aubrey knew there was nothing in the pocket but a box of extra .22 shorts. He moved his fingers over the pants to where the little revolver rested, trigger guard outside the holster.

"I can't find . . . ," said Aubrey, looking up in alarm. "Maybe they bounced out under the Jeep seat." He crouched, the better to fire from. "Could I take a look without you shooting that thing?" As he spoke loudly, he clicked his safety, and pointed his other hand at the Jeep.

Tobb's eye momentarily followed Aubrey's arm and in that instant Aubrey fired and hurled himself sideways from the crouch. No expert, Aubrey missed, even at this close range. Tobb's larger pistol went off, but the surprise had thrown off his aim.

Aubrey fired again, swinging holster, pistol, pants, everything at Tobb just as Tobb brought his gun back down to fire. In the momentary confusion, Aubrey scrambled like an animal across the slaty ground and put his shoulder as hard as he could into Tobb's shins, a torpedo tackle.

Younger and more muscular than Aubrey for all his pot, Tobb tried to brace a leg backward to keep from toppling, but the surprise was too much. He stumbled, then crumpled sideways.

Intent on only a single thing, Aubrey grabbed at the gun, butting into the Californian's sweaty shirt as his hands missed the gun but closed on Tobb's wrist. The pistol blammed again and Tobb swung around with his powerful left arm to thrust off Aubrey's grip.

Aubrey grasped the pistol barrel. It scorched his hand as he wrenched it outward. But Tobb's wrist was too strong for Aubrey to twist the gun away. And the hot metal forced him to let go. Tobb, at close quarters, could not point the gun at Aubrey, but swiped meanly with it at Aubrey's head and caught him an oblique blow that pitched Aubrey onto his back.

With little distance between them, Tobb fired. The slug plowed up a geyser of grit beside Aubrey's right eye. But before Tobb could bring the gun around to mush Aubrey's brains at point-blank range, Aubrey kicked Tobb full in his unprotected nose.

The barefoot blow stunned the Californian for a second, long enough for Aubrey to come up and grasp the pistol. With one hand on the gun, the other on his wrist for leverage, Aubrey rolled hard and brought Tobb's crouching body over and then under his own.

With a smart snap, Aubrey bashed the gun hand on the ground as Tobb sought to buck him off. Again, Aubrey slammed the gun hand on the hard earth, shouting in pain as his own knuckles took some of the impact. Tobb's fingers loosened for an instant and Aubrey twisted the gun's hot muzzle, wrenched it away. Tobb heaved him off at the same instant.

A more competent streetfighter than Aubrey might have tried to get his own fingers into the trigger guard of the heavy automatic. But Aubrey feared that the younger, stronger Tobb might again take custody of the pistol.

As Tobb clutched vainly at Aubrey's forearm, Aubrey swept his arm upward and outward, hurling the automatic in a high arc toward the ravine.

Tobb saw it in the air, scrambled up and with a heavy but inefficient kick at Aubrey's crotch, loped toward the cliff where Aubrey's heave had fallen short. The gun lay darkly in the dirt at the cliff's edge.

Aubrey grabbed up his coat and the damp trousers, feeling the reassuring bump of the little pistol in the holster, and ran for the Jeep. Frantic as he was, he was also exultant. Minutes ago he had been a dead man, his only hope that he could lure an evidentiary bullet from his adversary. Now he was alive with a chance of escape and unless reinforcements came for the gunman assured at worst a stalemate.

When he sprawled down in the dirt behind a tire of the Jeep and looked at the cliff edge forty feet away, he saw no sign of Tobb. The gunman had doubtlessly scooped up the pistol and was behind the mound of trash, hoping Aubrey would show enough of himself for a shot from the accurate long-barreled automatic.

Eyes fixed on the trash mound, Aubrey felt in the coat, withdrew two bullets from the box and fully loaded the revolver. For five, ten minutes, he lay cooking red on the rough earth. There was still no sound, no breeze whatsoever. High up, a hawk or vulture wheeled over the dry land. Even the insects seemed seared away by the merciless sun.

Aubrey's head hurt from Tobb's blow, his feet from the slate, his fingers from the hot muzzle, his knees and elbows from strawberries. As if that weren't enough, he was beginning to worry about Bethany. He did not think they would harm her. But it was not impossible. And if that was their intent, he must make an effort to return to her if he was to live with his conscience.

"Save my conscience, lose my goddamned life," he grumbled to himself as he wormed into the seersucker trousers and put on the coat to bar the sun from his back. The drying stain on the pants made him grunt with joyless humor. If he had not wet himself, Tobb never would have been stirred to his scornful joviality, would not have felt over-confident, and Aubrey might now be dead. Now, alive, he had to figure out a way to escape.

There was no real chance for him if he took to the fields. Abandoning the Jeep made no more sense than abandoning an overturned boat at sea. In the fields dogs and men with guns could do the job they failed to do on him at Ambourg-Repose. And he could not creep down the road without exposing himself to the gunman.

Aubrey cocked his head up to steering-wheel level for an instant. Tobb had left the key in the ignition. Aubrey snakebellied along the Jeep and peered out. The murderer was nowhere to be seen. Aubrey rose slightly from the dirt and reached into the Jeep. His hand just touched the gearshift.

At that moment Aubrey saw Tobb's dirty blond head pop from behind the mound. He dropped down again beside the Jeep wheel, and waited a few minutes. Tobb, Aubrey knew, would need a moment to aim. Again he crept to where he could reach the stick shift and gave it a gentle nudge. He would be able to get enough purchase on it to shift gears.

Again Tobb's head popped up like a cautious pika's, and down behind the mound. Aubrey positioned himself alongside the Jeep, left hand on the gearshift, right, with the pistol in it, along the hood.

With a sharp pull, he levered the stick out of gear and into neutral. Now, gun arm still along the hood he rocked the Jeep. It moved slightly, but the wheels were cocked. Aubrey cautiously turned the steering wheel to straighten them out so the Jeep would coast. Another heave and it began to roll slowly rearward. Tobb's head came up at the sound of the wheels on the dry earth and he fired. Aubrey squeezed off an unaimed shot to force Tobb back into cover.

The Jeep rolled ten yards with Aubrey moving beside it in a duck walk. Then it began to accelerate and Aubrey pressed forward on it as the gunman fired again. This time the slug crunched through the hood. Another shot slammed through the windshield.

Despite Aubrey's body pressure, the Jeep was moving faster. If it swung leftward sharply it would pitch into the gulch. A fourth shot tore the seat. Aubrey, low and jogging beside the Jeep, a hand on the wheel from outside, fired back wildly, hoping to buy an instant. The Jeep was barely under control.

He did not dare fire off the cylinder for fear Tobb would be counting and after six reports would take a chance that Aubrey's gun was a revolver and rush him.

The vehicle was moving too close for Aubrey to steer it from its side. The wheels jerked in the hard ruts and threw him off balance. It lurched into him, broke free. Aubrey went down to one knee. For a full second or two he was exposed to his enemy. Tobb fired. The slug caught Aubrey's coattail and he cursed with fright.

As Tobb fired again, Aubrey ran to the Jeep, vaulted over its low side and into the bullet-ripped seat. Bending so low he could hardly see out, he flicked on the ignition. He was too absorbed for the moment to worry about protecting himself with the gun he still held in his hand. He rammed down on the clutch. With a great grinding, he got the gears into reverse.

When he let out the clutch, the Jeep bucked, the motor coughed. But it did not catch. Before the Jeep could slow Aubrey jammed in the clutch again, let it gain a little speed as two more shots missed, and released the pedal. The engine coughed and started, and Aubrey eased out the clutch and guided the Jeep rearward under power.

As it careened to the rear, Tobb rushed from behind the mound. Jesus, Aubrey thought, ducking down, isn't that goddamned thing ever going to run out of bullets? But there was no shot. Aubrey bobbed up. Tobb was in the road, aiming with both hands.

Aubrey threw down his head as the shot went off. The Jeep, its driver without sight of the road, took evasive action independently, whipping off the road toward the edge of the gulch before Aubrey looked up and maniacally steered away from the drop. The Jeep tore across the road toward the vines, giving Tobb another broadside shot at it. The bullet tore into the side of the vehicle but missed Aubrey.

For fifty yards he hugged the vines, out of sight

of the man with the gun. Then he whipped the Jeep back onto the road and pushed it as fast as he dared until he hit a spot in the road that had been widened rightward to accommodate dropped-off hoes, rakes, wire, and whatnot. Careful to avoid a bundle of worn poles lying under the vines, Aubrey backed in, turned the Jeep around, and roared off.

Even though the rear mirror showed nothing behind, Aubrey neurotically imagined Tobb in the road, aiming the long-barreled pistol. It was so vivid that he could almost feel the burn between his shoulder blades, the black oblivion as he died from Tobb's bullet.

Twenty-six

THE DAGGER

Robert St. Gage had not been sure when he left London for Lisbon and Armanda whether it would be wise to make the acquaintance of the Baroness Bethany von Mohrwald, assuming she showed up. On balance, he thought that it was not a good idea. But she had been on his mind and he prepared for the possibility.

Meeting the American, Aubrey Warder, posed no such question. Tobb would make any meeting permanently unnecessary.

Now, at De Dona Armanda, in the one air-conditioned room of the large, otherwise sweltering casa a hundred yards up the road from the vineyard's other buildings, he lay in bed and read Mirabella Tjarna's essay "On Humiliation." Too prissy for hardcore pornography, St. Gage got the same effect from scholarly works into which he could interpolate himself and other real human beings.

From time to time he dozed, then awoke refreshed, read on, dozed, and awoke again. He was in one of these brief catnaps when there was a loud knock on the door. He rolled from the bed, alarmed and not sure for a moment where he was. It was one of the workers, passing word from Bridsey that the baroness and Warder had arrived and that Warder was in Tobb's hands while the baroness was in the vineyard office with Bridsey.

St. Gage washed his face, sleeked his hair, and quickly dressed in a dove-colored suit of cotton and orlon. Given the rural setting, he allowed himself a batiste sport shirt, open at the neck. In the mirror he saw a thirty-eight-year-old man, youthful, vigorous, with a trace of dash, as he preferred to think of it, in his eyes.

As he admired his reflection, he made up his mind to meet the baroness. The last section of the Tjarna essay had given him a dizzy, welcome but, it must be said, a self-endangering feeling about the possibilities.

' More rationally, the death of Maier had made his covert role in the wine conspiracy less maintainable. He had personally done the negotiations with the French bankers, revised the contracts. And already, although he had appeared supposedly only as a solicitor, he had met with financiers in London, Antwerp, Zurich, and Stockholm, not to mention some sewer dwellers in Liechtenstein. Besides—and the thought made him quaver momentarily with excitement—he would be ordering the climax of the enterprise in only two days. So why not make himself known to Bethany von Mohrwald?

There was even a practical reason for it. When

Warder did not return, he could present the "Portuguese worker's tale" of Warder taking off across the fields with more plausibility than Bridsey. She would not believe it, of course, but he could use it subtly to point up to her the dangers of further resistance to the cartel. If that was all that came of their meeting, it would still be worthwhile. But, he thought with another anticipatory shiver, this one of an entirely different nature from the first, perhaps that would not be all.

When St. Gage entered the vineyard office in the lower building, he found the baroness and Bridsey talking politely. The British wine magnate introduced St. Gage as his lawyer. St. Gage took Bethany's hand, made the gesture of bowing toward it without completing the kiss, and waited for her to signal him to be seated.

"I have heard of your courage, baroness," said St. Gage, "although I might reserve judgment as to the wisdom of it." He smiled and went on, "I would not want you to think me, or Mr. Bridsey, so naive as to believe that your visit to us is entirely to discuss possible sale of your splendid vineyards. After all, we would have been glad to visit Schloss von Mohrwald for that."

Mild as a well-trained Doberman, St. Gage waited for an answer. Bethany wished Aubrey or Franz were there. While she might be a match for Bridsey, the newcomer unsettled her.

"We need have no pretenses, Mr. St. Gage," she said. "There is a great deal known among the three of us here, as well as a great deal unknown. But let us deal first with the question of our acreage.

It may be that you will prevail where Mr. Bridsey, with the best efforts in the world, was unable to."

Bethany stopped, rather pleased with herself.

"Well, let me say then, baroness," he purred with a bit more acid than he intended, "that you and your husband have held out against the most generous offers that my clients have made any vineyard owner in Europe. You have hired this American snooper to trespass on Mr. Bridsey's properties in France. You do not, I suppose, wish to argue the point?"

"Go on," said Bethany, trying to keep any nervousness from her tone, hoping to get some useful information if not from the literal meaning of St. Gage's words, then from their order and their tone.

"In Washington, I should add, this detective threatened to kill a French citizen, one of Mr. Bridsey's partners," St. Gage said coldly.

Aubrey had not gone into any detail about why d'Edouard had been so talkative about Portugal and the cartel's interest in the Château Rossant and why the Frenchman had given up possession of the vial. She was curious and St. Gage acutely picked up on it.

"To be blunt, baroness, this Warder drew a knife and threatened to mutilate Monsieur Olivier d'Edouard, with whose vineyard you may have some familiarity."

"To mutilate him?"

"To emasculate him, baroness, if I may be explicit, as well as to cut his throat. It was by these means that you have come to believe that the American vines you seek are in Portugal."

Bethany was genuinely shocked. She was all too aware of the mad streak in Aubrey, but she did not think that he would have gone as far as St. Gage said.

"I don't believe you," she said. "It would be more in the style of your own group, Mr. St. Gage." But she realized that feistiness would dry up any chance of getting information from him or Bridsey. "I will discuss it with Mr. Warder," she said, still with more anger at her interlocutors than she intended.

"Please do," replied St. Gage haughtily.

Bethany felt her ire flame up again.

"I do not wish to be argumentative, but one of my earlier employees died in California under most mysterious circumstances. There is also a French wine merchant associated with this matter who is dead. You will grant me, I am sure, the difference between an empty threat even if it were made as you say and one that is carried out."

"I can tell nothing about that, baroness," said the lawyer.

In his seeming denial, didn't she sense something purposeful? Wasn't he saying, yes, I do know of the death of Wheatley-Smith and of the death of Auguste Maier and of the potential for more violence if you do not yield?

"I would like to believe that you know nothing about Inspector Wheatley-Smith's death," she said more primly than she had meant to. "I think if that and a number of other things could be cleared up, then my husband and I would be more amenable to further conversations."

"Baroness, you are spending money at present instead of making it," counseled Bridsey. "Reconsider. Do be practical."

"What other things?" asked St. Gage of Bethany, ignoring his supposed client.

"There is first and foremost just what is going on," she said. "Why are you paying these prices, Mr. St. Gage? Even with the market rising, and that may be because of your purchases, your offers have been extremely high."

St. Gage nodded, encouraging her to go on.

"There is the shipment of the Domaine McIntyre vines to Mr. Bridsey shortly before the death of Inspector Wheatley-Smith. There is the disappearance of the vine stocks from Ambourg-Repose. There is Monsieur Maier's death."

"You have been a very busy lady," said St. Gage smoothly. He liked her spirit. In this room, cooled only by a slight cross breeze through open windows, the sweat had formed above her upper lip and at her temples, darkening the strands of honey-colored hair. In the dimness of the office, she looked young, healthy, strong.

Suddenly he felt a powerful almost intoxicating rush of emotion. It was a familiar feeling. When he had channeled it into his matings with his cousin, Lady Montfalcon, and the others, it had led to such satisfying pleasures. Now, in this room, was the woman who had been the subject of his imaginings when he left Berkady's that day, of his thoughts only the other night. But his feelings then had been only the baby brother to this impulse.

St. Gage was shaken. Usually so controlled, even when presented with these drives, he sensed that this one did not want to let him go. He could feel his ability to say yea or nay slipping its hawsers. He relished the slightly sickening feeling of easing up his grip on his emotions, his actions. There was an element of surrender in it, of what the French called *je m'en foutisme*.

Bethany had seen something happen to the man. He had fixed her with his eyes, had been sparring with her. It was almost as if a part of him, his attention really, had taken leave of him and left her talking to a shell, a being no more St. Gage than the cicada skin, once shed by the insect, is a cicada.

St. Gage, with considerable effort, shook himself free of the spell, or at least won a hiatus from it. Bethany was talking.

", . . and if you could clear up some of these happenings then we would talk seriously."

St. Gage was thoroughly back in the room.

"We can, we shall," he said. "As a first earnest for our good faith, let me assure you, most honestly, that the vines are not here."

"Then where are they?"

"I am simply the attorney for Mr. Bridsey. I cannot meddle in the business of his vine stocks. Indeed, for him a scion is a grape twig, for me a legatee. Our professions are better kept separate."

He smiled, eyes clearly telling her he liked her. She was not unflattered by this turn, this sudden attraction. He was handsome, but it was a serpentine kind of grace, like a poisonous snake that one might admire, might even find beautiful so long as it were in a case behind thick glass.

"And the other matters . . ."

"Mr. Bridsey will be discharging me for garrulousness if I yield to your supplications, baroness." My God, she thought, he is flirting with me. At a time like this. She wished Aubrey would come back. There was something odd, unhealthy and yet not unalluring going on here.

"So you choose not to clear up any of the mysteries?"

St. Gage took an unaccustomed deep breath.

"On the contrary, baroness, I *am* willing to clear up mysteries. You have asked about the buying of land. That is a legitimate question. It gets down to why you should join in selling us land. I will answer it."

She did not believe him. Beneath his suaveness the words came out just a little too fast, and with a hint of nervousness. She waited for him to go on. Taking another breath, he did.

"My charts are at the manor house. The casa. I had not intended to be so obliging. But if Mr. Bridsey . . ." He fixed Bridsey with a glittering eye. The look made Bethany squirm.

"I leave tactics to you, Mr. St. Gage," said Bridsey, himself seeming uneasy. "Shall we wait for you . . ."

"No, I tell you," he said to Bethany, and now his tone seemed even tenser. "The manse has air conditioning. I find I swelter here and you, too, perhaps. The papers are cumbersome and while I could send someone . . ." He gave her a forced smile. ". . . well, come along with me and I will lay it out. I'll just be a short time, Mr. Bridsey, or rather, we . . ."

His urbanity had given over to something brit-

tle. Bethany did not like it. Bridsey stirred uncomfortably, obviously also in the presence of something
he did not entirely understand.

"Shan't I come along?" he asked St. Gage.

"Not necessary. Not necessary. If you like, you
can be digging up the material for us on Austria
and your efforts elsewhere. We shall be back
shortly."

Bethany began to feel roily in the pit of her
stomach. She had gotten little of value out of these
two although she did believe St. Gage when he
said the vines were not here. The heat oppressed
her; her clothes stuck to her skin; her hair was
going limp. St. Gage had promised her commercial
details, but he would only spar further. Still, the
momentum begun, she must run her string.

As they walked up the path, St. Gage made
small talk about the *vinhos verdes* table wines of
Portugal, affecting savoir-faire, a quality which but
a few minutes ago had seemed to come so naturally
in him.

Bethany's mind was swirling on a multitude of
other things. His attractiveness for her had dissi-
pated. She interrupted him, the rural bluntness of
her heritage bursting through the gentrification of
their talk.

"To be honest, Mr. St. Gage, I am more interested in the purchases of Mr. Bridsey and the *Witwe*
Pfeffermühle and the late Monsieur Maier than in
the astringency of the Daos."

"Quite so, baroness," he said. "And you shall
be satisfied in every respect. The heat is terrible in
Portugal," he said, trying to make the non sequitur
sound unremarkable.

She had stepped out a pace ahead of him on the double-track dirt road to the manor. He fell in behind her, saw the patch of moisture at her waist formed by the perspiration. He imagined the sweat running down her backbone. Beneath the flared skirt he detected the swing of her handsome buttocks.

"Hmmmm," he said involuntarily. He felt again the dizzying semi-ecstasy he had experienced before.

Bethany was surprised when they entered the comparative cool of the old stone casa to find the downstairs almost empty of furniture. St. Gage took her arm gently, a touch at which she flinched.

"We will go to the upstairs sitting room. Only there has my client seen fit to put an air conditioner. He is a frugal man." St. Gage was breathing hard. He hoped desperately that she would not notice it or would take it as the results of his exertion in the heat. His throat was as dry as the floor dust.

"I would rather . . . ," Bethany began. But his gentle grip on her arm enforced on her a strange passivity.

"Be careful you do not trip on these old stairs," he said. "They are, Mr. Bridsey tells me, made of Portuguese oak installed many years ago by English artisans." His voice had a soothing quality to it. "In that sense, Mr. Bridsey and I feel very much at home here . . ."

Keep babbling, St. Gage told himself with the scheming part of his mind. You are almost there.

If only she does not physically resist before we get to the room.

The diverse but complementary tides in his cerebrum set his pulses going far too fast. The pulse in his temple rapped against his skull as if it would break out in a sudden scream.

"I wish I could say the same," she said. "You may let go my arm, Mr. St. Gage. I am quite capable of walking up stairs by myself."

He let go immediately and she felt she had won a victory.

"The study is right here, just off the top of the stairs," said St. Gage, then went silent. His voice had cracked. He dare not risk more words. A control in him, advisory rather than injunctive, told him suddenly to stop, to consider what he was about to do. He paused, clouded by vertigo.

His inchoate urge again took command. You have taken certain chances to encounter her, it said. You have made preparations. They should not be in vain. It has been a long time since you did what you wanted to do with a woman, almost a year. Bethany von Mohrwald or her like will not come into your orbit soon again. She is noble, robust, spirited. Her body is young.

Bethany sensed a craziness in the air and turned at the top of the landing. But he blocked her. He took her arm, coercively now.

"My arm . . . ," she began, trying to pull away.

"You will slip on these ancient floors," he said, his voice sounding even to him high-pitched, nearly childish. He almost dragged her to the door, opened it with his left hand, and pushed her in. His throat had closed up in his anxiety. With an anomalous show of politeness, he motioned her to the easy chair, cushioned and covered with a bright print.

The sudden coolness of the room cut through her turmoil. She broke from him and grabbed the doorknob. But he caught her wrist and with the other hand shot the deadlock.

"What . . . ?" she demanded.

"A private talk," he managed.

She looked at his face. The eyes were impenetrable as if all the work of his mind were going on in some far recess which she could not reach, whose reflections did not even show in his eyes. Only his quick breaths indicated that she was dealing with someone who, at this point, was not going to worry about the future. She was in a bedroom far from any help with a man in the clutch of monomania.

If I could just get past, she thought as she stared at him. She considered for a moment the women's defenses that, even in Europe, were appearing in the magazines: the blow to the groin, the Adam's apple, the gouge at the eye. But he was wiry, well-conditioned. He would be too ready, too quick for her.

There was the window. But in the Northern Portuguese manner, it was barred with decorative framing of stone. Her heart beat so fast that she was giddy.

"What is it that you want?" she said at last, wishing it sounded firm, aware it did not.

St. Gage did not answer. He grabbed her wrist. His hand was so hot she was sure he was feverish.

He pulled her toward the room's closet. His face had become alive, vital, animated.

With a quick movement she bumped him so hard that he fell toward the bed. His arm hit a table and he let her go. She scrambled to the door, fumbled with the unfamiliar bolt. He snapped her arm away from the door. She swung on him left-handedly, caught him a good slap in the face.

He barked with anger and hooked back with his fist. It smacked into her cheek, knocking her to the floor. She had never been hit before, not by anyone. The blow shocked her. The pain and humiliation made her cry as she sprawled beside the bed.

"Get up, baroness," he ordered. His breath rasped from his mouth more excitedly than the exertion from the blow warranted. All the detachment that had beguiled her in the office was gone.

She sat stunned on the floor. None of this was possible. And yet there he was above her. Before she could even consider new action, he gripped her lower arm, pulled her to her feet and wrenched the arm behind her back with a grunt of satisfaction. She cried out.

He pushed her toward the closet again and swung open the door. To her horror she saw him snatch a scabbarded dagger, an ornate antique, from his suitcase.

"*Jessas Maria!*" she gasped. He was going to kill her!

He put the blade at the vee of flesh which her modest blouse left bare. His face was writhing with excitement, his eyes flat, hot, expressionless as if they were controlled by independent beings too deep inside him for her to even surmise their intentions.

"No," she said, her saliva making it sound more like a gurgle than a word. She cleared her throat. "I'll do what you say. Just say. Don't use that thing."

For an answer he lowered the knife and one by one with its razor-sharp edge snicked off the buttons of her blouse, the pretty smoky gray pearl buttons which had led her to buy it. She could smell his hard breath, a mix of breakfast sausage and garlic laced with an unrecognizable sourness.

"Arms out," he said, the words so much more portentous than what they commanded. She slipped her arms from the short sleeves. "Now the skirt." She unsnapped it in the rear, unzipped it, and let it drop to the floor. In the cool room, she shivered.

He lowered the knife to her stomach and she almost fainted, remembering what he had said of Aubrey's threat to d'Edouard. But it was to cut the waistband of her slip and her panties. He did the same with her bra. Paralyzed by the threat of the knife, she stood with the cloth still draped on her until, delicate as a milliner, he removed the severed garments and left her standing like a statue, naked and silent.

Without a word he backed her toward the bed, the stiletto touching the flesh just above her armpit.

She exhaled. He was not, at least at this moment, going to kill her. Her thoughts began to organize themselves. But what would a table lamp, a shoe be against his knife. She watched him undress himself, his eyes still on her.

Naked himself now, he returned the dagger to

the skin near her armpit and this time pressed the point until it pricked her.

"Oh my God," she said under her breath.

St. Gage was so aroused at the sight of the dagger dimpling her flesh that he could hardly avoid precipitancy. But, he thought, he must. He did not want all his preparations to be in vain. He tried to think of some unsexual scene, a sluggish, dirty river, say the Irrawaddy. It brought his ardor under control.

He blinked his eyes with relief and withdrew the knife. It had left a tiny drop of blood on her skin. It would be more exciting, he thought crazily, if he and the baroness could put on armor as he and his cousin had done all those years ago. But that was the stuff of lunacy in an adult, he knew.

He stared at her face. In its apprehension, it was plainer than it had seemed to him in the office. But nothing could be done about that. He touched the blood, looked at its diminutive smudge on his forefinger.

His hands trembled. He felt a disconcerting rush of passion again, paused, and again regained his self-control. He walked around her, Venetian stiletto in hand and regarded her. Lightly he touched the soft twin moons of her buttocks with the point. But he did not break the skin. She flinched and shuddered at the touches.

St. Gage wished he could do something with her hair—pull it back more severely.

"I want your hair back," he ordered. "Do you have hairpins?"

"In my pocketbook," she said, her voice barely audible.

He picked up the pocketbook from where it had been dropped and handed it to her, moving closer to her with the knife so he could be sure she didn't pull out a weapon and complicate things.

She dropped first one hairpin, then another.

"No stalling, baroness," he said, moving the dagger to her throat. It created a new problem with arousal. I must keep things in perspective, he thought. She pinned back her hair. It gave her the look of Marianne on old French stamps. "That will have to do," he said critically.

He moved up face-to-face, with the knife touching her between the shoulder blades so she could not pull away. He was proud of his body, considering it the heritage of the centuries, proud to have her feeling it against her. Again his passion strained. But this time there was no danger of precocity, he was sure.

Something totally rational in his mind reminded him that all this was somehow like something a long time ago, like a very little child showing off his risen part to a nursemaid, hoping she would admire it.

"If only you could enjoy this," he said to Bethany, almost pleading. "But that, of course, is unrealistic." It angered him that he should feel so defensive.

"I'm sorry for you," she murmured.

He wished her words were real sympathy, but they were not. They were as false as the words he encouraged the whores to say to him.

"You don't understand a damned thing about this," he said. "Do you?" Again he was irritated.

Why was he seeking some way of explaining himself? Why did it seem important?

"Of course," she said, then corrected herself. "Well, not entirely. Would you like to explain it to me?"

His face clouded and he backed away from her.

"I see what you are doing," he said, feeling tense, even dizzy. "It won't work." He came to her and put the dagger to her lying lips. Her mouth opened as if she were about to scream. None of that, he thought, touching the point to her upper lip. The scream died, aborted by a tightened throat. Her eyes were popped open in terror. He dropped the dagger to her nipples and touched them lightly, trying to stir them, but they remained soft, frightened.

"Please," she whispered. The sound of her voice redirected him.

He moved the baroness toward the bed again. Her heel bumped against one of the bed legs, making a creak, and he looked down. She was a little plump in the thighs, he thought, not exactly the muscular Valkyrie type, but then neither were the Valkyries he had seen on stage.

Now they faced each other. He contemplated her. So far, so good, he thought. But he saw her features suddenly disintegrate. The mouth turned into a round hole and a scream erupted from her lips. She's gone crazy, he thought, and it's going to spoil everything.

"Shut up, baroness," he ordered, bringing the knife to her left breast. Some dramatic gesture was necessary. He dropped the dagger on the bed. The sudden action surprised her, he could see.

She stopped screaming. He looked at her, her face still paralyzed in lines of horror. He surveyed her, her belly, slightly rounded, slightly marred by ancient lines of birthing scars, the dark, pronounced pubic hair, the thighs, the flesh seeming less inviting now.

This is what I want, he reassured himself. This is the woman I must have. His passion returned. His breath began to come faster. His face contorted as he felt almost a pain, a *pang* of old, splendid pride.

Even in his wildest imaginings about Bethany he had only planned to hold the knife in his hand as he made love to her. But now, alone with her and feeling secure, he conceived a dangerous and thrilling variation.

"Try to pick up the knife," he said. "Go ahead." He would risk the fray, give her a chance to win. With a formal—to him—gallant gesture, he pointed palm up, fingers all extended, to the dagger.

"Take it," he said between gasps of breath, his voice seeming thin through the roaring in his ears. He felt his loins harden. His eyes blazed with resolve. He stepped back another foot from the bed.

She did nothing for an instant. Then she showed her mettle. She snatched at the ancient hilt. He had left himself plenty of room to check her and lunged to put himself between her and the stiletto. But he stumbled.

Bethany jerked up the knife and crouched, even as he recovered. She moved toward him with peasant caution and he slowly retreated, eyes glittering. Midway to the wall, he swooped down and grabbed his pants, wrapping them quickly around his right arm. Still crouched, she crept forward.

At the door she stood only two feet from him. He felt her considering where to stab and held his wrapped arm forward, feinting slightly to left and right. Abruptly, she thrust toward his chest. He dodged, too agile for her. Her arm stabbed into nothing, throwing her off balance.

Quick as a mongoose he grabbed her wrist. She struggled to free it, but he held on, shaking his other hand from the trousers. She hissed in rage and fear. Rage and be damned, he thought.

St. Gage dragged her to the bed. He threw her onto it, still holding her wrist, the dagger still gripped in her hand. His nostrils drew in the cool conditioned air like a heaving warhorse. His ears hummed, not quite loudly enough to drown out a tiny, staticky but sane voice.

It said: this is crazy; you are ridiculous, just look at you. But in a moment he was back in thrall to his passion. His breath again came faster and faster. Yet, even as he dizzied with his special want, he saw the deadly blade of the dagger, the small maddened eyes of the naked woman as she tried to twist free her hand.

Circumspectly, he shifted his body to where he was astride her, holding her hand with the dagger in it tightly against the bed. Then he began to close his grip on her wrist to force her to unclasp her fingers from the hilt. He did not want to break any wrist bones. Harming her was not his desire.

The unrelenting compression popped what control Bethany had left. Temporarily more deranged than he, she bucked upward. Thrown off balance, St. Gage pitched forward; his genitals crushed against her shoulder and he howled in anguish.

Bethany ripped the dagger free. But she had not immobilized him. He flung himself across her in an effort to recapture her wrist. Cursing in outrage, he struck her shoulder. She was positive that he intended to kill her. Desperately she tried to get the knife into his vitals by lunging between the blows of this maniac's fists.

He hit her forearm a glancing punch, numbing it for the moment it took him to catch her wrist. The dagger dropped to the bed. He whipped it up and put it to her throat where a pulse throbbed from her struggles.

In his eyes there was anger and lust. A woman had almost thwarted him, cried the fury within him. A wiser voice urged as if in panic, Beware! Do nothing more than you planned. You'll destroy everything. Everything!

Carefully bracing his knees so no sudden motion by her could throw him off again, he remounted her. He increased the pressure of the point on the pulsing artery so precisely that each time her heart beat the point came a few micrometers closer to piercing the skin. He watched the point, waiting for it to draw blood, feeling in his loins forces that seemed to want to explode.

Twenty-seven

MAKING TRACKS

Aubrey knew that the little cluster of buildings of De Dona Armanda lay somewhere near. But to try to retrace his route through the maze of slaty, irregular tracks would mean delay. Instead, he counted on the cliff road eventually intersecting with something more substantial. As he hoped, he came to a graveled way which shortly opened upon the road to the vineyard entrance.

The Jeep, spry and well-kept for its age, roared healthily as he pushed it to its limit. His aim, his only aim, was to get Bethany and himself out of Portugal as fast as possible. To make a police report was to linger and thus invite murder. Unnerving as it was, he now recognized he was the target of an assassin.

At the entrance to De Dona Armanda he saw the taxi was gone from beside the lower building. He stopped for the few moments it took to reload the revolver, then crouched low and pulled up the driveway. There was going to be trouble. Bethany would not have voluntarily left in the taxi without him. Someone had ordered it away. And at this moment behind him the American would be puffing across the fields. The need for haste made Aubrey braver than he was.

He accelerated the Jeep up the drive, pulling it in to the porch so fast that it skidded in a quarter circle. He bounced out and up to the front door. Gun in hand, he pushed the door. It was locked. He moved to the window, pocketed the gun for a moment, and picked up a wooden bench. He rammed one end of it against the window, shattering panes and wood, then jammed it through, clearing out enough space to step over the sill.

As he did, a Portuguese worker ran into the room. The sudden dimness of the interior left Aubrey half-blind, but he saw the man's outline and rushed him with gun pointed. The man gasped and backed away but Aubrey put the gun against his cheekbone and grabbed him by his throat.

"Where's the baroness," he growled. The small worker gagged and stuttered, genuinely unable to understand. "The baroness," Aubrey shouted as if sheer volume would translate English into Portuguese. In answer, the man slumped to the floor in fear as if his body had turned to jelly within his clothes.

Aubrey barged over him and slammed full force at the doorway into Bridsey. Aubrey's superior momentum set back the husky Englishman, who retreated, bristling with outrage until he saw the little pistol.

Before Bridsey could recover his aplomb, Aubrey clutched his vest so hard that the man lurched forward. He poked the .22 revolver above the larger man's brushy mustache.

"Where is she?" Aubrey demanded. "Talk fast. If that gorilla you sicced on me shows up I'll blow your brains out, here and now."

Aubrey's own fright transmitted itself to Bridsey without an erg diminished.

"Not here," gulped the wine merchant. "I assure you, I . . ."

"You assure my ass!" barked Aubrey. The Portuguese had come to his elbows. "Down, you little shithead," he said, swiveling the gun toward him. The man got the message and flopped onto his back, his white eyes rolling.

Aubrey, still gripping Bridsey's vest, towed him back to the office. When he saw Bethany was not there, he gave the portly Englishman a shove that sent him sprawling into one of the leather chairs. Bridsey gamely tried to stand, but Aubrey rushed to him and this time actually put the muzzle into his nose.

"One more infinitesimal second of delay and this bullet goes nonstop into that stupid brain of yours, Limey. Where is she?"

Bridsey, in combat, had been a doughty man. But pluckier soldiers than he would have blanched at this half-dressed madman poking the muzzle of a pistol into his nose. His mouth tried to form words, but they came out only as a garble. At last in a weakened voice, he whispered, "At the big house . . ."

Aubrey, as much out of frustration as anger, caught hold of the rumpled vest and forced Bridsey up. With a grip on the collar and the gun in his back, he marched him through the hall where the worker still lay supine.

"Tell him not to call the cops," ordered Aubrey.

"I don't speak Portuguese," Bridsey said, at least a little of his huffiness returning with his courage.

"Then fucking learn quick," said Aubrey, putting the pistol to the back of Bridsey's perspiring neck.

"Non policía," Bridsey tried to oblige. The man looked at Aubrey in confusion. Clearly this was no police. What was the English boss saying?

"No teléfono policía," Aubrey snarled. "Try that." Bridsey repeated it. The man seemed to get it, but Aubrey forced Bridsey to say it again just to be sure.

"Sim Patrão," said the man, nodding from his back.

"Now, hairface, up the hill!" ordered Aubrey. As they walked up the two-track path, Aubrey, his bare feet smarting from the gravel, viciously jabbed Bridsey in the kidneys with the pistol. He cocked his head nervously over his shoulder every second or two, fearing someone would pot him from ambush.

"What's she doing up there?" Aubrey asked.

"I don't know."

"One more lie," Aubrey spat, his temper bubbling up. "Just one more and you are a dead motherfucker." He smacked Bridsey's jowl from behind him.

The man's head jerked but he said nothing.

"Talk!" Aubrey shouted at him, thrusting the pistol hard.

"My lawyer took her up there," said Bridsey.

"Hunh?"

"They're talking business."

Aubrey was dubious. But anything was possible.

"And the taxi?"

"I sent it home."

The manse was just ahead.

"Does this guy have a gun?"

"I don't know," said Bridsey.

Aubrey was all but out of breath. At the porch he paused, obsessed with fear that he might be shot at again, this time accurately. He moved in close behind the bulky Englishman.

"If your lawyer has got a gun you had better hope he loves you better than most lawyers love their clients. Because you are goddamn going to be my sword and buckler. Where are they?"

"Upstairs."

Aubrey pushed Bridsey at the first porch step, but Bridsey fell. Aubrey kicked him in the buttocks, hurting his big toe. He cursed and dragged the rising man to his feet. At the front door Aubrey opened it slowly and silently, then jostled Bridsey into the cooler interior. From upstairs Aubrey heard Bethany shriek. As a counterpoint, a tenor voice began shouting. Aubrey urged Bridsey up the stairs by his vest. The sounds stopped. As they reached the top, Bethany began sobbing loudly, interspersing her weeping with exclamations of outrage in German.

Outside the door Aubrey signaled with a hunch

of his shoulders that Bridsey was to help break it down. The Englishman stepped back with every appearance of determination. Aubrey, beside him, nodded and the two men rushed, shoulders forward, at the heavy oak portal.

They smashed into it simultaneously. The ancient hinges held, but the newer deadbolt inside burst from the jamb with a cracking sound. As Bridsey went down inside, and Aubrey flopped awkwardly onto his back, Aubrey saw the unimaginable.

Bethany, her head in an odd bun, lay on her back on the bed. She was naked, her knees veed up.

Between them, fresh from a lunge at her crotch, from the masculine look of him, was a thin, muscular man. His left hand held down Bethany's right wrist. In his right hand he gripped a theatrical-looking dagger, its point at her throat from which there trickled a hairline rivulet of blood.

Bethany and the man looked at Aubrey with equal astonishment.

For just an instant the improbable tableau held: Bridsey and Aubrey on their knees, staring upward; Bethany, eyes saucer wide, in the conventional supine position; Robert St. Gage poised to slay or to rape, whichever of the two actions had, a split second before, been coursing through his obsessed mind.

"Drop it! Now! Or I shoot!" Aubrey screamed at the nude man, aiming the pistol at his head. St. Gage seemed unable to comprehend what Aubrey had said. Then, as if he were coming out of a profound trance, he lowered the knife even as his lesser weapon drooped, until both pointed impotently toward the bed. At a second order from Aubrey, he dropped the dagger. It fell to the floor with a clunk.

The sound seemed to activate everyone. St. Gage jumped from the bed; Bethany took a game swipe at him with her fist as he went past her; Aubrey came to his feet, the revolver still outthrust at St. Gage. Bridsey crept backward to the wall.

Now the lawyer reacted more normally. His hands went straight up in the air, his eyes fixed on the pistol muzzle. Bethany was not so controlled. She righted herself, crawled across the bed, and grabbed up the knife. Aubrey had no doubt she would use it on St. Gage.

"Bethany," he shouted. She turned, her expression as wild as a maenad's. "No! We've got to go!"

His shout brought her to, but only for a moment. He had to rush around the bed and catch her wrist as she sought to stab St. Gage. She tried to pull free, still too enraged to be embarrassed by her nudity. Aubrey held her arm and at last tension went out of her body. She let the dagger slide from her fingers and he released her. Weeping, she bent to pick up her clothes. Bridsey modestly looked at the window.

St. Gage's face was as pale as a man in the midst of a heart attack. He looked aghast, perhaps at the turn of events, perhaps out of shame over the twisted regression to which he had succumbed, perhaps from both. Aubrey felt no sympathy for him. Far from it, seeing the condition to which he had re-

duced Bethany, he would, with only minor prov-
ocation, have killed him on the spot.

"How goes?" he questioned the weeping
woman, eager to get on the way, all too aware that
the murderer would soon be at the lower buildings
and might even now be moving on the casa.

"Okay," Bethany sniffled, far from okay. She
had put on her skirt and shoes and was fumbling
with her slashed brassiere. Aubrey, revolver still
ready, snatched the disordered sheet from the bed,
unable to see anything else but St. Gage's clothes
to offer her for the blood on her neck.

"Wipe your throat before you put on your
blouse," he said as gently as if he were talking to
a child. He helped her into the jacket, then retrieved her shoulder bag and handed it to her.

Eyes still on the two men, he worked his foot
into St. Gage's fine leather boots. They pinched
slightly. He picked up the lawyer's batiste shirt
and, with repugnancy, stuffed it into his coat pocket.

Bridsey, keeping a low profile, still knelt. Aubrey tested the boots' fit by giving the wine merchant, whom he suspected of conspiring in the
atrocity on Bethany, a jolting kick in the side.

"Up, fatso," he said.

Bethany, looking pathetically drained, waited
passively for Aubrey to tell her they should go.
Her defeated look exploded his anger. Without a
word he strode around the bed, snatched up the
dagger from the floor in his left hand, and pressed
its point to St. Gage's naked belly.

"I ought to gut you like a fucking fish," he said
to the strained, handsome face, and delicately

pressed in the point until St. Gage's face fell apart in terror.

And why not drive it home? thought Aubrey. But he could not kill that way. Instead, he drew back a step, flung the knife at the barred window, and hit the Englishman full force in the nose with a left hook.

The blood gushed, splattering the floor as St. Gage pitched backward against the wall, his cry hoarsened by pain. He crumpled to the floor, fingers reddening where he held his mangled face.

"If you follow us . . . ," Aubrey began, but turned away from St. Gage in disgust, the threat unsaid. Bethany was already out the door. Aubrey shoved Bridsey along behind her.

At the lower building the Portuguese on the porch ran in and slammed the door when he saw them coming. A dusty white Peugeot and two other passenger cars were parked behind the building.

"Keys," demanded Aubrey.

"In the office," said Bridsey.

Too much time, Aubrey thought. The American murderer scared Aubrey every time he thought of him. A second gun battle was the last thing Aubrey wanted, one that could rally the workers with whatever shotguns or rifles were around the place.

"Get in," Aubrey ordered the Englishman, gesturing at the Jeep.

"See here," Bridsey gamely protested.

Aubrey started toward him, already so heavily into violence that he would have no hesitation now in hurting Bridsey, and badly if that was what it took. The wine importer walked heavily to the Jeep and climbed in back.

"In front," said Aubrey. "Bethany, can you keep this pistol aimed at the back of his neck?" He watched her carefully, fearful she might flip out when the dulling protection of shock lifted. She took the gun without a word.

Aubrey and Bridsey knew the American would not think twice about firing at the Jeep. They crouched low as the Jeep pulled out of the gate and swung down the road. Unbidden, Bethany imitated them.

They were three miles down the road before Aubrey felt truly that they might escape.

"What's the closest way out of Portugal," said Aubrey to them both as they bumped along. Bethany lowered the gun to dig into her pocketbook for the map. Good girl, Aubrey thought, she's coming out of it. Bridsey replied, more politely than not.

"There is no direct road. You can go south to Trancoso but it is a long way. The main highway is north through Braganda, but that is even longer."

"Airfields?" Aubrey suggested.

"Come, come," said Bridsey, "this is Portugal."

"Well, the train goes to Spain," said Aubrey. To flee by public transportation, at first thought, seemed madness. But it would be faster, more direct than by road. There would also be the limited protection of other people. Besides, did they have a choice? "Where can we pick up the train?"

"At Pocinho," replied Bridsey. "You can't be sure whether it will be a regular train or a sort of trolley. But it runs to the main line at Salamanca."

"You're a cooperative enough son of a bitch now," said Aubrey nastily. "But I'm not letting you go. How often does it run?"

"Often, in the afternoons," said Bridsey, trying unsuccessfully to hide his disappointment over Aubrey's words. "I have ridden it myself to Salamanca in the interest of time."

"Could we pick it up *outside* Pocinho?" Aubrey was worried that St. Gage or the American might call ahead to alert someone in Pocinho to try to pull them off the train.

"I would think a road would follow the tracks some way past the station; I have seen the train stop for peasants along the tracks."

Aubrey drove on, thinking of Bridsey. They would have to take him at least to the border to keep him from calling his coconspirators. Once in Spain Aubrey was sure he and Bethany could escape.

In the back, Bethany dug again in her pocketbook and found a handkerchief. She dabbed at her throat. The bleeding had all but stopped. Still it left a small streak of blood on the cloth.

"Oh God," she said. Her voice was tremulous, and Aubrey realized how fragile was her seeming recovery.

"Baroness," said Bridsey with what sounded like sincerity, "I wish to assure you I knew nothing of what he planned. I was as . . ."

"You let the miserable pervert take her up to the big house," broke in Aubrey. "You . . ."

"I had no idea he had," Bridsey looked for the word, "a penchant in that direction. If anything, I swear to you, he has seemed more calculating, more well, rational than most . . ."

Aubrey was inclined to believe Bridsey, but that didn't make it much better. "You damned well knew where that murderous fake Portuguese was taking me," Aubrey reminded him.

To that Bridsey made no reply.

The wind was whipping through the Jeep now that they had left the protection of the vineyards and were in scrubby hill country. Aubrey began to consider what they could extract from Bridsey before they let him go.

"Bethany," he said. "Put the pistol up to Mr. Bridsey's left ear, pointed outward. I'm allergic to brains and it's Q and A time."

Bridsey said nothing as she complied.

"Now look," Aubrey said reasonably. "You are on the verge of me cutting you loose at the border. You must know I'm not a natural killer. But you bozos killed a fine guy, a friend of mine, the inspector. You killed this Frenchman. You tried to kill me. You raped . . ."

"Not quite," Bethany snapped bitterly. "Tried to."

Both men could hear the profundity of her anger.

"You *tried* to rape the baroness."

"I did none of these," said Bridsey loftily.

"Don't toy with me, Limey," said Aubrey angrily. "Cock the hammer, Bethany. Just pull it back a little notch. Be careful. Don't let your feelings get the best of you." He turned to Bridsey again. "You have got to know that the baroness might just pull the trigger not solely because you allowed that thing up there to happen, but simply right now because you're a man."

Bridsey understood immediately.

"Don't," said Bridsey, off his high horse. "I'm an army man. I know these cheap little pistols. Ask your question. Please, baroness, don't try to cock that thing."

"You can start with the American's name. His full name," said Aubrey.

Bridsey's game was complicated. He knew he would have to satisfy Aubrey, that the man was thoroughly worked up and therefore unpredictably dangerous. But Bridsey also knew that he must not give him enough so that he would take steps so precise that Tobb and St. Gage would know Bridsey had told all. In that case, he would assuredly suffer the fate of Maier. Therefore, he must only tell Aubrey what he could conceivably have learned elsewhere.

"I don't know. He is an employee of St. Gage."

"Bethany, cock it and keep your thumb on the hammer. If it goes off, shove him over the side so he doesn't bloody up the Jeep."

"I know him only as Pierce. Please, baroness," Bridsey begged. "I implore you, Mr. Warder, ask me something I can answer. You will find me more than forthcoming."

"Point the gun away from his head, Bethany," said Aubrey. "Okay," he said sternly to Bridsey. "Who's in this goddamned thing?"

"I am."

"And St. Gage."

"Yes." St. Gage had surfaced on his own volition, Bridsey rationalized. Besides, he felt rancorous toward the lawyer for letting his weird fetish get in their way.

"And the *Witwe* Pfeffermühle," said Bethany.

"Yes." They would already know this or have guessed it, Bridsey assured himself.

"And Maier," Bethany went on.

"Was," said Bridsey. "Was in it."

As the heat began to go out of the day, Aubrey pressed in with the persistence of the trained reporter, augmented by a gun literally at Bridsey's head. But no matter how he worked Bridsey around, used the pistol threat, the wine merchant denied further details on the deaths of Maier and Wheatley-Smith.

Relentlessly Aubrey braced him on the bottle of Château Rossant and Bridsey, as had d'Edouard, said he believed it was intended for research on phylloxera.

"But why?"

"I am not privy to that," Bridsey said.

Aubrey had Bethany put the gun to his ear. My God, Aubrey thought, I'm becoming an instant expert on the third degree.

"And the vines. Where are they?"

"I do not know." Aubrey felt Bridsey adjusting to the limits, sensing that Aubrey would not kill him.

"You know something about where they are, goddamn it."

"No," said Bridsey. "I swear it."

"Well, you've sworn to one too many lies," said Aubrey, slowing. He pulled the Jeep off onto the narrow shoulder. They were in a barren stretch bordered on their left by a copse of pines.

"What . . . ?"

"I'm stopping, Mr. Bridsey, because it's that

important," said Aubrey with cold resolve. He took the gun from Bethany and marched Bridsey toward the copse. Bethany followed. In the copse, out of sight of the road, Aubrey told Bridsey to stop.

"Last time," Aubrey said inflexibly. "Where are they?"

"I don't know. Dear God, Mr. Warder, I don't."

Aubrey looked at the heavyset older man from whom all the prosperous manner had gone. Bridsey could feel a change in him.

"The fun's over," Aubrey said, firm and quiet. "Kneel down and say your prayers."

"No, Aubrey," gasped Bethany, shocked from her own misery by her fear that Aubrey might just shoot. "It's murder."

"No more than he conspired in for us."

"For you. I don't think he knew about me . . . ," she pleaded.

"One's enough."

"No," said Bridsey. "I helped you. I cooperated." Now he believed Aubrey was serious. More practically, he did not want to stake his life on Aubrey's *not* being serious.

Aubrey kicked the heavy man in the ankle and when that made him stumble, pushed him over.

"On your knees. Die like a man," said Aubrey.

Bridsey was scared almost into irrationality. But he did not want to sign his own death warrant with Tobb and St. Gage unless he took Aubrey down to the last moment.

"No, no, no, no, . . . I am telling everything," he lied, the tears rolling down his face. He flopped over on his back, clasped his hands to Aubrey and began to sob, half feigned, half in earnest.

"Crocodile tears," said Aubrey.

"No, Aubrey," begged Bethany.

"Then die on your back like the coward you are," said Aubrey, taking aim, arm extended at Bridsey's face.

"No, I'll tell," screamed Bridsey, genuinely panicked at last. Aubrey relaxed and Bridsey got to his feet, embarrassed and shamed. "You shouldn't drive a man to behave that way," sniffed Bridsey not without dignity.

"Shut up," said Aubrey. "Talk!"

"There is a researcher, a scientist of some kind."

"The vines are with him?"

"I'm sure of it."

"Where?"

"I don't know."

Aubrey moved toward him, his eyes angry. Bridsey backed up in terror. He had told the truth and still this maniac did not believe him.

"Please," he said. "Ask me more questions. I'll answer."

"There is something about California. About its wine crop not being a problem for you in years to come."

Bridsey's mouth dropped open. He was sure Tobb and St. Gage planned to neutralize the California wine industry in some horrifying way. But even to speculate on it was to invite death. He thought for a vivid second of Maier in the Algerian wine tun.

"Talk!"

"I don't know. I don't know." Bridsey was headed back toward hysteria. Aubrey eased off.

"When is this California thing going to happen? When, goddamn it?"

"I don't know," Bridsey parroted himself.

Aubrey, eyes getting wilder, put the pistol to Bridsey's temple, then stood back as if to get clear of any backsplash of brains. Bridsey thought of his midnight meeting with St. Gage. The timing of whatever was going to happen in California was something he had no trouble guessing.

"Now? Months? Weeks?" Aubrey cocked the hammer unnecessarily, but it had an immediate effect on Bridsey. He tried to form words, but no words came. He shook his head side to side to indicate an answer before Aubrey shot.

"Days," Bridsey was at last able to whisper. "Days, I think."

Aubrey pulled back.

"How many?"

"Oh, God. God, I swear I do not know. It is only what I feel! Not very many days!"

The answer jarred Aubrey like a slap. Days! He had known the clock was ticking. But he had been thinking in terms of weeks. Semirational himself, he moved back up to Bridsey.

"*What* in California, man? *Where* is this scientist? Goddamn it, tell me!"

But Bridsey, looking like he might faint, had staggered rearward and put his back to a tree. He held to it, hands behind him, almost as if readying himself for execution, blubbering.

"I don't know. I don't know," he said like a child's chant when he is hurt.

Aubrey, calmed by this spectacle, waited for

Bridsey to get control over himself. He glanced at Bethany. She looked sickened. Bridsey reached into his coat pocket, withdrew a large handkerchief, and began blowing his nose and wiping his tears.

"I can't stand any more," he said.

"Then don't make me do this," said Aubrey. He felt guilty about the whole episode. First, d'Edouard and now this. In his heart he was as sickened as Bethany by it. But if there were only days . . .

"So, now *what* in California? *Where* are the vines?" He had gotten back his restraint and it showed in his voice. Bridsey finished repairing his wrecked face, tried to assume the manliness he had lost.

"I cannot tell you," he dissembled once more on the first question. "I do not know," he answered honestly to the second. Then, caving in, knowing that if his words ever got back to St. Gage, they would be his death warrant, he said, "The *Witwe* Pfeffermühle is the only one who knows anything about the research besides St. Gage and perhaps this American."

Bridsey had no real way of knowing how much the *Witwe* knew. But his answer had the ring of truth. Aubrey did not think he could extract any more.

"Back to the road," he said. "And fast."

Bridsey gave a moan of relief. He almost jogged to the Jeep. As they drove off, he appraised the damage. He had not made the ultimate revelation: his certainty that something dreadful was planned for California's vines. That surmise he had kept inviolate. He thought of Aubrey and that deadly, unreliable little revolver. If it had come down to it there was little, indeed nothing, he would not have told this ferocious man. Between him and Tobb he could not see a tuppence's difference. And Warder had been the man at hand with the loaded gun.

The three foreigners must have seemed odd passengers when they were picked up by the trolley-train. Although Aubrey had put on St. Gage's shirt, he was sockless; his suit—while the coat largely covered the dry urine stain—was badly wrinkled and dirty; Bridsey's suit was sweated through and filthy from his roll on the ground. Bethany's face was bruised and she had a small scab forming in the exact center of her throat.

The trolley looked a streetcar from the American fifties, but wider, with wooden seats on either side of an aisle, and a first class compartment on the other side of a low partition. First class's only luxury was wicker seats. The car had doors at both ends so that when it was hooked up with other similar cars, the passengers and conductor could pass between them.

Aubrey, Bethany, and Bridsey sat on one long seat, its wood polished by decades of peasant bottoms. The trolley moved along smartly. From a tattered schedule and route map plastered to the wooden interior wall, it appeared they would arrive at the border town of Barca de Alva in thirty minutes. There they would drop Bridsey and either take the trolley or a taxi into Spain and comparative safety.

The day was cooling rapidly now. Across the vineless land, almost desert save for a few runty trees, the sun was on the verge of descent. The bruise on Bethany's face where St. Gage had struck her was darkening and swollen. Aubrey felt creaks or scrapes in and on most of his body.

Yet they were on the way to freedom. He was sure of it. He looked at Bethany, so battered now, but calm. What a wonderfully brave and good person, he thought. She caught his sentiment but could not smile.

As they clanked along, Aubrey turned his thoughts to how they could force or cajole information from Frau Pfeffermühle. If Bridsey was right, they must derail the conspiracy, even if they could not destroy it, within the next couple of days. The old German woman was their last hope, frail as it was.

His anxious thoughts were interrupted by a rapid deceleration of the trolley.

The conductor got out and tinkered with the motor. The driver joined him and smoked a cigarette.

From the other passengers' brief head shakes, their murmured words and their lapses into dozing, Aubrey realized a stall on the line was not unusual. He and Bethany waited nervously, looking back and around, until the conductor and driver climbed aboard and the trolley was in motion.

Relieved, Aubrey and Bethany got out the map and were soon absorbed in how, once they had crossed into Spain, they could best be on their way to the *Witwe*'s castle. Thus, it was Bridsey who alerted them with a grunt of surprise to the second trolley that was pulling up on them from behind.

Twenty-eight

THE TROLLEYS

The conductor saw the approaching trolley at the same time as Bridsey. He ran up the aisle of the swaying vehicle to notify the driver. Aubrey grabbed Bethany's hand and they followed. By the time they came to the driver's stool he was already slowing, assuming there was some official reason for the pursuit.

The conductor stared at the couple as if they were crazy. The eccentric-looking foreigners had already caused him and the driver speculation.

Aubrey made his hand into a pistol and said, "bang, bang," pointing rearward. The driver and conductor boggled at him in incomprehension. "*Kidnapperos*," said Aubrey, knowing it wouldn't work.

"*¡Asesinos! Ladrónes*," Bethany said, a strong trace of her previous hysteria in her voice.

"*Bandidos*," shouted Aubrey remembering words from an old Zorro movie. "*Bandidos*," he said with

authority. The driver ordered the conductor back
to take a look. Aubrey and Bethany trotted after
him down the aisle of the decelerating trolley. The
three peered out the open portal. A chain was strung
across it and a small hinged platform was folded
back, exposing the coupler just below.

Not fifty yards behind, the second train was
pulling up fast. The look of terror on the face of its
driver and the English-dressed man with his nose
bandaged standing ominously right behind the
driver were sufficient to convince the conductor
something was amiss. As they scrutinized the second trolley, there appeared in the train's doorway
another foreigner, this one with a black automatic
in his right hand.

"*Pistola*," said the conductor.

"You're goddamned right it's a *pistola*," said
Aubrey, recognizing his would-be murderer.

The conductor turned and ran back through the
car. Halfway down he called out a warning to the
driver in a shrill voice from which Aubrey drew
the word *pistola* again. The word was picked up
and frantically repeated by the two dozen passengers. From drowsing in the hot, air-conditionless
car, they scrambled like ants under boiling water.
The timid hurled themselves under the wooden
seats; a few younger, bolder men rushed to the
rear of the car.

The driver sped up. The trolley jerked forward,
sending Aubrey down on one knee and those who
were not already crawling for cover asprawl in the
aisles or toppling over seat backs.

Aubrey and Bethany risked fleeting looks out
the rear door and Tobb saw them. No more than

twenty-five yards of track separated them. As the gunman aimed his long-barreled weapon, Aubrey bumped Bethany away from the narrow door and dropped to the floor.

The automatic's report scarcely sounded above the whirr of the rapidly spinning motor and the screech of axles unaccustomed to bursts of speed.

"Duck! Down!" yelled Aubrey. But his voice was drowned by the noise; in any event, the passengers, squirming under seats, needed no advice. From its holster Aubrey snatched the .22 and darted another look out the door. The heavyset Portuguese whom Aubrey had first seen on the porch with the American was leaning out the driver's window, trying to aim a pump shotgun.

Aubrey pulled in his head. Did he dare try to plink the man? To do so would endanger the passengers in the commandeered trolley. But the pursuers were gaining.

"Everything's in the maintenance," Aubrey said to himself, incongruously remembering those words of a racing car mechanic from a story decades before.

As the trolley drew up on them, a young Portuguese crept to the rear, a peculiarly shaped grafting knife in his hand. Behind the worker, the conductor came, pressing his body along the wooden side of one seat after another. In his hand he gripped a long-handled shovel, perhaps the tool used for putting sand on the tracks.

At least, Aubrey thought, if they try to board, it won't be without a fight. The three defenders hugged either side of the heavy wood framing around the door. The suspense was too much for the young worker, however. He peered around the corner, then hurled himself back as a shotgun blast went off, spraying the cabin.

In a few moments they heard the clank of couplings outside the door. Aubrey popped his head out and found himself staring into the frightened face of the conductor of the pursuing train. He was precariously straddling the folded up platform of his car, trying to join the two vehicles.

In the doorway, eyes full of wrath, was the American. He raised the pistol at Aubrey, who fell backward. The pistol blammed, splintering the wood at Aubrey's elbow. Aubrey rolled under a seat as a second blast sounded, making a *whing* sound as the ricochet struck a steel patch on the trolley's floor.

Before Tobb could fire again, the young man with the grafting knife moved. Holding the crude weapon in his left hand, he snatched the shovel from the hands of the paralyzed conductor and moved out into the open aperture.

Aubrey saw him thrust once, heard his satisfied oath, but could not see his target. When Aubrey peeked around the corner, he saw the American toppled backward. The worker pushed again, this time adroitly throwing the conductor off balance. It was all the uniformed man could do to keep from falling to the tracks. Like a crab retreating, he squirmed into the car, bumping Tobb who was trying to regain his feet for another shot.

Out of breath, the young man got back to his position of safety. Aubrey clapped him on the shoulder, with a loud "*Olé.*" The driver of the second trolley had slowed to protect his conductor, and the distance between the two vehicles was fifteen yards.

The greater gap gave the man with the shotgun space now to move back to his window post. He fired and the huge blast sent pellets ripping into the cabin, ricochetting and breaking two of the handful of windows that had been left up despite the heat.

Aubrey risked another swift look. The American again had the gun on the conductor who was weeping hysterically as he crawled to the open door for another try at the coupling.

Behind the trolley driver Robert St. Gage, dressed in a grey suit and smooth as a spaniel except for his bandage, seemed to be holding some sort of weapon at the driver's back. The antique dagger, Aubrey thought, wishing now he had killed him.

The second trolley was only feet away. The conductor was athwart the platform again. Tobb this time was paying more attention to the coupling than to Aubrey, bestowing on him only a vengeful glare without bringing up the gun. Again, the sobbing conductor reached down to join the two cars.

At that instant the brave young Portuguese, his knife discarded, whipped from cover and smacked the conductor's hands with the shovel. But the conductor had already dropped the U-shaped clasp over the hook of the fleeting trolley, coupling the two cars.

Aubrey withdrew his head as the young man scrambled back through the door. At the same instant, Tobb's pistol fired. The force of the slug hurled Aubrey's ally backward. The shovel flew from his hands and clattered to the floor.

Enraged by the shooting of this selfless man, Aubrey dropped his own pistol, grabbed the shovel, and strode to the door. The adrenaline pumped into his body.

The conductor was pushing down the platform to make a bridge to the first trolley. Aubrey jammed him in the chest. Then, before Tobb could aim, Aubrey flailed and sent the pistol caroming back into the train. At the driver's window the Portuguese with the shotgun strained to get his shoulders out far enough to fire.

Tobb, wildly cursing as he gripped his mashed hand, scrabbled to retrieve his pistol. Aubrey was in full fury. These people had shot a brave man; they were intent on killing him, Bethany, and God only knew who else. Aubrey, crazed and dangerous, his muscles hardened by his vineyard labors, kicked down his own platform and strode onto the treacherous walkway. Like a maddened caveman smashing at a mammoth, he clubbed in the trolley's front window. Had he missed contact, he would have pitched off into the roadbed.

In the aperture Aubrey saw St. Gage hurriedly handing the retrieved gun to his American henchman. With a long thrust he knocked both men rearward, and crossed half inside the pursuers' doorway. He rammed the shovel down on the American gunman's already injured arm. With a shriek, the man dropped the gun.

Face-to-face again with Aubrey, St. Gage retreated from behind the driver, the antique dagger, as Aubrey had surmised it would be in his hand. Using the shovel as a pike, Aubrey poked the lawyer violently in the chest, caving him in. Gasping for breath, Aubrey choked up on the shovel and, baseball bat-style, swatted the driver from his stool. The man grabbed for the controls as he went down. With one last slam, Aubrey demolished the small array of knobs and levers, decommissioning the vehicle at least temporarily.

The Portuguese with the shotgun did not dare risk a blast at such close quarters. Taking advantage of his problem, two passengers, a giant peasant woman and a man in a cheap business suit, fell on Tobb and St. Gage. The driver and conductor joined in.

Aubrey retreated to his car, folding back the two-hinged platform. With a final heave, he levered the U-clamp from the hook. The coupling clanged free.

Behind him he heard Bridsey's baritone braying orders to the passengers in a parade-ground cockney dialect to which he had reverted.

Fearing some new attack on his own trolley, Aubrey glanced back for an instant. To his astonishment, he saw the burly Englishman bending over the wounded Portuguese worker's upper arm, trying to staunch the flow of blood, calling for cloth to make a compress.

Aubrey had no time to ponder the ex-soldier's journey in time to a war in which courageous men risked their lives to save the lives of other courageous men. Liberated from its drag, their trolley lurched forward vigorously. Reverse inertia threw Aubrey onto the folded platform where he teetered above the tracks.

As he scrambled to keep from falling, the man with the shotgun, now in the decommissioned car's aperture, deliberately aimed at him. Aubrey saw the black hole of the muzzle, not ten yards away, though receding, and shut his eyes.

Good-bye, he heard himself saying, cleansed by his certainty of death of everything: anger, hope, memory. He turned his face out of some strange last-moment vanity, to take the shotgun blast on the side of his head.

As he did, he heard two reports. The first was the snap of the .22 revolver. The second was the roar of the shotgun which, when Aubrey heard it, he knew would not touch him. Its blast had gone over his head.

Aubrey opened his eyes. The man with the shotgun crouched gutshot in the door opening, his screams sounding even above the whine of Aubrey's accelerating train. Behind the man the American, broken free of his adversaries, jerked at the weapon more perhaps to try to control the insurgents aboard his train and make escape possible than to try again for Aubrey's life.

His body an exhausted shell, Aubrey turned his head. In the doorway, both hands still pointing the little gun, Bethany knelt frozen by the shock of shooting to kill. The last of the sun hit her honey-colored hair, still done up so severely. She was like some warrior maiden open-eyed in prayer, holding out her weapon for the Almighty's blessing.

Aubrey crawled past her. The upheaval within him from his rush of adrenaline and his crazed exertions were having their effect. He began to tremble. He closed his eyes again, hoping that if he could calm his thoughts, he could calm his body. In his chest he felt the wild thump of his heart.

In the middle of the car there was screaming. Aubrey opened his eyes. The shotgun blast had gone high enough to miss Bethany. That was obvious. But the ricochets from the metal roof supports, the fixtures, the hand bars had rained down on the interior of the trolley.

Aubrey tried to rise to help whoever was screaming, then fainted.

When he came to, not long after, Bethany was loosening his belt. He looked from her bruised face to the beet-red features of an old Portuguese woman who was pouring water from a wine jug onto her apron and swabbing his forehead.

"Are we . . . ?" he began.

"They're stalled. Out of sight back there," she reassured him. He lay still, eyes closed, luxuriating for a moment in the cool of the cloth and the ease now with which he could breathe.

"How long do they say before the border?" he said at last.

"A few minutes, if nothing else happens."

Behind them there were two small groups of people.

"The young guy?"

"I don't know."

Aubrey rolled over and got totteringly to his feet. He braced on a seatback, feeling very old, very stiff, and worked his way forward. The young man's right arm lay outstretched, the shirt ripped away. Bridsey's undershirt was bound around the wound and had soaked red. The conductor, come back to life now the danger was over, was putting on a primitive tourniquet made of a sleeve of his own shirt and a ball-point pen for twisting it tight.

"Bridsey?" Aubrey asked in alarm. Where was the surprising Englishman? Maybe I can turn him, Aubrey thought with wonder. In the clutch he performed. Maybe . . .

But now he saw what the second group was all about. From within the circle of passengers on their knees, the columnar legs of the wine merchant protruded. Aubrey staggered to where, above the bare, beefy chest, he could see Bridsey's face.

The eyes were open, one staring, as lifeless as a mugshot's. The other was like a squashed cherry. A lead pellet, either directly or on the bounce, had entered his eye and gone into his brain as neatly, as lethally as if it had been an ice pick.

"Oh God," Aubrey said. Bethany stood at his side, mouth and eyes three round O's. There was no sheet to pull over the face of the redeemed old warrior with his single staring eye, his mouth open as if in garrulity; Aubrey carefully picked up the Englishman's suit coat and used it for a shroud.

"What can we do?" Bethany asked, stupefied.

Aubrey looked again at the portly form. What could they do? Tell his wife that he had died a hero? That he had tried, and perhaps succeeded in saving somebody he never even knew? Aubrey's failure of words was the best evidence of how badly he felt.

"You were going to kill him and I was going to stand by," Bethany said, still almost as if in a daze. The words struck to his heart, making him want to cry.

"No," he said, his voice shaking. "I was not going to do that. No matter what, I wasn't going to do it." He knew that much was true.

Up ahead a cluster of houses showed beside the roadbed. In a moment there were a few low white-washed warehouses and big sheds. The trolley was getting to Barca de Alva. It slowed as they saw the tile roofs of the little town. The setting sun elongated the train's shadow which raced across the bare front yards of the boxlike houses. What a strange burden this train carried, this common-place little Toonerville trolley which had set out that afternoon on a trip that must have seemed to all aboard like any other trip.

Yet when it got to the station its arrival would be as agitating as that of an alien spaceship. Police, ambulances, city officials would mill about. The young worker would be rushed to a hospital. Brid-sey had to be pronounced dead and identified. Interrogations of the passengers about the gun battle would begin.

Up ahead now was the station, as sleepy as on any other evening. The train was creeping in for its stop. The people aboard moiled about, looking for possessions, talking rapidly and excitedly to each other. They were bound together as passengers are on an airplane that has nearly crashed.

The driver began to clang his bell over and over, summoning officials. A railroad employee with a round sign on a stick ran from the building. Then another. One of the elderly women passengers began to wail. Only the two tending the wounded man seemed untouched by the arrival.

As the train stopped the passengers crowded around the double doors in the train's middle. Once outside they talked with gesticulations to the officials, to anyone who would listen. Aubrey and

Bethany skirted the crowd and walked quickly through the station and out among the waiting taxis.

Aubrey picked the best-kept of the cabs. A few blocks away, with Bethany hiding her bruised face in the shadowy rear of the auto, they reached the border crossing. The Portuguese and Spanish guards, chattering separately about the events at the station, passed them with perfunctory questions.

In Salamanca, rather than waiting at the station, they sipped beer in a dark corner of a bar until the train came for Bordeaux. There, in the morning they would pause to buy presentable clothes before flying on to confront the *Witwe* Pfeffermühle.

Twenty-nine

THE *WITWE* II

The *Witwe* Pfeffermühle, dying in her castle keep, had fought the crawl of cancer with all her will. But her will was no match for the mindlessly errant cells within her.

Berkady had been to see her the afternoon before, bringing her some notes for safekeeping, part of his "insurance policy." He had said he would have some more in a few days. When the visit was over, the old scientist had held her dry hand in his moist one, too distressed to speak. Each good-bye seemed closer to their final one. He had flown back to Paris that evening.

Now her nurse was telling her that two visitors were seeking to speak with her. They were Bethany von Mohrwald and Aubrey Warder.

The *Witwe* had met Baroness von Mohrwald at a wine gathering in Frankfurt a few years ago. The older woman had felt the scourge of the baroness's contempt for her conversion of the great Marienwagner vineyards into the production of Jolly Priest wine. There had been the added whip of the baroness's nobility and her own mere gentryhood.

The *Witwe* smiled thinly. She had been untouched by the contempt. Four hundred years ago the von Mohrwalds had been only countrified vintners, and Austrians at that. The *Witwe* came from Prussian stock.

She had no doubt that St. Gage, once the cartel had made its coup, would find a way to dispossess the von Mohrwalds. Their markets would be choked off. Bankrupted, they would have to sell out to the cartel or to someone else. So much, then, for this prissy Austrian who had come calling.

Warder, on the other hand, had been dangerous. That she had gathered from Bridsey during their circumspect dialogue. An American detective! An envenomed thorn in their flesh. The thought of him gave her an instant's rancorous energy. But he, too, would soon be cast down. For this very day, Pieter was loading the insects into his plastic containers. In two days, they would be doing their vile job.

The nurse waited, then gently suggested that perhaps Frau Pfeffermühle did not want to see the visitors. The old woman closed her eyes, her face taking on the look of an aged turtle. After all, did it matter whatever this odd couple thought was so urgent? Visitors, even her beloved Pieter, tired her so.

Yet the *Witwe* was, above all, a person of duty. It was her duty to draw from these two any information that, at this crucial moment, might be useful to Pieter and to St. Gage. At worst, an interview with them, so long as it was brief, would be a diversion from the terrible pain that cored her night and day.

The nurse let the pair into the old-fashioned bedroom with its two windows looking down on the Rhine far below. The *Witwe* thought that Bethany, even discounting the ugly bruise on her face, had aged a decade since she had last seen her not two years ago. This craggy, irresponsible-looking Warder was something else. She smelled a reckless quality in him, a someone not quite proper, who, for whatever reasons, felt he had nothing to lose. It put her on her guard, with its challenge made her forget, if only for a short time, her impending death.

"Sit down, my dear, and you too, Mr. . . ."

"Warder," said Bethany, then nervously began a more formal introduction. "Frau Pfeffermühle, this is . . ."

The *Witwe* stopped her with a weary raise of a skeletal hand.

"No time for formalities," she said. "Tell me what it is you want. And, *bitte*, succinctly."

"We have been traveling since yesterday morning without real sleep, Frau *Witwe*," Bethany began a little disjointedly. "We are here to solicit your help."

The *Witwe* inwardly sneered. As well solicit the help of a dying king cobra, she thought.

". . . We know you are part of an organization set up to restructure the international wine market, that you have helped to buy up the European vineyards . . ."

"Get on with it," the *Witwe* interrupted Bethany. How naive could she be? "Why are you here?" She gestured to the American. "Surely you did not transport Mr. Warder all the way to Schloss Löwenfels to lecture me on the future of the wine industry."

"No ma'am," said Aubrey, "the baroness only wanted to lay out to you what we knew, the context in which we wanted you to help us."

"Let us assume the context," she said, purposely excluding Bethany, her attention focused on the man. She felt him studying her and it made her uncomfortable. There was a worldly shrewdness in his look. She must listen not just for his words but for his motives.

"You are in league with crazies, Mrs. Pfeffermühle," he said quietly and unpityingly. "Do you know that? These are people who have already killed three people . . ."

The words made her flinch. The English inspector, Maier. Could the third be . . .

"Three?" she tried to dissemble her anxious breath but it wheezed audibly up the ancient trachea.

"A friend of mine, Wheatley-Smith. The French wine merchant, Maier. And yesterday, by mistake, William Bridsey . . ."

"Bridsey," she said softly, simultaneously shocked and relieved. She closed her eyes to regain her sangfroid. "I do not understand," she said.

"The baroness and I were in Portugal. We are looking for American vine stocks which are being used in some way by your cartel. A Mr. St. Gage, one of your partners, tried to have me killed and there was some shooting and Bridsey was killed. By them, unintentionally."

It seemed to Aubrey enough to tell her for the time being. He saw no reason to confess to her that he had kidnapped Bridsey as a hostage for his and Bethany's escape.

In better times she would have processed this information as a bridge partner's three no-trump bid. Now she had to shut out the world, use her mind to blot out the pain briefly so she could sort things out.

Did this Warder have any idea about Pieter? That was what she wanted to know. Even more importantly, did St. Gage and Tobb suspect that Warder had any idea about Pieter? Once they had the insects and the samples of his antidote and its formula, then all that would protect him was his "insurance." For who in France or Belgium or any-where would really be concerned about him?

She thought of the little packet of films, tapes, and notes he had been entrusting to her. On his visit the day before, he and she had gone through them. She had kept them out, waiting to husband enough strength to meet with her personal lawyer. They were in her night-table drawer in a marzipan tin.

Because she was dying, there must be a fail-safe system in place for them. If Pieter died un-naturally, they must be surfaced in order to destroy St. Gage and Tobb. And if Pieter lived to die nat-urally, then the "insurance" must be destroyed.

Now she wished the marzipan tin was back in the safe. As soon as these two had gone, she would summon the lawyer, work it all out, then redeposit the tin in the safe in her husband's study, though it would use her last bit of strength to do it.

But for the moment she must learn just how much Warder knew, to surmise how much St. Gage and Tobb thought he knew.

"All of this is unfortunate," she said at last. "These dead people." It was not that she cared that much about any of them, although Bridsey had been usefully informative and she had been fond of Maier the way one is fond of a puppy. But so many deaths attracted attention. More importantly, they were evidence of how occupied Tobb was with death. She had known Nazis like that. To Tobb, as to them, another killing would be nothing, perhaps, even probably, a pleasure. And Pieter . . .

". . . you must know, Mr. Warder, that for me to help you there would have to be something substantial in return." Lead him on, lead him out, she thought.

"If this cartel thing comes off," he replied earnestly, "eventually the truth will out. All the facts of these deaths will be on a record and their prosecution will blacken everyone involved, even those of you who are comparatively innocent. Your illness"—read that death, the *Witwe* thought—"might preclude your being concerned at the moment. But surely the Pfeffermühle name is important to you. Would it not be useful to you for the baroness, for myself, to be able to testify that you were unaware of any wrongdoing, that you cooperated to help uncover the wrongdoing that did occur?"

Fool, thought the *Witwe*. Could you really think if I did not have other motives that such weak broth would cause me to help you?

"Go on," she said.

Aubrey deferred to Bethany who took it up.

"We are not so naive as to think you will tell us all you know. But we thought that one clue, a lead on where the American vines are could be spoken of without endangering you, and that we in return . . ."

"Now come, both of you," she said, unable to hold back. "Endanger? Surely it is obvious that *my* danger is not from without but from within." She allowed herself a ghostly smile. At that, in Warder's eyes she caught something similar to respect.

"Mr. Warder, let me ask you where you think the vines are."

"We do not know," he replied quickly and honestly. "Bridsey said you might know. He spoke of . . ." She could see he was reluctant to tell her everything, but that he correctly understood he must throw his last regiment into battle if he was to win anything at all. ". . . a scientist who . . ."

"*Sakrima Christa!*" she gasped. My fears are now fact. It was what she had been probing for and its discovery confounded her. The pain suddenly throbbed in her abdomen like a giant clock. She shut her eyes once more and put her head back on the pillow.

Following the cartel members' meeting in St. Gage's office, she had made her pointed but imprecise mention of a researcher to Bridsey for two reasons, both with her death in mind. First, it established with someone besides St. Gage that a

researcher—Berkady—had a legitimate claim on
the cartel's eventual profits. Secondly, more importantly and more subtly, if St. Gage should do
away with Berkady, then Bridsey, hearing of the
murder of a vine entomologist, would know St.
Gage or Tobb or one of their hirelings had done it.
Someday, somehow, Bridsey might use this knowledge to ruin St. Gage by setting the authorities on
him, thus carrying out the *Witwe*'s posthumous
revenge.

"A moment," she murmured. When, by raw
will, she had collected herself, she said in a voice
so low that her visitors had to lean forward to hear
her. "Do any of . . . the others know that Mr. Bridsey told you that?"

"About a scientist?" asked Aubrey.

"Yes."

"No."

God be praised, she thought, but her relief was
momentary.

"How did Mr. Bridsey come to confide in you,
Mr. Warder? Is it possible he confided in others,
as well?"

Aubrey thought a moment. He could refuse to
tell her, but that would guarantee her noncoop-
eration. He could continue to let her believe that
Bridsey, for whatever reason, had voluntarily told
them these things. But if she thought about it, she
would soon realize this was not credible. Or he
could simply tell her the truth.

"To be blunt, Frau Pfeffermühle, when we es-
caped, we used Mr. Bridsey as a hostage. Shots
meant for us killed Mr. Bridsey."

"Then," she whispered, closing her eyes,

knowing the answer, "Mr. Bridsey was in your . . . custody for some time."

Aubrey followed her thought, knew she had divined that he had physically or mentally tortured the information from the Englishman. Shrewd old lady, he thought, waiting for her to say more before he asked her more questions of his own.

The widow was upset. St. Gage and Tobb would know from seeing this man's brutishness that he would do what he needed to in order to extract every secret from Bridsey's fat head. And what were the secrets? Surely Bridsey had surmised the American wine industry was to be nullified. Surely St. Gage and Tobb would have known Bridsey suspected the American vines were being used for research to further that aim. St. Gage probably would wisely suspect that she had spoken to Bridsey about a researcher, perhaps even assume mistakenly that she had mentioned Berkady's name.

She almost choked out a sob. Gage, and his monster friend, Tobb, knew they could not trust poor Pieter. He was frail, susceptible to pain, to torture. They would know that this detective was a man as merciless as they were, one who would drain out everything Pieter knew within one ghastly hour. So even now, Tobb might be on his way to kill him. Angel of Death! Might they not take a chance on fighting the "insurance" in court rather than letting Pieter live to give his secrets to Warder and perhaps testify, if the pressure were great enough?

She began to get dizzy. There were so many imponderables.

How could she be sure Warder had not killed

Bridsey himself and might not now be seeking out Pieter to kill him and to thereby destroy the grand design. But surely Bethany von Mohrwald would not be party to such a thing. *Gott sei dank* for good Germans, even if they were Austrians.

Nevertheless, she thought of her former lover's body, first in the hands of Tobb, then in those of this Warder. These American fiends. As her options collated themselves, she saw imperatively that before striking any deal she must try to warn Pieter against St. Gage and Tobb on the one hand, and Warder on the other.

"Leave me for a few moments," she said to Bethany and Aubrey. "I must think of what you say. The nurse will have a servant bring you some wine." She looked with mild malice at Bethany. "Would you like to sample a recent bottle of my Jolly Priest, baroness?"

When they were gone, the *Witwe* took a sip of water. They would assume she was getting them out of the way for some selfish purpose, perhaps one dangerous to them. They might well think she was calling St. Gage. Let them. Everyone at this stage was desperate, she included. The day of the phylloxerans was at hand and they were all going a little mad.

She breathed deeply to steady herself and dialed Berkady's number. If only he were there and not just his blithering wife. The telephone rang but there was no answer. She dialed again. Tobb would never harm Pieter until he had delivered the insects and the antidote. The nasty little creatures were like a magic circle of fire, protecting Pieter from St.

Gage and Tobb. But once the plastic containers were loaded . . .

Alone in the tower chamber she groaned unhappily. She could not go to Neuilly herself. She could not trust this Warder. Weariness swept over her like a tide cluttered with debris. There was only Bethany von Mohrwald. Even if warning Pieter meant aborting the project, she must risk that.

She buzzed for the nurse.

"Send in the baroness. The other person can wait outside."

Bethany, as she came in, protested the exclusion of Aubrey, but the *Witwe* interrupted with a forceful hiss, "He is detestable."

Bethany recommenced her protest and again the *Witwe* silenced her.

"There is no time. Now listen to me. I am going to tell you where the vines are. You must follow my instructions to the last umlaut. You must *swear* to follow them."

"I believe I'd have to hear first what it is I am to swear to," said Bethany.

The *Witwe* felt an instant of blinding anger. This snippity Austrian! But she had no choice.

"I am going to give you the name of a man and his address. When you get there you must have him call me. When I have ascertained that you are with him, I will tell you where the vines are."

Having won the first round with the old woman, Bethany was unintimidated.

"Not enough. We will give him the message to call you only after we find the vines."

"You will . . . ," the old woman began, her voice

rising, then dissolving in a cough. She felt the extent of her dire helplessness. Bethany awaited capitulation.

"The vines are at the address I am giving you," said the *Witwe*, "I will write a note to the man at this address telling him to show you the vines and asking him to call. You will swear now to carry this out, above all to have him call me." There was no need to tell Bethany that speed was everything.

"I swear," Bethany said, somewhat disdainfully. "You're making the whole thing awfully Wagnerian."

"Do you think this business is some confection of a Strauss waltz, Frau von Mohrwald?" said the *Witwe* bitterly, emphasizing her failure to use Bethany's title. "It is your American gangster who has been talking of death, not I."

"I am not unserious about this," said Bethany. "But since you refuse to tell us what is going on here, or in California, or wherever, it is a bit difficult for me to deal with you sympathetically."

The *Witwe*'s only answer was a searing look. She returned to the note she was writing, with painful slowness.

Bethany tightened her lips. But as she watched the skinny wrist, saw the death's head behind the ivory skin of the old woman's face, she could not hate the *Witwe* Pfeffermühle.

When Bethany had gone, the *Witwe* counted: an hour to the Frankfurt airport. A plane was due out a few minutes after that. An hour flight to Paris. An hour, maybe less, to Neuilly.

Meanwhile she would keep calling Berkady. If

she got to him before Warder and von Mohrwald did, she could warn him of St. Gage and Tobb and, at the same time, tell him to refuse to speak to Warder and his Austrian puppet. She could urge him, when St. Gage and Tobb appeared for the phylloxerans and antidote, to have armed guards on hand and to reemphasize that new arrangements, outside his control, had already been made to put his "insurance policy" into effect if he died suspiciously or by manifestly violent means.

She must quickly get her lawyer to the tower, must, in addition to verbal instructions, write down what he was to do in the case of every eventuality. After that, the marzipan tin would be in the safe, an earnest of her love and a guarantee of Berkady's continued life.

The strain on her had set off the iron strides of the cancer within her. She sobbed softly in pain. From the night table she took two deep blue pills.

During the forty-five minutes before they took effect, she lay back, listening to the pain's retreat as if she were receiving advisory reports from an enemy front. In a few minutes the agony would have withdrawn enough for her to call the lawyer. Perhaps, out of caution, she should deposit the tin in the safe until he came. She would summon the nurse now. But it was the nurse who knocked on her door.

"It is a messenger from Dr. Berkady, or so he says," she whispered when she entered.

"So he says?"

"He is an American. Or English."

Who? wondered the *Witwe*. St. Gage? Tobb? Or some friend of Berkady drafted to run an eleventh-hour mission as she had drafted the von Mohrwald woman and her desperado employee.

"What does he look like?"

"A dark mustache," said the nurse, "a small beard. A heavy head of hair, also dark. A thick, strong-looking person."

Neither Tobb nor St. Gage, thought the *Witwe*.

"He says he has a small packet from Dr. Berkady that he can deliver only to you," the nurse continued.

So be it, thought the *Witwe*. But why didn't Pieter bring it himself? Perhaps because he was too involved with the packing and transfer of the insects. Yet was it not dangerous to trust anyone else? And why so soon after the last delivery? Her vertigo came back over her like the agitated wings of a great black bird. *Lieber Gott*, she thought, it is all so hectic. I, who am in pain and am dying, only want peace. Even from Pieter. And yet, I cannot afford peace.

"Let him come up," said the *Witwe*, rolling on her side to push the marzipan tin far back in the drawer of the bedside table.

When the visitor came in, she saw instantly that it was Tobb in an absurd disguise. Why? Why try to hide his looks from such discreet servants as he must know she would have? Then she saw the menace implicit in his concealment.

"You look ridiculous," she said rapidly. "What is happening? I am told that Bridsey is dead. What do you have from Doctor Berkady?" She said nothing of Bethany and Aubrey's visit.

"Berkady brought you some things last night.

I want them. And the other things he has brought."
His eyes darted around the room.

Her breath rushed out. Tobb had been to Pieter,
forced him to betray himself. Her mind burned
with a brilliant cold light.

"My lawyer has them. I gave them to him today. If you harm me or Pieter . . ."

"Your lawyer was in Frankfurt today. Your maid
confirmed he has not been here. You were waiting
for another delivery. They are here someplace. Save
yourself pain. Where are they?"

The *Witwe*'s heart banged in her chest like a
trapped bird. Given time, he would find the marzipan tin. Even in the safe, he would have found
it. Nothing stopped such men. In their violence,
in their recklessness, they were resourceful. Again
she thought: they are like the worst of the Nazis;
like the S.S.

She opened her mouth to call the nurse, had to
clear her throat and, in that split second, he was
beside her. His hand shot out like a snake's tongue
and covered her mouth.

"I want Doctor Berkady's insurance policy," he
whispered to her. "I am going to change the ben-
eficiary." He was smiling as he stared with his
leopard's eyes into hers. He waited for her own
eyes to signal an answer was forthcoming.

She tried to bite his hand, but that was hopeless. She could not even move her enfeebled jaws
under his steel grip. No, she thought, no. I will
not yield. The papers, the tapes are all that are
keeping my Pieter alive. I will not conspire in his
death.

Or had Tobb already done the worst: killed Pieter and rushed here. Her head spun. Anything was possible. Was not the impossible happening to her at this very moment? The only impossible was that she would betray her lover.

If only the American and Bethany von Mohrwald reached Berkady in time. She knew that if Pieter called and found that she was. . . . Now she understood. When or if Pieter called she *would* be dead. But in such a case he would know with scalpel sharpness that she had been killed and that he was the certain next victim. He could save himself. Her body, dying anyway, would redeem his.

With a fierce shudder of strength, she tried to shake her head: to shake it against telling Tobb anything; to shake it against her own murder.

Tobb was still smiling as he gently reached under her head and, his one hand retaining its grip on her mouth, pressed the pillow firmly on her nose. She tried to thrash her legs as she began to suffocate. But suddenly she felt the covers, heavy as a leaden apron, weighing on her. Tobb had lain on her body, lovelessly, lustlessly, to keep her dying struggles from making any last sound.

Thirty

THE LABORATORY II

The wrought-iron gate at 14 Rue de l'Horloge was locked. Aubrey pushed the buzzer. When there was no answer, he walked across the sycamore-lined street to where he could look over the box-woods at the upper stories. Light glowed from two windows. He buzzed again and again but without response.

"Oh shit," he murmured apprehensively. Should they wait until someone came back to the house? Things were moving too fast for that. Besides, maybe no one was coming back.

"The lock?" asked Bethany.

"I never learned to pick one," he said.

"Some reporter; some detective," she said, touching his arm to let him know that, even now, she meant her jibe to be humorous.

Aubrey thought of smashing the lock with a bullet, but on the quiet street it would draw immediate attention.

"The hedge?" Bethany asked.

It was too thick for them to breach. Aubrey considered the gate a brief minute, then said, "Bethany, I'll have to boost you up over the gate. There just isn't any other way."

She pressed her lips together in reluctant assent and he went on, "You'll have to be careful of the pikes on top and sort of roll to the side and over the hedge before you drop. Can do?"

She gave him a weary grin as if to make a point of the absurdity of it all and began to take off her shoes.

Aubrey pulled out his pistol and said, "Wrap the muzzle of this thing in your scarf. Shoot it directly into the keyhole, standing flat up against the door so if there's any splatter it won't hit you." He took her upper arm. "I'm sorry. If you could boost me up, but . . ."

"Oh, Aubrey," she said, "stop whining." She was concentrating on how she could land on the other side without twisting her ankle. She looked up and saw his hurt expression. "Do I need to know anything else about that thing?" she said to make him feel better, nodding at the pistol.

He checked the safety on the pistol and watched her rather cavalierly drop it down the front of her blouse.

"When you've shot the keyhole, take this"— he pulled out the switchblade—"and clear away the junk. You should be able to pry the tongue out of the latch plate."

It took all his strength to push her up the gate's side, then support her feet while she scrambled over. She hit the ground with a hefty thump.

"Donnerwetter!" she exclaimed and he knew she was all right.

"Here comes the shoes," he said, and tossed them over to the left of where her voice had come from.

For more than two minutes he waited. Then there was a muffled report like a large firecracker going off in a box. He hoped no one in the quiet faubourg had heard it. In a moment the buzzer should sound, but there was nothing. At last, there was a second shot. She had not been able to shatter the lock sufficiently the first time. In a moment the gate lock buzzed. He pushed open the gate and strode rapidly to the front door.

Bethany was just inside, the pistol still in her hand. He took it from her and they listened. There was no sound within the house, nothing. Quietly, they searched the downstairs. It was as neat as if it had just been Thursday-cleaned. They crept into the cellar which smelled strongly of the chemicals stored in the boxes, jugs, and bottles. But aside from these and other scientific arcana there was again nothing.

Pistol drawn, Aubrey went up the stairs to the second floor. At the top he recoiled. On the hall carpeting, crumpled, her black wool skirt immodestly above her ungainly knees as if from a struggle, was a heavy, aged woman. Her throat was cut and the blood made an incongruously modern abstraction on the Victorian floral design of the rug.

Aubrey tried to turn Bethany away from the sight and back down the staircase, but she pushed past him, only to gasp when she saw the terrible gash. An open pocketbook lay beside the dead woman. Had her murderer wanted to make the police think robbery was a motive? Or was it that the killer had sought the key to lock the old-fashioned front door as he left?

Aubrey pushed open the first door in the hall and saw a bedroom as neat as the downstairs with a night lamp on. The room was the kind to which old married people would retire gratefully at the end of their day.

Further down the hall to the left was another ordinary wooden door. Aubrey opened it and inside was the metal laboratory door.

"This is it," he said, trying the handle, relieved the door was not locked. It swung open onto darkness and a strange, murmuring sound as of water running quietly, but ominously. A rash of tiny, flying somethings touched his face. He cursed and smacked at them, drawing back involuntarily. He reached in for a light switch, feeling more of the objects on his forehead. It was like being touched by many hairs.

He flicked on the light and illuminated suddenly a scene so unbelievable that he grunted aloud while, behind him, Bethany uttered a sharp cry.

The laboratory, in its disorder, seemed huge, high. A pigeonhole desk was overturned, its papers strewn on the floor. A chair was thrown atop a broken glass case like a piece of trendy sculpture. From the jagged broken sides of this and other cases dirt had poured like sawdust from a torn doll.

The contents of the cases were gone. Aubrey stared at the decayed and necrotic rootage on the floor. This was the place they had sought so long: the last of the peripatetic American vines!

Most shocking were the insects. Crawling, flying, glued nastily to the shards of glass, were swarms of small licelike things, yellow, brown, winged, unwinged, hideous phases of a single species.

As Aubrey opened his mouth to speak, more flew in. He spat in disgust, almost retching. Behind him Bethany was using her fingers to try to comb the horrid mites from her hair.

"Aphids," he said. "Phyl . . ."

". . . loxera," they finished together.

Her eyes bugged. She dropped the root, knocking off more of the vile animals. Their tiny wings flickered effulgently in the bright lights.

"Oh, *Jessas*," she said, shaken by her own assumption. "They were being used to test the phylloxerans. The American vines should be resistant. They aren't to these . . ."

"They've developed a strain," Aubrey interrupted, "that will . . ."

"Eat the California vines just like they were European."

They looked silently at each other.

"We've got to call Duddman," he said. "Everybody."

He looked wildly around for a telephone.

"Who'll believe you?" she almost screamed at him. "Who'll believe it? Proof, Aubrey! You've got to find proof! There's bound to be something in here."

Immediately, he saw the truth of what she said, but he stood stock still, stunned at what they had discovered. Their theory had to be right. It fit with everything. This was the guarantee that California would be nullified. But unless they could give the

American authorities more than a speculative warning, who besides Duddman and Hernandez would believe him?

Bethany wasn't merely speculating. She grabbed up a piece of paper, looked at it an instant, then discarded it. Aubrey began doing the same, making a heap of those he had looked at, unfolding the crumpled ones and putting them, too, in the looked at pile.

As he moved toward the overturned desk, he saw a rivulet of blood coming from beneath its corner. In it a battalion of phylloxerans had already drowned. He peered over the desk.

There, a grin of yellowed teeth above the fatal grin of gore on his throat, was Berkady, his white robe front clotted with still more blood. The lice swarmed over him. His good eye stared up at Aubrey but it was clogged with insects. Aubrey recoiled.

"Berkady, dead," he said, his voice cracking.

Bethany started in his direction, then stopped.

"Murdered, like the woman," he said.

"What . . . ?"

"Police. I'll call. We've waited too long already." He searched for the telephone while she stood upright. "Keep looking," he said. "Don't stop."

The telephone lay behind the tumbled wastebasket, uncradled. Aubrey followed the wire to where it had been torn from the wall. He put the receiver between his head and shoulder, newspaper style, and scratched the phone's wires to the bob-tailed leads protruding from the wall. But the phone, perhaps smashed internally by its rough treatment, was as dead as its owner.

"Aubrey," Bethany called and he rose and hurried to the center of the room where she held a slip of paper. It was an invoice, the merchandise described in a rude scrawl.

"*Abeilles*," she read. "*Recipients*. Bees. Containers for bees. Two hundred twenty of them."

"Jesus Christ," he said. "That's enough for . . ." Then a second wave of shock hit him. "What's the date?"

It was four days ago.

"They're on the way to California," she said, almost with awe.

They understood simultaneously, but he spoke first.

"These just got left behind . . ."

"Yes. The others. The two hundred containers of them . . ."

"Will be on the vines out there in a few hours. That's why they killed this guy. They had what they needed from him and they didn't want any whistle-blowing." He was breathing hard from the shock. "We've got to find something else, some evidence that we're right. Fast, fast." He went wildly to work, scanning flat sheets, uncrumpling others.

"Hey . . . ," he said over one of the pieces of paper, smoothing out its wrinkles. It was in handwriting, odd backward-leaning handwriting, and with a fountain pen. Aubrey's nervous, moist fingers picked up ink from it.

"Fresh," he told Bethany as she studied it.

"He was writing it when . . ."

"They killed him."

The writing appeared to be false starts on some kind of formula. There were chemical abbreviations, lines scratched out.

"If he was writing on it when they came in, then why would it be balled up and thrown on the floor? Why not just drop it in a wastepaper basket?"

"Unless he was in a panic, writing it to *avoid* being killed."

"Formulas?"

"To protect these things, keep them alive."

"Or to protect the European plants, the cartel's vines, against them. They would never use these things without . . ."

"An antidote," she said. "He was giving them the antidote."

"He *gave* them the antidote," he said. "And after they got it they killed him anyway."

"If we could find the formula, we could save . . ."

"We could save California." But they wouldn't be so foolish as to leave behind anything complete. Still, he fell to, looking for similarly crumpled papers. They found two more false starts, nothing more. Aubrey would have to call Duddman, try his theory, hope Duddman would be willing to help on the basis of the thin evidence they had turned up.

There was still Berkady's body. Might there not be something there. With repugnance, he went behind the desk, reached under the corpse, but felt no wallet. He checked the pockets one by one. Nothing. The murderer had foreseen a search and vacuum cleaned him.

As Aubrey rose, he glanced down at the dead

man's hands. They had been half-closed when Aubrey first looked at them. Now, Aubrey shivered. They were, ever so slowly unclinching as a result of Aubrey shifting the corpse. Rigor mortis was tightening the muscles on the back of the wrists, prying open the hands as if by pulleys.

The ghastly phenomenon revealed an odd ink marking on the left thumb. With distasteful care, Aubrey held back the fingers but it was too dark behind the desk to discern the mark.

"Bethany," he called. "Brace yourself. I need that gooseneck lamp on the floor." She tested the light and brought it around the desk, grunting in dismay at the sight of the corpse.

She held the light close to the palm. There, only slightly distorted by the ink seeping into the whorls, were several letters. They were backward. Berkady had made them by pressing his thumb on the drying ink of his notes, obviously unnoticed by his killer.

One letter was a distinct backward C. The others, at a slight angle to the first, were more difficult.

"A-One," suggested Aubrey. "A-One? Top flight."

It's also a steak sauce, he thought, but that's crazy even by this case's bizarre standards. Even top flight made no sense.

"It would be words from the formula. That's what he was working on," said Bethany.

"Or chemical symbols," said Aubrey. "C is carbon."

"CA-one?"

"Ca is calcium but that's a capital *A*."

"Not A-one," Bethany said. "A-ell. Al."

"Aluminum. Carbon aluminum? Nothing."

"CA-ell. Cal," she said. "California. Even I . . ."

Aubrey let the dead arm flop to the floor.

"Yeah," he said. "Yeah. It's got to be."

Aubrey paused for a moment amid the disorder to try to think whether there was anything further they could discover before they went out to seek a pay phone. Nothing occurred to him. He picked up the crumpled papers with the aborted formulas, knowing he should be leaving them there for the police. But that could wait on his copying them for anything his and the von Mohrwalds' scientific friends could make of them.

Fingerprints? he thought as he prepared to go. But there were too many. Theirs were all over the place. They'd have to give a set to the French police anyway. He wondered whether the killer or killers had taken time to erase theirs. Probably.

It was a long walk before they found a corner bistro. They were able to convince the proprietor to give up almost his entire supply of jetons. First Aubrey had Bethany call the police. His next gambits depended in part on the murders becoming a media event, one that would give credence to his implausible warnings. And the media coverage depended on the French police acknowledging they were working on a double murder, the husband a scientist pursuing phylloxera research.

Aubrey had Bethany tell the French police that she would meet them in front of 14 Rue de L'Horloge, that a famous entomologist-botanist and his wife were inside with their throats slashed and that she was the Baroness von Mohrwald from Austria.

Lived there a desk sergeant with soul so dead or *pourboire* pocket so full that he would not phone his favorite Paris popular press journalist or Agence France-Presse stringer upon getting such a call?

Behind Bethany, a customer waited to make his call. As she spoke, his eyes widened, until, unable to maintain his Gallic sangfroid, he walked over to the bartender.

"*Mais c'est les Belges . . .* ," Aubrey heard the bartender say. They slipped into excited argot. The patron ran for the door to be first on the scene, the bartender close behind him. But he realized someone must mind the store, and with an anguished "*merde alors*," he returned to where he could, at least, hear Bethany's words.

The police notified, Bethany worked with intense frustration and determined politeness to get the French telephone operator to dial and redial Schloss Löwenfels until the busy signal gave way to the ring.

A man's voice, cold and cautious, answered. Bethany demanded to speak to the *Witwe*. For answer, the man asked who she was.

Thinking fast, perhaps at some deep level, anticipating who the man on the other end of the line was, Bethany said only that she was an old friend of Frau Pfeffermühle.

"She has been sick. I was worried," said Bethany, not having to fake any sense of anxiety. "Is this her doctor?"

"No," said the voice.

"Well, who is *this* then? I do not recognize *your* voice."

"Madame, this the police."

"The police?" gasped Bethany. "Is there something wrong? Please let me speak to Frau Pfeffermühle. Tell her please that the Gräfin von Höffenstatler is calling."

The voice on the other end of the line hesitated. Bethany knew her Germans well. Titles, even for women, had their way with the lesser folks.

"Gräfin," said the policeman, still cool, but more cooperative. "It is my sad duty to report that Frau Pfeffermühle has passed on. If I may ask without presumption, had you spoken with Frau Pfeffermühle recently, or could you give me any information . . . ?" Bethany hung up and turned to Aubrey, taking his arm to steady herself. She saw he had divined her conversation from her side of it, still she said, "They've killed her. He said 'passed on,' but from his voice . . ."

In the wretched light of the bistro, Aubrey looked in his little black book for a home phone number for Hernandez. Again Bethany cajoled a French operator and finally Hernandez was on the telephone, uncomfortably accepting a collect call from Monsieur Aubrey Warder in Neuilly.

"Where's Neuilly?" said Hernandez, when he heard Aubrey's voice. "Why collect at home?"

"Oh, goddamn it," said Aubrey too tired to be angry. "It's outside Paris and I'll pay you back. Now please for Christ's sake, try to listen . . ."

He looked up at Bethany, nodded that it was okay for her to go back to the house to meet the police, and rolled his eyes as if to say, "Dear God, what next." Bethany reached to his wrist and squeezed it both to encourage and reassure him.

Concise as the newspaper crime reporter he had once been, he told Hernandez what had happened since d'Edouard's pigeonry.

". . . and so I'm sure of it, crazy as it sounds. They are flying these things to California and they think, and I think, too that it'll work. So somebody's got to get a watch put on two-bit airports and landing strips. And somebody's got to get the vineyards looking out for strange trucks and planes. I don't know how the hell they plan to get these things onto the vines."

"Oh God," said Hernandez, so effective in one-on-one police work, so inadequate when it came to political action. "Aubrey, I believe you. But the evidence. Jesus, ink on a stiff's hand. It's as crazy as the rest of it."

Hernandez agreed to call his chief, to try to get the state police and wine country localities to put out some kind of alert. Aubrey, pessimistic about what Hernandez could do, thanked him for trying and got Duddman's home telephone number from him.

The coroner was as gloomy about any action as Hernandez, but slightly more resourceful.

"Look, I believe you. And no, you don't have to tell me what kind of fucking hero I will be if I save the farm. But do you understand how insane your evidence is . . ."

There it was again. Aubrey tried to interrupt him, but Duddman was half-raging over the burden Aubrey had put on him.

"Of course you know. Why do I ask? But *I* know this state. Until these little shitbirds hit the fan . . ."

". . . ground," Aubrey could not resist.

"Very funny. Until they do, I'm going to look like an Orange County nut and I'm not even from Orange County." He too promised he would try:

with the local prosecutor, the nearby U.S. Attorney, a couple of state legislators he knew.

Aubrey, with four fifty-dollar bills in escrow with the bartender against the toll charges, now called an old friend at NBC, hoping he would put something on radio or TV on the strength of Aubrey's words. Good story, said the man. He'd get on it first thing in the morning, but until he could get substantiation, he wouldn't dare go with it.

Aubrey's acquaintance at the State Department took a gruffer but similar view, as did an ancient source at the FBI who had been appointed to one of the less important assistant directorships and whom Aubrey had reached through the bureau's switchboard.

As Aubrey implored, he felt more frantic. For all his good years of reporting, his sound reputation, the story was just too weird, the evidence interesting, but too sketchy for instant action. Aubrey felt like Laocoön.

Bone-tired, worried about how Bethany was doing with the French police, he checked back with Duddman. The coroner was almost in tears. Aubrey was touched in spite of his own woe. Duddman had finally risked his own emotions on the case. He was a believer, he too trying to convert the unbelieving.

"Everybody," said Duddman, "between me and Hernandez, we've tried everybody we even thought of knowing. I called up a classmate in the governor's office I haven't talked to in twelve years."

"The State Agriculture people, don't they understand what can . . . ?"

"They're the worst. Asshole bureaucracy at its

hairiest. It never happened so it can't happen. At least the governor's guy got the state cops to promise to get the locals to make special checks on abandoned airstrips in the wine areas."

Well, that was something, Aubrey thought, but not much. If he were doing it, he'd jet the bugs over in an old 707 cargo plane to Mexico and transfer them to prop planes that could land on a highway if they had to. Or more likely the planes would simply sow the things like they were Agent Orange. Or maybe they were going to be dropped in bombs and blow all over the place. Or crop-dusted, for that matter. Whatever the case, he would guess a few desultory checks by local cops not even knowing what they were looking for, probably thinking it was drug flights, were not going to turn up the phylloxerans.

"Keep trying," said Aubrey. "And thanks for believing."

Desperate, at last, he called his old paper, the *Washington Eagle*. It would be morning before they would go into print with it. And morning would be too late.

Even at the *Eagle* he had to hold until the new managing editor could be called at home. How fast things change, Aubrey mused, feeling useless, defeated. When finally, the night rewrite man, an old comrade, came on the telephone, Aubrey began, "Slug it 'Bugs' and dateline it Neuilly, France, that's N as in Nellie, E as in Easy . . ." Before he began the body of the story from the quick outline he had prepared while waiting for the managing editor's okay, he told his friend bitterly, "And, Harry, make sure they spell the byline right."

Thirty-one

ADIEUS

On the way to Berkady's house, Aubrey slipped the pistol and holster into a rain sewer, feeling nervously unprotected as he walked toward the glimmer of many lights down Rue de l'Horloge.

Once there, it was like the old days when he was covering a major fire, explosion, or police raid. No simple murder could have brought so many whirling lights, pulsating sirens, marked and unmarked police cars, ambulances, bullhorns, uniformed and plainclothes cops, TV trucks, press radio cars, and gaping citizens.

As he worked through the mobs toward the police barricades, he saw that the command post was inside the hedge. There, portable floodlights raised a glow that luridly lighted the face of the old dwelling.

At the barricade, Aubrey found a corporal, flashed his detective credential and tried to assert in French that he was a *témoin*. But it didn't gel until an onlooker began to translate for him. Aubrey explained that he, like the Austrian baroness who was surely now inside the hedge, had been on hand when the bodies were discovered.

The corporal, studiously cool, listened intently, then ushered Aubrey under the barricade. From corporal to sergeant to homicide detective, he was led through the gate to where Bethany sat incongruously in an imitation Louis Quinze chair brought from the living room of the house.

Squatting or standing around her, like postulants around a worn but still chic Delphic oracle, were the detectives.

Bethany looked up at Aubrey with relief.

"There he is," she told her chief interrogator, a lean young man with shallow, bright eyes, "the man I spoke of. Our investigator."

It was evident from her tone that her story had not seemed entirely credible to the French cops. Aubrey would be more in their element. He showed the dapper inspector his Virginia private investigator credentials and, using Bethany as translator, neatly and precisely recited the main facts of the story.

He omitted both the effort by St. Gage to rape Bethany (out of respect for her modesty) and his pressures on d'Edouard (out of fear of the Frenchman's pull on his home turf).

He hit hard on the earlier deaths of Wheatley-Smith, Maier, Bridsey, the *Witwe* Pfeffermühle. These were events ascertainable within minutes from French and neighboring police. They would give substance to the other bizarre aspects of the case.

The inspector nodded, interrupting briefly and

somewhat self-importantly to comment that he was aware of the Maier death and that of the esteemed late Scotland Yard inspector whom he had the honor of having met once in London.

As Aubrey spoke, he kept his eyes on the inspector, glancing from time to time at Bethany to pick up her nods as he stressed points she had already made. The coinciding of their stories, he knew, was an element in believability.

When he finished, he begged the inspector to ask the Foreign Ministry to alert the American Embassy, late at night as it was, that there had been a report that the vineyards of California were about to be attacked.

Bethany's voice was intent as she translated, but Aubrey could see the unbending look in the Frenchman's eyes. This is a police case, monsieur, the look seemed to say. In the morning, perhaps, we will speak with our Foreign Ministry liaison, the look seemed to add.

"All proper steps will be taken, I assure you," said the inspector when he had heard them out.

Discouragement weighed on Aubrey like a stone slab. The inspector took him and Bethany to a newly refurbished precinct office in a decaying building in Neuilly, where they retold their stories into a tape recorder. Then a sleepy-eyed male French typist wrote up summary statements in French which Bethany had to translate for Aubrey while the inspector read the French over her shoulder.

At last, after signing affidavits that they would return to France at the call of the gendarmes, the inspector had them driven to the Sofitel Hotel at

Charles de Gaulle Airport. By the time they arrived, it was almost dawn.

Aubrey was too vanquished, too considerate of her to think of asking her to sleep with him. He went with her to her room, knowing that she would want to talk, if briefly, before they got—separately—the few hours sleep they would have before parting.

First, she tried to call Franz. Aubrey felt awkward, for he had no one who needed to know how he fared. He went to the bathroom and washed up. When the low murmur of her voice stopped, he went back into the room.

"He's in Vienna," she said, sitting on the bed by the telephone. "They don't have a number." As he looked at her, her face, already so drawn, crinkled along the age lines and she began to weep. Silently the tears flowed down her cheeks while he stood by helplessly.

Aubrey's mind was all but numbed by his weariness, so tired that only the most basic facts would form in it, and without subtlety. She has been such a fine comrade, he thought. She has done everything bravely and well and she has tried to call her husband to get approval and solace and he is out of town screwing his girlfriend.

The unfairness of it would have stirred him to anger had he not been so exhausted. Now he acted simply, compassionately rather than passionately. Respecting her tears, he did not try to dry them, or pat her or hold her.

Knowing how his own body ached and where, he went to her and knelt creakily in front of her.

Carefully he untied her scuffed shoes that had picked up the dirt of four countries since she had last changed them. He took them off and put them side by side on the floor, held her feet under the arch, one in each hand, and softly kneaded them.

At first she seemed taken aback. Then the tears came faster if no less silently. He watched them roll out of her eyes and down her cheeks. She dried them on her sleeve and in the same motion leaned to put her hand in his grimy gray hair.

At last, abruptly, she rose and went to the bathroom where she blew her nose. When she came back her face was red but dry and Aubrey had taken off his own shoes to rub his own tired feet. He looked up from where he sat on the bed with a smile but her face was still serious, as if some long filibuster in her own mind were drawing to a close.

Bethany walked to where he sat, dropped down beside him, and took his face in her hands. Tender, as familiarly as if they had been kissing all their adult life, she pressed her lips to his.

Aubrey felt now the peace of defeat. They had done all they could ever have been asked to do. And it had not been enough. Aubrey's mind moved away from all that and to the pressure of this woman's lips. They had a roughness to them, as lightly pressed as they were. Small wonder, he thought. My God, his must be like bark. And he hadn't washed for days or brushed his teeth. He needed a shave. Bethany, too, smelled a little less than dainty.

They broke and he looked at her. She had not opened her eyes. Nor did she for a moment. When she did, he saw the kind of resignation in hers that he felt in his own.

"We did everything right," she said.

"It's not the end of the world," he said.

"No," she said. "It's not." She sighed, deeply as if to wash all that out if she could. "Stay here tonight."

"I'd like that," he said, then wanting, for her sake to make it sound a little less like a proposition. "We'd have to talk someplace anyway about what we do next." Both of them knew he did not mean about them, but the case.

"Tomorrow is soon enough for that," she said.

He wondered a little anxiously how he was going to get from this romantic posture out of his clothes and into the shower and then back into the bed and into her arms. But it was not as if they were adolescents.

She took his hand and pulled him up even as he rose. Arms about each other's waists they walked to the shower stall, Aubrey thinking that it would feel good to have her scrub his back and to scrub hers in return. Beyond that he was not prepared at the moment to imagine.

Thirty-two

THE PHYLLOXERANS

Pierce Tobb, caught up in a dream of dawn patrol, watched from the crop duster he was piloting as another biplane below him released its phylloxerans on the vineyards. They wafted down like toxic snow.

Tobb, in spite of jet fatigue, had eagerly filled in when a flier he had hired failed to show up at the community airport outside Dos Palos, one of several landing fields at which his small bomber force had been loaded just before sunrise.

The little Ag-Cat he was watching moved like a gliding bird above and parallel to the vines. Then, the field seeded, it shot up swiftly but gracefully and was off to its next assignment.

Tobb, his pulse beating with the excitement of the job, banked his Stearman and headed northward where his first target lay: a toy cluster of barn, farmhouse, and other buildings against the backdrop of the immense Sierras.

The day was perfect for the phylloxerans. There was enough breeze to waft the streams of them over the vines, giving maximum coverage, without being strong enough to blow the precious insects uselessly into woods, unplowed fields, and roads. The sky was the most dulcet of blues, still aquarelled with pink from the California dawn.

So high were Tobb's spirits that he did not think of the ends of the conspiracy, only its means, this feeling of youth and adventure that had nothing to do with St. Gage or the millions they would reap from the present morning's work.

As he swerved and prepared to drop down on the westernmost row of the vineyard ahead, he did not see above him at five o'clock the California Highway Patrol Cessna 180 overtaking him.

Tobb's plane fell more steeply than he had intended. He drew back on the stick with a self-admonishing oath, leveled off, and a little disappointed with himself, began the row further along than he had planned.

"Rusty, rusty," he said.

At fifty feet, he pulled back the release handle that opened the hopper beneath the plane. A yellowish stream of insects billowed out. As he swiveled backward he saw them settling onto the fields. The glance also showed him the police Cessna not two hundred yards off his left elevator.

Tobb had assumed that some of his pilots would be caught. They could honestly say that they had thought the dusting material was a pest-killer. Tobb had carefully covered any inadvertent discovery of the insects by the crop dusters by telling them some few hoppers contained tiny parasitic wasps to eradicate vine moths. None of the hired fliers, he was sure, were entomologists enough to tell the difference.

When Tobb had been unable to resist filling in for the truant flier, he had known he, too, could be caught. As a precaution, he had moved his rented car from the airport to a spot off the approach road a half mile away. When he finished his task, he planned to land the efficient converted World War II trainer on the road, abandon it, and drive off. Not for him a welcoming party of cops and sheriffs. And, in case there was trouble, he had brought with him his long-barreled automatic and a sawed-off 12 gauge, both of which were within reach on the cockpit floor.

The police craft drew up almost wing to wing with him. When Tobb shot a look at the cockpit, he saw it was manned by two policemen. The one not piloting the plane was talking into his microphone, no doubt seeking instructions.

"Trouble," Tobb said aloud. "Tru-u-u-ble." He held to the rows, this section of the vineyard almost finished.

While the one policeman sought instructions, his pilot flew wing to wing with the Stearman, moving away when Tobb made his turns at the end of rows. Tobb wondered spitefully how far up the line this pissant cop would have to go before someone told him to stop flying in formation and do something.

Tobb's radio was fixed on the tower channel. He wished he had been able to hear what the policeman and his headquarters were saying. It wasn't long. As he bore westward toward the mountains, his radio, full of static began to growl.

"Stearman seven-five-six Foxtrot," the radio hailed him. There was a pause. Tobb made no response. "Stearman seven-five-six Foxtrot. This is Merced tower. The police plane in your vicinity informs us you are under arrest. Proceed to Merced and await clearance. Acknowledge please."

Tobb continued impassively on his course as if he had not heard, and in fact most of the crop dusters either lacked radios or had sets that were inoperative. He finished the last row and banked upward, the motor roaring throatily. It was futile for him to try to dust anymore. He had shown his defiance. Why wait until Air Force planes swept in with guns and rockets? He was adventurous, not suicidal. And it was time to figure how best to escape these dumb air cops.

The Cessna was back on his wing. The man beside the pilot popped up his side window and slipped out a long paddle on which was a printed message. Purposely Tobb looked toward the front, but the police plane shot ahead and there was no ignoring the message. "U R UNDER ARREST," said the strong black on white letters. The officer flipped over the paddle. On its reverse was "FOLO ME."

"Not on your ding-dong," said Tobb. "Nossir."

The high-wing 180 was much faster but also less maneuverable than the Stearman. But maneuverability was not much of an asset. True, Tobb's little radial-engined plane was reliable and would get him back to the road where it could safely land.

But the Cessna would be over him all the way, signaling ground police to pick him up before he could drive a mile, coursing over him as he fled in his car.

Tobb mused over the cop with his paddle. By the numbers, he thought. They sure do it by the numbers. The man drew the paddle back into the airplane. Tobb looked at the mountains. He could try to shake the police plane in the valleys and crags of the Sierras.

But by that time, even if he were successful, half the California Air National Guard would be on the lookout for him. It was just the sort of exercise they would love. And their antinarcotics efforts of the last few years probably had made them pretty sharp pilots.

As Tobb chugged on at an unchallenging 110 miles an hour ground speed, the window of the plane beside him opened and this time the policeman thrust out a double-barreled shotgun, probably one stowed in the plane for riot duty.

Tobb started to pull up his own shotgun and blast away. But that would be foolhardy. He had not done anything yet but defy commands to land. He was not fleeing, not making any movements that threatened the other plane.

In constitutionally-minded California, the police would not simply shoot him down for failing to obey an order. But it was conceivable that this guy would try to shoot out his motor, force him to crash-land on the stony ground below. Tobb feigned a look of alarm, slowed his plane, and docile as a bull following a steer from the ring, skillfully fell in behind the 180. The police plane made a wide sweeping turn to lead Tobb back toward its head-quarters.

For more than a minute Tobb played along. Far ahead he could see the ocean. The mountains were behind him now. When he had been a boy, well a college student, well a sometime college student, he had surfed just down the coast.

Momentarily poised on a crest of danger, his mind quirkily summoned up a scene. He remembered a wave, big as an elephant, and himself glancing quickly to see his foot position, glimpsing the blond hairs burned blonder on his leg, knowing his plant was right, perfect for no matter what wave came on. And then the wave rose under him, higher, higher, forever rising, and his heart and soul with it. His balance had been true for those instants, longer than any orgasm. He had felt himself to be only wave and wind and sun and trustable board. The board and he had swooped with the wave, and the wave with the earth and in his ears had pounded a line which some English class had fixed in his head, despite himself, ". . . and the world turned a little while with me." And he had wanted to cry for the joy and the cleanliness of it. At such times there had been no need to hurt, no possession by the thing in him that made him run violently, self-destructively counter to what his father, society wanted him to do.

But these free moments did not last, could not. And their substitute, their flip side, although he did not like that way of putting it, had been these other things he had done that gave him the same sense of heart beating faster, or danger, or importance.

He thumbed the safety of the shotgun on and then off again, just to be sure, and laid it across his knee, holding the plane's course with one hand. The Cessna ahead moved like a straightedge with its two straight cops, bringing home the bacon so they believed.

Pigs! he thought derisively. Brave beaters of blacks and Mexicans. Two such cops, plainclothesmen, had lied when they testified against him after his drug arrest. Oh, it was not that he was not into drugs, not that he was not dealing then. But they had testified to two ounces of heroin, nearly uncut, when in fact it had been a half-ounce and cut.

He gave the plane full throttle and roared fast and sure up above the plane in front of him and to its left. At the precise moment when he was abreast of the Cessna, he dipped his right wing so that nothing but twenty-five feet of air separated him from the police pilot. Indeed he could see the man's surprised face through the plastic. He throttled the Stearman a few yards ahead of the Highway Patrol plane.

Tobb put his knee to the stick to steady it, quickly aimed the shotgun at the wind-screen and simultaneously squeezed off both barrels. The blast jerked the gun upward wrenching Tobb's wrist.

The police pilot had already thrown the plane into a dive at sight of the shotgun, but the dive had come too late. The triple-ought buckshot shattered the wind-screen dashing plastic and lead into the two men's upper bodies.

Tobb felt the exhilaration of a bull's-eye shooter. He lowered the shotgun to the floor and banked the plane up and around. Beneath him, the Cessna pitched into a steep dive, then a spiral as its powerful engine plunged it ever faster toward the ground.

Tobb did not circle to watch every movement of its fall, but glanced back at instants as he flew toward the mountains. When the patrol plane finally dashed into the ground, it disappointed him because it did not catch fire as planes do in the movies. To avoid radar, Tobb dropped the Stearman to a few yards above the ground, a posture for which it was made in any case.

By this time, all over the California vineyards, the insects would be at their work, coming out of their stuporous state to affix themselves to the fall vines. He only regretted that he had been unable to discharge the entire contents of his hopper. But now his thoughts were for his security, then London, or perhaps the Italian Riviera would be where he would follow the developments stimulated by this rain of phylloxerans.

In a few minutes, if he had calculated right, he would be above the road near the community airport. He looked back, instinctively feeling that again he had been seen by a hostile party.

This time he saw the approaching plane while it was still no more than a speck. If it was an Air National Guard jet, then his only chance would be to crash-land and flee afoot, particularly if the shattered police plane's silence had alerted its dispatcher to some disaster.

If it was another Highway Patrol plane, then the odds were only a little less than equal for him, and mildly short odds had never really worried Tobb. After all, wasn't he still here, still viable, still alive and full of his fierce joys?

Tobb flew on, as if innocently, hoping the second plane's occupants had no knowledge of how he had dispatched his earlier combatants. At the same time, he reloaded the shotgun. The plane drew closer and he saw it was the twin of the first. More state pigs, he thought. Then ahead, he saw still another plane, this one a Maule Five. He felt a surge of something, not fear, but, as best Tobb could put it during the moment before his mind turned to action, bad karma.

He must instantly decide whether to give up, go in with them, stand trial for murder of the two other state policemen and God knew what else, or try to escape. The second after he had set up his options, he had made his choice.

He was already just above the ground where his maneuverability would most daunt his new enemies. They would have to take the same chances he was taking to get near enough to hurt him. Because there were two of them, he must assume they knew something of his previous air encounter. They would try to destroy him from out of range of his shotgun, if possible, and that meant an assault rifle. He had to assume the planes were equipped with them. The damn things had everything else aboard.

So tactics: his smarts against their firepower.

The Cessna was already over him, but far up. It was only moments before the Maule fell in a little lower and to the left. He wished the damned radio had a channel other than the tower. The thing crackled and he heard a cop voice coming in on the tower channel.

"Stearman seven-five-six Foxtrot, head that thing toward Merced. That's five degrees west of due north," the voice said, then paused. "If you don't you'll be shot down."

It was as simple as that. Apparently the state police were handling the whole job. He wondered where the Air National Guard was. With their jets, it would be hopeless for him. With these there was a chance, though even Tobb recognized how slight it was.

For response, he rode the controls back and forth, but unevenly, giving the plane the motion of a wounded insect, wobbly, hard to fix on with a hand-held weapon. As he did, he looked up, and the nearer plane's window snapped up; the black stick of a gun slipped out. He hit the rudder again, saw the puffs of smoke from an automatic rifle, but knew the shots were wide.

Christ, he thought, I'm like a tied duck in this open cockpit. He swerved the plane more drastically, looking upward. The automatic rifle sputtered again. This time the shots pitted the wings. Gotta do something, he thought, if they lead me on one of these turns, I'll fly right into a slug.

He gave the plane full throttle and swooped rapidly upward hoping to duplicate his successful stratagem against his first victim. But his new adversary, perhaps combat trained, peeled away and was behind him as the less powerful crop duster almost stalled. This time the Cessna had the clean shot, but the man with the rifle missed him, the bullets taking a piece of strut from above Tobb's head.

Frantically pulling out of the stall, Tobb was an easy target for the higher Maule, which slanted past, raking his fuselage. As it went by, Tobb jerked up the shotgun and fired at the side window, but could not tell if he had hit. Just then he felt a sting, no more, in his left leg. He dropped his hand from the controls for an instant, touched wetness, and knew he had been wounded, though not in a bone. But the blood would have to be dealt with.

His will still iron, he reckoned his moves. He had more shells and he had the automatic. He recalled for a moment a long-ago picture of a pilot in World War I aiming a pistol at another plane from the cockpit. He could not remember whether the man with the pistol was a German or a Frenchman. He gave a "humff" of amusement, seeing himself now in that same makeshift role.

The 180 swept up toward him and he dived back down toward the ground, pulling out just above the underbrush. Leveling, he felt again at the wound. It was gooey but not sopping. A vein then, and not a big one. Good luck, he thought, and "humffed" again with humor. If this was good luck, God protect him from the bad.

The Maule Five came at him from nowhere and he pushed the rudder pedal hard. But the Stearman did not respond. He knew a slug had disabled it. Still he flew on, slumping back in the cockpit so he could use the windshield as a brace in aiming his sawed-off shotgun.

Slugs spattered across the plane just back of the

cowling. My God, he thought, they're hitting me at eighty yards! What kind of goddamn marksmen are these guys? All they have to do is move a volley four feet closer and I'm hamburger.

Tobb worked the elevators and ailerons. They functioned. But without the rudder he'd be about as evasive as a fat duck.

His mind, though, was working as smoothly as the plane was ungainly. The police were firing M-16s, he reasoned, or some such. That meant a good deal of reloading. There was still an odds-off chance for him if he could just use the intervals to do some magic with the crippled Stearman.

The Cessna dove at him. He fired at it, missed, and jerked the ailerons and elevators, rolling the plane away precipitously, belly-up, fast enough to forestall a clean shot.

But the plane's automatic fire minced his windshield, flinging bits of plexiglass onto his face and into the cockpit. He was cut and the wind in his eyes made flying, much less reloading, almost impossible.

His mind disoriented for a moment, he held the plane steady by instinct. Then his faculties came back with a rush.

"Tobb's last stand," he said, no panic in him, rather a certain pride. Strongly, he felt ennobled, vindicated by the odds against him. He could not shoot. He could not escape. He could only fly.

"Cowardly pricks," he muttered, kicking the plane laboriously into a left roll, right roll as the Cessna pulled up above him preparatory to another dive.

"Oh you mothers," he said, biting on his determination as if it were a cold piece of steel. "Dive close, oh please dive close!"

The Cessna did dive close. This time instead of veering away, Tobb waited until the last second and kicked the aging crop duster's nose directly down toward the diving plane's tail. The police gunfire went wild.

As the police plane pulled out of its dive and slowed, Tobb gave his Stearman the gas, cut across the parabola of the patrol plane's dive, and accelerated toward its tail. The pilot saw what Tobb had done and tried to evade the sawing prop.

But the whirling blade ripped at the sleek plane's tail, the clatter like some great iron thing ripping apart. The Stearman shuddered, almost flinging Tobb from the seat. He sunk low to avoid the wind and the flying bits of metal, holding the stick stable with all his might.

The attack cost Tobb his prop and almost cost the policemen their lives. The Cessna careened dangerously close to the ground, its guidance system maimed, then struggled for altitude.

For a strange few moments, the two planes were upreared side by side. Tobb and his enemy stared with hate into each other's eyes before each went back to trying to save his aircraft.

The Cessna continued to climb. Although it was wobbly, its ability to turn left or right all but destroyed, its motor was intact.

Tobb's powerless Stearman almost stalled. No more than two hundred feet up, he looked down and saw beneath him, so close he could almost count the grapes, a small vineyard.

There was no time to pick and choose. He could only try to make his landing as near tail down as possible. The quasi-stall had dropped his speed so wind was no factor. He pulled back on the stick, got the tail in place with a jerk that left the stick totally useless in his hands.

The Stearman sat down heavily, still going too fast. The sturdy vines tangled the wheel struts and caught at the wings as if they were live creatures of revenge. While Tobb frantically banged the release on his seat belt, instinctively fearing fire, explosion, the left wing crumpled, and the plane did a cartwheel.

Tobb was knocked unconscious as he was thrown from the cockpit. The immense noise of the crashing plane quickly gave way to silence. There was no fire. When Tobb came to a moment after the crash, he felt whole save for vague pains in his chest and his legs.

"I'm gonna get out," he said. "I pulled it off." His spirits, buoyed by his animal courage, his intrinsic optimism, almost made him sing. He sought to roll out from under the section of wing which lay on his chest and right arm.

But when he did, there was a pain so sharp that he grunted. The wreckage held his torso pinned. Something inside his chest had cracked, ribs perhaps, so that any movement was anguish. And now his previously uninjured leg was beginning to throb.

"Oh shit," he said.

Shock had protected him briefly but soon the pain would crest over him, he knew. A rib was broken, that was clear. And his leg perhaps, too. Was it bleeding? There was no feeling in it below the knee, only the throb of his thigh.

"Femur," he said to himself. He tried to collect his thoughts. Gingerly, with his free left arm, he sought to push off the wreckage, but it was too heavy. Part of the fuselage was on the top of it, he could now see. Was there anything he could reach to pry it upward so he could roll free? Feeling the pain in his chest each time he moved his arm, and grunting with its enormity he nevertheless felt on the ground around him, then up toward the hopper which held the insects. He fingered the hopper's ruptured aluminum side, jagged as a ripsaw. When he brought his hand down, bloodied from where he had touched his face, it was covered with live phylloxerans.

Disgusted, he wiped his hand hurriedly on the wing but the sudden motion caused him excruciating pain in his chest. He began to curse to himself now, to fend off the terrible pain. What now? He put his mind to it.

Someone would come, he thought. Someone would have seen the crash and would summon a rescue squad which would jack the terrible weight from his chest. In the midst of the pain, in the midst of the tears of agony that were coming into his eyes, he imagined the rescue squad arriving, saw brawny men raise the wing, put him on a stretcher, inject him with morphine to take away this awful pain that was replacing the shock's brief easements. He saw himself in the hospital, under guard to be sure, recovering use of his body which had served him so well. He saw his lawyer. St. Gage would have to give him the best of defenses.

St. Gage's name snapped him back to a moment of total lucidity. The smooth Englishman was comfortable in London. He had played them all, Maier, Berkady, Bridsey, the *Witwe* , even him, Tobb, like a marionette-master. He had exposed his flank—Tobb grimaced with the start of a raw laugh—only once when they were chasing that newspaper maniac in Portugal.

A spasm of pain shook Tobb and he slipped back into his dream. He saw the judge giving him a long sentence, imagined a few months in jail, a perfect behavior record until he could find some way to escape, again with help from outside, for St. Gage would have to aid him or face the temple crumbling in on him, with Tobb as Samson.

Suddenly his mind came clear again. He felt the wrenching, scraping pain in his chest. He felt the weakness that he knew must come from substantial blood loss. They must come, he thought. He licked his lips, tasted his own blood, and something else.

With repugnance, he swiped his hand across his mouth and drew it away. The blood on his lips was aswarm with insects. He looked up. Crawling from the bright sunlight on the fuselage into the shadow where he lay were legions of phylloxerans. Some made short flights, landing here, there, their wings iridescent.

Tobb thought of Berkady, dead behind the desk, and the insects swarming out of the glass case he had smashed. And now they were here, and he as helpless to defend himself against their relentless march as Berkady's corpse. The disgusting bugs and St. Gage had conquered all.

They dropped from the wings, creeping in straggly regiments along his shoulders and on his neck, like tiny lemmings drowning in the blood from his face. They were inside his shirt, crawling down his body. Revolted, he squashed them. Others fell from his jacket and onto the ground. They and their fellows were on the move. They were headed in the tens of thousands into the vineyard, into the fields to do what Tobb and St. Gage had planned for them to do.

"Ugh," Tobb said and tried to wipe the bugs from his face, from his chest. But the yellow and off-yellow creatures merely stuck to his bloody fingers. He rubbed his fingers on his shirt, but the shirt, too, was fouled with blood from his face and with dying bugs. The blood and plant lice were covering him like some grotesque cake icing.

"Ugh," he said again, his mind swirling. He tried to grab again at the dream that he would be saved and began to cry "help." His voice sounded as if it came from someone else, far off. It only made his ears ring. As he called, the pestilence invaded his mouth. He shut his lips, imagined that he was calling, but tasted the mix of blood and bugs.

"Oh, no," he said almost sadly, at last recognizing he might not escape, that no one might come. "No." The idea of death made him frantic. Life, a life of vigor and in his terms the greatest fullness had been all there had been for him. He had gloried in life, living it as he saw living at its most rewarding. That no longer possible, there was only an abyss.

With all the strength in his left arm, he tried to push up the wing. It seemed to move a little, but in his chest there was a pain such as he had never known before. He let the arm flop down and screamed, his mind groping toward the pistol which he knew was still in the cockpit, or somewhere but not available to him, not where he could at least take his death in his hands as he had taken his life in his hands. His fingers clawed at his bloody, insect-infested chest to try to get at the pain. But it would not go away.

"Oh," he screamed. "Oh God, God, God." He could not stand it. At last the pain in his chest turned him bestial. There was only his voice, screaming and screaming, and the terrible pain. Just those two.

The insects heard nothing, felt nothing, or if they did it did not move them from their course into his open maw. Their sisters, like untrained militia, straggled out into the sunshine and toward the vines.

Thirty-three

VINCET ST. GAGE

St. Gage stood by the window looking out on the Thames as he had all those months ago when his plan had seemed so problematical. Behind him on the table of the conference room, a place he loved well for its view, *The New York Times* was outspread.

In its front-page story, the newspaper had done an astonishing job during the single day since the rain of phylloxerans of piecing together the puzzle.

The insects, it said, had been speedily identified by the California Department of Agriculture as phylloxerans. At first, the scientists had thought the whole thing was the work of some lunatic. After all, it was well known that American vines were, in the language of oeno-entomologists, "tolerant" of the pests. The phylloxerans, which had displayed a virulent vigor in going for the vines, were immediately tested with conventional insecticides. They were found to be almost impervious except in dosages which would poison the grape crop as well.

After the *Times* story had dealt with the breaking aspects in California, it had picked up large sections from an article by the abominable Warder in the scurrilous *Washington Eagle*. It was clear the *Times* was chary of both newspaper and reporter, the one because of its reputation, the other because he had deserted journalism.

Nevertheless, through quotes from Warder's story, the *Times* did allude to St. Gage's role in Portugal. He was humiliated at the sight of his name in print. Not only did he fumingly regret ever going there, but, so profoundly catastrophic had the effect been on his psyche that he had come to detest the aberration which had led to his debacle.

The *Times*, still quoting the *Eagle*, had picked up Warder's charge that St. Gage "had physically abused a prominent Austrian vineyard owner, a baroness." The name and details had been withheld by Warder probably in order not to further unsettle Bethany von Mohrwald. St. Gage was also cited as present when William Bridsey was shot to death.

More respectably, but as dangerously, St. Gage was named in the *Times* story as a lawyer who had figured in the buy-up of European vinelands. Both the *Times* and *Eagle* stories had been circulated in Europe by the wire services as St. Gage knew from calls to him for comment.

He had dodged them all. To counter the reports, he had prepared and one of his law partners had read to inquirers a statement saying the references to St. Gage were "fabrications by a seedy private detective and a European vineyard owner, both of them parties in interest. Indeed, the detective and the Austrian vintner trespassed on Mr. Bridsey's land in Portugal, and the detective brutalized a Portuguese worker and struck Mr. St. Gage, requiring medical treatment. The woman," the statement wound up, "was a participant in the kidnapping of Mr. Bridsey, which felony was the direct cause of his death." A forceful counterattack, St. Gage felt.

The law firm had let St. Gage know after an emergency polling of the partners, that he would have to find an unembarrassing way to depart. No matter, St. Gage had told them with some dignity: he had planned to move his operation to new quarters in any case.

His dominant feeling now was fear that the insects would not attack the vines as they were supposed to do, but would simply die. Gradually, he calmed himself on that score: one way or another, he would know in a few hours. There was nothing he could do that he had not done.

Tobb's death had affected his emotions in a more complicated way. *The New York Times* had played the crash story as a sidebar, identifying Tobb from FBI fingerprint comparisons. The paper had not yet put him together with the "associate" of St. Gage who, Warder said, had tried to murder him in Portugal.

When it did, St. Gage was prepared to deal with it. True, the American had been the one indispensable partner during the dramatic first stage of the scheme, as well as St. Gage's sole confidant. There were still tasks that Tobb and no other could manage.

On the other hand, Tobb alive held St. Gage's destiny in chancery. Dead, he could become the focus for all the efforts by law enforcement people to affix blame.

It was Tobb, not he, who had leased jet transport planes through a Liechtensteinian straw corporation to get the phylloxerans out of France; Tobb had arranged for the falsified cargo declarations, hired the propeller-driven cargo planes to fly the insects from Mexico to California, found the marginal operators who had lined up the crop dusters.

St. Gage, if he were called into court, could testify that Tobb had exceeded in staggering fashion all bounds set by the enterprise. With Tobb silent, St. Gage could have his solicitors build stone walls to protect him, confident that there were no longer any loose stones to fall from the wall. His attorneys could help him to sanitize documents and endlessly stall official inquiries.

The London papers, always fearful of libel, could be counted on to be less probing than *The New York Times*. A few threats from his lawyers to their owners would calm them even more.

St. Gage had only scanned the Paris papers. Their hastily put together stories on Berkady varied wildly. One need not take the Parisian popular press seriously.

As for Berkady himself, the loathsome Belgian and his manipulatively empty eye socket had been as disgusting as his creepy little wards. It was a pity about the death of Mme. Berkady, and, although it had put her out of her misery, that of the *Witwe*. St. Gage had liked the *Witwe*'s pluck, her iron-hard honesty. But Tobb had to do it. He dearly hoped that Tobb had not lied when he said he had burned the whole tin of "insurance" as soon as he had crossed from Germany into France on the way to his final mission in California.

During St. Gage's wait for news from California, he had been anything but passive. He had risked everything on success. Through straws, he had shorted, bought puts, and sold calls on the New York exchanges against every major conglomerate and independent with large vineyard holdings in California.

When their stocks plummeted, as they would surely do that very day (and had showed signs of doing late in the session yesterday), St. Gage, on paper, would be worth still more millions.

By committing his fortune to such option deals, to selling on the margin, he was making his millions do the work of a billion or more. This kind of leverage insured returns of up to ten to one, or if the phylloxerans did not take, losses of the same dimension.

In a few days he would know whether he was a billionaire or a bankrupt.

He thought of the horrid insects swarming the vines all over California as they had in Berkady's laboratory. How exquisitely perverse. When American phylloxerans had destroyed Europe's wine industry a century ago, America's sturdy root stocks had been the cure. Now Europe was returning the curse of the long-ago pestilence to America—and was withholding the cure.

The days that followed astounded even St. Gage. Stocks associated with American wines fell off the precipice. National Distillers was down seven, Seagram nine, R. J. Reynolds twelve. Beer stocks raged bullishly.

A number of smaller vineyards that had laboriously worked up their reputations with fine Cabernets, Chardonnays, zinfandels, and Gewurztraminers let it be known that they were for sale.

Speculators, putting only tiny percentages down, bought the properties, but at scandalously low prices, driving vineland even lower as they played one panicked owner against the next. Even giants like Cloister Wall and Bel Amore were the objects of frenetic brokering.

The first federal reports leaked from the Department of Agriculture and were called in to St. Gage by his representative in Washington. Samples of the infected vines had been flown from California to the Department's research center at Beltsville.

They showed the phylloxerans were boring in, preparing for the winter cycle, healthily getting down to the business of egg-laying, and the prodigious production of young.

"Thank you, God," said St. Gage, in a rare moment of weakness deferring to a power higher than his own intellect. "Thank you."

The Beltsville study, tentative as it was, was confirmed within hours by similar studies using slightly different methods at Davis and at Cornell. All had a "so far . . ." hedge to them, but all were portentous enough to stir the more cautious European markets into motion.

The first symptoms were calls from vineyard brokers to St. Gage with offers even higher than the high prices his cartel had paid. He told them he would take all proposals under consideration, knowing the word would spread that he was willing to do business, quite the contrary of the truth, but certain to run up the value of his holdings.

Chilean and other South American vineyards soared in value and began to change hands like shells in a con game, each time at a higher price. They and every other winegrowing country put an immediate ban on import of American root stocks and the few grape imports that occurred in the off-season.

Twice during these heady days, he had been obligated to meet at his office with inspectors from Scotland Yard. His lawyer, the best of his kind in England, had been on hand. The questions had dealt with the rain of insects in California, the death of Berkady and the others, the Portuguese events.

His solicitor, more than he, had suggested that the compulsive American Tobb had been the villain, not the unwitting St. Gage. In Portugal, where St. Gage had personally been much in evidence, the lawyer had gently inquired whether British law was involved, and whether anyone had been pressing charges. The answer, of course, was no. The police had left empty-handed.

During the next few weeks St. Gage had nothing but success and as sole proprietor, he was also sole profiteer. The money gave him the kind of power that only the once-neglected can feel. It made his self-esteem flourish. It was as if all the slights to his father, to him, to the long line of younger sons he represented were being righted by one financial coup after another.

One day after closing out a particularly profitable short on the New York market, he said to himself in the splendor of his new office, "Today, honor thy father." He had already decided on how to do it; now he would.

Although St. Gage père was a suicide, blood had won over religion and his prominent relatives had permitted him to be buried in the family cemetery at Seymour-by-the-Slopes fifty miles south of London. St. Gage had gone there over the years to put flowers beside the simple stone—all he had been able to afford at the time his father's legal fees had been toted.

Only last week, by cajoling and a promise of a thousand pounds for general upkeep of the cemetery for a year, he had gotten permission to build a mausoleum for his branch of the family, including reburial there of his grandfather and great-grandfather, and a place for himself. On the walls would be engraved his branch's honors and genealogy, preserved for as long as marble lasts.

St. Gage had taken a London architect with him; the plans for the tasteful but impressive marble structure had been approved by his fourth cousin, the head of the family, a dealer in woolens but a knight. The job would be completed by spring.

The marble oblation seemed to bring to St. Gage hundred-fold returns from Bacchus or more fiduciary gods. Throughout the world, his holdings multiplied, not just land but warehoused wine.

Merchants of table wines, knowing how much dearer the coming European vintages would be with a half billion gallons of California wine knocked out of the world market, began to raise the over-the-counter prices of their continental wines.

Such rises were still more manna for St. Gage. They made the European vineyards producing cheap wines that were popular in America all the more valuable. When young wines from St. Gage's tens of thousands of acres went on the market in the fall, then he could stagger the prices higher yet.

In January French vineyard workers struck, then rioted over demands for a greater share of the coming European wine bonanza. They closed off the French channel ports to wine exports and used their trucks to blockade Italian and German crossing points for hours at a time. The French government's inability to control the situation brought the usual demarches from the rest of the Common Market.

At about the same time, laid-off vineyard laborers in California marched on Sacramento, and shortly thereafter on the Capitol in Washington seeking emergency aid. By then it was clear even to the White House that the phylloxerans were not conventionally eradicable and that without a miracle, a great deal of California's wine acreage would be destroyed. And what was not yet infected by the spreading insects, would be as tainted in the public's eye as the wine soon would be to the palate.

By February, St. Gage was spending more on computer experts than on his substantial office rent, but it was worth it. He could buy, sell short, take land options, exchange puts and calls faster than anyone in the wine business.

Daily printouts helped him particularly in his

refinancing, for he was paying off the high interest notes with which he had bought the vineyards and refinancing at lower rates based on the increased value of his holdings. His empire was beginning to look less rocky and more rock hard as his 18 and 19 percent short-term promissories were converted into 12.5 percent long-term loans.

He had also computerized his fact-gathering network as an underpinning for his financial complex. A British intelligence employee, bribed by St. Gage, slipped him a copy of a United States Central Intelligence Agency document on the subject of the cartel. It recognized St. Gage (misspelled St. Guage) as the head, but said the masterminding behind the late Tobb's assault had been the work of the Cuban government, explicitly the CIA's Cuban rival, the DGI.

An American evangelist, meanwhile, blamed the California wine disaster on that state's immoral life style. He suggested a national cleansing, pointedly urging the Roman Catholic and Episcopalian churches to forgo wine in favor of grape juice.

A more pertinent bit of intelligence reached St. Gage from his industrious man in Washington. The Agriculture Department, St. Gage was told, had run some tests on a bottle of 1885 Château Rossant. St. Gage was sure Warder had something to do with it. His own tests on the diluted fluid sopped up by d'Edouard had yielded nothing but traces of sulfur and he was sure Warder's sample had been equally useless. A few days later, prodded by St. Gage, his Washington operative reported Agriculture's tests, too, had produced nothing.

The thought of Warder irritated him. Warder!

If St. Gage had not wanted to avoid all further violence, he would have found another Tobb to do away with the American. The California authorities were still making sounds about the British inspector's death, or so his informants in San Francisco had reported. He knew Warder was behind it. It was hopeless for the ex-reporter, ex-detective to keep it up. But it was a burr.

These ruminations turned St. Gage's mind to the von Mohrwalds. Because they had held out, their land had become all the more valuable. Despite St. Gage's efforts to block them from the market, they were borrowing money on their vineyard and keeping up modest wine sales.

For a moment, when St. Gage thought of Bethany von Mohrwald profiting from *his* efforts, *his* elevation of property values, he was overcome with rage. She had humiliated him. She had seen him humiliated.

He closed his eyes until the ire passed.

"She'll pay," he said, so controlled it sounded matter-of-fact.

Thirty-four

CALIFORNIA SUN

By spring, throughout the wine lands of California, Berkady's horrendous legacy was wasting the plants. Galls were forming on the tender leaves, on twigs, and beneath the soil. Roots were beginning to swell, first with nodules, then with grotesque bulges and bulblike protuberances.

The genius of the old Belgian was his breeding in both virulence and multiplicious reproduction. It was many years before the first phylloxerans discovered in Languedoc in 1863 spread into Médoc. The insects did not wreak destruction on Jerez until 1894. But Berkady's louse-size monsters were breeding so rapidly and spreading so adventurously that while California's fall vintage would not be wiped out, it would be ruinously diseased. To the north, grape fields in Oregon and Washington already were reporting specimens.

By summer, many vineyards were scenes of desolation and destruction. Some owners simply burned off the vegetation, unable to sell the land except for future use as fodder acreages.

Others gallantly tried to treat their vines, ripping up the most diseased ones, burning the galled woodage, the scant yellowed leaves and the spongy deformed roots. When pulled, the vines listlessly left the ground, rotten-rooted and shedding phylloxerans in various stages of their four adult forms, one of them parthenogenic, and numerous immature phases. Even on the vines least affected, the grapes were hardening, the wine expected to be thin and bitter.

Aubrey Warder, back in his vineyard in Maryland, was actually having a modest success. The grapes' luxuriance already held the promise of juiciness. This vintage would be more appetizing than his first Spartan pressings. It might also be his last.

No matter what embargoes had been put on export to other states of Western grapes, the itinerant phylloxerans were certain to make it to the east. The eastern states would have this one great shot at the American market before all of America was given over to foreign wines.

Warder, defeated in the investigation, all major leads closed down on him, his enemy St. Gage able to block every legal action he had been able to help muster from California, was as soured as the California wines.

Bethany had written him honest angry letters. She and Franz were still holding on, ironically kept afloat by the increase in value of their land. But their distribution outside Austria was all but shut down. It was only, she felt, St. Gage's absorption with other matters that kept him from putting enough pressure on Austrian wholesalers to dry up even the von Mohrwalds' Austrian sales.

Bethany had done nothing either to prosecute St. Gage for his attempted rape or to publicize it. Because it had occurred in Portugal, she would have had to pursue the case there, drawing Aubrey from America as a witness. Eventually, if she were involved in legalities, their two interludes of love-making would, if they were honest, come out. And neither was given to perjury if it could be avoided. Besides, there was no certainty that St. Gage would be punished or, indeed, suffer any more than appearing bizarre or ridiculous.

In her notes to Aubrey, she made no mention of their nights in the *cave* and Paris. Nor did Aubrey, alone with his Cabernets, his Chardonnays, and the old, day vineyard worker who still assisted him, allow himself the luxury of mooning about her.

Only a few times, when the humid Montgomery County nights made the stars glow with soft fuzzy coronas, did he think of Bethany, her humor and bravery. Then he groaned and turned with what diligence he could to his translations of the *Bucolics*.

One night, thinking of her, trying hard to focus on rhymes, he bumped with surprise on a line in the *Bucolics* which defeated his best purposes:

> *How beautiful you are; if half so true,*
> *Here could I live and love and die with you.*

With a long moan and a hole in his heart the size of the great night outside his country kitchen, he shut his book and trudged up to bed, thinking gloomily of age and loneliness and hopelessness and death. And what a romantic old fool he was.

Cadwalder, the middle-aged manager of Domaine McIntyre, walked between the rows of dead and dying vines. Like a minor god inspecting a field of dead children, he touched this vine and that, noting the festered bolls where the insects dwelled who had killed his fields. The sun was hot on him, but he took no pleasure from its warmth.

"Oh Lord," he sighed, alone in this world of moribundity. His workers were laid off. His owners were trying to sell the land to an agricultural conglomerate for a song. In a few days he, too, would go, to work for a former lover who owned a string of warehouses outside San Francisco.

Aubrey Warder and the Mexican-American policeman, Hernandez, had visited him shortly after the phylloxerans had fallen. The two had convinced him, not in an accusatory way, but merely solemnly, that the very vine stocks he had innocently sent to France had played a significant role in the carnage, or rather herbage, around him.

During that bitter afternoon as they walked the rows, even as he was doing now, Warder had made plain his desire to destroy a man named St. Gage who they believed had killed the Scotland Yard inspector at Domaine McIntyre and had then gone on to kill its vines. He had come to trust the harsh detective and his kinder but equally shrewd companion. And if he could help them annihilate this

St. Gage, he would welcome the chance, and hope the murder of the man who had murdered his vines would be as gradual and as grisly as the death of his vineyard.

The only healthy thing on his vines now were the predatory insects beneath the yellow leaves. He split a gall with his thumbnail and several fat, yellow, licelike bugs tumbled out. Further on, he saw a gall different from the others. Like the rest, it hung to the underside of a withered leaf, but in this case, the gall itself was also withered. He creased it with his long nail, but no bugs fell. Instead, its insides were desiccated as were the phylloxerans, mere shriveled bits of insect matter.

So much the better, he thought. He tugged the plant to see whether it had the strength to hold in the soil. It had not. The plant slipped from the ground with its underburden of necrotic mandrakelike roots.

Most of the nodules on the roots were plump with their destroyers. But beneath the adhering sod, he saw one that was cracked and empty. He brushed the dirt from another. It, too, was dry, about to crack, unlike the fatally pregnant bolls which afflicted the plants he had inspected over the past weeks. He popped it too. It was so fragile he hardly had to run his thumbnail along it. The phylloxerans inside were as dead as those in the galls of the leaf above.

The manager had not been aware that there was a phase in these vigorous pests' lives when they died en masse, as some insects did—although later in the fall. He dropped the plant and looked further down the row.

This part of the vineyard was atop a rise and thus got sun both in morning and afternoon. He found two more plants in which the phylloxerans had dried up. And yet this was a part of the vineyard in which he had not tried any of the experimental insecticides which he had bought under the wishful directions of the Phylloxera Crisis Center at Davis.

Back at the deserted winery he went to his office where most of his papers were in old wine boxes, awaiting removal. On his desk was his folder on the phylloxerans. He had followed their phases with the deathly fascination of a man with a terminal tumor reading about the course it would take.

Nowhere in it did he find an early fall phase when the insects dried up and died, not even under the category "Deviate or Abnormal Stages." A meticulous and scientific man, he quickly called up his regional contact at the Crisis Center.

As he told what he had observed, he could almost feel the tension building on the other end of the line. At last the Davis scientist spoke.

"Mr. Cadwalder. If you will, rope off the area where those specimens occur. If I'm not mistaken, there's a big bare space in front of your pressing shed. I'll be there by helicopter within two hours."

"Helicopter . . . ?" asked Cadwalder, dumbfounded.

"This is the third report since yesterday. Of course we're not sure, but it could be important. The goddamn things shouldn't be dying that way . . ."

"Well, why are they?" asked the manager.

"I don't know and I don't know whether three

reports make a trend. But something funny is going on. Of course, they bred faster than any normal phyllox; they attacked faster and they spread faster, too."

"But, why . . . ?" persisted the manager, his heart beating faster. "If they are more, well, more horrible than normal phylloxerans, they ought to be all the more hardy."

"You'd think so," said the scientist, his own voice cracking now with excitement. "But Jesus, maybe they die faster, too. Just think of this, think, don't believe, okay? Suppose that what looks like its working great in the lab where these godawful things were developed, just doesn't cycle out when they're in the field."

"Maybe too much sun . . . ?"

"Or air, or clouds, or oxygen, or wind . . ."

"Kills them."

"I'm a fool for getting carried away. But . . . I'm wasting our time. Get out there, Mr. Cadwalder, and fence off these plants and I'll be there as soon as I can locate a pilot."

The McIntyre manager was dizzied by what he had heard. For a moment he did not rise from his chair in the denuded little office. Then, almost frenetically he searched up a roll of heavy vine twine and carefully tied off the area where he had found the dried-out galls.

By the time he saw the helicopter, a dragonfly-size spot in the hot, hazy sky, he had found another hillock with its clutch of dead insects.

The scientist, an excitable man in his thirties wearing khaki chinos, work boots, and a Levi's jacket, marched behind the manager to the twined-off areas and, careful as a surgeon, snicked off root, leaf, and twig specimens. Then he uprooted two entire vines and with the help of the manager wrestled them into a gigantic plastic bag.

As the two men carried the vines back to the helicopter, the manager peppered the scientist with questions. At first the younger man tried to be taciturn, but the urgency of the questioning and his own ebullience quickly conquered him.

"Look, for Christ's sake, not a word, okay . . . ?"

"Of course," said the manager, more excited now than ever.

"Well, on the radio, while I was on the way here, I got two more calls. I mean, that's five we know about in two days. If you want to know what I think, and this is strictly off the record, I think the little bastards are dying. I think the good old California sun is just too much for them."

The manager first called McIntyre's president person-to-person in San Francisco. The official cautiously told the manager to stay in touch and resolved to stall the sale of the vineyard he was on the brink of consummating until more information was forthcoming.

Cadwalder, on his own, and because he had promised to keep him abreast of *anything* affecting the wine disaster, called Hernandez and explained carefully and conservatively what he had discovered and what the Davis scientist had told him.

No sooner had they hung up than Hernandez called Aubrey whose old reportorial contacts and instincts served him efficiently.

He knew the officials at the Crisis Center would

clam up if he called. Instead, he implored a California Congressman on the House Agriculture Committee to get an Assistant Secretary at the Agriculture Department to call Beltsville and require them to find out exactly what the experts at Davis had come up with. Roundabout as it sounded, Aubrey had what he needed before nightfall.

"My ass will fry if this is in the paper in the morning," said the Congressman. "They've got some kind of tight security on it until they're sure."

"Well, how sure are they?"

"Pretty damned sure. The little fuckers are dying off, well, like flies. Can you stall a day? I thought you were out of the news business anyway."

"I'm half out of it. I'll stall half a day which means it'll be morning after next before I break it. Do you want me to give you a plug?"

"Shit no. Forget you know my name on this one. Just remember that you owe me a big one." When they hung up, the Congressman instructed his broker to buy a heavy assortment of calls on the American wine group stocks, then phoned some of his most important financial backers to urge them to do the same.

Aubrey, for his part, called Bethany and excitedly told her to get Franz on the other line.

"What is it?" she delayed long enough to ask.

"It's wonderful and I love you," he said.

"My God, Aubrey," she shushed his indiscretion.

Franz had only a single day to capitalize on his information. But the scrambling he had done to keep the vineyard alive had prepared him. He had contacts with every land broker and bank of any consequence in Austria.

First, he mortgaged every bit of land he had, giving second liens where he could get anyone to take them, writing promissory notes against the Schloss itself, the paintings, the silverware, borrowing from every relative he could scrounge a groschen from.

With the money, he took options on all the wine land he could find in Austria, Germany, and the Tyrol. By making the options short-term, a month at the most, he was able to tie up much of the land that St. Gage had missed and some which, as in his own case, was owned by families who simply did not want to sell to the cartel.

What this meant was that Franz had the right to pay for the land at a fixed price in a month. If he did not, the land reverted to its owners and Franz was totally bankrupt and entailed.

Bethany understood the financial coup planned by her husband and ran for phone numbers and records to help, but interrupted his frantic calls only once.

"There's Claudio . . ."

"Yes, we must. Call him and tell him to take every land option he can get, then sell . . . oh hell, he'll never be able to understand it. Tell him to send me all the money he can get his hands on, with a telex draft before supper, all right?"

Bethany called the prince and tried to explain what Franz was doing, but Claudio could only say, "But *cara*, couldn't you have Franz explain it to my lawyers, my accountant? I don't fully understand . . ."

"No," she said. "It'll be too late. Claudio, just do what I say, please. It will make you so much money, so much."

"Enough to buy back my vineyards from those pigs, right?"

"Yes, and then some."

Franz, meanwhile, had gone into the second phase of his plan. From banks and brokers to whom he had not previously gone for money, he now sold the land options, but on a short sale basis. What this meant was that while the bank, taking a sizable commission in the process, paid Franz at today's high prices for the land, Franz would not have to deliver the actual title until a month down the road.

In other words, the bank was betting that the land value would remain stable or follow the upward trend it had been on ever since the phylloxerans fell on California. What Franz knew was that the bottom was going to drop resoundingly out of the European vineyard market as soon as word got around that the insects were dying, that California would recover, and that within a year or two, the California vineyards would again be pouring cheap wine onto the world market.

When prices plunged, Franz would buy the land at bargain prices and deliver the deeds to the bank, keeping the giant profit he had made on his short sale. Even after he had given Claudio Martino e Stelio his portion, he would be able to redeem every lien on his land and breathe free on the proceeds for years to come. Nor did he forget his supporter in Krems. He paused long enough in his wheeling and dealing to call the old man and explain what he was doing. On the second explanation, the vintner understood.

"Franz, you're sure?"

"Sure enough to be betting the Schloss on it."

"Then let me off the telephone, man. I'm behind already."

At the end of their hectic day, the von Mohrwalds called Aubrey again, more for reassurance than anything else. They had risked everything on his information. He did not disappoint them. Bethany, bound again to Franz by his vigor and optimism, his dash and intelligence, still felt a tingle when she heard the older man's voice.

"Yeah, I'm sure, surer now than ever. I've been working on the thing as a story for my old paper. It's solid as a rock."

"When . . . ?" began Franz.

"The story will run in the morning. It'll say, with the proper hedges, that the plague is over."

"Then the cartel is over," said Franz.

"Unless St. Gage can sell one helluva lot of land in one helluva hurry," said Aubrey.

Thirty-five

THE MAUSOLEUM

All the money Robert St. Gage had paid out for computerization, for informants, for consultants, all his acumen in setting up his intelligence network, all his care in providing numbers where he could be reached day or night did not protect him from the surprising death of the phylloxerans.

It was particularly ironic that St. Gage got the news later than he might because he had taken off a rare three hours to visit the newly completed mausoleum he had built for his father.

When he returned to his office from Seymour-by-the-Slopes at seven in the evening, his secretary burst into tears.

"I have been desperately trying to reach you," he made out through her lament. She handed him a slip of paper with the name of his Washington operative on it. "He is almost hysterical," she said, not far from that state herself.

"Grab your desk, Mr. St. Gage," the man began, "Davis is finding a pattern of unexpected mortalities among the bugs."

"A pattern?"

"Enough to notify Beltsville."

"Just the alates?"

"No, it seems to cut across the phases."

St. Gage was stunned.

"Anything else?"

"I'll stay on it and call."

Within two hours, St. Gage had ascertained the worst. The phylloxerans were indeed dying. So virulent *in vitro*, they were drying up under the rays of the California sun.

While they had wiped out or made undrinkable a substantial fraction of the California vintage, there was still going to be some cheap potable wine this year. With the kind of zealous replanting the Californians could be counted on to do, the next vintage would be 80 percent of the normal production, the year after that 90 or even 95 percent.

There was, St. Gage knew, one last desperate chance. Already the American wine stocks had turned bullish. An over-the-counter called Early California which he had used as a bellwether jumped a point and a half—50 percent just on the first inconclusive reports. American land prices would also be going up and the European vineyard markets, in contrast, were going to be scuttled.

He didn't need a computer to tell him what he had to do. He must buy up as much of California's wine lands as he could and, at the same time, dump his European land, his warehoused wines, his options to buy. He had to purchase, instead, options to sell—as many as he could.

But his whole operation had been geared for the buying of land, with only selective selling of wine-related securities when he needed cash and when they were inflated even by the standards of the inflated market he had largely brought about. He was not set up to dump stocks and bonds on the market, to refinance loans at higher rates for the funds he needed to buy California land with dollars. He was, in fact, a slave chained by his own financial genius. For every investment he had made was based on the exact opposite of what he now must try to do.

St. Gage had his secretary call in his computer men, his analysts, his loan specialists. As the acidulous night wore on, he contracted to buy California land, giving the brokers only time to call his bankers at home to ascertain that he had liquidated enough land and securities to make payment.

St. Gage was not alone. Others had followed his road to profits. They were now doing the same frenzied things to avoid disaster. Panic midnight selling in London led to awakened bankers, vineyard brokers, warehouses, wine speculators of every mark in New York, Paris, Rome, Budapest, Brussels, and Amsterdam. The hectic buying and selling spread to Hong Kong, Tokyo, Sydney.

When St. Gage ordered his aging Australian financier partner to liquidate, explaining why, the man had spluttered over the thousands of miles of radio-telephone and cable and finally cursed, "You filthy British bastards, it's another Gallipoli."

By two A.M., St. Gage had begun pledging property twice to different banks, risking that a rise in the prices of land he had been able to solidify in California would allow him to pay off his fraud. At five, he was reselling the California lands to try to cover demands in three languages by bankers who had discovered the treacherous game he was playing. The prices he was getting were high. But they were nowhere near sufficiently high.

By dawn he was studying a single page printout brought to him by his bleary-eyed chief technician who knew, not just from the numbers on it but from his boss's expression, that they were all going to be out of jobs in an hour or two.

Left alone in front of his polished birch desk, St. Gage looked in the wall of figures for an egress. There was none. He thumbed almost aimlessly through the urgent telephone slips that lay on the desk like fallen leaves.

To his surprise, he saw drops of water falling on the slips. His eyes had begun to run tears, and in his dismay he had not been aware of it. He wiped them on his sleeve and stood up. There was no way out: he was bankrupted, and many times over. He had committed millions of dollars worth of fraud on the banks who had greedily or foolishly trusted him. Soon, like his father, he would be a national scandal.

He sagged to the window. Such a short time ago it seemed that he had stood by a window in his old offices while the cartel's members gathered in hostile accord and decided to take the plunge. That decision had cost them all their lives.

The bells rang faintly through the glass, just as they had on that other day when Tobb had come to tell him of Wheatley-Smith's death. Death. He let his unloosening mind wander to when he had first thought of it. At a time, he was sure, when his mother was still with them, his nurse, his father, long before Cambridge, in the big house with the old tapestries, the armor, the remnants of a name.

The bells still rang. Betjeman, he thought, oh poet of bells.

"I ask my nurse the question, 'Will I die?' " he said to himself.

"As bells from sad St. Anne's ring out so late . . .
. . . I caught her terror then. I have it still."

He wished he could remember more of it.

When the rest of the wine world had begun its maniacal buying and selling, the von Mohrwalds were just ending theirs. They had moved so swiftly and in such a variety of ways that their notes were on scraps of paper.

At the desk in their office, Franz made his final computations while Bethany, looking over his shoulder, suggested an addition here, a correction there. The little hand calculator they had used was barely up to the arithmetic, the sorting out of their profits.

While they could not reach an exact figure, it was clear they were not going to have just enough, but much more than that. The essential paperwork done, Franz turned and put his arms around his wife's body, pressing his head gratefully to her stomach.

"Meine kleine Bäuerin, we—you—did it."

"We all did it," she said, touching his dark hair at the back of his neck with unqualified affection, "beginning with the poor Englishman . . ."

"And our friends in Krems, and Claudio, and most of all your splendid Warder."

"Yes, most of all. But not *my* Warder. He took the case. We paid him, but as you say . . ."

"It was not just the money."

"Yes. He was a dogged person."

"More than dogged. Without him, certainly, the cartel would have foundered. But us with it. This information he gave us . . . He developed it after *his* case was over."

"Ah, Franz, he'll be happy with his news story. He seemed to me anyway more journalist than detective. And his vineyard."

"Damn it, Bethany, where's your gratitude? It's not like you. Look, that rosé we've been working on. Consider: Mohrwalder Warderrosen. It even sounds German. And for him, a vintner, well a sort of one, he would understand the gesture."

Perhaps too much, she thought. "Oh, Franz . . . ," she said, suddenly and genuinely moved by her husband's generosity. And how Aubrey *would* love it, to have for all time a good European wine named for him.

But she could not. It would make a hypocrite of her: her husband and their children and so on as long as the vineyard lasted would be made the unwitting accomplices of an affair which, however brief, however justified, was still illicit.

"Then yes?" he inquired, mistaking her hesitation.

"No. And for this reason. Part of him, if I read

him right, would love the honor. But as a journalist he would consider it somehow improper. He would feel, I think, he had been paid for doing a job, had done it well and would be embarrassed to have us give him more."

"Then we could offer it to him. You could approach him."

She thought a moment about that, tempted, but not for any reason that Franz would assume. She would like to see him again, be held in his gentle bear arms, feel that insistency, unfamiliar and powerful. But that would be using dishonest means for even more dishonest ends.

"Believe me," she said. "I think he would rather just be paid for the time he spent and did not bill us for. And in any case," she said, not really believing it, "I don't like the sound of it that much, it looks and sounds too much like *Wärter*"—a guard or keeper—"like we were naming a wine after a jail warden."

Franz mused on that a moment before he agreed.

"Then, a check. We'll get it off today against whatever accounting he's willing to make. How much do you think?"

"Let's try him with $10,000."

"Better $15,000," said Franz. "It's a wonder he's not dead like the rest of them. Remember, he didn't just save the Schloss. He saved the life of its mistress."

In the big kitchen, a cup of midday coffee and the check for $15,000 before him on the table, Aubrey tried to figure up what the von Mohrwalds actually owed him for unbilled services. He knew

that he could not take $15,000. He also knew that
Bethany's approval of sending any money at all
meant that she wanted things between them to be,
at least for now, business and not personal.

He sighed, decided to take $10,000 and to use
some of it to dot the i's of the case. There was still
his own debt to Wheatley-Smith. For while St. Gage
was bankrupt, he was not yet unmasked as an
accomplice to the British inspector's murder.

From Gatwick, Aubrey called Varner Leason,
the *Globe-Informer* reporter who had put him on to
the pathologist and asked him what he knew about
Robert St. Gage.

"Aubrey my boy," said Leason peppily, "I never
believed that cock-and-bull story you gave me about
insurance for a moment. But, I'm buggered if I
thought you were on to anything that good."

"You liked?" said Aubrey, pleased.

"Our Washington man stole your whole story
from your first edition. Is that a kudos?"

"Nothing finer imaginable. St. Gage?"

"You're outdistanced by events. He's skipped."

"Skipped?"

"He's disappeared. One jump ahead of the subpoenas. His creditors got one court order for all his
documents and another for him to appear for tes-
timony. When they got there . . ."

"Where's his house?"

"No use. Everything's gone. I just got back."

"What's the address? Maybe . . ."

"Old Relentless," said Leason, and gave him
the address. "I'm telling you it's cleaned out."

"Well . . ."

"But if you find anything you can tell me about, call me, right?"

At the door to St. Gage's town house, Aubrey's ring was greeted by a haggard maid whose face looked like she had just finished fifth in a six-horse claiming race. Aubrey reverted to detective and showed the sixtyish woman his Virginia credentials and she began to look as if she had finished last.

Aubrey carefully explained that St. Gage had some debts in the United States and he had been retained to try to recover them.

"And not just there," she said morosely.

"Not just there, what?"

"Not just *debts* there."

Aubrey picked up a personal note.

"Surely he discharged his personal debts better than his professional," he said with a kindly crocodile smile. "Even the most exorbitant business venturers are careful to pay their own servants." He doubted the truth of it, but the concept served his purposes.

She prissed her lips.

"I shouldn't talk."

"Could my clients offer you some help? You must have family. I assure you that you could pay it back on your own time."

"I know what you're doing. The reporters already said they would pay me to help them do things. But I'm not that sort. I won't take money. Besides, the court people took everything."

"May I see?"

"No."

"Dear lady," said Aubrey. "Then let me pay you a week's salary in advance as the maid for *my* employers."

"That's ridiculous," she said, piqued at his outrageous proposition, but not merely piqued. He sensed her ambivalence.

"Well, it's not so ridiculous at it is novel. Look, I am actually going to pay you, right now in good British pounds, to work for me a week. All I want is for you to show me around the house of a man who has welshed on your salary for a week . . ."

"Two weeks. He owes me for two weeks."

"Then I'll hire you for two weeks," said Aubrey. "Constructively you don't even work for him anymore."

"No, I'm not trying to make you pay me more, just setting you straight on how he treated me."

"Then one week. Beginning right now."

He looked at the simple face, saw her wavering, seeking some way she could morally take the money which she obviously needed.

"It'll be between the two of us," Aubrey said. "Your name won't appear in the papers. I won't even ask you what it is. I won't take anything from the house, just look around. You can accompany me every step of the way."

She stared back at him for a long moment.

"How much?" he asked, softly but bluntly.

"Fifty pounds," she said.

He peeled it off, folded it and put it in her hand. Then he followed her down the long hall toward the rear of the house.

St. Gage's study was serene, with statues on

pedestals, a painting of a dignified woman, a single suit of armor in the corner, and a crossed mace and halberd on one of the walls.

Without risking a request for permission, Aubrey went methodically through the desk. There were a few personal notes, one from a cousin. It congratulated St. Gage on his good fortune and asked for a donation to a church charity. His creditors' lawyers had used their subpoenas to clear out everything else that related to money.

Aubrey looked again at the suit of armor and followed the empty helm's sightless visor across the room to an empty corner. With the rest of the study filled with memorabilia, almost cluttered, there was an imbalance in that emptiness, something unesthetic.

On a hunch, he walked over and saw the wall was slightly paler in the corner. With a table light, he scrutinized the rug. Lightly on the thick fabric were the prints of two pointed feet.

"Did he have another suit of armor?" he asked the watchful maid.

"Yes," she said. It had, she thought, been handed down from generation to generation. It had disappeared with St. Gage and she thought he must have sold it, for it was no doubt valuable.

"That hard up?"

"Yes," she said. "Just so." He had sold the Rolls Royce, fired the chauffeur, and was trying to sell the country home he had begun.

"When he had it, he spent it," commented Aubrey, playing with the dial of a wall safe. "Do you know the combination of this thing?"

"No, sir," she said. "And it's empty. The court people had the locksmith open it. They took out everything."

"So he tried to sell everything."

"Everything he could," she said. "Some he couldn't."

"Couldn't sell?" If he was selling the armor, he was selling everything. But then, why not the rest of the armor, the painting, the old weapons? The maid was answering.

"He built this marble house, mausoleum, for his father, down at Seymour-by-the-Slopes. Not much chance of selling *that*."

It was particularly galling to the maid, obviously, that the older St. Gage, despite his scandal, was honored with a tomb, while she got stiffed on her wages. To Aubrey, building a tomb for his father was one of the few decent acts he had ever heard about St. Gage.

"Mr. St. Gage was very fond of his father, in spite of . . . ," the maid was saying.

"I know . . . ," answered Aubrey mechanically.

"And he was down there telling them how to build it, even how to polish the marble . . ."

"To buff it . . ."

"Yes, right down to those details. In fact, the last trip the chauffeur took with him, poor young fellow, like me, not a penny paid on his last two weeks, was to Seymour-by-the-Slopes."

"When did he take that trip?" asked Aubrey, things going click-click in his head: ornate dagger, armor, heraldic old study, honor, forefathers, dishonor, father's suicide . . .

"The afternoon before everything went to

pieces," said the maid. "When he got back, he never really was the same."

"After you show me the rest of the house," Aubrey said, "I want you to tell me how to get to Seymour-by-the-Slopes."

From the window of the rented car, Aubrey saw, far down the dirt road toward the hills, the glistening white marble mausoleum. It seemed garish among the graying lesser tombs and sepulchres. Far off, the blue sky making it almost too picturesque, was the village that gave the place its name, nestled beneath the brown of the hill slopes.

At the cemetery, heavy trucks had left their tracks in the unaccustomed earth. Aubrey let himself in through the iron gate. The day was hot and he was both anxious from this trip to the mausoleum and weary from jet lag. The graveyard was quiet except for the buzz of summer insects and, far off, a birdsong.

Among these quiet tombs, the St. Gages, the collateral branches, Mulberrys, Pells, Hawtherbines, how could there be anything untoward? He followed deep cart tracks through the ancient stones toward the marble structure.

On the mausoleum's frieze the name "St. Gage" was deeply incised, with the family motto, "Ne Quid Nemis"—nothing in excess. Aubrey thanked his crude Latin for letting him appreciate the irony.

The barred bronze door was ajar. Aubrey's heart beat faster. St. Gage would never have left it so, and the workers had finished their work on the mausoleum.

Cautious as a cop on a drug bust, Aubrey put

his cheek to the cold marble wall beside the door and listened, wishing he had the little pistol. He heard nothing.

With a quick motion, he swung open the door and darted his head into the aperture. Inside it was dim. He made out walls on which names had been graven and in the center a rectangular tomb with a classically reclining figure on its lid. The smell was of damp, recently finished construction work.

In two steps, Aubrey was beside the tomb, knowing that this was no carven knight atop the lid. He pulled up the visor and, still in the darkness, saw the features of a man, almost as pale as the stone. He touched the face and found it clammy, the skin of a man not too long dead.

He recoiled, shocked in spite of finding what, in his heart, he had believed all along he would find. As his eyes became accustomed to the gloom, he gently took off the helm from the armored figure and saw, in repose, the aristocratic features of Robert St. Gage.

Thirty-six

PHOEBE HILLS VINEYARDS

Aubrey walked among his vines, fondling—there was no less sexual word for it—the luscious grapes. The sturdy Chelois and Seyval Blancs were as lovely to the eye as the plump Chardonnays and Cabernets he was growing experimentally.

These latter, he was sure, would, if not this season then next, produce wines which even his discerning sometime friend, the Baroness Bethany von Mohrwald, might not have sniffed at. "Might not have," was the way he thought of her, for in his last talk with her, when he had told of finding St. Gage in the tomb, he had felt her commitment to her husband, to her accustomed and good life.

That was, after all, the way things happened. The politician's wife who had loved him long and well was still in Sri Lanka. When she came back, who could tell but what they would rediscover the wonder of their dangerous adultery before her husband had died and left them free to decide—as they did—that their paths had diverged.

Bethany had chosen the wise, safe way as why should she not. Why exchange a slightly straying but thoroughly decent husband for a man with two heart episodes in his background, fourteen years her senior, and a devotion to a forgotten Latin poet and a dubious vineyard? C'mon, he told himself with a smile, partly bittersweet, partly resigned.

There were affairs, he thought, looking at the lines of neatly tied vines, which are no more lasting than a young Moselle, and every bit as fresh and sweet. He was glad that he had experienced such wines, glad that he had experienced the sweetness, the goodness of Bethany von Mohrwald. He was glad that he was alive, when he might, several times in the past few months, have been dead. His escape from Tobb in Portugal, particularly, had been narrow. By all rights, he should be dead, a tangle of bones and dry integuments, if that, in a gulch. But he was not dead. He was reasonably healthy, reasonably happy, and with good prospects of fulfilling years, moderately rewarding vintages ahead.

But to more specific things. A cluster of Chardonnay grapes in the row he walked looked particularly ripe, inviting. Their rich, not really sweet flavor would be an interesting complement to some goat cheese he had picked up in Rockville where he had gone for some state agriculture forms, some shopping that morning.

For his main dish he would use a recipe for baked chicken he had clipped from Marge Tyler's column in the *Eagle*. He considered inviting her out to share the dish, then thought no, maybe next time.

Tonight, after supper, he would start copy-reading the fifty pages of the *Bucolics* he had finished. Not too far to go now. When he was completely done, he would try to peddle them to the university presses, and failing that, maybe find some good little press in New England and vanity-publish them.

He'd send copies around to his friends. It wasn't every newspaperman who had translated Vergil, even fairly simple Vergil. No, nor won a Pulitzer, nor loved a fine woman until the time came when she died, and later loved well one more fine woman and then worked with and seriously made love to a baroness of quality and humor.

"Son of a bitch," he said softly, even admiringly, grunting with humor for self-congratulation was not a luxury he often allowed himself.

As if it had summoned up a genie, a tremor of concern, an instinct made him rise and turn, just as he had under similar circumstances more than a year before. He saw a ribbon of dust wisp up behind the trees over toward the main highway.

This time he watched until it came up on his side and then became a black car in his own drive-way. The matter of the cartel had made him more cautious than was his wont. He kept a 12-gauge loaded and had bought himself a Colt revolver which he kept beside his bed and, during the d ay, on the porch.

He walked toward the pistol. When he saw the car's diplomatic plates and observed the liveried dandy step from it, package in hand, he sensed there was no danger. Still, he wanted the pistol within reach.

The thin chauffeur spotted him now and made for him, an ingratiating smile on his face, his hat off and in his hand. People who intended to kill you, Aubrey reasoned, did not occupy one of their hands with holding a hat. Aubrey came forward, wondering what was in the package, no bigger than a wine bottle.

"Mr. Warder," said the chauffeur diffidently. "I am from the Austrian Embassy. Forgive me for not calling, but this is for you, from our diplomatic pouch."

"From . . ."

"Austria. I do not know whom. I was told only to surprise you with it." He smiled. Aubrey saw the man was timid and tried to help.

"Well, I'm surprised. Can you use a cup of coffee, a glass of wine? It's a long way out from town."

"Not necessary, not necessary," said the man, "I will be on my way."

Aubrey watched the diplomatic car disappear and pulled off the brown paper on the outside of the box, then a layer of floral feminine wrappings. He knew the box contained wine and that it came from Bethany.

Inside the box was a sealed white envelope, its paper thick and costly. Before he took out the wine, he opened the envelope. The note bore at its top an embossed but unintimidatingly colorless seal.

"I will visit you again, Aubrey," it said, "when you are among the things you love. *Trink voll. Auf-wiedersehen*." It was signed with a modest "B."

So, he thought, smiling, mouthing the word "wonderful" without saying it. He would see her again after all. He stuffed the note and envelope in his pocket and walked into his house, holding the wine by its neck.

There, in the kitchen, with the westering sun pouring through his window, he looked at the label. It was a four-year-old Mohrwalder Maximiliansehre, its tiny replica medals dancing in the sunlight.

Efficiently he opened the bottle and poured himself a small glass. He held it up as if for a toast. The sun's rays streamed through the wine. Its color was as golden as honey.

Les Whitten is a prizewinning investigative reporter who has worked as co-byliner with columnist Jack Anderson, for the *Washington Post*, and for Hearst newspapers. In his thirty years of journalism, he has covered Vietnam and other wars, Watergate and most major political scandals before and after, natural and manmade disasters, and other ills the press is heir to. He has eleven published books, including novels, poems, and translations of Baudelaire, plus short stories, and innumerable articles. He won the American Civil Liberties Union's Edgerton Award for refusing to reveal his sources despite jailing by the FBI in a celebrated case during the Nixon years. He was a visiting associate professor at Lehigh University, has lectured at the FBI Academy, the Naval War College, and numerous universities. He is one of the few Blood Brothers of the Iroquois, reads to blind people, and won a varsity baseball letter at Lehigh, from which he was graduated magna cum laude. He avidly skis, bicycles, and golfs.